Pine
Bugs
and
.303s

Library and Archives Canada Cataloguing in Publication

Title: Pine bugs and .303s / Ernie Louttit.
Names: Louttit, Ernie, 1961- author.
Identifiers: Canadiana (print) 20220398739 | Canadiana (ebook) 20220398755 | ISBN 9781988989518
  (softcover) | ISBN 9781988989525 (EPUB)
Classification: LCC PS8623.O887755 P56 2022 | DDC C813/.6—dc23

Printed and bound in Canada on 100% recycled paper.
Cover Design: Heather Campbell

Published by:
Latitude 46 Publishing
info@latitude46publishing.com
Latitude46publishing.com

We acknowledge the support of the Ontario Arts Council, Canada Council for the Arts, and the Ontario Media Development Corporation for their generous financial support.

Pine
Bugs
and
.303s

a novel

Ernie Louttit

46

To my first grandson, Adler

PART 1

Prologue

It was one of the few remaining troop trains making its way across Northern Ontario in 1945. The train did not even have a name, just a number: 277. It seemed to have been shuttled into every siding between Halifax and where it was now, a place in Northeastern Ontario with a small section house and some outbuildings, called Angus. The train sat steaming and hissing as it waited for an eastbound freight to pass.

It was warm for September and opening the windows of the old passenger cars only invited the acrid smoke and mosquitos in. The air inside was already heavy with cigarette smoke and the smell of unwashed men anxious to get home. The conductor, a First World War veteran with a slight limp, was apologetic and understanding. "Same thing happened to me, boys, after the first one. We were one of the last of the units demobilized and it seemed everyone forgot us, and we weren't a priority anymore. You just have to be patient boys. We'll get you home. It will be over soon enough," he said.

Elmer had gotten good at reading white people over the past

four years. A Cree man from a small reserve three hundred miles east of Fort William, Elmer had volunteered for the infantry in 1941 at Fort William after his cousin was killed in a training accident in England. Prior to joining the army, he knew very few white men and could not really count any among his friends. During the war, three of the five Cree and Ojibwa soldiers who had joined his unit were killed. Most of his unit were either English or French Canadians.

As Elmer watched the conductor speak, he could feel the sadness that came with the conductor's knowledge and experience. He knew the conductor was only telling half-truths. Elmer knew it would not be over when they arrived in Fort William. Too much had happened, and everyone had changed. What the future was would be wide open.

A young officer, Lieutenant Bell, had come to his quarters about a month before Elmer received his discharge date. Bell talked like a priest to Elmer, even though Elmer was 33 years old and a combat veteran. Bell meant well and Elmer was too polite to call him on it. The officer explained to him that because Elmer had been overseas for more than four years, he would no longer be considered a status Indian. The officer had made some correspondence with the war office because he wanted to make sure all of his men knew what benefits were available after they were discharged. The Lieutenant expressed his shock and disappointment to Elmer and told him he would talk to the commanding officer to see what could be done. Elmer sat quietly when he was told this and felt sorry for the young officer. Bell was genuine in his concern, though Elmer knew from experience Bell would be swallowed up and nothing he could do would change things. Elmer was not told this when he signed up but acted like he had known it all along when Bell told him. Just another thing like missing a moose during the hunt, Elmer thought.

The roar of the eastbound train speeding past jolted him back to the present. The train rushing by pushed air into the car. Interwoven with the train's smoke was the smell of Jack pines, Tamarack, spruce trees, and fresh clean water. His train

4

jolted and started to leave the siding, slowly pulling onto the mainline. It was a far cry from the claustrophobic North-West Europe which had been tamed by the population density and ravaged by war. It had been thick with the smells of destruction and death mixed with the coming of fall even months after the war had ended. Elmer smiled at the thought of the vast forests, lakes, and rivers of Northwestern Ontario, without people everywhere you went and tried to nod off, letting the motion of the train and the rhythm of the steel wheels on the track put him into a half sleep.

Gilbert sat across from Elmer. Gilbert had been playing cards in another car earlier but had gotten bored and was feeling a little sleepy himself. He looked at Elmer as he drifted off. Elmer Wabason had been in his regiment from the start and came from the Indian Reserve across the highway from his hometown. The highway was called the King's Highway and later the Trans-Canada Highway after 1943. He had never met him before the war, and was surprised when he learned they had grown up less than three miles away from each other. After four years, he still did not know a lot about Elmer. Elmer and the other Indians kept to themselves. Three had been killed in battle. One in France and two in Holland. The other Indian, Richard Sutherland from around Red Lake, was caught in a hellish mortar barrage that killed and wounded several men two weeks before the war ended. Though he was not wounded, he had not spoken more than a few words since, even to Elmer. He was sitting in the last car on the train, alone as usual.

Gilbert knew Elmer had a wife named Mary, and two children. When Elmer was telling him about them, a Sergeant callously interrupted and said, "Chief there probably has a lot of squaws waiting for him Gil," and walked away. Elmer had flushed and stopped talking. Whenever someone said something like that Elmer usually clammed up and tended to his equipment. It seemed to Gilbert that Elmer cleaned his rifle a lot.

The train was not crowded, and Elmer was able to stretch his legs out to the next seat. He woke up when the train went over a poorly maintained switch that cause the train to bang and jolt hard. Elmer looked around the car for a moment. Everyone was dozing or staring out the windows, lost in their own thoughts. The train reflected the incomplete planning and wastefulness Elmer had become accustomed to over the past four years. The journey had been laid out by some rear echelon officer in Ottawa. They did not consider casualties, or the men who had volunteered to remain in the occupation force at the war's end. The empty seats were reminders—silent, empty reminders of what the past four years had cost.

The train had been booked on the Canadian Pacific Railway line rather than Canadian National, which meant almost everyone from the regiment would pass their homes in the northern part of Ontario during the night. They would have to travel back the way they came while angling north after being demobilized in Fort William. For some, with vehicles and family meeting them, it was not a big deal, but for others it meant long days travelling home by whatever means they could find. Elmer dozed off again. Gilbert was watching him across the aisle. Elmer had a soldier's ability to fall asleep anywhere. At the speed they were going, barring any unforeseen calamities, they would be in Fort William tomorrow around three in the morning. Gilbert would try talking to him again in a bit, he thought. The motion of the train combined with the shots of rum he had earlier made his eyes heavy, and he too dozed off.

When Gilbert woke up it was dark outside, and the train was stopped in a little town taking on water. Some soldiers were off the train talking to people on the platform. One of the locals was passing a bottle around and the soldiers were handing out tailor-made cigarettes to the men, who all seemed to be railway workers. Elmer was not in his seat. Gilbert got up and went to the vestibule so he could get out and stretch his legs. Elmer was in the vestibule on the opposite side of the platform staring out the window into the woods.

"We'll be home soon Elmer," Gilbert said.

Elmer turned and smiled his big smile, which he reserved for special things. "I can feel the land," he said. "What are you going to do once you are home?"

Gilbert was surprised; Elmer was rarely this straightforward. Only in combat did he ever start conversations. Gilbert's answer was immediate, so Elmer knew it was an honest answer. "Well, my Cree friend, I am going to get rich dealing with people's shit. Everyone does it, nobody wants it around. I am going to get rid of it and people are going to pay me to do it. Do you want in?"

It was Elmer's turn to be surprised. This white man was offering him a chance to go into business together. Elmer had always trusted Gilbert, especially during the hard and bitter fighting in Holland. What you saw was what you got from him. He knew his own strengths and his weaknesses. He also knew Elmer's and they covered each other's faults automatically. They did not have to talk all the time like a lot of the other soldiers. Elmer replied, "Can we do firewood too?"

"Yes," Gilbert answered.

The conductor hollered, "All aboard fellows," and the soldiers came rushing aboard smelling of cigarettes, whiskey, and rum. The conductor closed the vestibule with a clang and the train started moving in a cloud of bellowing hissing steam. The conductor moved down the train telling everyone their journey was almost over. "No more drinking boys. You have about five hours to sober up before you meet your sweeties, and for you young ones, your mothers. Your war is almost over."

Chapter 1

The rear echelon officer from Gil's regiment had telephoned Frances two days ago. Frances answered the phone and listened with her hands trembling as the officer told her Gil's train would be in Fort William in two days, but he did not know the exact time. Their hometown of Lac Ville had received individual phones in late 1944 when it seemed the war would end in an Allied victory. Frances had spent two weeks of Gil's pay to have it installed. When she hung up the phone, she immediately began planning his homecoming. She grabbed a sheet of paper and began to write all his favorite things down. After a moment she crumpled the paper. It had been four years. She had no idea what his favorite things were anymore. Gil was a good man but not much of a letter writer. He wrote a letter every two weeks. Frances received a total of 212 letters in four years. It seemed like a lot but most of the letters were a best a page long. They always ended the same way:

I hope you are well. I am alright. We are winning.
I will be home soon. My love to you always.
  Gil

There was no detail, no insight, and no way to read what was happening to her beloved Gil. Frances knew more about the Indians in Gil's regiment than any of the other soldiers. She found this curious, like it was okay to write about when they were killed or wounded but not about other members who suffered the same fate. Gil and Frances had married after high school and had fallen in love awkwardly because Gil was a man of few words. When she first set eyes on him, she had swooned. He was a tall, dark, heavily muscled young man with sparkling dark eyes. He was known around Lac Ville as a hardworking man with a bright future. When he smiled at Frances in their senior year of high school, Frances knew she would be his wife.

What had intrigued Frances the most was Gil couldn't care less that she was the prettiest young lady in Lac Ville. She turned down the richest and most handsome men for miles around. Frances had green eyes and the full-bodied figure of the movie stars. She was the object of desire to almost every red-bloodied man in the region. All of that meant nothing if she could catch the eye of Gil.

She did, one hot summer day by the lake. She was fishing by herself. She landed a five-pound northern pike and as she was pulling it from the water, she realized someone was watching her. She turned and saw Gil with his fishing gear. He smiled and asked her where her friends were. With her heart pounding, she replied that she liked to fish alone. Gil smiled and said, "I am going to marry you, Frances."

They married in 1938 with the approval of their families, the church, and almost the whole town of Lac Ville, except for the many heartbroken men and women who had desired them both. Gil worked hard as a cutter and harvester of pulp and softwood lumber. He rose to foreman in the first two years of their marriage. They bought a small two-bedroom house right on the lake. When the war broke out in 1939, it did not seem real to either of them.

News took a long time to arrive, and the radio only broadcasted when the weather was clear and ideal.

Not a lot of young men from Lac Ville rushed to volunteer. Frances heard some boys from Georgetown forty miles up the highway had enlisted but she did not know any of them. Gil became obsessed with the news. He subscribed to the paper in Fort William. It came with the mail every few days and was several days behind the headlines. The first Canadians began to die. Mostly sailors and airmen; each time Gil read of their deaths he would slam the table. An Indian from the reserve across the highway who had joined up in 1939 was killed in England. Gil did not know him, and most people in Lac Ville had not known anyone from the reserve who had joined. Gil became moody and often lost in his thoughts. He even began to lose interest in hunting and fishing.

In January 1941, one of the coldest Januarys in years, Gil told Frances at breakfast he was going to Fort William to enlist. No amount of tears or smashed china could deter him. Frances could be fiery and vocal. It did not matter to Gil. He had made up his mind.

On January 15th, Gil's boyhood friend Alphonse drove him to Fort William in Gil's truck. Gil left money for everything. The fuel and food were taken care of. Gil had shown Frances how to use his 30-30 rifle and shotgun. He promised to write often, and then he was gone.

In the first few months and for the next four years Frances renewed the subscription for the Fort William paper and scanned it anxiously every time it arrived for news of Gil's regiment. Because they had been raised in Fort William, they were often front-page news. They had been converted to an armoured or motorized regiment after they arrived in England. Frances was not sure what it meant. Surely this was a good thing, she thought.

It did not take long before the men who were not at war began coming around. In the years since she had married Gil, she became nothing if not a more beautiful and mature woman. Within a month of Gil enlisting Alphonse lost his trigger finger in a wood cutting accident. Several more men from the town mysteriously lost their trigger fingers in the following weeks making them all ineligible for service. She became accustomed to the men knocking on her door asking if she needed anything. She knew in her heart the needs these men were looking to satisfy were not her own.

The women in town took notice as well. The weaker and jealous ones spread rumours. The stronger ones could only marvel at Frances's strength against temptation. All of them had needs, and in the confines of a small town sometimes they acted on them. Her family and the church helped her occupy the days, then months, and eventually the years Gil was away.

Frances had purchased her gas ration whenever she could. She rarely drove Gil's truck and her father had no need of it. She had more than enough gas to go to Fort William. She hoped it would run alright after sitting for so long. Frances excitedly walked to her father's house to tell him the news. Jean, Frances's father, smiled warmly as she knocked and entered the house. Her mother Louise looked up and said, "Someone has some news, Jean. Look at her smile."

Frances quickly related the call she had just received, and Louise stood and hugged her warmly. Her father seemed oddly indifferent. Frances picked up on it right away. She decided she would wait and ask her father what was going on in the truck away from her mother. He would be more honest and less guarded. Frances was their only child and he told her things he told no one else. Maybe it was because her father had been able to spend so much time with her over the past years, and now she would be with Gil, she thought. She quickly dismissed the thought. Her father was not like that.

It took Louise about an hour to prepare a lunch that could feed four men for three days. Jean was checking the truck, inspecting the tires, belts, and spark plugs. Frances picked a simple blue dress suitable for travelling and packed a small bag with pants and blouses. Frances had a very practical side as well and did not want to be in a dress if they had trouble on the road. They would stay at her uncles in Fort William if they arrived too early and had to stay overnight while waiting for the train. With a flourish of hugs and well wishes from her mother, they headed out onto the highway. Jean had insisted on driving. As he was shifting gears and concentrating on the road, and before she could even ask him, he answered her questions about his reaction to her news this morning. Looking straight ahead he said, "My girl, I am worried. War changes men, even a good man like Gilbert. We could be going to meet someone totally different from the one your young heart remembers." He stopped. Frances let his words sink in and loved him for his concern. She put her hand on his forearm and waited. She knew he was not done talking. "People will treat him differently. Some good, some bad. The men who did not go to war will resent him. It will take a while before things will be the same as they were. They may never be the same," he said.

Frances looked at her father until he turned to gauge her reaction. "It will be alright Father. You will see," she said and turned to watch the road.

Frances started to think about what her father had said. She knew Alphonse was not the friend Gil thought he was. He had come around more times than she could count while Gil was away. When he was with his friends at the store or at the coffee shop, he was always leering at her and making comments about how much work there was to be had during a war. Frances's eyes always found their way to his healed hand and his missing trigger finger. It said everything she needed to know about Alphonse. Frances knew Gil and Alphonse would never be friends again. A cow moose and her calf broke cover and dashed across the road, interrupting her thoughts. Jean downshifted and started laughing. "Too bad we don't have time to shoot her and the calf. Can you imagine what Gil would say if we showed up with them in the truck?" he said. They both started laughing. Frances had happier things to think about.

They were about an hour out of Fort William and were rounding a curve when Frances saw an Indian man with two boys standing hitchhiking at the side of the road outside the entrance to a small reserve. The man looked in his 30s. The boys around eight and six years old. They had a small rucksack and suitcase. Frances looked at her father. Surely, he was going to stop and let them get in the back. Instead, he stopped whistling and accelerated. His face grim and angry. Frances knew the look; it was not a time to challenge or comment. Frances could see the man and boys in the rear-view mirror watch the truck pass with what appeared to be conditioned resignation. A mile or two later, Jean began to whistle again. The rest of the trip went by uneventfully. Frances tried to enjoy the pleasant September day and the scenery. Jean was content to whistle and drive.

Chapter 2

The woodpile was almost completely used. The last two rows of blocks were mostly wet from sitting over the summer. The cover for the wood had been damaged during a storm in August. Mary only used the wood for cooking in the summer but the beginning of fall without a fresh supply made her anxious. Elmer's brother Everett had brought firewood for four of the years while Elmer was overseas, but he had not brought any for months. Mary had skillfully spurned his advances over the years. He tried everything. "Elmer will never know. He is probably with all the French, English, and Dutch girls he can get, Mary. You have needs."

Mary told Everett she would not hesitate to tell his wife Wilma and the elders if he ever touched her. It always seemed to do the trick and Everett would back off.

Everett was Elmer's older brother. Two years older he was a big brutish man who would take or force himself on any woman he could. On a reserve of six hundred people there were not a lot of secrets. He was crude and powerfully built. Elmer was his opposite.

Strong, handsome, and intelligent, he courted Mary since they were children. It seemed only natural they would come together. They married when she was sixteen and he was eighteen. He was a good provider. Elmer trapped, hunted, and took jobs wood cutting whenever he could. They tried to have children for years. Eight years passed before Mary became pregnant. The elders had almost lost hope before Mary gave birth to their daughter Helen. Two years later their son Elias was born. Both children were healthy, and Elmer told Mary there would be more. Their life was comfortable and uneventful.

In 1940, when Elias had just turned one year old an Ontario Provincial Police officer with a priest from Georgetown drove onto the reserve and went to Elmer's Auntie Rita's house. His cousin, Auntie's son Richard, had left the reserve and joined the army in 1939 after the war in Europe had started. "An adventure, Elmer. I don't want to be stuck here like you married with kids," Richard had said, laughing. The war was a distant thing, and everyone thought Richard would be back with many stories in a short while.

Because the reserve was small, almost everyone had stopped what they were doing when the police car drove in. Within a few moments, a mournful wail came from the house and everyone knew Richard had died. Elmer went to the house, as his uncle was on the trap line and days away. Richard had died in a training accident, he learned. His body would not be repatriated, and he was buried in some place called Aldershot in England. The elders came to the house shortly afterwards. The police officer and priest were visibly uncomfortable in the presence of the elders, and after telling Rita that Richard's belongings would be sent home as soon as possible, they got in their car and left. Auntie Rita in her grief had so many unanswered questions. Elmer, always a leader, told her he would find out everything she needed to know, even if it took years. He left her with the elders and went back to his house.

Mary had been watching Auntie Rita's house as the children played in the kitchen. She saw Elmer walking out and coming back to their home, his face set in a grimace and his shoulders straight. Mary knew that look. Mary guessed what he was going to say before he opened the door. "Richard was killed in England. I am going to enlist," Elmer said, looking directly into Mary's eyes.

Mary felt weak in her knees. Elmer was a good man. Kind and thoughtful, he was also as stubborn as anyone Mary had ever known. She knew nothing she could say would dissuade him. "When?" she asked. It was the only word she could say.

"I will get everything you and the children need. I will head to Fort William within the week," Elmer replied. "I will hitch a ride with Luke."

Luke was a truck driver who had married Eva, a mixed-blood girl who lived on the reserve with his auntie Ethel. There was a story there, but Elmer had never asked. Luke gave rides to people who had doctor appointments or other reasons to leave. He never asked for anything. He just did it because he liked everyone. Luke was partly crippled after his truck was hit by a drunk driver just outside Nipegon. He never complained afterwards, he just took it in stride, always working. Luke had a rough edge to him, but he was always smiling. Elmer thought Luke was just one of the characters you found on the reserves from time to time. Luke was accepted without voiced judgements and welcomed for his spirit.

Elmer went outside without further comment. He was heading to his brother's house. Mary grasped the end of the table to steady herself. Elias crawled under it with Helen giggling in pursuit. She slumped into a chair. Just like that Elmer had made up his mind and Mary knew all she could do was support him. She knew he did not have to go. He was married with children. He could be exempted—or, if not, he could find a way to stay in Canada. Mary knew he would never accept that. He did not go on hunting parties just to paddle the canoe. When he made up his mind, he always took the lead and the risks. One of the reasons she had fallen in love with him was his resolve, and now she would have to bear its burden. Mary picked Elias up and patted Helen's head. They were both smiling.

Everett slammed his hand down on the table. Cups and plates flew in the air. Everett's wife had retreated into the bedroom when Elmer came in. "It is not your war, brother. We have already lost our cousin. It makes no god damn sense for you to go," Everett shouted.

Elmer held up his hand. "I have already decided. All I am asking is you watch over Mary and the children," Elmer said calmly.

Everett regained his composure. Breathing heavily, he knew Elmer was going. As long as Elmer had not volunteered, then there had not been any pressure on him or the other men to do the same, he thought selfishly. "You will be the death of us Elmer," Everett muttered and added, "I will watch over Mary and everyone else while you are away, brother."

"That's all I can ask Everett, thank you," Elmer replied, and let himself out the door.

Mary was frying bannock when Elmer came back. There was a pot of tea on the stove and two cups on the table. Mary did not turn around when he came in. Elmer paused. He stood staring at her, taking in her long black hair and a figure any woman would be envious of. He knew she was upset and hoped she would turn to look at him. He knew in Mary's mind he was already gone. It was how she coped whenever he had to leave. But this is different Mary, he thought. The children broke the silence. Helen squealed and started laughing as she ran towards him, throwing herself in his arms. Elias sat up and stared. Elmer squeezed Helen tight then put her down. He walked behind Mary and put his arms around her. A foot taller than her, he gently rested his chin on her head. He loved the smell of her and knew he would miss the warmth of her embrace. Mary did not respond. For her, Elmer knew he was already gone. Her coldness hurt him. He loved her so much, but he understood. It was his Mary's way.

Within three days, Elmer had shot a young bull moose and a bear. One hundred miles north of the northern tip of Lake Superior, the area around the reserve was thickly forested and criss-crossed with rivers, swamps, and small lakes all set into and on the many rock outcroppings of the magnificent Canadian shield. It was rich with game and fish, even with the growing number of people the forestry and mining industries had brought in since Elmer was a boy. The other women were helping Mary to dress the animals. He had gone to Lac Ville and purchased bags of flour, cans of lard, salt, and tea. It was enough for a couple of months until he started receiving his army pay. He had packed a small bag and had kept ten dollars for incidentals. On the morning of the fourth day, Luke pulled up in his truck. He was hauling broken machinery from the sawmill for repair in Fort William. Luke called to Elmer, "Come on, times a wasting."

Elmer waved from the front door. He hugged Helen and Elias. He then took Mary in his arms. "I love you," he said.

Mary looked him in the eyes and said, "I love you too. You better go."

Elmer stepped out the door and she closed the screen door behind him. Elmer shrugged, walked over to Luke's truck, and jumped in the passenger side door. Luke put the truck in gear. Elmer looked toward the house and could not see anyone. Luke eased the truck out of the reserve, onto to the highway and they were off.

Mary cleared breakfast from the table and began to cry. She cried for a long time with little Helen wiping her tears and asking why she was crying. Elias was on the floor chewing on a towel.

Mary closed her eyes at the memories and brought herself to the matters at hand. The war was over. The fist of dread that had gripped her heart for so long loosened. Elmer had survived and was coming home.

Mary knew she had changed. She had become very independent and had learned to run the house and raise the children on her own. Elmer's army pay was more than enough even with the portion held back by the Indian agent. The law allowed the agent to hold a portion of Elmer's service pay in trust because it was thought Indian women would not be responsible or savvy enough to handle the money. Mary kept an accurate ledger of how much she and Elmer were owed. She would be sure to tell Elmer when he got home. Mary had become a leader in the community, especially among the women. She had advocated for a school to be built on the reserve so the children would not be taken to the residential schools.

She had written a well-reasoned proposal to the government that outlined the cost effectiveness of a small school. She had learned that with Indian Affairs, anything which saved them money was considered with uncharacteristic bureaucratic speed. She also learned that the less the band was seen or heard from, the happier and more compliant Indian Affairs was. The school with two classrooms opened in 1943. Mary made sure the men felt they were responsible. Everett boasted to the other men about how he had got things done. He was hired as the foreman when the school was being built. Mary knew he was bitter and resentful of Mary's pivotal role. The job also kept him out of the war when the casualties were the highest and the need was the greatest, something Everett would never acknowledge.

Mary was brushing her hair and fussing with the children. She was doing her best to keep them clean. Helen was roughhousing Elias, who had grown into a solid young boy. Helen talked constantly and Elias said little; he was, however, always smiling. Elias was a spitting image of Elmer. Helen was a combination of them both. Mary knew Elmer would be home today or tomorrow at the latest. There was nothing more to do but wait. Mary had spent the last four years regretting how she had said goodbye to Elmer. She had been so cold. It was how she covered fear and hurt. Elmer's letters, more like notes, had revealed nothing untoward. They became sparse when the fighting was the fiercest towards the end of the war. They became more detailed and frequent when the war ended. Mary would know how things were when she saw Elmer and not a moment before.

Chapter 3

The conductor was true to his word. It was about four in the morning when the train pulled into the Fort William yard. It was dark except for the lights at the station, and it would be several hours before sunrise. The early morning was cool and misty with the moisture of Lake Superior heavy in the air. The engineer only blew the whistle once because the city council had admonished the CPR about waking up the people in the hospital and surrounding area when troop trains came in late. The war had been over for months and the people who were going to meet the train would be there. The rest of the city was trying to sleep and move on. Everyone on the train went anxiously to the windows and vestibules to try and get a glance at loved ones waiting for them. The cool air revitalized their energy and excitement after such a long and tiring journey. The crowd was small. For many soldiers their welcome home would have to wait until they were actually home. Most of the men in the regiment were from isolated communities and travel was always a major undertaking especially when the day they would arrive kept changing. Inside the railway station, the regiment's rear party and welfare officer had set up a discharge centre. The soldiers would receive their last pay and sign out before leaving with or going to find their loved ones.

The train screeched to a halt and billows of steam belched into the air. Gil saw Frances by the door of the waiting room. She was with her father. He watched as Frances scanned the train looking for him. The Regimental Sergeant Major had told the troops they would have about fifteen minutes to greet everyone before they would parade and be mustered out. Gil wanted every one of those fifteen moments, and he jumped off the train as soon as the conductor opened the door. Frances was still scanning the rush of soldiers when Gil grabbed her waist. She spun around surprised and was greeted with a bear hug and a kiss.

Elmer had let everyone with people meeting them get off before he did. He shouldered his kit bag and stepped onto the platform. It felt good to be off the train. Elmer knew Mary would not be there. In her last letter she had told him she would wait at their home for him. The city was not a good place for her and the children. Elmer knew it was possible other letters may still be out there and in transit, but he knew she and the children would not be here this morning.

Elmer looked for Richard Sutherland hoping to talk to him before they went their separate ways. He saw him by the baggage wagons looking in his kit bag. As Elmer walked over, the company sergeant majors began calling everyone to fall in. Loved ones groaned and muttered, but the discipline of the regiment held as they reformed for the mustering out parade. Everything was done in alphabetical order so Elmer knew it would be a while before he was signed out. He figured he would catch Richard Sutherland before he left. Gilbert Bertrand would probably be long gone before he was done. He had seen Gil's wife meet him shortly after they had de-trained. She was more beautiful than Gil had said. Elmer longed for his Mary. Mary's beauty took his breath away. Soon, Elmer thought, soon.

Elmer waited patiently. He heard one of the sergeant majors

call out "Private Nelson R." the soldier came to attention with a slam of his boot and marched to the table in the waiting room. Private Nelson R. saluted, signed some papers, received a thick large manila envelope and stepped back. He saluted again and then turned to go out the back door of the train station onto the city streets, a civilian once more. Soldier after soldier followed. A regiment bonded by fire and shared experience, disappearing into the misty morning as the first hints of sunrise shone through the station windows. The commanding officer and senior staff stood by the ticket counter. All of them would soon be returning to their former occupations unburdened of the responsibility for their men's lives. The commanding officer had wanted to parade them through the twin cities so his men could feel the appreciation of the civilians they had fought to protect. It would have added another two days for the men before they could go home. The Senior NCOs dissuaded him. This was how it was going to end.

Elmer's name was called. Elmer came to attention, slamming his boot to the station floor. He marched up, halted, and saluted. The clerk turned his discharge papers to him and presented his envelope. Elmer signed and saluted. The captain at the table said, "Good luck Chief."

Elmer turned and walked to the station doors. He stepped through them and except for a few stragglers saw very few uniforms. Richard Sutherland was gone. Gone without a word. The sun was rising. There were civilians moving down the streets. Hardly any of them gave him a second look. It was about a two-mile walk to the bus depot where he would begin the last leg of his journey home. He hoped he could find a coffee along the way. He hoisted his kit bag onto his shoulder and started to walk.

"Elmer," someone shouted. Elmer turned and saw a 1938 Chevy dump truck about fifty yards away in the station parking lot. Gil was hanging out the driver's side waving. "You need a lift, Elmer?" There was another soldier sitting in the dump truck box already. Gil recognized him as the Finnish kid, Walter Enio, who lived on a lake ten miles north of Georgetown. He had come as a replacement late in the war, but he had fought like a veteran. They would never let him do sentry duty because his accent was so thick a nervous soldier would have shot him as soon as he started talking. Elmer walked toward the truck. Frances was in the middle and a man he had never met was on the passenger side. Frances smiled warmly. The other man scowled and avoided eye contact. Gil got out to meet Elmer. "We were waiting for you. We are going the same way. It won't be as comfortable as the bus, but it will be quicker." Gil turned to introduce Elmer. "Frances, this is Elmer Wabason. The fellow I wrote you about. This is Jean, Frances's father."

Frances smiled and said, "Pleased to meet you, Elmer."

Jean grunted something and looked at Gil. "I guess we need to get going," Gil said. "There are some horse blankets in the chain boxes. Try to make yourselves comfortable. We can grab some coffees and food once we are out of the city," he added.

Elmer threw his kit bag into the wooden box of the dump truck and climbed up. Walter smiled and tossed him two heavy blankets. Before Elmer had even sat down Gil put the truck in gear and was turning out of the parking lot. Elmer half fell against the back of the box and quickly put the blankets under his buttocks to save them from the slivers. Walter laughed.

It took about twenty minutes to get out of the city. Fort William was a city of contrast; old fashioned and modern caught between the remnants of pre-war depression and the benefits of wartime prosperity. It was the gateway to Northern Ontario, so its population reflected it in their dress and mannerisms, with some people looking as if they just came out of the bush and others in suits and ties. "All these people Elmer, moving around like there was never a war," Walter said with his heavy accent.

Elmer just nodded. He had not really given it much thought. He had plans, but they were small and all based on Mary and the children. He had never really considered how much the rest of the country had been changed. He began to think about last night's conversation with Gil. Gil believed septic systems and sewage would provide their future. He was sure they would be popular, and if they were willing to work, they could corner the market in Lac Ville and Georgetown, maybe even further. Elmer shuddered as he thought of the smell of the dead bodies baked in the sun he and Gil had passed in Europe. Sewage would not bother him. Gil was right; they could do this. Elmer smiled to himself. Walter who had been watching him asked "Thinking of your woman, Elmer?"

"Yes," Elmer lied. He had not really spoken to Walter at any length. Elmer and the older soldiers were always stand-offish with replacements during the war. It was a hard habit to break even though the war was over. A conversation would help pass the time. "What are you going home to Walter?" Elmer asked.

Walter grinned and replied, "My trap line, if no one stole it, and my cabin if it is still standing. I'm also a carpenter. When I get tired of the bush, I will start a business and find a woman. Do you know any who would like a man like me, Elmer?"

Elmer was surprised for the second time in as many days. Walter seemed like a good man and Elmer's cousin Lucy's husband had drowned in early 1944. As far as he knew she had been alone ever since. Maybe he could introduce them. "I might be able to arrange something, Walter," he said. Walter gave him the thumbs up. He knew Elmer was as good as his word.

About an hour out of the city, Gil pulled the truck over by a lake. Elmer and Walter had been taking in the smells and scenery while talking about everything from trapping to storing wood, and had not noticed the time. Elmer found he had to really listen close because of Walter's accent. Walter, he found, was a practical young man with a dry sense of humour and very knowledgeable about the North. You either could or could not live in the bush. If you were one of the people who could not, he probably would not have said more than a few words to you. Gil got out and said, "Frances says there is enough sandwiches in the chain box to feed everyone and three thermoses of coffee filled at three this morning."

Gil stretched as Frances came out the door behind him. She smiled at Walter and Elmer and brushed her hair back. Elmer opened the chain box and took out a basket and the thermos. He handed them to Gil. Walter jumped down and went into the bush to relieve himself.

"You know it took Walter a year before the army accepted

him because his father was Finnish. They were not sure where his loyalty lies. Walter made the trip three times to Fort William before they let him join," Elmer told Gil.

Gil laughed. "They should have seen him in action. There would have been no doubts."

The passenger door opened and Jean got out. He spoke quietly to Frances and ignored Gil and Elmer. It was awkward and uncomfortable for everyone. Gil and Elmer looked at each other with knowing glances. Jean was being like the German middle-aged men when they occupied Germany: full of hate without the courage to express it. Gil quietly said, "Elmer, I did not know about this part of Jean until this morning. It has been a quiet ride so far. Let's not let it wreck our day. We will be home in a couple of hours."

Elmer shook his head in agreement. Frances looked over and Elmer could tell from her eyes and expression she was troubled and embarrassed by her father's behaviour.

Walter returned, face and hands wet with lake water. "Smell this air my friends. Feel this land," he almost shouted with a smile. Walter was oblivious to the tension between everyone else. Walter was in his mind already home. They ate the sandwiches and drank the coffee quickly while Jean smoked and talked softly to Frances at the front of the truck. When they were finished Gil said, "Let's mount up boys." He smiled at Frances and in turn ignored Jean.

They never really got going over 45 miles an hour. Gil's truck was not built for speed or highway driving. He was very proud of his truck and had paid cash for it in 1938. Every load and haul he made before he went to war had been profit minus the fuel and maintenance costs. He worked long days between his job as a foreman and his hauling business. It occurred to Gil he had not really arranged to keep everything in place while he was gone. Getting his old job back would be a good start. Gil saw the sign for Georgetown and started gearing down. The town site was about a quarter mile off the highway and Gil put his turn signal on. Walter tapped on the roof. "Right here is good enough."

Gil pulled over and got out. Walter grabbed his kit bag and

jumped down. He reached his hand up to shake Elmer's and then shook Gil's. Gil said, "Walter it is still ten miles to the lake. I will drive you."

Walter replied, "I am going to the tavern for a beer and a ten mile walk afterward is nothing. Thank you. You know where I live. Your truck would never get up that trail they call a road anyways. Come and see me when you can my friends."

With that, Walter tipped his cap and started walking. Gil looked up at Elmer, shrugged, and got in the truck. As Walter walked away, Elmer thought of something. Walter, Gil, and he were among the few soldiers he knew who aimed their shots during the battles they were in. Most of the lads just unloaded in the general direction of the enemy. He knew where every shot went, every time he missed or hit his targets. Gil was the same. Walter had said in his deadpan way that it was because the ammunition was too heavy to haul around, so he did not want to waste it like the killing was an afterthought. Elmer thought differently. He knew it was because they were truly warriors, and no one would ever take that away from them.

Frances looked at Gil as he drove. He looked older and a little harder than when he left. It only made him more handsome to her. His smile could still melt any woman's heart. But he was hers and now she had him back.

Gil downshifted again and pulled onto the road leading to Elmer's reserve. Someone had shot the sign that someone else had taken time to paint and erect more than once. Elmer noticed the bullet holes as well. Elmer double tapped the cab roof as Walter had done and Gil stopped the truck. "I want to surprise everyone by walking in. If you drive in everyone will come out to see who it is," Elmer said.

Gil jumped out of the truck. "Aren't you a sneaky bugger," he said. Elmer grabbed his kit bag and jumped out. Gil surprised him by giving him a hug. "I will come and see you in a few days. What is your house number?" Gil asked.

Elmer looked him in the eyes. "Twelve. It's the one with the flag out front," he replied. "Thank you for the ride," Elmer said, waving at Frances.

Jean stared out of the passenger side window. Frances waved back and said, "Good luck Elmer."

"Thank you, brother," Elmer said to Gil and turned to walk the four hundred yards onto the reserve.

Elmer was marching. He could not help it. His left hand secured his kit bag, but his right arm was swinging. He felt proud of his uniform. He wished his boots were shined. The gravel would have wrecked the shine anyway, he corrected himself. He saw smoke rising from a couple of chimneys and heard children playing. Someone was chopping wood. Elmer began to feel a little light-headed with every step. He was almost home, he thought. A young boy who was throwing rocks in a pond and a dog that started barking were the first to notice him. The boy immediately ran into a house. Three more boys appeared in short order. Then their father, Douglas, came out waving. Elmer put his finger to his lips for them to keep quiet. He saw his house, and that the flag was still there. It was everything he could do not to break into a run. He reached the front step and pretended not to notice the people who had all come out of their houses to see what was going on. He quietly turned the doorknob and entered the kitchen. Mary was scrubbing Elias' ears with vigor. "Elias, I do not know where you find all this dirt," she was telling him. Helen first noticed Elmer, the father she had not seen for five years. She shyly looked down with just the hint of a smile and touched Mary's shoulder, pointing towards Elmer.

Mary turned. Her eyes widened. She dropped the washcloth and ran to Elmer. Elmer opened his arms and pulled her close. Elias was having none of this and put himself between them trying to push them apart. Elmer and Mary both laughed. Mary reached down and told Elias, "It's ok Elias, this is your father." He looked up and turned away. He walked about five feet then just stood and stared at Elmer. He had no memories of him and had only seen his picture. He trusted his mother and she looked happy, so this was good enough for him. He went to Helen and held her hand.

✦

Gil drove the last three miles into Lac Ville. People waved as they drove through the town. Gil drove Jean to his house. Louise came running out, thanking God, Jesus, and the Virgin Mary repeatedly as she kissed the three of them. "Come in the house. I will feed you," she said.

Frances looked at her mother and shook her head. "We will come back later, Mother," she said.

Gil thanked Jean for coming to get him. Frances winked at her mother and said, "I want to get him home."

Her mother winked back. "Go get settled. We will see you in a while."

Jean went into the house, followed closely by Louise.

Chapter 4

Mary was brushing Helen's hair while Elias finished his oatmeal. Elmer was chopping wood and filling the woodbin. Mary was smiling. She was sure she was pregnant. For the last five days Mary and Elmer had been like newlyweds. They had come together every time the children were not around or sleeping. It was not like they were trying to make up for lost time. Elmer had said it best, "It is like when two bodies of water are separated by a beaver's dam and the dam is broken. They quickly come together again to be one. It is what is right."

Elmer was an awkward romantic. Elmer came into the house with an arm full of wood blocks and dropped them into the bin by the stove. He smiled at Helen "Beautiful, like your mother," he said.

Helen smiled shyly. She had warmed up to him quickly. Elias was already starting to walk like Elmer, and imitate his father's mannerisms. He still did not say much. He watched everything Elmer did. When he finished his oatmeal, he took his bowl to the dish pan. He started making his own bed every morning as soon as he got up like Elmer did. He placed his boots neatly by the door like Elmer did. "All right you two, off to school," Mary said.

Elmer looked at Mary with a sly grin. "The school you made happen, Mary," he said.

On his second day at home, he had walked with the children there and looked it over. Mary had told him the story and how Everett had been the foreman during its construction. The school looked solid enough. Elmer was just happy it was here. "Pride is a sin, Elmer. Everyone did something to make it happen," Mary said.

Elmer glanced out the window and saw the children, with Helen hovering over her younger brother, joining up with other children on their way to school. Then he saw Gil's truck coming down the road. Elmer heard the now distinctive gearing down and watched as Gil slowed, searching for his flag and house. A moment later he was in front. Elmer stepped out the door and walked over. Gil was out in a flash and gave Elmer another bear hug. Elmer knew everyone was watching. Not many people from Lac Ville came to the reserve. Elmer turned towards his house. "Come on in and meet Mary," he said. Mary was standing by the open screen door. Gil was momentarily speechless. Mary was a beauty. Her dark eyes were mesmerizing, and her smile could make a man weak. Mary held the door open, and Elmer introduced Gil. He shook Mary's hand.

Mary was impressed. Elmer had described Gil to her, but his actual demeanour was powerful. He had presence and purpose like Elmer. She could see how they had gravitated to each other. He was rugged and handsome as well. Elmer had developed a taste for coffee in the service and there was a freshly brewed pot on the stove. She poured coffee for them and felt a twinge of resentment towards Gil. He had spent the past five years with Elmer, and he knew more about what her husband had been through than she did. They talked like the brothers Elmer and Everett should be. "Envy is a sin," she thought and put the feeling aside. Mary began to busy herself cleaning up the breakfast dishes.

Elmer and Gil talked for about an hour, Gil laying out his plans for their new business and how they were going to pay for it. He said, "With all the army surplus material, we should be able to find a powerful pump. With luck we could find a water trailer we could convert to put sewage in. The military grade water trailers would be the best there was."

Elmer was making notes and had suggestions. Mary watched them, thinking, this man Gil sees her Elmer as she does, a man worth walking with and an equal. She had never experienced this before. Mary also felt a bit apprehensive because she knew a lot of people would not feel the same.

Her thoughts were interrupted by a quick rap on the screen door before Everett let himself in. Everett had done this many times while Elmer was gone hoping to catch her asleep or half dressed. She knew in her heart the only reason he had not taken her forcefully was because she was Elmer's wife. He always had an excuse or pretext for coming over. Mary waited for it now. Everett asked if he could borrow Elmer's mallet and log splitter. Elmer introduced Gil and Everett to each other. Mary knew Everett just wanted to know what Gil and his truck were doing at Elmer's house. She watched Gil. Gil was cordial enough with Everett, but Mary could see he instinctively did not like him. Reading Everett came easily as well. Everett was intimidated, and when he was intimidated, he always would find an underhanded way to balance the scales at some point. These men were sometimes like open books. Her apprehension about Gil's and Elmer's plans was beginning to gather momentum like an impending storm. Everett having at least partially satisfied his curiosity nodded to everyone and went out to the shed to grab the implements he asked for.

Gil and Elmer finished the coffee and, having outlined their plans, said goodbye with pats on the back and a handshake. Mary stayed in the house and waited for Elmer to come back in. She had some questions.

Gil pulled onto the highway, reflecting on how his meeting had gone with Elmer. This trip had been his first ever to the reserve, even though he had lived his whole life in Lac Ville, which was only three miles away. It took a war to get him to do what he should have done a long time ago. Gil had appraised the reserve as he drove in. It appeared to him the Indians were given possibly the worst piece of land available: two miles square with the railway tracks and highway on the south side and the swampy end of the lake on the north. To the east was the river and to the west was scrub brush. There was not a lot of room for it to grow. The land to the west looked wet and uneven but it was the only way the reserve could expand. It could be done with a lot of back fill and drainage planning. He would talk to Elmer about the possibilities the next time they got together.

The first few days at home had been eventful for Gil and Frances as well. They had no children to interrupt or regulate their pent-up passions. There was days Gil thought his strength would fail him. Frances was a lover other men could only dream about. At nine o'clock in the evening on his second day home, Alphonse and some of the fellows he grew up with showed up in a pickup truck. They were drunk and began banging on the door like teenagers. Gil went to the door and saw they had a couple of cases of beer with them. Frances looked at Gil with concern. This would be the first time Alphonse and Gil had met since he had returned. Frances knew Alphonse had taken Gil's job as a foreman when Gil was serving. Frances also knew from the town gossip he was not willing to give it up now that Gil was back. Alphonse had told the boss he had earned it. Gil knew none of this and Frances thought Alphonse was supposed to be in the bush for another week.

Gil thought Frances was just put off because of the interruption of their evening. He opened the door and stepped out on the porch. One of the men used a knife to pop off the cap of a beer and handed it to Gil. Gil raised it up in a salute and guzzled half the bottle. Alphonse stepped forward and hugged Gil. "Welcome home soldier," he said and raised his beer to the others. They cheered and began sitting all over the porch. Alphonse was already close to having had enough. His speech was slurred, and his eyes were glassy. He went to light a cigarette and Gil saw his hand. His trigger finger was gone, and the socket had healed poorly. Gil felt a wave of anger rising up inside of him. He thought of the men who had died in combat alongside him. Men who never doubted their purpose and went forward despite their fears. Now his best friend from boyhood sat on his porch without even being self-conscious of the injury that in some people's minds would always mark him as a coward. Then he saw that Daniel, another boy he grew up with, was missing two fingers on his right hand as well. Had to make certain did you, Gil thought. Pine beetles thrive after forest fires. In his mind Gil switched from having celebratory beers with his old friends to an intelligence gathering role. Gil spent the next two hours getting as much information as he could about the people he thought he knew. He knew these people would be some of the new obstacles he would have to overcome.

Frances never came out of the house when the men were out front. She did not like any of them and knew they would eye her up and down whenever Gil was not looking. She was nervous about what he had heard and how it would affect him. Gil came in the house sober and smiling. He told her he purposely spilled most of the beer he was given. Frances held her breath waiting for Gil to ask her why she had not told him about what some of his friends had done to avoid the war. He turned down the lamp, took her in his arms, and lifted her nightgown over her head.

The next day Gil went to the superintendent's office of the company he worked for as a foreman before the war. The superintendent welcomed him in and offered him a coffee. He asked some questions about the trip home and quickly came to the point. "Are you wanting your old job back?" he asked.

Gil replied honestly. "Yes, I was hoping to pick up where I left off."

The superintendent was a straightforward man. Gil always liked that about him. He told Gil that Alphonse had been the foreman for the past four years. He was going to keep Alphonse in the position out of fairness. If Gil wanted to start again as a cutter, he was welcome to. He had needed Gil during the war, and it was not the company's fault Gil had chosen to enlist. Pine bugs plant their eggs in the stumps of trees while they are still smouldering after a forest fire. Pine bugs thrive after a calamity, natural or caused by men, Gil could not help thinking. Gil swallowed his pride and took the job, asking for a week to get his affairs in order before he started. The superintendent truly had no idea of the significance of what he had just done to a returning veteran. He was a company man through and through. "See you Monday," he said shaking Gil's hand.

When Gil got home, he told Frances he would be going back to work Monday. He did not tell her the details.

The next couple of days, Gil and Frances visited different people in town for coffee and to catch up with everyone. Frances saw and felt what her father had told her on the drive to Fort William to get Gil. People were treating him differently. Some acted like he never left and others were cautious, as if Gil was damaged or so changed that they did not know what to say to him anymore. It was the worst at her parents. Jean and Gil hardly spoke to each other anymore, and her mother tried too hard to pretend everything was the same as before Gil left. Frances began to worry. Gil just seemed to be taking it all in with a detachment that frightened her. When they were alone, he outlined his plan for the business he wanted to start with Elmer. He was animated and excited when he spoke. Frances asked him why he wanted to work with Elmer so badly, knowing some people, especially as he had found out her own father, would not like it. Gil looked at her and said, "He has all of his fingers, and he is not a pine bug." Frances understood the first part but did not have a clue what the pine bug reference meant. Gil, who rarely did, had shown the depths of his feelings about what had happened since he came back. She made up her mind that whatever Gil had planned, she would support him. The next morning, Gil went to the reserve house number 12 with the flag in front of it.

Chapter 5

Alphonse was having coffee with some of the men from his crew in front of the post office. Everyone was talking about the landings in Normandy. It was a beautiful morning. The mid-June sun was warm and the air rich with the smells of late spring. "Now the real fighting will begin," Robert, the postman, said.

The other men agreed, nodding their heads. Alphonse grew uncomfortable and changed the subject. "If the black flies do not carry us away, we should get back to making some money tomorrow," he said.

They would start cutting pulp trees in the low-lying area thirteen miles north of the lake in the morning. The Ministry of Natural Resources had closed the area to harvesting in 1930, and believed it had recovered enough to allow harvesting again. Robert and the other men knew Alphonse never talked about the war, despite the fact his best friend Gil had been in it for three years now. When he lost his trigger finger to a log chain in '41, Alphonse appeared devastated. Devastated, until home brew loosened his tongue and he told everyone that whoever had volunteered for the war was a fool. He could and would take whatever he could from them while they were gone. "Fair was fair." he said.

The war, except for losing a finger and nearly his arm to subsequent infection, had been good to Alphonse. It took a year before he was promoted to foreman in place of Gil. The sailing had been smooth ever since. He was making good money and there were plenty of girls who liked a man with money. More than once, he had assigned one of his men to stay in the bush for the weekend so he could spend it with the man's wife. Alphonse knew he was not as handsome as Gil. He was, he knew, well endowed, and married women seemed to love that about him. He did not even have to try to be a good lover. Home brewed beer and spirits allowed Alphonse and the men to circumvent the rationing system. Frances was the prize to him, and the stuck-up bitch would not give him the time of day. Even though she was Gil's wife, all the men had bet they could partake in her charms. All of them had failed. Still, Alphonse fantasized about her. He plotted and schemed constantly. He knew his desperation made him look pathetic and weak to Frances. He hated how it made him feel. Every woman he was with was Frances to him. As long as the war continued, Alphonse knew one way or the other he had a chance, even if a German bullet was the cause.

On the evening of May 8, 1945, the news that the war in Europe had ended reached Lac Ville. Everyone was celebrating and drinking to a victory many of them had no part at all in. Frances was with her parents, and they urged her to stay at their house because so many men were drunk. She refused, saying, "I have spent many nights alone and this one is no different." She was happy, and was going to have a glass of wine and go to bed. When she was home, she locked the door and drew the curtains. It was a warm night, and she slid the window in her bedroom open about 3 inches. A gentle breeze off the lake rustled the curtains. Around eleven o'clock she heard shooting, yelling, and laughing. Some men were firing their rifles in the air to celebrate the war's end. This usually only happened on New Year's Eve, but it did not scare her. She sipped on her wine and was thinking of the day Gil would be home.

She heard a noise at the back of the house. Too loud for a small animal, and she knew a bear would not be that noisy. She heard heavy breathing and she turned the lamp as low as it would go. Fingers, seven she could see, started to slide the bedroom window upwards. Frances grabbed the .30-30 rifle and cocked it. The window stopped. Frances shouted, "Alphonse, if you come in, I will kill you. If you are lucky, I will not tell Gil." Next, she heard crashing in the bush behind her house. She ran to the window in time to see a figure smashing through the trees. The rest of the night was quiet, though Frances hardly slept.

Two days later Frances heard a story about Alphonse at the store. He was scratched all over his face and hands. He had nearly lost an eye to a branch. His story was he had gone to the reserve to see a willing girl and had been chased off by a pack of reserve dogs. Frances knew better, but said nothing. It was almost funny, if he was not such a single-minded bastard.

Now that Gil was home, Alphonse was confident Frances had said nothing. Gil had to know by now he had taken his job as foreman. From what he could remember the next day, Gil was friendly and asked a lot of questions when he and the boys had gone over for beers. Gil seemed to have accepted the changes without question.

"That's what happens when you leave to fight someone else's war, Gil, my friend," Alphonse said out loud to himself as he prepared for work on Monday. He was not done with Gil or Frances yet.

A week earlier, three miles to the west on the Lac Ville Indian reservation, Everett had stomped onto the steps. Everett had come home from Elmer's in a temper. He threw the mallet and log splitter in the porch and sat heavily at the kitchen table. There was no place his wife, Wilma, could go to be out of his way.

"I don't know what Elmer is planning with that guy from Lac

Ville," he said. "It's like Elmer has forgotten who his real brother is. Just because those two were in the war together doesn't mean things are going to change around here, Wilma. He was always a bit of a fool," Everett said, almost shouting spittle and spraying the table. Wilma tried to make herself small like she always did. It did not help. Everett turned to her. "This fuckin house is a mess," he yelled. He threw the salt and sugar trays at her. It's too early for a beating and the kids will be home for lunch, Wilma thought as she quickly cleaned the broken glass, spilt sugar, and salt. Wilma kept her eyes down. When she dared to glance up, Everett was gone.

Everett was fuming as he walked down the path on the west river side of the reserve. Leaves were starting to turn and there was the smell of fall in the air. At the very edge of the reserve was his cousin Lucy's cabin, barely visible from the path. Lucy's husband, Peter, one of Everett's drinking buddies, had drowned in early 1944 when he tried to get a jump on the pickerel spring run with a dip net. He was more than half cut, slipped on the wet rocks, and fell in the rapids. The cold fast water took him in a few minutes. Everett had bought the strong homemade brew from an ugly guy from Lac Ville named Alphonse and sold it to Peter and the other men on the reserve.

Everett turned onto the path leading to Lucy's cabin. There was a curl of smoke coming out of the chimney. Everett hoped there were no elders visiting. He stopped and listened. He did not hear any voices. He threw the door of the cabin open. Lucy was drinking a cup of tea. Her eyes went wide. She threw the teacup at him. He knocked it aside and closed the door. He pushed her down and turned her over. Lucy knew he was too strong and mean for her to fight him again. In the past, he had beaten her body (though not her face) so badly she had peed blood. He raped her as he had been doing ever since Peter had died. When he was finished, he stood up and fastened his pants. He went out the door without a word. Lucy lay on the dirt floor and thought someday she would kill him, and started to cry.

Everett stepped out of the cabin and looked left and right to make sure no one had seen him. Even if they had, he did not think anyone was brave enough to say anything to him. He was almost out of home brew. He would have to see Alphonse this weekend. They both made a healthy profit from this arrangement. Everett still sold the brew on the reserve. He had offered up Lucy to help cut his costs. Alphonse only came at night. Lucy knew better than to protest. "I don't know how that bitch doesn't get pregnant." he thought as he went home to see his children, who should be home for lunch. He was hungry as well.

Chapter 6

This was the fifteenth time Gil was at house 12. Helen and Elias had taken a shine to him. Mary was comfortable and looked forward to his visits. When Gil and Elmer were together, Elmer was relaxed. She did not know all the details, but it seemed whatever they had been working on was coming together. Gil had told Elmer he had gotten a letter from the officer who had overseen the motor pool in the brigade their unit had been attached to. This officer had a line on a 300-gallon water trailer with a hand pump. It was declared surplus. The forest protection branch of the Department of Lands and Forests had bought all the big trailers at rock bottom prices. They had overlooked this one. It was sitting in the vehicle park in Port Arthur at the armoury. The commanding officer who knew Gil told the officer he could have it for five dollars if he could get it out of his compound before December. The hand pump was not ideal, and it would be labour intensive. Still, it was a good start.

Gil bought a surplus 15 cwt General Service truck for two hundred dollars on the same trip. Elmer was able to put in fifty dollars after writing a letter to the Indian agent who had withheld a portion of his pay from Mary. He had been assured the agent would release the money to him. He knew the Indian agent would not want to meet him in person. Gil drove his dump truck home. Elmer drove the familiar army truck and trailer. The surplus truck was relatively new, and it had a powerful 95 horsepower Ford engine. The truck had been used by the home force and had never been deployed overseas. Gil insisted Elmer keep the truck and trailer on the reserve and he use the truck to make money in whatever way Elmer thought he could. Gil kept a notebook of all transactions and he showed Elmer everything he wrote so everything would be "on the up and up," he said.

As winter set in, Elmer insulated the trailer with canvas and began hauling water for the school and the residents of the reserve. He hauled firewood and made grocery runs. It was cold work. Elmer loved the brisk clean air. The smell of the lake water and the wood kept him warm. He did not charge much; just enough to pay for gas and a small profit to provide an income. Even at the low prices he charged, he quickly accumulated enough to pay Gil the other fifty dollars for the truck to make it a fifty-fifty venture. Gil smiled and wrote the transaction in his book when Elmer gave him the money. "We are just getting started my friend." Gil said.

Mary had been busy as well. When the children were in school, she sometimes went with Elmer on his rounds, using the opportunity to talk to everyone who normally bunkered down for the cold winter months. Mary knew homebrewed alcohol was becoming a problem in some houses and she gathered as much information as she politely could. "Whenever a dark cloud appeared, Everett was usually involved," she thought. Mary had been so blissfully happy for the past months she had missed a lot of what had been going on. Mary decided she would do everything she could to put a stop to the flow of alcohol onto the reserve. She would tell Elmer what she was doing when the time was right. "Good strong men could sometimes be very naïve," she thought.

Mary had convinced the nuns who were teaching at the school to let her use a classroom at night as an office. She was organizing the women to improve their everyday living conditions. They shared everything so no one would go without. Clothing, food, and tools were shared until they were so worn out, they had to be replaced. A lot of the men from the reserve worked in the Georgetown gold mine, so there was money around. The men, however, controlled it in a lot of households and Mary saw a need for what she was doing.

Mary worried about Wilma, Everett's wife, and all the wives of Everett's drinking buddies. Everything about Everett said he beat her to Mary. Then there was Elmer's cousin, Lucy. Mary had not seen a lot of her since her husband had drowned. Lucy was only five feet tall. She was blessed or cursed with an ample bosom and a beautiful face. Men would trip over themselves to get her attention. Before Peter died, she was always around, laughing and carelessly flirting. Now the light seemed to have left her and she rarely smiled. There was a pain behind her eyes and Mary knew there was something else besides the grief over her husband's death. Elmer knew Mary was suspicious of Lucy. He always brought Mary with him when he brought Lucy wood and water. Lucy had a small business tanning hides and making gloves and moccasins. She seemed to be getting by. Mary vowed to get Wilma and Lucy alone the first chance she had. Mary wished her mother was here so she could ask what she would do. Both Elmer's and her parents had moved to Moosonee on the shore of James's Bay after they were married. They were very traditional and did not speak a lot of English. None of them had learned to read or write. They thought the reserve was in a bad place, and it would only lead to sadness. Mary had not heard from them for years. In truth, Elmer and Mary did not even know if they were still alive.

Gil had his notebook opened on the table. "Frances, my girl, Elmer is already making money with our truck and trailer. Come spring we should be able to really get going," he said.

He waited for Frances to comment. She seemed distracted. He got up from the table and walked over to her. She was staring out the window at the snowy field leading to the lake. She turned and looked at him. God, she is beautiful, Gil thought. "Gil, I am pregnant," she said with a smile. She undid the buttons on his shirt. "Pregnant, not broken," she said, laughing before he could say anything.

Gil could not have been happier. Frances was up and frying bacon for a late breakfast. "Have you told your mother yet?" he asked her.

"Everyone including my mother will know in about three months. Now tell me how you and Elmer are going to make sure our children have food for the rest of their lives," she said with a smile.

For the next two and a half hours Gil explained how everything was going to work and how it was going to get paid for. When he finished, he asked her if she thought she could do the books and handle the paper end so Elmer and him could work without distractions. "Of course," Frances replied beaming. I have married the right man, she thought with satisfaction.

He slid his notebook across the table. "Good, you can start today," he said, laughing.

Gil worked long hours on Alphonse's crew. They hardly talked at all. Alphonse was a bully as a foreman, but not to Gil. He just had the smugness of a weak man who had taken advantage of an opportunity. Gil watched and listened to him interact with the other men. If he had been with them in the war as an officer or senior NCO, Alphonse would have been involved in an accident with a grenade, Gil was certain of that. Gil wondered how he could not have noticed all these things before the war when they were growing up together. Closeness could gloss over ugliness the same way time and distance could shine a light on it, he thought. The money was good, and Gil knew in the spring, at least three hard months of winter away, he would be done with all of them. As long as there were people, they would always produce what material he and Elmer would need for their business. In fact, the more people the better.

Elmer was comfortable enough with Gil to come to his house on the town site. People would stare. Elmer did not care. The

Germans had stared when he was in their country too, he thought. Elmer came early one morning in late January. He told Gil, "Grab your snowshoes and a rifle, I have to show you something." Frances made Elmer promise not to keep him too long. Gil came out of the house with his snowshoes and his .303 Lee-Enfield No. 4 Mk I. "Kept yours too, Gil," Elmer said, not as question rather an affirmation of how close they had become.

Gil just smiled. The truck still had rifle racks and Gil saw Elmer's rifle still sporting the green issue strap secured on the driver's side. Elmer drove east on the highway for about five miles. He pulled over where he had tied a red ribbon to a tree. "We have to walk from here," he said. It was bitterly cold but there was no wind. The sun was just starting to rise, and Gil felt invigorated by the fresh cold air. There was a faint outline of an old cut trail leading to the north. The snow was deep enough they had to don their snowshoes after a couple of hundred yards. Gil's curiosity was getting the better of him, but he did not ask Elmer where they were going.

After about two miles they came to a place that had three small rocky hills forming an open U-shape. There were no streams or bodies of water within the two miles they had covered. At the open end of the U there was a field with a few sparse trees. Elmer walked into the centre and began kicking the snow away. When he reached the ground Gil could see it was loose gravel. "This where our cess pits will be. Agreed?" Elmer said.

"You are an amazing man, Elmer," Gil replied. This site was perfect.

The clerk at the Department of Lands and Forests in Georgetown was a veteran. He worked out a deal where Gil could lease the land in question for fifty years. It had no timber value and no natural waterways close to it, so no one had ever expressed an interest in it. He told Gil that Elmer could not be a co-leaser because he was an Indian, as far as the clerk said he understood the Indian Act. Gil was going to tell him Elmer had lost his status because he had been overseas for more than four years. Elmer had told him not to because he was not sure if the clerk would officially record Elmer as having lost his status. Elmer just let everyone assume he was a status Indian. So far it had not been a problem. It just seemed easier not to draw government officials into what they were doing if they did not have to.

While they were in Georgetown, they ran into Walter outside the store. They had not seen him since the end of the war. He had come off his trap line to get some supplies. His crazy blue eyes were blazing as always. He had a full beard and was carrying his .303 rifle. He had four dogs pulling his sled. "Georgetown is getting too civilized. You think these girls had never seen a dog team," he said with his heavy accent. "Let's grab a beer," he added.

Gil and Elmer knew Elmer could not legally drink in the tavern. The law in Ontario was very clear about serving Indians. They did not really know the constables in Georgetown and did not know the tavern owner either. Elmer shook his head. Gil understood right away. Elmer was not going to do anything to draw attention to himself until their business was up and running. "After that, who knows?" he had told Gil. They politely declined.

Walter shrugged it off. "Hard enough to keep these dogs on the trail without having beer on board," he laughed.

Before they parted company, Elmer extracted a promise from Walter to come to house 12 after the spring break-up. He had a woman he wanted Walter to meet. Elmer told him to be sure he brought a moose hide as an introduction. "Sounds like my kind of woman. A soldier's promise is better than gold brothers. I hope she is near-sighted, Elmer. I will see you in the spring," he shouted, laughing as he mushed his team towards the tavern.

Chapter 7

The spring of 1949 saw the lake and river full of logs that had been skidded out of the bush over the winter. There were more logs than Gil had seen for years. The changes to their business that spring were sometimes hard to keep up with; tractors and trucks had largely replaced the horse teams from his youth. Most of the workers stayed in camps surrounding Lac Ville. There were a lot more foreigners cutting and skidding now. Former German prisoners of war, Portuguese, and Finns made up more than half of the work force. Lac Ville was growing steadily. Gil and Elmer's business had taken off. Whenever the framework for a new home went up, Gil approached the builder and offered to install a septic system at cost plus five percent if the owner agreed to use their septic cleaning service for five years. Gil often brought Frances with him to explain the paperwork. Her beauty and charm often helped to seal the deal. Gil and Frances had been blessed with a healthy son they named Rejean in '47. Frances's parents watched Rejean when she was helping Gil. Elmer and Gil had found another truck and two trailers last year in Fort William. It was not army surplus but the ¾ ton Ford was reliable and rugged. Elmer kept the original trailer for his water hauling business. One of the new trailers was a five-hundred-gallon tank on a dual axle trailer. The other trailer was a flatbed trailer for hauling septic tank material.

Elmer stayed in the background while in Lac Ville and quietly did his work. Gil was doing the same when they were working on reserves. They both laughed about how doing this did not offend anyone's sense of how the world should be. Gil's father-in-law was not so easily fooled. Jean resented the success of Gil and Elmer and the clear bond they had, even though he knew his daughter and grandson could only benefit from the work they did together. Perhaps, as he had once told Louise during one of his rants about the business, in the end they alone would. Outside of the reserves and Lac Ville, they worked as a team at the fishing and lumber camps in Georgetown. The odd person would make a comment but for the most part people were just happy the work was getting done.

The business grew every month as word spread about the quality of the work and their reasonable prices. Elmer had apprenticed four young men from the reserve. They worked out well because as well as doing the labour, Elmer and Gil taught them so they could do the work independently if need be. Gil surprised everyone by hiring two former German prisoners of war. They had been repatriated to Germany after the war and returned when they found nothing at home for them anymore. Gil told Elmer the two had been captured in North Africa and he was sure they had not killed any of their friends. They were hard workers and worked alongside the men Elmer had hired without any problems. Kurt, one of the Germans, had been a mechanic in the Africa Corps and he could keep any piece of machinery running. He improvised a piston pump for emptying septic tanks that was better than anything they could have bought.

Gil had developed the cess pond location Elmer had shown him. They had cut and corduroyed the road to the site and had built a small hut for the men to keep warm during the emptying of the trailers in the winter. Gil had found a parcel of land halfway between Lac Ville and the cess ponds. Elmer and Gil built a garage with an office and a fenced compound for the trucks and trailers. They used water from a small creek to clean the trailers out after they had been used into a large septic tank on site. The work was not for anyone with a queasy stomach. It was, however, very profitable, and people were talking.

Frances looked forward to going to the credit union in Lac Ville to do her deposits because her friend Carol worked there. Frances and Carol had known each other since Grade One. Every week, when Frances came in to make the week's deposits, Carol would smile and ask about Gil and young Jean. She would talk about how Lac Ville was growing and how exciting it was. Frances, always open and forthcoming with the women in Lac Ville, would give her all the details and tell Carol what Gil and Elmer were doing to grow their business. Carol would listen carefully and provide words of encouragement. Frances always enjoyed making the deposits and catching up.

Every second Saturday, Alphonse would come to Carol's house. It worked out because Alphonse was out of the bush for four days and Carol's husband was a train engineer with a regular run to Winnipeg. They would drink and parade around naked until they ended up in bed. Sleeping with Alphonse felt hedonistic to Carol. It was her way of punishing her husband for not paying enough attention to her. Carol told Alphonse about the large deposits Frances made and what Frances had told her about Gil and Elmer's business. She told him Frances and Gil thought they were better than other people in Lac Ville. Carol knew it was not true, but Gil had rejected her advances years ago. It was not that Carol was unattractive. She turned down more men than she could count. Gil just was not one of them. Carol had even opened her shirt to show him her breasts at the lake when they were teenagers. The humiliation of him telling her to put those away stung to this day. Alphonse always listened carefully.

Mary was happy and felt a little guilty about it. As Elmer's and Gil's business grew, Elmer ended up working long days and was gone a lot. She had gotten used to the independence she had when he was overseas. Now she had the best of both. Elmer's work allowed her to run the house and raise the children without a lot of interference. Elmer would give her money and approved of almost everything she was doing. Most nights she could count on having his warm strong body in her bed with her. Helen and Elias loved their father. They seemed to like how little his being home had changed their routines. Elmer made good money, more than they needed. Mary had opened a bank account in Georgetown. It was a painful experience with the bank manager explaining everything to her as if she were a child until Elmer came in to see what was taking so long. The bank manager was intimidated by Elmer knowing he was a veteran. Stories about the wartime exploits of Walter, Elmer, and Gil had somehow found their way into the gossip of this area of Northern Ontario. Elmer did nothing to make things less intimidating and Mary had her bank book a couple a minutes later. In the months afterwards, she grew afraid the quickly growing balance would come to the attention of some government agent for Indian Affairs. For whatever reason, Elmer's and Gil's success sometimes left her feeling uneasy. Elmer was not aware that he was sometimes paid with his own money when he provided water, wood, or sewage services to people on the reserve. It was one of Mary's ways of helping the community.

To Gil's delight, he and Frances were working hard to have a second child. Frances told Gil she was pregnant on Christmas Eve of 1949 after they got home from church. Gil did not say a word. Instead, he ran out of the front door and laid in the snow. He made a snow angel, got up, came inside covered in snow, and took her in his arms. Jean was asleep in his bassinette. He smiled and asked Frances, "You are pregnant not broken, right?"

Frances laughed. "You remembered," she replied.

Later, as they laid together embracing, Frances watched as sleep took Gil. Frances reflected on the years since Gil had come home. Gil and Elmer had worked hard to create a business which gave them everything they needed and more. Some people in Lac Ville were happy for them and others could not resist opportunities to make remarks about shit and money. Some people did not like the undeniable fact Gil and Elmer were a good team. Father Andre had told her, "Indians were like children, and even Elmer with his intelligence and strength would someday look to Gil as a parent." Frances was so shocked she did not reply. She had come to know Elmer as a man of purpose, integrity, and resolve. He would never be dependent on anyone. It was her father who made her the most uncomfortable. Jean was the father she knew when it was just her and Rejean at the house. He loved her and his grandson, Rejean. When Gil was around, he always found excuses to be somewhere else. He would not even say Elmer's name. Her mother would give the signs only mothers and daughters understood when Frances was talking about Gil's and Elmer's business, so Frances would know not to say anything else. The duplicity hurt Frances. A nagging sense of more difficulties to come made her hug Gil while he slept and rub her stomach to reassure her new child. It was early Christmas morning when she finally fell asleep.

Chapter 8

Frances's father Jean was in a foul mood. Frances had told him last night she was pregnant with her and Gil's second child. He was happy for her and Gil. His wife Louise was overjoyed. Louise spent every minute she could with their grandson, Rejean. Even this good news had not changed his mood this morning. He knew he had failed to keep up with the times. At 57, he found himself struggling financially. In the years before the war, Jean ran the stables, livery, and blacksmithing operations to service the horses used to skid the harvested trees to where they could be floated down the rivers to railway sidings. When tractors began to replace the horses, Jean bought several and leased them to the cutting operations. They were prone to break down in the harsh conditions of the Northern Ontario winters. He had managed to keep them going during the war despite a shortage of parts and rationed fuel. The cutting firms were not renewing his leases because bigger and better tractors were available since the end of the war. Jean knew he could not afford to replace machine for machine. His tractor leasing fleet went from 24 machines to six by the spring of 1950. They were more reliable and unfortunately more expensive to operate. Independent skidders who bought their own machines caused Jean to lower his lease rates year after year to stay competitive.

Jean was a prideful man, and he hid his concerns from Louise and Frances. Gil and Elmer's success also stung. "How could I have not seen the same opportunity?" he asked himself. Jean had carved a good life out of the forests around Lac Ville. He was well respected in the community. The frustration from his current situation sat like bile in his throat. He wondered if anyone in Lac Ville suspected he was in trouble. The last humiliation would be anyone feeling sorry for him. Jean drove to the coffee shop to meet Alphonse. Jean had known Alphonse since he was a little boy. He always liked the brash ugly kid because he was a go-getter, like Jean had always been. Alphonse was Jean's inside man with the cutting operations. When an operation was having trouble getting or keeping skidders Alphonse always gave Jean the heads up so he could take advantage of the situation. Alphonse always refused any money Jean offered him. Jean knew it was because Alphonse hoped Jean would tell Frances about the work and money Alphonse had brought to her father. Jean knew Alphonse still had hopes he would someday be with Frances. When Frances married Gil, Alphonse stayed drunk for a week. When he sobered up, he went to the bush and stayed in camp for a month. Alphonse loved his daughter and had not gone off to war. Jean secretly hoped Alphonse's devotion would someday be rewarded.

When Jean opened the door to the café, he saw Alphonse in a booth with several of the men from his cutting crew. Alphonse got up and shook his hand. Alphonse and Jean went to an empty booth in the back of the café. After the waitress had poured them coffees, they exchanged some talk about the cutting operations going on to the south of Lac Ville. After five minutes, Alphonse, who had been dying to share what he had learned from Carol, told Jean about the amount of the deposits Frances made weekly. Jean did his best not to look surprised. Alphonse, who lacked any semblance of subtlety, went on about his concern for Gil and Frances. He told Jean, "I do not know exactly what the rules and laws are about a white man and an Indian working together, but I am sure what they are doing could not be legal. I do not understand why Gil had left his cutting job and rarely talks to me anymore."

Jean listened and nodded his head to acknowledge everything Alphonse was saying. When Alphonse was done, Jean stood up and shook his hand. "You are a good man Alphonse, thank you for looking out for Frances and my family," he said.

Alphonse, feeling very satisfied with himself, replied, "You are like a father to me. It is the least I can do."

Jean left the café and went to the law office of Claude Talbot. Jean and Claude had been friends for years. Claude did all of Jean's legal papers. Every contract, sale, or lease Jean had ever done had fallen under the watchful eye of Claude. When Jean walked in Claude greeted him warmly. "What brings you in today, my old friend?" Claude said, extending his hand.

"I have some questions I need answered. I am concerned for Frances and my grandson," Jean replied.

Claude led Jean into his office and closed the door.

After Jean left Claude's office, he drove to the lake to think about everything he had heard and learned over the morning. Claude was honest and forthright about his limited knowledge of the Indian Act. Jean knew Claude would take it upon himself to learn more. The most interesting thing he had learned was that, to Claude's knowledge, there was no contract or formal agreement between Elmer and Gil about the business. Unless they had done it in Georgetown or Port Arthur, Claude would have known. Even if they had done a contract or agreement outside of Lac Ville, the legal community was small in this part of Northern Ontario. Claude was certain he would have heard something about such an unusual arrangement. When Jean drove home, Rejean was there. Frances had dropped him off so she could work on the business books. Jean smiled as he took off his coat and boots. He blew on his hands to take the chill off and lifted Rejean in his arms. Jean then walked over to Louise and kissed her. Louise smiled and said, "Someone is in a good mood, Rejean," and winked at him.

✻

Alphonse left the coffee shop after his meeting with Jean and drove four miles to the cabin of Sam Little. Sam was a former gold miner living off a small pension. He was possibly the most bitter and meanest man Alphonse had ever met. He drank every day. He hated all women and had no use for children. Sam had built the cabin he now lived in in the 1930s. He purposely built it in the swampy end of the lake where the mosquitos and blackflies were the worst. Sam told Alphonse, "It was so no one would bother me or build anything close."

Alphonse was hunting when he came across Little's cabin. He found Sam unconscious after a tree he was cutting while drunk fell and hit his head. Alphonse carried him to his cabin and when Sam came to, Sam offered him a drink. Sam took a liking to Alphonse because as he said, "It takes a real bastard to know a real bastard."

Over the past eight years, Sam ran Alphonse's stills and stored the illegal homebrew over his property. Alphonse paid him some money, but mostly he kept Sam in the juice. Everett came to the cabin to make his purchases and give Alphonse his share of the proceeds. No matter how cold it was, all deals were done outside because Sam did not want "that ugly Indian in my cabin." Everett used to yell at the cabin because he knew Sam could hear him. "Someday I am going to come in your cabin, shit on your floor, and laugh as the animals pick your bones." After Everett was loaded up, Sam would yell with sincerity, "I hope that shit kills you and your friends, you ugly Indian." It was the same conversation every time Everett showed up, and Alphonse knew they both meant what they said. Alphonse and Sam checked the stills and how the current batch was coming along, then they had a drink together. Sam was talkative for a change, and he told Alphonse they could expand their operation in the spring. He had found a rock outcropping with a small cave under it which was perfect for another still. Alphonse got back in his truck and drove back to Lac Ville. It was not even ten in the morning yet and Alphonse was already having a great day.

🐜

Claude watched as Jean drove away from his office. Claude knew Jean was having money troubles. He had not reviewed anywhere near the same volume of lease agreements for Jean as he had in past years. Claude was dismayed Jean could be so transparent about how he felt about Gil's and Elmer's partnership. He had known Jean for years. It was a surprise and disappointment to learn his friend had a deep and irrational hatred for Indians. He took down his copy of the Indian Act from his bookshelf. He rarely referred to it and had never read it in its entirety. Indians were the responsibility of the federal government. Claude dealt with the department lawyers and he could not recall a single incident where he was asked to litigate any issues involving the Indian Act. As he opened it and read the preamble, he hoped there was nothing in it that Jean could use to hurt Gilbert and this Elmer fellow, the Native war veteran who he had never met. They seemed to Claude to be providing a service no one else wanted to do, and they were doing it well. Claude finished the thought by saying out loud, "Be careful what you wish for and why, my friend." Claude knew that whatever he learned, he would follow the law because that is what he lived.

Claude called in his articling student, a young man named Gabriel Cote. He wrote down some questions he wanted researched. Gabriel grew up near Ear Falls and had studied law down south. Claude hired him because he was passionate about social justice. Claude suspected contract and civil law would someday include enough social justice law to keep a firm like his busy for many years to come.

🐜

Everett thought Elmer somehow had become an even weaker man since the war. It had been five years and Elmer still did not know how to take what was his for the taking. Elmer sold his services cheaply on the reserve. He even dug and created a landfill for all the garbage on the reserve which featured an incinerator. Mary seemed to be in charge and, worse yet, Elmer was working with a white man from Lac Ville. Not only working with him, but even the elders called them brothers because of how well they worked together. Almost all the children from the reserve were going to school regularly, and they were becoming smart ass white kids, in Everett's opinion. Not his children, though; they only went to school when he let them, and his boys Peter and Lawrence felt the back of his hand or belt when he caught them reading. He never hit Wilma in the face. She knew better than to try to tell him what she thought. Everett was comfortable about who was a man on the reserve and who was not. Elmer got a pass only because he was his brother.

The moonshine business was going well, and the men he sold to and drank with had no idea he was having sex with their wives if they passed out. He had perfected his method of rape years ago, or as he called it, whiskey seduction. All the women he exploited were terrified of Everett and his threats to tell their husbands they had given themselves willingly to him while their husbands had been passed out. Everett knew the men's guilt over their lack of self-control was the security he needed to keep doing what he found so satisfying. Everett's legal job was caretaker of the school, which he made Wilma and his cronies do. Everett had no idea some of the women were talking.

It had taken Mary years to gain the trust of the women in the community. She did it so gradually people hardly noticed at first. She had enlisted the elders to establish her creditability. When Elmer had gone to war, many women believed he would die like Richard, and many treated her like a widow after he had left. Mary was always very private, and some women resented this. Gradually, other women began to see Mary as a leader. Some of the men saw her as a troublemaker. Others sided with the women. When Elmer came home, the two of them emerged as a team who got things done. Nothing they did put anyone out and it always benefited the reserve. The first woman who told Mary about Everett was terrified. She believed because Everett was Mary's brother-in-law, she was placing herself in danger. She tearfully told Mary that Everett had raped her when her infant children were in the same room. Everett had drunk homebrew with her husband until her husband passed out. She thought Everett would go home when she saw her husband nod off. Instead, he pushed her into the wall and forced himself onto her. Everett hissed into her ear he would tell everyone she had waited for the opportunity and gave herself willingly at the first chance.

Mary heard the same story with different variations ten times over the course of the past two years. Elmer, for such a strong man, seemed to have not had a clue. Mary struggled with how she could tell Elmer about Everett and all the pain he was causing. Mary had only ever been with Elmer, but other women had told her the best time to talk to a man about anything that mattered to women was after making love. One night as they lie together catching their breath, Mary said, "Elmer, I need to talk to you about your brother."

Chapter 9

Gil was on his way home from Georgetown late in the evening of June 30, 1950. He had spent the afternoon at the gold mine with one of the engineers learning about the mine ventilation system. The engineer was a veteran from the armoured division Gil's regiment had been attached to during the war. Gil had taken him for supper in gratitude and then he visited Walter. He did not realize how late it was until the sun started to set. Gil knew Frances, who was eight months pregnant, was going to be more than a little mad. He had been gone since seven a.m. He would make it up to her if his new plans to start a construction company panned out. Gil was driving about forty miles an hour because wildlife, especially moose, began moving after the sun started to set. Passing through the numerous rock cuts was challenging enough in the daytime; at night it required all his concentration. He entered a curve. On his right-hand side was a rock face about forty feet high and on his left a drop of about thirty feet into a creek bed.

Alphonse and Jack had gone to Fort William that same day.

Alphonse had bought a new 1950 Chevrolet Styleline Deluxe, a black four door. Alphonse paid cash and put it in his friend Jack's name. Alphonse wanted a fast, reliable car when he was making runs with his homebrew. He did not want the police to know the car was connected to him if they ever did stop it. After buying the car, they had supper in Fort William and headed back to Lac Ville. They stopped in Georgetown for a few beers at the tavern. Alphonse met with a few of his customers and worked out some more deals. It was dark when they left Georgetown. Alphonse told Jack to drive and opened a jar of his brew. Jack had the car up to eighty miles an hour as they raced through the rock cuts and curves. Alphonse was laughing and encouraging Jack to see what the car had. Jack was more than half cut and he pressed down on the accelerator.

Suddenly, as they rounded a curve, the headlights lit up a truck in front of them going half of their speed. "Holy shit," Alphonse yelled. Jack swerved to pass the truck and caught its rear driver side bumper. The truck spun to the right as the car passed it. "Floor it," Alphonse yelled, and they sped down the highway without looking back. Both Jack and Alphonse started laughing.

Gil only caught the flash of headlights in his mirror. A second later his truck was spinning out of control. He counter steered to avoid hitting the rock face and plunged over the embankment towards the creek.

After speeding along for ten miles, Alphonse announced he had to piss. Jack pulled the car off to the side of the road. They got out pissed and lit cigarettes. Alphonse looked at the passenger side front. It was not too badly damaged. There was a three-foot scrape. Some green paint had become imbedded along the scrape. Alphonse, drunk or not, knew he would have to clean it off. Jack, more sober, now looked at Alphonse and said, "Do you think we should go back and check on whoever that was?"

Alphonse looked at Jack and flicked his cigarette at his face. "You really are as stupid as you look. Fuck whoever that was. At worst they will have to walk," he answered. "Let's go home," he added and got back in the car.

When they were about two miles out of Lac Ville, Alphonse had second thoughts. He told Jack to kill the lights and they drove the car to Jean's old stables. They parked the car inside and went to the bar to catch last call.

🐜

Luke, the truck driver who married Eva and lived on the reserve when he was not on the road, was on a late-night run from Winnipeg with supplies for a mill about three hours east of Lac Ville. He was tired and he was going to stop and spend the night with Eva so he could make his delivery first thing in the morning. He was gearing down for the difficult curves on the stretch of highway about fifteen miles out of Lac Ville. As he rounded a curve, he saw what he thought was a faint light down by the creek. It was unnatural; he knew that if not for his elevated position in the cab he would have missed it altogether. Then his headlights showed the skid marks and the broken wire barrier where a vehicle went over the side. He finished negotiating the curve and pulled over as soon as he could. He got out of the truck, grabbed a flashlight, and ran towards the break in the wire. After driving for so long it was hard to get the legs going, but a rush of adrenaline moved him along. Out of breath, he arrived at the edge of the drop off. There was a vehicle down there, and one unbroken headlight was still on, fading as the battery was dying. Luke took a deep breath to calm himself. The forest was silent as he slid down the hill grabbing branches to slow his descent. When he got to the bottom, he turned on his flashlight and went to the crumpled cab of a truck.

Luke recognized Gilbert Bertrand immediately. He was the soldier Elmer was in business with. Luke had seen him several times at Elmer's house over the years. He also knew Gilbert was dead. His eyes were open, and his head was covered in blood. It took all of Luke's resolve to check for a pulse he knew was not there. When he had confirmed Gilbert was dead, he sat down on the rocks. The forest came back to life now that Luke was not moving around. He had seen other accidents and dead people on the highway before; it was a sad part of being a truck driver. He never knew them, so this was different. He sat there for a while thinking about what needed to be done. A wave of sadness washed over him, and he started up the bank. The forest went silent again.

Sergeant McNeil and Constable Brooks from the Georgetown detachment of the Ontario Provincial Police met Elmer, Luke, and Jean at the accident scene at eight in the morning. They had brought the coroner and Bill Waite, who ran the funeral home in Georgetown, with them. Elmer had been there since five a.m. He wanted to make sure no animals violated his friend's body. Luke and Jean had shown up after seven. The sergeant went down to the crash and began taking photographs. Several carloads of people from Lac Ville showed up either to rubber neck or offer help to recover the body and truck. The coroner was a First World War veteran and he was not able to go down the hill into the creek bed. Instead, he made notes and interviewed Luke and Jean to confirm the identity of the deceased. Constable Brooks asked Elmer to help him measure the skid marks on the highway. Jean looked on, aghast Elmer would be included by the police in helping with the investigation. Constable Brooks asked the people who were watching to stay back unless they were called upon. The morning sun was burning bright, which assured the day was going to be hot. Sergeant McNeil wanted to recover Gilbert's body as soon as possible and get him to the morgue. Both McNeil and Brooks knew the real evidence was on the roadway. Constable Brooks did not have to tell Elmer this was not a single vehicle accident. Constable Brooks was impressed by Elmer. He prided himself as an officer who was able to get a quick read on people. Elmer reflected his experiences; the wisdom and compassion that shaped his character was apparent in the way he carried himself. Elmer was thinking on the same lines. Constable Brooks seemed sharp and dedicated. His eyes reflected his intelligence and determination to do the right thing. He was like Gil: what you see is what you get.

Elmer and Luke were part of the six men who carried Gil's body to Bill Waite's hearse. He was covered by a blanket. Constable Brooks watched everyone who had come out to the accident scene while he pretended to make notes. When the door to the hearse closed, Luke gave Elmer a hug. Jean turned around and went back to his truck. Brooks did not pretend when he made a note of this. A tow truck arrived from Lac Ville as the hearse drove away. Brooks told Elmer and Luke that the truck would be towed to Georgetown for a mechanical inspection. When Luke went to talk to Jean, Brooks told Elmer, "You will hear things before I do in all likelihood. Call me when you do."

Elmer nodded to acknowledge the mission.

After Gilbert's body was in the hearse, Joseph, one of the guys from Alphonse's crew, drove from the accident scene to Alphonse's house. Alphonse heard the pounding on the door. He pushed the naked waitress from the hotel out of his bed and yelled he was coming. He opened the door naked, blinked at the brightness of the sun, and, seeing it was one of his guys, motioned him to come in. The waitress yelled at Alphonse, "You are such an asshole."

Alphonse went in the bathroom and emptied his bladder, loudly. The waitress covered herself with a blanket. Alphonse stuck his head around the corner and told her to get out. "What did you wake me up for?" Alphonse asked.

Joseph told him, "Gilbert Bertrand is dead. He went off the embankment by Sucker Creek. I saw the body and Gilbert's truck."

Alphonse was instantly awake and the fog of the booze he drank last night was gone. Alphonse asked him, "What else do you know?"

Joseph answered, "Jesus, Alphonse, what else can I tell you? Gilbert is dead. I came over because I knew Gilbert and you have been friends since you were boys."

Alphonse thanked Joseph and told him he would be at the coffee shop in fifteen minutes and to meet him there. After he closed the door, Alphonse punched the bathroom door. "God damn it," he whispered, and his mind raced with thoughts of all the problems this would cause for him.

Chapter 10

Gilbert Bertrand's funeral was the largest ever in Lac Ville. It was the hottest July day in memory. Even the breeze off the lake was like someone opening an oven door. There were hundreds of people, more than the church could hold. The service was done on the front stairs of the church. Father Andre was not happy about it, but Frances insisted. There were soldiers from Gilbert's regiment, townspeople, and all the men who worked for his company. Louise told Frances she had no idea how many people Gilbert had touched during his life. Frances was a pillar of strength and dignity in public, but her mother knew she was almost inconsolable in private. Elmer and Mary were in the front row because Frances demanded it. Luke and his wife Eva were right beside them. Jean and Louise were beside Frances, and Louise held Rejean as the priest began the service. Louise and Frances saw Eva, Luke's wife, for the first time at the same time. Both took a sharp quick breath almost in unison. Eva could be Frances's sister if she was not a mixed blood. Louise looked at Jean. He was stone faced and stared directly ahead. Louise and Frances looked at each other for a moment and then turned to look at Father Andre. Mary caught the interaction and realized the significance immediately. Until she saw them at the same time, it had never occurred to her who Eva's father could possibly be.

Frances was near full term and the baby kicked her constantly throughout the service. Frances told her mother later she hardly heard a word anyone said, and it took all her strength not to faint in the heat. Elmer and Jean supported her arms when Gilbert was laid in the ground. Jean did not ask Elmer, Mary, Luke, or Eva to come to the house after the service. Frances did not notice because she was dehydrated and emotionally spent when Louise helped her into Jean's truck. Elmer and Mary were walking to their truck as people were milling around when Elmer heard a familiar voice. "Is this your woman, Elmer?" Walter said, walking towards Mary with his hand extended.

Mary looked startled as the bearded man with the wolf-coloured eyes took her hand. His face broke into a big smile when he saw Elmer's face go from grim sadness to a smile. Mary, watching Elmer, smiled because she knew this crazy looking young man with the heavy accent was just who Elmer needed to see on such a sad day. She was struck by how Elmer and Walter greeted each other like brothers. It was like that with Gil as well, she thought, and Elmer had taken Gil's death hard. Elmer introduced Walter and they walked together talking about what had happened since they had last seen each other. Elmer, looking over the crowd, saw Constable Brooks in plain clothes talking to some townspeople. When their eyes met, Brooks held his finger to his lips to make sure Elmer did not acknowledge him as a police officer. Walter saw the exchange and told Elmer he had hitched a ride with the policeman and gave Elmer a knowing wink. Elmer had told everyone from the reserve who attended the funeral to come to his house for lunch afterwards. Mary had prepared a fish fry and the bannock just had to be cooked. Elmer asked Walter if he wanted to ride with Mary and him. Walter told him he would be coming with Brooks in just a bit. Elmer told him, "Alright brother, house number twelve."

Walter added, "With the flag in front of it," as they parted company.

Frances was laying down and sipping water on her parent's bed. The house was full of people. Jean was taking condolences with Gil's parents who had made the long trip from Sherbrook, Nova Scotia, where they had moved after Gil had married Frances. Louise and the women from the church were serving sandwiches and cold drinks to everyone. Every time Louise passed Jean, she looked at him. Jean avoided eye contact. His behaviour confirmed her suspicions. She had forgiven his dalliances years ago when he was that type of man. Louise had no idea there had been a child. Frances was thinking about Gil's parents. This was the first time they had seen their grandson, Rejean. Gilbert Sr. and Susan were the type of parents who raised Gil right, and when they were done, they were done. It was a wonder Gil was as loving and compassionate as he was. Frances was startled when the front of her dress was suddenly wet. Her water had broken.

Alphonse showed up at Jean and Louise's home just as everyone was starting to scramble around because Frances was in labour. Jean acknowledged him with a nod. Alphonse tried to look forlorn but when he realized no one was watching him he decided he really did not need to. He had made his appearance and left. Carol's husband was on his weekend run and he needed some distraction.

Always practical, Alphonse viewed the funeral as a business opportunity. He knew the bar in town would be hopping and the owner would need some of his home brew. The owner sold just enough of the heavily taxed legal liquor to satisfy the provincial liquor inspector's need to know he was being a responsible tavern owner. The profit margins from Alphonse's brew was way higher. There was some risk, but it was manageable for now. When the Ontario Provincial Police were done building their new detachment in Lac Ville, he would have to be a lot more careful. For now, though, it was good times for both, and with Gil out of the picture, who knew what the future held.

Elmer got the fire pit blazing and put the large metal grid overtop. He had cleared a large area at the back of his house and had used the stumps to make chairs. A long homemade table was covered in pans, which were covered with cloths, containing pickerel, pike, and whitefish. The whitefish was for the elders; they seemed to prefer it to the other fish. Platters of bannock ready to cook and pitchers of cold spring water and lemonade were ready. Mary and some of the wives were working on getting the food ready. Helen was playing some of the younger children and Elias, now 10 years old, was watching his father's every move. Walter and Constable Brooks showed up about an hour after Elmer and Mary got home. Elias stood behind Elmer when the men showed up. He studied Walter and laughed every time he talked because of his strong accent. Elias with his full head of hair and his chubby cheeks was the kind of kid everyone wanted to jostle. Elias took it in stride when both Brooks and Walter rubbed his head, laughing.

There were more than thirty people in Elmer's backyard to show support for Elmer. Nearly everyone knew how close Elmer and Gil had been. These people had also benefited from the work they had done together.

Everett looked out his window and debated if he could stomach all the elders and other people talking about Gil and showing support for Elmer. He could tolerate Elmer as long as he did not interfere with what he was doing. Everett had gotten hired to work on the new detachment building being built in Lac Ville for the police. He hated that town and almost everyone in it. He had a continual scowl, and because he was a big man no one ever talked to him. He liked it that way. Everett and Elmer hardly spoke at all since January. Everett did not like the way Elmer was looking at him. He was sure Mary had something to do with it; he just could not put his finger on what the little busybody knew. She was too close to the other women. Elmer and Mary acted like they were the chiefs. He went to his stash and pulled a jar of Alphonse's homebrew out. Wilma said nothing and went in the bedroom.

After everyone had eaten, Walter, Constable Brooks, and Elmer took a walk. Elmer wanted to be alone with them so giving them a tour was a good cover. Brooks told Elmer his first name was Robert. Brooks's commanding officer had convinced Robert that some men had to stay home from the war to police the ones who did not go. Robert had grown up near Wawa and knew he wanted to be a police officer since he was a boy. Robert had a low tolerance for cowards and criminals, and he believed they were one and the same. He had met Walter after the news spread of Gil's death in Georgetown. Walter came to the detachment and offered his services. Walter had told Robert that Gil, Elmer, and he had served together, and he needed to know how Gil had met his fate. Normally, Robert would explain that it was a police matter and decline. However, Walter's keenness and sincerity made Robert accept. Robert already firmly believed Gil's death was a hit and run; what he was not sure of was whether it was a murder or criminal negligence. "Either way," he told Elmer, "I will not stop working on it until I find the driver of the other vehicle." He told Elmer he found tire tracks the day after the accident where someone had pulled off the highway at speed. He made casts of the tire impressions and the casts appeared to be the same as the skid mark impressions from the accident scene. He believed there were two people in the vehicle because there were two different cigarette brands on the butts he had found. He thought the two people were both men because they had pissed standing up and right beside the road. The urine impressions had dried but still stunk. Elmer knew Walter must have been with Robert when he found where the suspects had pissed. During the war, Walter was a man hunter, as many Germans found out before their lives were extinguished by a .303 round. He specialized in stalking Nazi officers and snipers. After every kill, he would tell Gil and Elmer "I bear them no malice," and prepare for the next mission.

Lucy was weeding her potato plot with her back to the path when they were walking by. Potatoes and carrots were about the only vegetables she got to grow over the years. Elmer said "hello Lucy," and Lucy jumped. She did not like to be surprised, especially when she feared that pig, Everett. Walter laughed and apologized, "I am sorry we have startled you, ma'am."

Robert and Walter noticed how pretty she was right away. Elmer introduced them to Lucy who shyly brushed the hair out of her eyes. Elmer told Lucy that Walter was a trapper and Robert worked in the gold mine at Georgetown. Lucy, despite herself, blushed as she looked at Walter. Elmer extracted a promise from Lucy: she would come and see Mary and the kids. The men said goodbye and started back to Elmer's house. Lucy watched as they walked away. She looked down when Walter turned around to look at her again.

Robert and Elmer both saw the instantaneous attraction between Lucy and Walter. Elmer looked at Walter and saw he was totally distracted. He said, "I think she likes you, sniper."

Walter looked at both them and replied, "It is a good thing, yes. I will see you at the house." He turned around and walked back to Lucy's. Lucy was putting her tools away when she saw Walter returning. He stopped about twenty feet away and asked, "May I call on you again, Lucy?"

Lucy's heart was pounding. "Yes," she said. She went into her cabin and closed the door.

Francine was born at one in the morning. Frances had a difficult delivery, with enough bleeding to cause the doctor to be called. She was a healthy little girl weighing seven pounds and one ounce. Frances was exhausted when she put Francine to her breast. Louise, Susan, and two other women wiped Frances with cool wet cloths and gave her sips of water. The doctor was talking to Jean and Gilbert Sr. telling them, "The bleeding is from a tear, but it is not life threatening." Frances would need bed rest for a few days. Rejean was brought in to see his sister and then taken away to bed. Jean took a flask from his vest pocket and poured the men a drink. Everyone was exhausted, and after their drink they took their leave. The women would stay the night with Frances and the baby and sleep in shifts. The night was still warm and the air muggy as Jean sat on his porch alone. He took stock of the day as he sipped from his flask.

It was not the first time he had seen his daughter Eva. The previous time, she was five years old and with her mother, who had four hundred dollars Jean had given her. They were on their way to Winnipeg. Four hundred dollars was a lot of money back then. He thought it was a steep price to pay for peace of mind. Now he was angry, like he had been cheated in a business deal. He had forgotten about her until today. He had no feelings toward her, just resentment that she had found her way back to the reserve and Lac Ville. She was beautiful, though, like her mother, he had to admit. Even though Frances and Eva had different mothers, their resemblance was unfortunately hard to miss. He had seen Father Andre cross himself after he had looked at Frances, Eva, and him during the service.

Constable Brooks went back to Georgetown by himself. Walter said he was going to see if he could get hired to build the new detachment building in Lac Ville. There was always work for a carpenter in this part of Northern Ontario. Elmer had some projects in mind as well. Walter had a few other motives. He was going to see if there were any rumours floating around about Gil's death, he told Brooks. Elmer knew Walter was smitten. Walter took a moose hide out of the trunk of Robert's car and put it into Elmer's shed before Brooks left.

Chapter 11

A month passed before Elmer saw Frances, intending to give her the money and cheques he had received for the work the company had done since Gil was killed. He had gone every week and Jean had turned him away every time, saying Frances was too weak to see anyone. Jean was always abrupt and did not ask if Elmer had a message for Frances. Elmer tolerated his rudeness only because Frances was Gil's widow. When he pulled up, Frances, Louise, Rejean, and Francine were on the porch and Jean's truck was gone. Elmer did his best to hide his shock at Frances's appearance. Grief and a difficult childbirth had taken a toll. Her hair was limp and appeared not to have been washed for days. She was pale and thin. She gave the baby to Louise and walked toward Elmer as he got out of the truck. She smiled weakly and hugged Elmer. She spoke in a whisper asking after Mary and the children. Elmer stood for a moment before answering that they were fine. He gave the large envelope to Frances and told her briefly what had been done. She appeared to be half listening and distracted.

Frances apologized for not being available to keep the books. She explained, "I have not been to my home since the funeral. I will be on top of things as soon as I can. I am sorry I have not been very helpful."

Elmer looked her in the eyes and told her, "There was no hurry."

Frances took Elmer's hand and lead him onto the porch to see little Francine. Elmer looked her over and thought he got a smile. It was important to take in as many details about the baby as he could because Mary would not accept anything less. He told Frances, "I have come every week because I did not want things to pile up and be overwhelming when you feel better." Frances looked surprised, and Elmer immediately suspected Jean had not even told her. From the look on her face, he knew she had the same feeling. Frances looked at her mother who looked away, embarrassed. Frances turned towards Elmer. He saw a familiar spark behind her eyes and colour come to her cheeks. She spoke in a louder, clearer voice: "There is much we need to talk about, Elmer, and we have a business to run. If you'll excuse me, I will get to these papers as soon as I wash my hair."

Elmer smiled and replied, "Of course Frances, just call at the house as soon as you are able." Louise, the intended recipient, cringed when she thought of what Jean would say.

Two days after Francine was born, Jean had gone to Frances's house to get clothes for them. While he was in the house, he looked around for any documents he might find useful. No one had mentioned or asked if Gilbert had left a will. Looking through a desk, Jean came across the books for the business and confirmed what Alphonse had told him. Underneath a stack of letters from Gil to Frances he had written during the war, Jean found a soldier's will. All soldiers were required to make them after they enlisted. It was dated 1941 and looked like it had been thrown in the drawer as an afterthought. Surely, Jean thought, Gilbert had made a new one since he had come home. He searched for another twenty

minutes and was unable to find a more recent will. He picked
up the soldiers will. Gil had left everything to Frances as was to
be expected. It was signed before the business had existed and he
found nothing to contradict it. To his immense satisfaction, Jean
did not find a business agreement or contract. Gil's vehicle and
business keys along with his personal belongings the police had
recovered were in a box, untouched since Constable Brooks had
delivered them. Jean opened the box and took the keys. The key
ring was heavy and, knowing he could not conceal them on his
person, Jean put them in the chain box in the back of his truck.

Jean was at the law office of Claude Talbot when Elmer had
given Frances the deposits. Claude listened as Jean detailed what
he knew about the business of Gilbert and Elmer. Claude, who
had a lot of experience with contracts, could see where Jean was
going with this information. He felt a certain sadness at discovering
what a shallow and mean-spirited man Jean could be for a second
time. Jean had come to him years before to check and see if Eva's
mother had any legal recourse after Eva was born. She did not,
but Claude had advised him to give her the money and send her
away. He knew Jean could be ruthless in business, but he never
thought for a moment Jean would take advantage of his daughter
Frances' tragedy. Claude knew his professional obligation was to
give sound legal advice to his client, as distasteful as he found his
client's motives. Claude would reconcile his feelings with a steep
bill for every moment he had to listen to or research the questions
Jean posed.

When Jean got to the will he had seen and the fact there was no
business agreement or contract Claude wished he could go to every
school and teach children the importance of wills and contracts.
Legal wills provided enough legal work, never mind the work they
created when they were challenged. It was so unnecessary if people
were prepared. Not having them gave men like Jean a licence to
steal, which he was sure Jean intended to do.

Claude lit a cigarette and continued making notes. He wrote
power of attorney because he anticipated Jean was about to go
down that road. A minute later, Jean began talking about Frances

and her children. In a sickeningly false tone of concern, Jean talked about how difficult Gilbert's death had been for all of them. Frances, he said, "was so weakened by grief and overwhelmed with the immensity of being widowed with two infant children she was incapable of taking care of her own affairs." Claude knew the courts would see Jean as a determined strong father looking out for his daughter and likely would side with him because he was a man. Women, he knew from experience, rarely fared well in the courts, because the courts were entirely male-dominated in this part of the country. Gilbert's will had not even been seen by an executor yet and already Jean was working to ensure he benefited from it.

When Jean left, Claude poured himself a three-finger drink of scotch. He felt weary and older than his sixty-five years. Five more years and I will retire to Montreal, he thought. People like Jean made him wish he had been a prosecutor.

In the days after Gil's funeral, Walter moved into Elmer's shed. It was comfortable. Elmer had put a bed and table in years before. There was a small wood stove Elmer used to heat the shed when he was skinning furs. Walter got hired at the building site for the new police detachment. It was being built as an eight-man detachment with barracks and a large garage. The main building had been framed and the rest of the job would take Walter through until trapping season. The foreman was a government employee who had been building police detachments for years. He quickly took a liking to Walter because he needed little supervision and did quality work. The other men on the crew teased Walter about his heavy accent, but he soon became the go to guy when there were technical questions. Walter had met Everett on the reserve when Elmer was hauling water. Even without Elmer's obvious dislike of Everett as a cue, Walter found Everett to be a thoroughly disagreeable sort of man. He used his size and height to try to intimidate everyone he met. If he could not intimidate someone, he looked at them for any weaknesses. Walter had met many men like Everett before. When they met, Walter looked him in the eyes and felt he got a good measure of the man. Everett was a bully and a coward to Walter. Walter knew he was also an enemy to be wary of.

Walter walked to the job site every morning. He was always early, and by the time Everett arrived Walter was already working. Everett could barely hide his feelings about Walter. Walter was not afraid of him—that was obvious when they first met. Everett believed Walter and Elmer thought they were better than him because they had been soldiers together. It was like that with Gil before he died, too. This gnawed at Everett every day. The anger he felt made him work harder and faster than he normally did. Between Everett's bootlegging and the job, he had not seen Lucy for more than two weeks. Tonight, he thought, I will pay her a visit.

Lucy had come to Mary and Elmer's house every day since the day after Walter had arrived. She was her old self again, flirting shamelessly with Walter and laughing. Even little Helen told Mary that she thought Lucy was in love with Walter. Lucy helped with the children and preparing meals for the men. She waited until Walter got back from work every day. To Mary, she seemed reluctant to go back to her cabin. Lucy told Mary, "Most of my hides are not ready to be processed into clothing yet, so I have plenty of time to spare."

Mary knew it was Walter's infectious enthusiasm for everything, especially Lucy, keeping her around.

Everett got home from work and had a couple of swigs of homebrew while eating his supper. Wilma quietly served him as he ranted about the people he worked with and the crazy-eyed bastard that Elmer was letting stay in his woodshed. Wilma cleared the plates away and took the children into the other room. Everett took a long hard swig of his jar and yelled, "Suit yourself, Wilma. This place better be clean when I get home," as he got up and went out the door. He took the long way around the reserve to get to Lucy's. When he got there, he saw the door to her cabin was padlocked. He was furious and frustrated. Where can that little bitch be? he thought. His mood was getting darker and darker as he took the shortest route back to his house and his homebrew. Just before he got home, he saw Lucy and Walter in the fading daylight walking and holding hands.

🐜

Around 11 p.m., Elmer heard the bell by the school clanging. He woke up and went to the window. He saw the glow of a fire at the edge of the reserve where Lucy's cabin was. He pulled on his boots as one of the elder's was coming to tell him about the fire. He jumped into his truck and started it. He was getting out to attach the water trailer when he saw Walter and Lucy drop the hitch of the trailer onto the ball. Elmer smiled despite the situation. Lucy had been staying with Walter and it made him happy. Elmer, Walter, and Lucy got to Lucy's cabin and saw it was totally engulfed in flames. About forty people came to help but everyone knew all they could do was keep the fire from spreading into the forest. Walter saw Everett briefly in the glow of the fire at the edge of the crowd. He looked drunk and smug.

Chapter 12

Claude Talbot interviewed the head Indian agent for the area for three hours. James Price, the agent, was very helpful and over the course of the interview he consumed three quarters of a bottle of Claude's scotch. Price had told Claude that Elmer had never obtained any permits for the work he had done as required under the Indian Act. As a veteran, he had received about 2500 dollars as a veteran's benefit. He did not qualify for the larger benefit available to other veterans because he could not buy land on the reserve. Elmer's status as an Indian was in question and Price had written to Ottawa for clarification on how to proceed. Price, who had been an agent for thirty years, told Claude about the troubles he had with the Indian veterans from World War One. They had volunteered in large numbers from his region; many had been killed or wounded and some had been decorated for bravery. He treaded lightly on many of the reserves under his supervision. The reserve across from Lac Ville was one of the few that did not have a veteran's contingent from the Great War.

Price was candid about how he did his job in this area. If he did not need to, he did not go on the reserves. Only when he had no choice did he try to exercise government policy. The area was to spread out and the core of veterans challenged him constantly. If a reserve was running well and not causing him problems, he was content to let things be. "If Ottawa was happy, I'm happy," he laughingly told Claude.

Claude sat listening and wondered how Price was able to keep his job at all. Price's cheeks were red, but it seemed he was holding his own with the scotch. Price straightened up and looked directly at Claude and asked, "So what is it you really want to know?"

Claude raised his eyebrows. He had underestimated Price. "I have a client who wants to get his daughter, now widowed, out of a business with Elmer Wabason with the fewest complications as possible," he answered.

Price, remembering the defiance of the Great War veterans in the reserves to the north, saw the opportunity to nip it in the bud here. "I think we will be able to work something out Mr. Talbot," he replied, and drained his tumbler.

After Price left, Claude made notes. It was clear to him there would be little interference from Indian Affairs for any legal action he initiated on Jean's behalf. Claude loved the law and the order it brought. For a moment he almost felt bad about how heavily the law was going to work in his favor. He wondered if he would have been up to the challenge of representing Elmer Wabason.

Gabriel Cote was next door to Claude's office doing research and overheard almost all the conversation between Price and his boss. He made some notes in the small notebook he kept in his pocket. This was not the kind of law he was going to practice once he was on his own. Men like Elmer would need men like him sooner than later. He looked forward to the day.

Louise worried about Frances. Frances, except for brief periods of time she spent on the porch, had not left her and Jean's home since Gil died. She slept whenever the children did. Frances was listless and only did what she had to. When she was awake, she rarely smiled and only talked when she was spoken to. Louise told Jean this sometimes happens to a woman after a child is born and it was only further compounded by Gil's death. Father Andre and the doctor both told them that only time would bring Frances around. Rejean was with his grandfather and Francine was in bed with Frances. Louise stood looking out her kitchen window and started to cry softly. The mixed blood girl she had seen at the church was about a year older than Frances. There was no doubt in Louise's mind Jean was her father. Jean, who had always been secretive, was even more guarded about what he was up to and where he was these past two months. With whom and with what was Jean going to hurt and humiliate her now, she thought. Francine started to cry. Louise dried her eyes and went to check on mother and daughter.

✦

James Price heard a knock on his hotel room door. He had sobered up a bit since supper because he was expecting a visit from Alphonse. When he opened the door, Alphonse brushed him aside and quickly came in and closed the door. Alphonse pulled out a bottle and sat at the small desk in the room. He poured both a drink and got right to the point. "Why were you at the office of Claude Talbot? Is there trouble I should know about?" he asked in his gruff voice.

James was used to Alphonse's paranoia and answered, "No Al, it had nothing to do with our arrangement relax."

Alphonse knew if Price as the Indian agent ever reported alcohol abuse as a problem on the reserve, the police would be all over it. Alphonse put fifty dollars on the desk, drank his drink down, and left. Price sipped his and thought about how comfortable his retirement would be in a year or two.

✦

Constable Brooks talked to one of the barmaids, Cathy Turner, of the Georgetown Tavern almost once a week. Brooks had arrested a man who had assaulted her and ripped her shirt open at closing time. He had been respectful and compassionate when he dealt with her. He had even told the tavern owner to be quiet when he told her not to make a big deal out of the incident. Cathy felt this police officer had no ulterior motives and genuinely cared for her. "A real straight shooter," she had told her mother in a letter. She had a room above the restaurant where Brooks took his lunch in every second afternoon. Sometimes she would work the lunch shift to help pay her rent. Whenever she did, Cathy took the opportunity to pass on information she heard. One afternoon she was pouring coffee for Constable Brooks and slipped a note under his cup. When Brooks opened it after leaving the restaurant he smiled as he read:

> Some guy named Jack from Lac Ville was bragging about clipping a vehicle and the cops not having a clue last night. He said he was with a guy named Al who everyone was afraid of. He was talking to Jeremy who works at the garage and he was drunk.
> Take care

Walter and Lucy were having tea in the woodshed three days after Lucy's cabin had burned down. Lucy had lost nearly everything she had. Walter watched her as she sipped her tea. She had not shed a tear either during or after the fire. Lucy to him seemed like a burden had been lifted from her. Walter's mother had told him years ago that "a good woman will only tell you her secrets when she has nothing to gain and trusts you." Walter watched her dark eyes sparkle as she looked into the light of the lamp. He would wait, he thought; she was worth every minute.

Elmer felt lost without Gil. Even though they worked on separate job sites half the time, they always met up and exchanged notes. They had never discussed what would happen if either of them should die. Elmer was content to let Frances do most of the paperwork, except for getting paid and turning over the proceeds to Frances. Elmer did not have a clear idea of what their company looked like. Mary had told Elmer more times than he could count, "Elmer, stop being so trusting and get things on paper." Elmer could not even bring himself to ask Gil for more papers confirming what their business relationship was. He told Mary he thought it was disrespectful to do so. It caused the rare argument. Mary insisted it was just good business and Gil would understand. Elmer loaded his truck for the trip back to their compound and knew in his heart his beautiful Mary had been right all along.

As he started driving his anxiety grew as he began to think about Everett and what Mary had told him. Elmer had seen enough violence in his life. He felt he had already led three lives. Everett beat him from the time he could remember. Not satisfied just beating him, Everett tormented and went out of his way to humiliate every chance he got. It only stopped when Elmer grew big enough to fight back and win when they reached their mid-teens. Elmer knew everything Mary had told him was true because he had seen the beastly cruelty of his brother before. Elmer's second life began with Mary. With Mary, he needed no one else, and once the children came, his life was where he always wanted it to be. Elmer's third life was the unexpected and all-consuming war. Elmer felt each year in the army equalled five years everywhere else. The experiences were so intense and overwhelming, he had welcomed the lack of conflict with a reverence bordering on a monkish discipline.

It infuriated Mary that Elmer did not get angry when he should. She could not understand it, and Elmer knew. She never said it out loud, but Elmer could see the frustration in her eyes. Elmer knew he could not explain to her how closely fury and violence sat underneath his calmness. When Mary had told Elmer about Everett's bootlegging and rapes, Elmer pictured driving his bayonet through Everett's forehead. He pictured it, smelled it, and felt his brother's brains and blood flowing over his hands. Elmer knew he could never tell Mary that. He drove on, thinking how to put a stop to Everett's reign. Maybe the elders would banish him if they knew. Elmer felt like a stranger in his own community. He had been working so hard, he had been blind. He was not sure who he could trust. This is his fourth life and he had to do something before it spiralled out of control.

Chapter 13

Louise watched and listened as Jean convinced Frances he would look after Gil's business until she was herself again. Frances had perked up for a few days after Elmer's visit, then slipped back into her lethargy again. She watched and listened as the man she married masterfully manipulated his own daughter, who was suffering from the baby blues and weakened by grief, into doing exactly what he wanted. Frances, usually so sharp and high spirited, was unable to see what her father was trying to do. In spite of herself, Louise could not help admiring the skill and cunning of a man she no longer loved as he single-mindedly achieved his goals. Louise knew she would benefit from Jean's efforts and guiltily she thought it was what she would have earned for the years she had been with him.

When Jean presented a paper to Frances that Claude Talbot had prepared to give Jean control of Gil's business, Frances signed it. Claude witnessed the signature and his articling student Gabriel Cote signed as well. She knew Frances had signed it because she trusted her father. Louise knew Jean would not hurt his daughter or grandchildren if he did not have to. She also knew he could and would hurt everyone else to get what he wanted. It had taken him almost two months since Gil had died to spin this web. In the past couple of weeks, Jean was almost like his old self. He was driven and in good humour. He must have known this moment was coming. She watched as Jean hugged Frances and shook hands with Claude and Gabriel. His smile was the brightest she had seen in the past year. There was a handsome widower at the church. He had caught Louise's eye and she had caught his. Louise would pay Jean back soon, she thought, as Claude and his student left with the papers Frances had signed.

Jean wasted no time afterwards. On the first Sunday following Frances signing the papers, he went to the compound with Alphonse and four men from Alphonse's crew using the keys he had lifted from Gil's effects. Jean was surprised the mechanic was there. Kurt, the ex-prisoner of war and now Gil's and Elmer's mechanic, told Jean, "I like to work on Sundays, so everything is good to go for the week."

Jean regarded him suspiciously and asked, "Is Elmer on a job?"

Kurt told him, "Elmer gave everyone the day off because it was Sunday." Kurt knew Jean was Frances's father so he did not say anything as Jean took all the papers and keys he could find.

Jean told him, "You can continue to work here but I am now the boss. We can work out the details later."

Kurt stared back and continued working on a pump engine he was overhauling. The five men with Jean said nothing and Kurt made a special effort to remember their faces so he could tell Elmer. He also kept a heavy wrench close at hand. The ugly one who seemed to be their boss looked at Kurt like he wanted him to protest. Kurt did not take the bait, instead muttering, "Kleine Manner."

Jean and the others drove to the reserve in three trucks. They drove in fast, forcing children to run off the road. They stopped in a cloud of dust outside of house 12. Elmer came out the door as the men were getting out of their trucks. He motioned Mary to stay inside. When Elmer saw Jean, he knew this was what Mary had feared. Jean was abrupt and announced in a loud voice, "Frances has signed over the business to me. I am here to take the vehicles and trailers."

Elmer felt his blood rise. He took a breath to calm himself and answered, "These vehicles are mine, Jean, bought and paid for."

Alphonse and his men came alongside Jean. Elmer could see they had chains with locks in their hands. Jean motioned them to stop. "Do you have the papers to prove this?" he asked Elmer.

Elmer answered, "I do not have to prove anything to you, Jean."

Alphonse gathered his chain around his hand and started smiling.

The arrival of the trucks caused most of the people on the reserve to come out of their houses to see what was going on. Several of the men grabbed axes and started to go around the back of Jean and Alphonse's crew. One of Alphonse's men tapped Alphonse on the shoulder and whispered in his ear. Alphonse in turn tapped Jean. Jean glanced around and immediately looked deflated. Everyone stopped when Walter racked a round into his .303 rifle and stepped out from behind Elmer's house. Jean knew he had lost control and in a higher pitched voice than he intended told Elmer, "This is only the beginning. I have the law on my side." He glanced around, almost yelling, "All of you people will soon learn I have the law on my side." He motioned to Alphonse, and everyone got back in their trucks.

As they drove away, spinning rocks and gravel and being chased by dogs, one of the boys from the reserve put a rock through the back window of Jean's truck. As they pulled onto the highway, Alphonse saw Jean had lightly wet the front of his coveralls. He did not say anything. The smell said everything.

They drove to the picnic area near the lake. Jean had regained his composure by the time everyone was out of their vehicles lighting cigarettes. Jean stayed in the truck and spoke out the window. "Well boys, we sent a message," he said. "Thank you for coming with me. You may not believe this but that went better than I planned. They brought a gun to a business discussion. Does anyone know who the wild-eyed crazy man is?"

One of Alphonse's men did. He answered, "He is a veteran who served with Gil. He is working on the new police building."

"Very interesting," Jean replied. Perhaps the morning had gone even better than he thought. Knowing who Elmer's allies were was going to be useful in the coming days.

The next morning, Jean was in Claude's office relating his version of what had occurred at house 12. While Claude was making notes, he was thinking: You, Jean, are a bastard on so many levels. Jean had made this unplanned move to try and save on legal fees. He was so fixated on what he wanted he did not even think Claude would notice. Oh, my friend you better hope this business is as lucrative as you think it is because your legal fees just doubled, he smirked to himself.

When Jean was finished, Claude outlined his many options. Claude did not want Jean to call the police. He believed calling the police would cause too many problems. If the police questioned the legality of Jean's brash move of going onto the reserve, and questioned why he brought five men with him, it could go badly.

Claude instead recommended Jean wait while Claude's accountant and he went over all the papers Jean had taken from Frances and the office. In the interim, he would file complaints about illegal services Elmer had provided with the Indian agent, James Price. "Any price," is what Alphonse called him when he talked to Claude a week ago. The Indian Act allowed the agent to veto or approve services provided by status Indians to non-native people off the reserves. That Elmer might not be a status Indian because of his military service could be a problem later. For the moment, it was to everyone's advantage if people believed he was. He would have his articling student and secretary send letters to everyone on Gil and Elmer's ledger suggesting there could be trouble with their taxes because they had dealt with an ill-defined and possibly illegal partnership between Gil and Elmer. The letter would suggest Jean was remedying the situation and would be the contact person in the future. Claude recommended any services that had been contracted with government agencies be left as is. Jean should personally visit every one of those government sites and continue to provide services even if the service was at a loss. The last thing Jean wanted, Claude told him, is the government double checking an existing contract.

When Claude asked what would happen to the 24 employees Gil and Elmer had working for them by late 1950, Jean told him they had already been contacted and 18 were staying on. The other six had been replaced by a group of Portuguese workers he had hired from the railroad on the promise of better pay. What Jean did not tell Claude was he had been working on this from the payroll he had found at Frances's weeks before he visited the reserve. Alphonse and Everett had visited every employee except Kurt and told them how things would be. There were a few beatings along with threats against families, but everyone except the original six from the reserve Elmer had mentored came on board. Of the six who quit, two agreed to silence, two left the reserve right after Jean's visit, and the remaining two could be monitored by Everett. Knowing someone's family and their history made Everett's job easier, something Jean had suspected when Alphonse told him about Everett.

Claude made more notes. There were some details he knew he did not need to know.

🐜

In the days after Jean's visit, Elmer and Walter took the batteries out of the vehicles as they did every night. The trailers were chained to trees and new locks put on. Mary was quiet. She was not one to say I told you so, Elmer thought. Helen and Elias came home right after school every day. They shadowed Mary and Elmer wherever they went. Mary told Elmer to be patient with them. "They know and see more than you know," she said.

Elmer had gone to the compound and found a heavy chain locked to the gate. Kurt came out and told him what had happened. He told Elmer he did not have the key for the lock and the only vehicle keys he had were for the vehicles he was working on that day. He told him Jean had taken all the rest and only gave him keys when he needed them. Kurt said in his thick German accent, "He took all the pumps and keeps them in town my friend. I will work for him because I have to. I will work for you whenever you need work done. There is no honour in what happened here." With that he turned and went back into the shop.

The story about what had happened on the reserve took on a life of its own. People in Lac Ville had heard Jean and the men had fought the men on the reserve to a standstill. Other people heard from people on the reserve that Jean and company had run with their tails between their legs from Elmer and Walter. Though only a few people had seen Walter, everyone claimed they seen him with a .303 aimed at Jean. The stories eventually made their way to Louise. Louise asked Jean what had happened when Frances was busy with the children. Jean was expecting this sooner or later. He told her in a firm steady voice he reserved for when he wanted to make it clear he was taking no further questions, "I secured the future for Frances and our grandchildren." He put on his coat and left.

The story had reached Sergeant McNeil of the Ontario Provincial Police detachment in Georgetown as well. He was on the phone to the regional superintendent in Fort William when Constable Brooks came into the office. As he hung up the phone, he looked at Brooks and said, "I am taking the Indian agent to the reserve outside of Lac Ville. Apparently there was some incident involving townspeople and Indians a week ago. Have you heard anything?"

Sergeant McNeil was a police officer from the old school. He was very rank conscious and expected immediate respect from everyone. He also lacked subtlety. Brooks had heard the real story from Walter three days ago and hoped it would have died away until he got out there. Brooks answered, "I heard a rumour, Sergeant. I was not going to say anything until I knew more," which was half true.

Sergeant McNeil clucked. "Ah, to be a young constable. Constable Brooks, I need to know everything no matter how small a whisper. Do not let this happen again," he admonished.

Brooks took advantage of the fact Sergeant McNeil would

automatically assume his source was better than Brooks and made no further comments except, "Understood, Sergeant."

Chapter 14

Mary watched Elmer getting his truck ready to haul water for everyone in the even numbered houses on the reserve, which he did every Saturday morning. He was quiet at breakfast. He had not spoken much in the past couple of weeks. There was little to be said he had told her. Her heart was breaking for her husband. Where had the fight in him gone, she wondered. It was like he was accepting defeat the way he used to when his brother and the other boys used to beat him up when he was young. Mary knew him then and remembered how he would just go silent and sullen with every humiliation. Mary liked him back then and tried to get his attention whenever she could. Even though they were children she knew he was the person she was going to be with. Elmer would withdraw from everyone, and Mary knew she would have to patient. Now she knew the stakes were higher and she did not know if she could be patient again; Helen and Elias's future was at risk as well.

Walter rapped at the screen door and let himself in. Mary was startled. She was so deep in thought she missed him going by the window. Walter quickly read Mary's face and guessed her thoughts. "Mary, in the war Elmer finished every fight. He thought he was done and put it behind him. He knows a fight is coming again. He will not let you or the children down," he said.

Mary looked at him, waiting for more. Walter smiled and went out to join Elmer. Helen heard the screen door close and came into the kitchen. "What did Walter want mom?" she asked.

"I am not sure," Mary answered.

"He must have forgot what he forgot," she added with a smile.

As Elmer drove to the fast-running creek where he drew his water, he realized how hot this past month had been. He had been so distracted and lost in his thoughts he failed to note the drop in water volume in the creek. Walter had not. He told Elmer as they fastened the hose to the pump to fill the tank, "One good lightning storm and we all could be busy for a while, Elmer. I have never seen it this dry before."

Elmer nodded in agreement. He looked at the grass and trees dry as tinder and felt apprehension like he had not felt since the war. He tried to shake it off. Walter looked at Elmer for a moment. Walter had the same feeling; they did not have to say it to each other and went back to the task at hand.

Sergeant McNeil knew from experience that whenever there was a problem between white communities and Indian communities it was often easiest to deal with the Indians. They were not demanding lawyers right away and the elders knew from their experiences the Indian agent could make things difficult if there was not a consensus. Sergeant McNeil's sense of justice and fairness told him the deck was often stacked against the Indians. This did not stop him from taking advantage of the inequality when it came to keeping the peace. Thirty years into his career, he did not need the regional superintendent writing him up for allowing trouble between communities under his watch. Indian Agent Price was sweating alcohol out his pores as McNeil was driving towards the reserve. McNeil was not averse to drink; he was, however, contemptuous of people who let it dominate their lives. He had the windows down in the sweltering heat. Even the warm breeze did not help. McNeil frowned. If he could smell Price, the elders would too, he thought.

Price was complaining about his job. "I swear, Sergeant, they are the most difficult people sometimes. By far the worst are these veterans. They think the laws do not apply to them anymore because they fought in the wars. They even want to vote now. They want to be able to drink in the bars," he said, shaking his head. "I have a whole list of complaints filed with the Indian Affairs bureau office about this Elmer Wabason. Trading and selling services off reserve, providing services normally done by the government on the reserve, moving about without permission and letting non-Indians live on the reserve. I don't know where to start with this one," he added.

McNeil looked over at Price and replied, "Maybe if you had done your job from the start, you would not have to have a police officer with you today." Price frowned and watched the road ahead. Sympathy is between shit and syphilis in the dictionary, Mr. Price, Sergeant McNeil thought to himself. The Indian Act violations meant nothing to him. He was going to the reserve to determine if a criminal act had occurred. If there was no crime, he would lay down the law with both communities so Headquarters in Fort William would leave him alone.

McNeil remembered this Wabason fellow from the fatal accident involving the young man from Lac Ville. Constable Brooks had seemed quite taken by him which was the reason he did not assign the Constable this investigation. Wabason had a soldier's bearing and seemed bright. Perhaps McNeil could get this sorted out quickly and be back in Georgetown by the morning, he thought. McNeil knew the death of Gil Bertrand had something to do with this unrest and regretted not having re-read Constable Brooks's file before leaving.

As McNeil drove around the corner where Gil had been killed, he saw the sky to the south darkened by storm clouds. It looked ominous, and as suddenly as they appeared, the atmosphere changed. There was a sudden drop in temperature and the wind picked up. McNeil accelerated slightly; he wanted to get to the reserve before this fast-moving front hit.

Elmer looked up when the air changed. "You had to say something, didn't you, Walter," he said as they finished filling one of the elders' water tank.

"The forest needs the rain, but this is going to be a hell of a storm," Walter commented.

They had four more houses to go to. Elmer hoped they could get them done before the storm arrived.

McNeil and Price arrived at house 12 just as Elmer and Walter pulled into the yard. Elmer saw the police car and recognized the Sergeant and Indian Agent Price. "I have brought this trouble, Elmer, my friend," Walter said.

"No, this is on Jean, Walter. Let's see what they want," Elmer replied.

As they exited their vehicle the sky completely darkened. Price got out of the police car with a bundle of papers in a manila folder. McNeil exited and put on his police cap. There was a tremendous clap of thunder, and lightning struck very close. Elmer's husky came around the back of the house running, tail straight and teeth bared. Before Elmer could shout a warning, the dog clamped on Price's thigh. Price shrieked and dropped his papers. The wind scattered them as heavy drops of rain started pelting them all.

Elmer ran up and pulled the dog off Price. McNeil and Walter both grabbed Price and started carrying him to the house. He was bleeding badly. Mary, who had seen everyone arrive, threw open the door and yelled for them to get in the house. The sky opened and unleashed its fury, accompanied by lightning strikes every couple of minutes. Elias and Helen watched as the policeman and Walter cut Price's trouser leg to get a better view of the bite. Blood was pouring out. Elmer, Walter, and the sergeant had all seen wounds many times and knew it was serious but not life threatening. The dog had missed the main artery, which would have caused Price to bleed out quicker. The husky had hit a minor artery; a tourniquet was placed on Price's thigh. Price was whimpering. Mary looked on in contempt. This was the man who had withheld part of Elmer's pay. He was arrogant and pompous the last time she had seen him when Elmer was not there. Elias stood by his mother and repeated something Elmer had told him years ago: "Dogs know bad spirits. Trust the dogs."

Mary shushed him. Mary offered to cauterize the bite with her iron. Sergeant McNeil was not sure if she was joking are not.

Price insisted on seeing a doctor, and the men helped him to McNeil's police car, getting thoroughly soaked. McNeil told Elmer and Walter he would be back in the morning and to please be there. Price, in the passenger seat, watched as some of the papers he had brought swirled around the reserve or stuck to trees and windows. With a nod to the house, Sergeant McNeil drove off to Lac Ville in the pouring rain.

Chapter 15

There were eleven forest fires burning by morning. Six fires were south and east of Lac Ville and the other five between Georgetown and the reserve. The dawn broke humid and bright except for the haze from the closest fire. Elmer came out of house with a cup of coffee in his hand and saw Walter sitting on a stump beside the table in the backyard. Mary, Lucy. and the children were still asleep. Elmer's husky trotted up and Elmer stroked his fur. "Should we wait for the policeman, Elmer? Or go see how bad this is?" Walter asked, quietly.

"He will not be here until after breakfast, Walter. Let's do a reconnaissance," Elmer replied.

They jumped in Elmer's truck and drove out of the reserve. They drove to the high ground just north of Lac Ville, four miles from Elmer's house. Walter was silent as he looked at four columns of smoke rising from the forest about ten miles south of Lac Ville. Walter knew they were too close to each other and would probably merge with even a slight breeze. Elmer could see columns of smoke all around, but he too knew the main threat was where Walter was looking. The reserve should be safe. For once, being given the worst-situated piece of land was a benefit. The lake, highway, and swamp should shield it from the worst effects of the fire. Lac Ville was not so lucky, having been built right on the high ground beside the lake and backed by a thick forest. The trees behind Lac Ville had been harvested years ago and a poorly managed harvest left the area full of densely packed new trees, deadfall, and scrap wood.

The sun was obscured by the haze and, as if on a cue, a wind started to blow from the south. Elmer looked at Walter. "Jesus, you did not say anything this time, did you Walter?" he said.

Walter replied, "No, that was all on its own this time."

"We have to warn Lac Ville. It is Sunday and most of them won't be up for another hour," Elmer said as he jumped in the cab of his truck.

The breeze combined two of the fires together quickly, and it was moving along at a pace of five hundred yards an hour to start. It picked up speed with each gust of wind. Deadfall and tree tops began to ignite from the intense heat as the fire gained momentum. The forest sizzled as any moisture the rain had brought evaporated.

Elmer drove straight into town and directly to the church. There were people outside of their homes who were just now waking up to the danger the fire poised. When Elmer walked into the church, Father Andre was at his morning prayers. Father Andre motioned to not interrupt him with a flick of his hand. Elmer grabbed his elbow, yanked him to his feet, and led him outside. Father Andre was pointed to the south. He crossed himself and looked at Elmer. "I will ring the church bells," he said.

"Loud and often," Elmer growled.

Elmer and Walter watched as everyone in Lac Ville began to pour out of their houses with looks of horror and confusion clearly etched on their faces. He saw Sergeant McNeil's police car coming toward the church. McNeil stopped by Elmer's truck and got out. Elmer wasted no time and told him, "We may need to evacuate the town, Sergeant. Walter and I give that fire five hours at the most before it is here."

McNeil nodded his head in agreement.

Mary awoke to the incessant clanging of the church bells. Even at three miles distant, the steady ringing brought a feeling of dread and apprehension. Elmer was not in the house. She ran to the window and saw his truck was gone. Elias and Helen woke up with the commotion. Mary ran to the woodshed, "Lucy wake up. Is Walter there?" she yelled.

Walter had tossed and turned until three in the morning. Lucy had only fallen asleep a couple of hours ago. Lucy reached for Walter as she woke up. She yelled back before her eyes were even open, "No, he is gone," she answered. She came out into the smoky daylight and realized what was going. "Can you see the fire, Mary?" she asked.

Elias and Helen were out of the house when Mary pointed out the three columns of smoke to Lucy. Mary turned to Helen, "Go tell the elders to come to our house." She turned to Elias, "Go tell your aunties and cousins to come to our house. Quickly."

Helen and Elias ran off. Everyone was an elder to Elias, he would have gone to every house. Helen knew where to go. Everett came out of his house, looked at Lucy and Mary, and went back in.

Sergeant McNeil, Elmer, and Walter marshalled everyone who showed up at the church by the police car. Father Andre provided information on the elderly and the infirm. The principal of the school agreed to have two teachers record what was being done. Jean and several businessmen showed up with men. Jean took his orders from Sergeant McNeil while glaring at Elmer and Walter. McNeil said sharply to Jean, who he did not know, "We don't have time for your issues, whatever they maybe, sir." He tasked Jean with rounding up any heavy equipment he could find to build a firebreak on the east side of town. Walter told him there was a road which ran north and south of town which could be expanded into a firebreak. Jean knew the road and nodded to Walter. Another teacher was tasked with rounding up all the senior boys to stand watch for sparks landing on houses. Elmer was thankful people were responding to directions for the most part.

After an hour, a semblance of order emerged as people showed up and were tasked to do whatever needed to be done. The smoke was everywhere now, acrid and burning to the eyes. People became uneasy. The fire was moving very fast now. Everyone could feel it. Mary and about forty men from the reserve showed up in just about every vehicle from the reserve. Mary saw Elmer with a group of men and only caught his eye long enough for a smile. Mary approached Father Andre and told him the women and children would be relatively safe on the reserve and to her surprise he agreed. Sergeant McNeil concurred. With the help of many people who had never given the reserve, her home, a thought, vehicles were loaded with women and children for their first ever trip to her community. The men from the reserve reported to Elmer. Elmer did not want this to be how work crews were divided. Despite the enormity of the emergency, he saw this as an opportunity to build some bridges. He sent twenty men to Jean's fire break. He was clear on the fact they would take orders from Jean. "Work shoulder to shoulder," he yelled as they set off. Ten men from town and ten from the reserve were sent to the highway to monitor the fire from the north. Elmer told them to extinguish any fires started by sparks and he would find some pumps for them as soon as he could. He had just finished saying this when Kurt showed up.

"Do you know where Jean keeps the pumps, Kurt?" Elmer asked.

Kurt replied he had heard one of the men say they were in the old stables at the rear of Jean's property. Elmer told McNeil he was going to send Walter to collect some pumps. Walter grinned when Elmer tasked him. He took Kurt and four men with him. When he broke the lock on the largest stable door, Kurt rushed past him. A moment later, Kurt yelled, "Meine Kinder, I have found them." The pumps were indeed like Kurt's children. He had modified and created the powerful machines. When Walter entered the stables, he saw a car. It looked brand new, save for the dust and some damage to the passenger side front panel. The other men were busily loading the pumps and did not notice when

Walter scraped off green paint from the damaged area and put it in his cigarette case.

Alphonse woke up, hung over, to the peeling of the church bells. His head was hammering with each chime. He looked out the window and saw the smoke from the fires. "Damn it," he cursed. Alphonse had watched the storm from the balcony of the hotel until three in the morning. He got up and drank a beer. Alphonse pulled on his pants and grabbed his keys. He had to check on Sam and his stills.

Chapter 16

The fire was consuming entire trees in seconds. The intense heat was causing trees to ignite before flames even reached them. The wind was now pushing the fire at about five miles per hour. Elmer's original estimate of five hours before the fire reached Lac Ville was cut in half. Sergeant McNeil and the mayor of Lac Ville agreed with Elmer. The town site would be the frontline. If they could create enough of a fire break, they could keep the fire from taking structures. Floating sparks and embers needed to be extinguished as quickly as possible. If a house caught on fire it would have to be abandoned. Everyone seemed to be working well together. There was fear and trepidation in the air, though; Elmer could see and feel it. Panic was always only one step away in a calamity. "Keep everyone busy," he told the mayor. Terrified small animals scurried through the town site making for the lake. Elmer watched them running and knew if one man did the same, the town was lost.

Almost every man in town was on the line with Jean and the lumber camp superintendent working on making a firebreak. The amount of combustible fuel was disheartening. In the years before the municipal dump was built, people dumped their garbage in piles scattered around the outskirts of Lac Ville. Lumber companies discarded machinery and empty oil containers in pits. The Department of Lands and Forests had mandated site clean-ups, but as always, the centres closer to the offices in Georgetown received attention first. The companies in Lac Ville had been given a reprieve until the following year. Many of the men, including the camp superintendent, wished that they had not been given the reprieve now.

Sergeant McNeil wanted a house-by-house check done to make sure no one was sheltering in their homes unbeknownst to the rest of the community. He called Elmer over and told him to take Father Andre's apprentice and two men from town with him to check the houses closest to the path of the oncoming fire first. At the most, they had about forty minutes to get this done before the fire was at the firebreak. The sky was dark with smoke, ash and embers swirling as they set out. The first five houses they checked were all clear. In the sixth house, they found Jack Turk still passed out from drinking with Alphonse the previous night. When Elmer shook him awake. He woke up throwing punches and demanding to know how Elmer got in his house. Elmer parried the punches and grabbed Jack's arm, twisting it behind his back until he got to his feet. Jack went limp and the two men from town carried him out and threw him in the box of Elmer's truck. They carried on checking all the houses on the bush side of Lac Ville without encountering anyone else. They did not have time to check any of the houses on the lake side before the fire reached the fire line. It came in roaring, with flames dancing higher than the tops of the trees. The wind caused flames to snap and lash at each other as if in anger. The fire was the fiercest and most intimidating Elmer had ever seen. Elmer dragged Jack out of his truck, threw water on him to wake him up, and sent him on his way. Elmer reported the houses nearest to the fire line were clear to Sergeant McNeil and sent Father Andre's apprentice to the church steeple to watch for spot fires.

The principal of the school had all his senior boys ready to respond to the apprentice's alarms.

Elmer respected and feared fire. He had seen Canadian tank crews burn to death in the war. He had seen Germans burned to death by Canadian Churchill Crocodile flamethrower tanks. The screams of the burning men still haunted his dreams. Sergeant McNeil called him back to the police car. "Mr. Wabason, I need you to go and check the fire line and then report back to me," he instructed.

Elmer knew McNeil was contemplating a total evacuation before it was too late. He jumped in his truck and drove quickly to where Jean was. Jean and the superintendent had done a lot of work in the short time they had. They had used bulldozers to push trees down and away from the road. They had men sawing down the tallest trees and felling them into the fire to keep the fire face as low as possible. Elmer pulled up beside Jean "What do you need?" he asked Jean.

Jean stared at him for a moment and answered, "Water for the men."

Elmer nodded and headed down the line before heading back to report what he had seen. When he got to the south end of the fire line, he saw this area was the least threatened because it was the swampy area just before the forest met the lake. The fire could burn up to the lake and then it would have no fuel. He drove back to Sergeant McNeil's location. "The men on the line need water but I think they will hold the fire," Elmer said.

McNeil's face showed relief. They were not out of danger yet, but the worst was over. The fire could still claim some structures in town. Between the highway north of town, the firebreak, and the swampy ground to the south, the fire's fury would be spent and it would become starved for fuel.

Louise was in the school on the reserve with the older women from Lac Ville. Frances, Francine, and her children were with Mary at her home. Mary had organized everything she could and made a list of everyone who had been evacuated to the reserve. She made sure everyone was as comfortable as possible. One of the men had taken her list to the police officer. Everett had the boys patrolling the reserve, watching for spot fires. Lucy was making tea for everyone when Luke and Eva drove in. They were both covered in ashes and smudged. Luke told them about the fires to the west of the reserve. "There are two fires close to the highway. They are moving westward away from the reserve and Lac Ville." Luke told them the Lands and Forests crew were fighting a big fire close to Georgetown. He was oblivious to the women's reactions when Frances and Eva were face to face for the first time. Mary kept acknowledging Luke as he was talking, but she watched as two sisters looked each other over for the first time. Eva smiled shyly at Frances and asked if she could see Francine. Frances picked up her baby girl and removed the cover from her head. Mary realized Frances knew, but Eva had no idea she was looking at her niece.

Alphonse made it to Sam's cabin before the fire did and found Sam half in the bag. "I thought I was going to have to get in my boat and head to town, you stupid bastard," he snapped. "Help me load the truck, then sit tight here until the fire gets close, then take your boat to town. It is better people do not know we know each other."

"Loading is your job. I just guard this. Besides, I already carried these cases," Sam replied.

Alphonse knew there was no point arguing with this cantankerous fool. The fire may or may not take his stills, but he had a hundred and fifty gallons of product he needed to get to safety. After he had loaded up, he gave Sam a twenty-dollar bill. "Get a room at the hotel. I will see you tonight," he added.

Alphonse's head was starting to clear after last night. As he drove the trail back to Lac Ville, he saw for the first time how dangerous this fire was. It was moving much faster than he had anticipated. He thought about turning around and heading to Sam's, but he could not be sure he had not left when he did. He had about a mile to go and the fire was only feet from the road now. The soft wet ground had slowed it down, but the fire was jumping the treetops. Alphonse drove as fast as he could. The trail was rough, and his load of tin gallon cans was bouncing. He could not slow down or the road would be closed by the fire. He cleared the trail and drove out onto the south end of the firebreak. Elmer was delivering water to the men when Alphonse emerged from the trail. Alphonse had no idea his load was on fire. Sparks had lighted the high-octane alcohol that had spilled out of ruptured cans. Elmer saw the fire and waved Alphonse down to tell him. Alphonse geared down and recognized Elmer just as the alcohol exploded. Alphonse jumped from his truck and ran about fifty feet before he turned around. His truck was engulfed in white hot flames. Elmer was on the ground. The men working this end of the fire break ran up and dragged Elmer away from the fire. Blood was pumping out of his neck where a piece of tin had struck him. Within two minutes, Elmer Wabason was dead.

Chapter 17

Alphonse walked over to where Elmer lay on the ground. Elmer was in a pool of blood, more blood than Alphonse had ever seen. The blood smelled so sickly sweet even the smoke could not mask it. The men around Elmer's body had no idea what had happened. One of them drove to see the superintendent to summon him to the scene. The fire was still raging but everyone knew the fire would burn itself out for lack of fresh fuel in the next 24 hours. Alphonse was dehydrated. Between his hangover and the last few hours, he had nothing left. He watched as someone covered Elmer with a tarp. Everything turned black. He felt himself losing his balance. He fainted and fell to the ground. The camp superintendent arrived shortly afterwards. He ordered a couple men to take Elmer's body and his unconscious foreman to the church and then turned his attention back to the fire.

The wind had stopped. Mary noticed it right away. She walked outside to be sure. Mary was about to turn and tell Frances and Eva when a large black crow flew to the top of the parked trailer in her yard and cawed loudly at her. The crow's beady black eyes held hers for the longest time and then he flew away. She grabbed the door jamb to steady herself. Helen opened the door and grabbed her hand. "Mother, what is it?" she asked.

Mary let herself sink onto the steps. "Something has happened to your father," she answered. Helen stroked her mother's face and started to cry.

Everyone noticed immediately when the wind stopped. The face of the fire stood there like a beast at bay, burning straight up, gaining no further ground, and now rendered impotent except for embers and sparks. Jean and everyone on the fire break redoubled their efforts. Energized by this turn of events the bulldozer operators laid on the gas pushing back trees to fuel the fire low before it could rise and jump the road. Cheers erupted from the parched and smoke blackened men. Indian and white they hugged each other and smiled at their good fortune. The cheers died as word filtered up the fire line that someone had been killed.

When Jean was told Elmer was dead, he leaned on his truck and turned his back to the young man that had told him. He could not let his lack of emotion become a story in town. The man who told him thought he was overcome with the news and stepped back. Jean waited a moment or two before he turned around in what he thought would be a perceived show of strength from a leader and said, "We must carry on. Back to your station young fellow. Tell everyone we must carry on." That is a story that would spread, he thought with satisfaction. Jean sat on the bumper. His lungs and eyes were sore from the smoke. He was as tired as he had been for a long while. Things were coming together now faster than he had anticipated. Except for some loose ends, he had achieved his goals.

Walter and Kurt were reporting to Sergeant McNeil when the truck with Elmer's body and the still prostrate Alphonse pulled up. Walter recognized Elmer's army issue boots sticking out from beneath the tarp. He knew his friend was dead. One of the men yelled for the nurse to attend to Alphonse and they carried him into the church. Walter and Kurt looked at each other and silently acknowledged that Alphonse had something to do with Elmer's death. Walter stood and listened as one of the men who had brought the bodies explained to Sergeant McNeil that Alphonse's truck came out of the bush from a trail at the south end of the fire break at speed and on fire. Elmer tried to flag the truck down to warn the driver when the vehicle exploded. The man qualified that he had not seen the whole sequence of events. This is what he had pieced together from what he and the others had seen.

Sergeant McNeil walked to the truck and lifted the tarp. Walter went with him. Elmer had a jagged wound in his throat and several small shrapnel wounds. He did not have a lot of blood left in him. His shirt and pants had been soaked. The blood was beginning to crust but it was still wet enough to glisten. Walter reached and pulled a tin shard from a wound in Elmer's leg and showed it to the sergeant. Townspeople were starting to gather. Father Andre told them to show respect and move back. McNeil took out his notebook and began making notes, commenting to Walter, "Damn shame a man can live through a war and then be killed by pieces of tin." He told Walter to go to Alphonse's truck and gather any evidence he could see and protect things until he got there. McNeil reached into Elmer's pockets and fished out his truck keys. "Bring his truck here, if it still runs." he said as he handed the keys to Walter. The keys were still wet with Elmer's blood. Walter hesitated. "I will make sure your friend's body is taken care of until you get back," McNeil said. He instructed two men to drive Walter and Kurt to the wreck of Alphonse's truck. "We will tell his wife as soon as we can," McNeil shouted at them as they drove away.

Walter, hardened as he was by the war, felt tears welling up. Kurt punched him in the arm. "Not now. Later. Over Schnapps. If you were Elmer's friend, you are a friend of mine now," Kurt said.

Walter braced up. "God damn Germans. No wonder it took so long to beat you bastards," he said, grinning his crazy grin.

Father Andre performed last rites over Elmer as Sergeant McNeil told the mayor to get a body bag from the funeral home. McNeil removed all the pieces of tin he could find from Elmer's body. The tin puzzled him. Fuel was carried in Jerry cans. The steel gas containers adopted from the German design, which were far more robust than the tin cans the commonwealth had used at the beginning of the war, were pretty much standard around the world now. Maple syrup and molasses sometimes came in tin cans as did olive and canola oil. Surely none of those liquids would explode, they would just burn. With a sudden realization and a surge of anger, McNeil wrote "Homebrew?" in his notebook. He needed to know who the man was who had been carried to the church and question him as soon as possible. As the only man in uniform, he could not delegate the leadership of the crisis to another until he was sure the danger had passed. It would be several hours before he could begin his inquiries.

Alphonse awoke to a nun wiping him with a cold wet cloth. She gave him small drinks of water. A nurse and doctor were talking by a table. Alphonse overheard the doctor tell the nurse, "He is just dehydrated. I could find no injuries. Booze is still reeking out his pores."

The nurse laughed. "Sounds like the Alphonse I know."

Alphonse got up and stood for a moment. His legs were a little wobbly. He took a deep breath to steady himself, then silently walked out the side door of the church opposite of where the police car was. The doctor, nurse, and nun looked at each other. The doctor said, "Let him go. We can only help those who want our help."

Walter and Kurt found five burst gallon tin cans in the area surrounding the burnt truck. The rest were in hundreds of pieces scattered everywhere. It looked like the bed of the truck had taken a direct hit from a mortar round. Elmer's truck had been riddled with small shards of tin. Walter questioned all the men who had been in the vicinity when the explosion happened. No one could really offer anything new, they were just happy no one else had been killed. Walter put the tin cans in the back and drove back to McNeil's location after a thorough search. He was not a policeman, but he knew the tins would be important. He hoped he had not missed anything.

It was late in the evening when Sergeant McNeil, Walter, and Kurt arrived at house 12 with the body of Elmer. McNeil and Walter went to the door and Lucy let them in. Mary and Frances were at the table. Helen was with the children in the corner amusing them. Elias stood behind his mother. Mary looked at Walter, and as soon as their eyes met, she knew what she had feared was true. Before McNeil could say a word, Mary asked in a quiet and tired voice, "Did he suffer?"

Surprised, McNeil answered, "No, Mrs. Wabason. It was an explosion. He was killed instantly." This was a white lie. McNeil he had told many over the years when he believed the absolute truth served no purpose except to cause further pain.

Mary stared at McNeil, doubting it was true but hoping it was. Elias hugged his mother then shook hands with Walter and McNeil. He turned and looked at everyone and then ran out the door. Walter made to go after him. Lucy grabbed his arm and said, "No, Walter, he needs to be alone. He does not want anyone to see him cry."

Walter had worked until four in the morning building a coffin, quietly sawing and using a muffled hammer to drive the nails. Lucy had sat with him. Neither of them spoke. They exchanged glances and let their sorrow speak for them.

Elmer was buried the very next day, twenty-five yards behind house 12. The women had washed and dressed Elmer's body. Sergeant McNeil made the decision to forego an autopsy because of the lack of a proper storage facility precluded preserving the body and because the cause of death was so obvious. It was his call; such was the way of policing in the North.

Walter, Kurt, and Everett dug Elmer's grave in silence and refused help from anyone else. With Frances and Lucy by her side, Mary received the elders and others from the reserve arriving with food and condolences. Helen took care of the children and Elias watched everything in silence. Father Andre, on his own volition, arrived and conducted the ceremony. Mary and Elmer's backyard overflowed with people from the reserve and people from Lac Ville. Word had spread of Elmer and Walter's timely arrival to sound the alarm, and everyone wanted to pay their respects to one of the men who had saved their town.

Jean had sent friends to pick up Louise and the other women from the reserve school and did not attend the funeral. Alphonse was lying low in Sam's hotel room until the policeman went back to Georgetown. He bitched to Sam because he had to pay for and drink government alcohol.

After the funeral, Sergeant McNeil told Mary he was not done investigating and he would be back as soon as he could to see her. Mary thanked him, but she knew that whatever the outcome, her Elmer, the love of her life, was gone, and nothing McNeil learned could ever change that. Frances and she were both widows in two completely different communities. Being widows was a bond because, for all the differences in their communities, no one really knew what to say or how to act around them. Mary knew she was the stronger of the two, for now. She had no idea what the future held for all of them, Lucy and Eva included. As strong as she was, they were now at the mercy of men like Everett, Jean, Alphonse, and Indian Agent Price.

When McNeil pulled up at the hotel to collect Price, Alphonse was looking out the window. He cursed and went into the hallway. There was a drop-down staircase leading to the attic. He quickly pulled the rope and climbed into the attic to hide. McNeil knocked on Price's door and a moment later Price limped out of his room. They went to his police car in silence. Price was whimpering as he limped. McNeil did not avoid any bumps on the drive back to Georgetown.

Chapter 18

The late August fires burned out within the week. The fire protection branch of the Department of Lands and Forests lowered the fire risk signs to moderate with the coming of steady rains and the end of lightening. Elmer Wabason's death was the only recorded fatality. Thousands of acres of forest had burnt, and some structures were lost, but overall the fire season came late and ended quickly.

Constable Brooks was saddened by the news of Elmer's death. He asked Sergeant McNeil, "Can I be assigned the follow-up investigation because the Gilbert Bertrand investigation requires me to go to Lac Ville anyways?" For weeks, the day-to-day calls for the police had been delaying Brooks from getting to Lac Ville. A stabbing of a miner in a drunken fight, vehicle accidents, and accidental deaths all held him up.

The fire at Lac Ville had taken more out of McNeil than he cared to admit. He began to think about an office posting in Fort William or a training job in Southern Ontario. He had enough of the bush and lack of support from headquarters. He would, of course, never tell a constable such a thing. He framed the assignment of the file as an opportunity for Brooks to gain experience and signed off on it. In McNeil's initial report on the fire and the death of Elmer Wabason he did not include his suspicions about the fuel being homebrewed alcohol. He did not need headquarters to think he was not in control of his area. He wanted Brooks to make inquiries before he brought attention to something as serious as this. He had written down the name of Jack Turk, the drunk found during the house search. After the man walked away, McNeil asked one of the nuns who he was and wrote his name in his notebook. He had gotten Alphonse's name from the nurse. He told Brooks, "I want this Alphonse brought to the Georgetown detachment for an interview as soon as you find him." He had taken off before McNeil had a chance to talk to him. McNeil did not know why he had recorded Jack's name, but he wanted Brooks to have as much information as he could before he went to Lac Ville. McNeil showed Brooks the tin containers Walter had brought him. He instructed Brooks to get a statement from Walter to prove continuity of the exhibits.

As Brooks recorded all of McNeil's information, it was everything he could do not to jump up and head right to Lac Ville. The "Jack" that Cathy had written about in her note had to be Jack Turk. It would not be too much of a coincidence if Alphonse turned out to be Al, but like most police officers Brooks trusted coincidences as starting points in investigations. Walter would, he hoped, fill in the gaps.

A couple of days after Elmer's funeral, Walter put his .303 in Elmer's truck and drove to the south end of the fire break. He found the trail Alphonse had emerged from and followed it for a mile before parking the truck and continuing on foot. He walked a couple more miles before he saw a small cabin. The swampy ground had saved the cabin from burning. He went wide around the lake side so he was in the back of the cabin where he would not be seen. There were small foot trails leading from the back of the cabin to a small rocky hill. The person using the trails had put scrub to conceal them from anyone who was on the door side of the cabin.

He followed the trail to a small cave and saw a still. There was a two-burner naphtha gas stove under it on a low burn. No smoke; you are a clever one whoever you are, Walter thought. He laid in some dense brush and waited. An hour later a man he did not know came up the trail from the direction of the cabin. He looked half drunk. The man shut the stove off and replaced the tank and restarted it. In a lean-to about 20 feet from the still and under a rock outcropping, Walter saw a stack of tin containers which were the same size as the ones he had given to the policeman. Walter placed his rifle sights on the man's face right below the nose and above the upper lip. He had seen enough. When the man went back to his cabin, Walter stealthily moved away and once he was clear of the cabin walked back to his truck.

In the days since Elmer was buried, Frances had moved back to her house with the children in Lac Ville. Louise tried to convince her to stay. Frances politely insisted it was what she needed to do. Elmer's death and the fire had snapped her out of a long period where she felt as if everything was muted. Her inability to concentrate and lack of energy lifted like a fog. She dusted the ash which had seeped into her home from the fire while Francine slept and Rejean played. Frances made the bed she and Gil had shared. When an overwhelming feeling came to her to lie on it and try to smell Gil's presence, she resisted. She pulled the sheets tight and threw the covers over the pillows. Later, she thought. For the first time, she noticed her desk drawers appeared to have been gone through. She tensed up and clenched her fist. Frances went to the box containing Gil's effects, which the police officer had had her sign for months before. When she lifted the flaps, she saw all of Gil's keys were gone. Her father was the only one who had been in her house when he came to get clothes for her and the children. Frances looked at Rejean and quietly said, "What has your grandfather done, my son?"
Rejean looked up and smiled sweetly.

Mary took stock of what she still had. Elmer's two trucks and trailers would allow her to keep providing water and wood. Walter and Lucy helped her. Walter's job at the police building construction site would be done by winter. Mary was not sure if he would go back trapping or stay on with Lucy. Wood cutting might not provide enough income to them all. She knew how to work the water run but getting wood would be a challenge. Elias, now 11 years old, worked with her whenever he was not in school. 13-year-old Helen cooked and took care of the house. Anyone who knew Mary knew she was grieving. Mary grieved by keeping busy. If she cried, it was when she was alone. Anybody who did not know her would wonder how she could be so focused so soon after her loss. Mary did not care what anyone thought. She only wanted Elias and Helen to be provided for. She still had not opened Elmer's kit bag, and all his clothes hung where they were when he had died. She knew she was not ready to deal with those things. Elias would want everything his father had. He walked like Elmer, arranged his clothes like him, and took care of his kit. He called everything he owned his kit. Elmer had told him many times that "a man who takes care of his kit can take care of everyone else when he needs to." Helen was like Mary in so many ways. She took her cues from Mary and kept busy. She had been excelling in school since Elmer came home. She told Mary she would continue to do so because that was how she would honour her father. The nights in their home were the hardest, as all of them in spite of themselves kept looking at the door as if they were expecting Elmer to come in.

James Price took two weeks off before he finally came back to his office. The bite on his leg had become infected and he had to take powerful antibiotics to make the pus from the wound stop festering. When he retrieved his mail, he found a letter from the main office in Ottawa explaining that because Elmer Wabason had spent more than four years overseas, he was no longer considered a status Indian. The supervisor urged Price to be cautious if he took any actions against Corporal Wabason. The Indian veterans had been raising Cain since the end of war. The minister did not want any undue attention prior to the next election. He put the letter down and grabbed his copy of the Indian Act. Wabason is dead, he thought. Mary Wabason was now the wife, correction, widow of a non-status Indian. He double checked and found she could now technically be stripped of her status as well. He took his flask from his pocket and took a swig. He wrote a question down on a pad of legal paper "Do I have to tell Ottawa?" The question was rhetorical. He knew he would eventually. He imagined sending a letter two days before he retired. The isolation of the north and the length of time it took for communications had worked to his advantage many times over the years.

Everett took Elmer's death in stride. It was hard to bury his only brother. It was done and now it was time to move on. He announced he was letting his name stand for the next election for chief of the band. The current chief was in ill health and wanted to step down. Elmer had been the only other real contender. Everett knew Elmer would have won and Everett could never have taken the humiliation of losing to him. Things change, Everett thought as he was preparing for work. Things change.

Chapter 19

Jean was in Claude Talbot's office ten minutes after he received his bill for the legal services Claude had provided from the post office. "Jesus, Claude, what has cost so much? You could have called me or dropped over," Jean said as he put the bill on Claude's desk.

Claude gestured for Jean to sit down. He explained the bill step by step. He wanted Jean to know he had asked for and initiated every action Claude had taken on his behalf. That Elmer Wabason had died did not affect what he had to do. He had made Jean the sole proprietor of Gil's and Elmer's business. Frances on paper had been willed the business. The will was weak and outdated. The power of consent Frances had provided was legally sufficient to give Jean control. Claude knew on the surface everything looked legal and binding. He also knew if anything he had done was challenged in a superior court, it could fall like a deck of cards. Jean, Claude knew, only heard what he wanted to hear, so Claude was just selling Jean his bill. Claude's accountant had revealed the net worth of the business. Jean would not be the only one who benefited from the tragic deaths of Gil and Elmer, Claude thought to himself.

Jean paid his bill and left Claude's office confident there were no loose ends. He could now turn his fortunes around. He began planning on how to find someone who could do the distasteful work for him so all he had to do was collect the profits. A moment later, he slapped the steering wheel and laughed to himself. "Alphonse here is your chance. You may be my son-in-law yet."

Constable Brooks made arrangements to go to Lac Ville and the reserve shortly after Sergeant McNeil had assigned the file to him. He arrived at house 12 early Sunday morning. Walter came out to greet him with a cup of coffee for each of them. Mary waved from the house. Lucy and Mary were busy making bread. Elias came out and sat on the stairs. Walter had transferred the paint scrapes he taken from the car in Jean's old stables into a small glass jar. He turned them over to Brooks while explaining the circumstances of how he had found them. Elias knew something important was happening because the policeman took what Walter had given him and starting writing in his book. Elias watched them as they talked. They were like two hunters who had just come across fresh tracks. They were both smiling when Walter was drawing a map on the hood of the police car. Elias knew then he was going to be a hunter like them someday.

Walter explained to Brooks, "The fire has stripped most of the cover from the trail to the cabin where I had found the still. Going in a police car would only invite trouble and possibly put us in danger."

Brooks in turn told Walter that Sergeant McNeil insisted Brooks be in uniform when he sent him to investigate. "The community needs to see the police are working and that is done in uniform, Constable," McNeil said.

They made a two-part plan. First, they would seize the car from the stables and then they would apprehend Jack. The still would have to wait. If the still was making money, no one would be in a rush to dismantle and move it. Before they left the reserve,

Walter went into the woodshed and grabbed the Walther pistol he had liberated from a German officer years ago.

In a small town like Lac Ville, stories circulated for weeks, growing and shrinking with each telling. The story of the confrontation between Jean and Elmer always included the wild-eyed man who pointed a rifle at Jean and his crew. People had figured out Walter was the wild-eyed man. They either saluted or avoided him. Jean had as many enemies as friends because of his manner of conducting business. The garage owner was not a friend, and he was only too happy to follow Constable Brooks and Walter to Jean's old stables with his tow truck. He did not ask a lot of questions because he knew he was going to be part of something important. People would come to his garage to hear the story. They would use the pretext of getting gas to try to get information, and the business never hurt.

When they arrived at the stables, Constable Brooks noted that no one had replaced the broken lock. The door was partly ajar. Walter swung the door open. The car was still there, covered in a thick coat of ash. It looked to Walter like no one had been there since the fire. Brooks made notes and recorded the plate number. He looked inside the driver's compartment and saw there were no keys in the vehicle. He did a walk around and drew a sketch of the damaged area. He took another notebook out of his tunic and flipped the pages to his notes from the accident investigation. The tire impressions were a match. A moment later he motioned to the garage owner. "Hook it up, sir," he said. Brooks instructed the garage owner to take it straight to Georgetown and present the vehicle to Sergeant McNeil. Brooks told him he would meet him there and square up the bill as soon as he could.

There was no way they could work unnoticed and soon telephones would be ringing as people called each other to find out what the police were doing in Lac Ville. As the tow truck driver drove away, Brooks and Walter jumped in the police car and drove to Jack Turk's house. When they were about two hundred yards away, Brooks let Walter out. Walter walked to the back of the house and stood by the back door. Brooks drove to the front and knocked on the door. Jack saw the police car as it stopped in front of the house. He saw the policeman was alone. He grabbed his coat and ran out the back door. Walter tripped him as he came down the stairs. Jack tumbled into the dirt. Walter reached down and gathered Jack's collar in his fist. "The policeman wants to talk to you, my friend," he hissed into Jack's face.

Jack said nothing as Brooks handcuffed him and put him in the back of the police car. Before the door even closed, Jean and several men rolled up in three vehicles. Jean eyed Walter as he got out of his truck. The other men fell in behind Jean. Walter did not see Alphonse among them and moved closer to Brooks. Brooks stood his ground. Jean asked Brooks, "Why were you at my stables and what did you take from there, Constable?"

Brooks replied in a clear, confident tone, "I believe the vehicle involved in the hit and run which killed Gilbert Bertrand was hidden in your stables, sir. Do you know how it came to be there?"

Jean looked genuinely surprised. The men with him looked at Jean and the menace came out of them in a flash. Jean stammered, "I have no idea, Constable."

"For your sake, sir, I hope this is true," Brooks told him and got in his police car at the same time as Walter.

Everyone could see Jack in the back seat. One of the men held his hand over his mouth so Jack could see him as Brooks drove off.

When Brooks and Walter arrived in Georgetown, Brooks booked Jack into a cell while Walter wrote out a statement for Sergeant McNeil. Brooks came out and began making phone calls to the Fort William police to have them track down the vehicle registration. Brooks wanted to have all the information in his hands before he interviewed Jack. Walter went to have lunch at the diner while Brooks typed his initial report and worked on getting more information. Every half hour, either Sergeant McNeil or Brooks checked on Jack. He sat quietly in his cell and asked for nothing. After three hours, Brooks got up and took the cell key from its hook. The registration for the car was in Jack's name and the car had been purchased in Fort William on the day Gilbert was killed. Sergeant McNeil would monitor as Brooks interviewed Jack. Brooks could not see Jack when he went to the cell door and thought he was sitting in the corner. He undid the heavy door and stepped into urine on the cell floor. Jack was blue and his fists were clenched. He had hanged himself with his socks from the bars on the cell window. His weight allowed the knot to become untied after he went unconscious. Brooks yelled for the sergeant and pulled the sock ligature from his neck. Jack was still warm but there was no sign of life.

"God damn it," Brooks said in frustration

Walter, who was waiting in the office for a ride home, heard Brooks yell and rushed to the cell. McNeil took one look at Jack; the bulged eyes, clenched fists, and body posture were enough for McNeil to know he was past saving. McNeil told Brooks, "He is dead, Constable." He then turned and looked at Walter and said, "Get the doctor and the funeral home manager."

The news of Jack's arrest and a car being seized from Jean's old stables spread quickly. Frances, Louise, and the children were just getting home from church when her neighbour came over and told them. The neighbour, Gillian, a retired schoolteacher, said, "I heard there was a murder. Who was murdered I do not know. Of course, Jean had nothing to do with the car in his stables. The murderers must have hidden it there." Gillian realized she did not have any more information. Satisfied she had said something important, Gillian went back into her house.

Louise turned ashen. Frances helped her to the porch and then retrieved the children. Louise stared at Frances. "Why would a car be in the old stables? How did it get there, Frances?" she asked. The questions were more for herself than for Frances.

Frances answered, "I do not know, mother. Let's wait for Father before we jump to conclusions."

Feebly, Louise shook her head in agreement.

It was an hour before Jean showed up. Rejean was delighted to see his grandfather and ran into his arms right away. Both Louise and Frances stared at Jean until he said, "What have you heard?"

Frances quickly related what Gillian had said. Louise said

nothing. Jean sat down heavily while holding Rejean. "It is true there was a car in the old stables. I did not know it was there. I swear this, Louise." He looked at Louise as he said it. He turned back to Frances and continued, "The police officer said the car was part of the investigation into the death of Gilbert." He paused to let the words sink in for the women. "I got a call the police had been in my building, and I went to where the police car was parked at Jack's house to ask him what he was doing. When I got there, they were arresting Jack," he finished. Jean did not add he took several men with him in case there was trouble.

It was Frances's turn to go pale, then crimson. If Gil had been killed by a criminal, why would the criminal be comfortable enough to hide a car in her father's building? Her father must know this person, she thought, and this person must be from Lac Ville. She looked down because if she looked in her father's eyes, he would have seen the suspicion and rage welling up inside her. Francine began to fuss, and Frances picked her up. Your grandfather has many secrets, my girl, she thought, and she held Francine in her arms. Jean watched quietly as Frances rocked her. Louise said nothing.

The police officer had given the garage owner a printed card with the criminal code section which compelled a citizen to come to the aid of a constable in a lawful investigation or arrest or face being arrested themselves. The constable told the garage owner to show it to anyone who gave him a hard time when he got back to Lac Ville. He knew he would need it when Jean came to his garage. He put the card on the shelf under his till right next to his shotgun. The garage owner also knew he would not have to wait long.

Constable Brooks lent Walter his personal vehicle so he could get back home. He got home late Sunday evening. Mary and Lucy were waiting. The news from town had reached the reserve. Lucy wanted to know if Walter was in any danger. Walter just grinned and shook his head. Walter reported to work on Monday on time. People were staring and whispering. Walter did not care. In his lunch box in the original holster was the Walther pistol, loaded and ready to go.

Jean sat by himself in the kitchen thinking, I had ordered the pumps he had taken from the business to be stored at the old stables; I should have gone there myself. He had sent Alphonse and a couple of Alphonse's crew to secure them in the stables. No one had mentioned a car being parked there. On Monday morning, he went to Alphonse's house and Alphonse was gone.

Chapter 20

Claude Talbot sent Gabriel Cote to Georgetown to inquire on the status of Jack. Talbot instructed Cote to see if charges had been laid and to gather as much information as he could. Jean was paying the bill. When Gabriel arrived at the detachment, he saw several police cars parked outside in the lot. He knew there were more cars there than the detachment warranted. When he entered the detachment, he saw an officer who appeared to be an inspector and two plain clothes detectives talking to Sergeant McNeil, who he recognized from the August fire. McNeil looked tired and was without his usual tie. Gabriel cleared his throat to get their attention. McNeil looked up and yelled to the back office, "Constable, there is someone here. Take care of him will you."

A moment later, Constable Brooks came out. Cote introduced himself and explained his purpose. Brooks countered with questions. "Do you know if Jack Turk had any relatives in the area?" he asked.

Cote answered he did not know.

Brooks told him politely he could not provide Cote any information and showed him the door. Dejected, Gabriel went to the tavern. After ordering a beer and a sandwich he asked the owner if he knew why all the police were at the detachment. The owner smiled. "That smart ass Constable Brooks arrested a guy in Lac Ville yesterday and the guy hung himself in his cell is what I heard. I hope they fire his ass," he said.

Cote drank his beer quickly and took his sandwich to go.

McNeil, the inspector, and the two detectives laid out what would happen in stark and clear terms to Brooks. There will be a coroner's inquiry, they told him. There are no more suspects and Brooks will close the investigation with "death of suspect by suicide." This will make the coroner's inquiry a straightforward affair. Brooks would receive a commendation for his work on finding Gilbert Bertrand's killer and the matter will be closed by summer. There will be no further complications that could embarrass the force. The inspector closed his notebook and stood up. "Are we clear on all this, Constable?" he asked.

Brooks answered, "Yes sir."

The Inspector added, "After the inquiry, we can have you transferred if you wish."

As the inspector and his driver were leaving the detachment, one of the detectives put his hand on Brooks shoulder and said, "It's all for the best, young fellow. Keep your chin up."

McNeil went into his office and closed the door.

Walter returned Brooks' car the following Sunday, his first day off. As Brooks drove Walter back to the reserve, Walter told him how the news of Jack's suicide had spread in Lac Ville. The people in Lac Ville were divided on the news. Some felt Brooks had not proven Jack was responsible for Gil's death and others were glad for the justice. All of this happened, of course, before Brooks even had a chance to tell Frances what had transpired in an official capacity. He was going to Frances' after he dropped Walter on the reserve; he hoped Jean would not be there. Walter told Brooks, "The rumour in town is Alphonse has high tailed out of Lac Ville after he had heard about Jack's arrest." Walter had not personally seen him at all.

"The still and Alphonse," Brooks told Walter, "will have to wait again."

Walter was anxious to see the man he believed was responsible for Elmer's death brought to justice. He could wait, though, he told Brooks.

Constable Brooks knocked on Frances' door. Frances opened it and invited him in. There was no surprise on her face. She had been waiting. When Brooks came in and removed his coat. Frances got up and locked the door. "I want to hear every word you say, Constable, and I want no one to interrupt us," she said. Frances had made sure her mother had taken Jean to church. They would have at least an hour to talk.

Brooks opened his notebook and held it in his hand in case he needed to check facts. He did not as he told Frances everything he knew about the death of her husband and his investigation. When he got to the part about the investigation being shut down, he decided not to mention "Al" because he would compromise his informant. Frances listened carefully and dabbed at the corners of her eyes when the tears came. Rejean was playing with his toys and did not disrupt them once. Francine cooed and smiled at Constable Brooks. An hour passed quickly and Frances heard a truck pull up. "Someone must have told my father you are here," Frances said. "Thank you for everything you have done, Constable. I have one last question if you don't mind."

"Go ahead," Brooks said.

"Do you know how the car came to be in my father's stable?"

Brooks looked her directly in the eyes. "No, I am sorry, Mrs. Bertrand. I never got the chance to ask."

Brooks' answer shook Frances to the core. Suspicion and doubt about the complicity and motives of people she knew, loved, and lived with had been growing, and now they began to swirl into a storm. Jean rattled the door. Frances opened the lock. "I am sorry, Father, I must have locked it out of habit," she said.

Brooks pulled on his coat and told Frances, "If you have any further questions do not hesitate to call me, Mrs. Bertrand."

Jean glared at Brooks and Frances glared at her father.

It was the first week of October, twenty days after Jack Turk had hung himself, before Constable Brooks was finally able to pick up Walter to raid the still. Brooks had brought the game warden with him. They left the patrol car at house 12 and headed to Lac Ville in Elmer's truck. Mary was happy to lend it if it meant an end to the flow of homebrew onto the reserve. Mary and Lucy watched as the three men drove off at seven in the morning into a light rain. The heavy grey clouds seemed appropriate for the tasks at hand. "Seems like everything happens on Sunday," Lucy said as she rubbed Elias's head.

Elias had asked Walter if he could go, too. Elias was disappointed at first when Walter told him, "No, you have to stay here and keep watch over your family. You are the only man here right now." Elias had nodded in agreement and when he realized he had an important role, his disappointment was replaced with pride and purpose. Elias had his .22 caliber rifle ready and had to put it back in the rack.

The day before this, Alphonse had sent a message to the police building work site for Everett. Alphonse's man gave Everett the note and walked away. Everett read it and then crumbled it into a ball before sticking the note in his pocket.

Before the sun even came out on Sunday morning, Everett and two other men from the reserve launched his boat. They paddled through the remnants of the early morning fog until they were under the highway bridge going over the river before he started the motor. Everett steered around the lake at a low speed. Anyone looking out from Lac Ville would assume it was a boat full of fishermen getting an early start. Everett drove to a little sand spit behind Sam's cabin and cut the engine. The momentum carried the bow into the soft sand. All three men got out with their rifles ready and walked the trail to the cabin. There was no smoke coming out of the chimney. "He must still be drunk," Everett said to the others. Everett cautiously went to the door and called. "Sam, you degenerate. It is Everett. I have a message from Alphonse."

Everett did not want Sam taking a pot shot at him, so he made one of the other men push the door open. The gray dawn gave just enough light for Everett to see Sam laying on the dirt floor of the cabin. His face was contorted, and his fists were balled tightly across his chest. It looked as if he had been dead for a few hours. "Heart or liver probably. Who gives a shit." Everett laughed and kicked the body. "He is as stiff as cordwood," he said. The other men did not laugh and looked at Everett wanting to know what to do next. Everett looked at them as if they were stupid. "Load the finished product and toss the still in the lake," he ordered. He quickly checked for money and anything else Sam would not need anymore. He left the cabin door open. "Animals got to eat," he said.

Brooks, Walter, and the game warden had walked the last two miles on the lake side of the trail leading to Sam's cabin because it gave them better cover. It was wet and cold going. Walter raised his hand to motion them to stop about five hundred yards from the cabin. When they stopped, they heard the unmistakable sound of a metal boat being loaded. "Shit," Brooks said, picking up the pace.

When they were about three hundred yards away an outboard motor started. Walter looked at Brooks and said, "Go to the cabin." He broke right and scrambled up a hill leading to the lake. When he got to the top, he saw a boat at full throttle heading north with three men in it. They were about five hundred yards out, the bow throwing up spray with every wave they hit. Walter let his breath slow and sighted his .303 on the driver. "Everett," he whispered.

Walter came down the hill and found Brooks over Sam's body making notes. "Looks like a heart attack but who knows," the game warden said.

Walter nodded in agreement. Walter went to the location of the still and lean-to. The still was gone. There were tracks leading to the water's edge. He followed them and saw a stain on the water. The still had been thrown in the lake. It was too cold to go in and get it. Walter did not know if it would even have any evidentiary value. There was nothing in the lean-to. Except for a small stove and some copper tubing, there was nothing left. Brooks knew there was no way the men could walk back to the truck and get to Lac Ville before the boat was docked. Although Sam's death looked like a heart attack, he still had to investigate it. He was done for the day. He sent Walter and the warden to get his police car with his equipment and camera. "Son of a bitch," he muttered as they walked away. The daylight only highlighted how dull and gray the day was.

Chapter 21

Constable Brooks and the game warden went back to Georgetown after bringing Sam's body to the funeral home at Lac Ville. The doctor in Lac Ville did not hide his distaste about the police officer bringing him extra work. He wanted to know where to send his bill and findings even though he already knew. The local coroner had only recently been appointed and did not really know what he was doing even with the short training in Fort William. Brooks could not help feeling he had failed Elmer, Mary, and Walter. It was late when he arrived at the detachment. He walked in, and after hanging up his jacket, Brooks felt as tired as he could ever remember. Deflated, he suspected if he closed his eyes sleep would take him in seconds. The sergeant had turned the oil stove to its lowest setting when he left for the day and Brooks shivered as he loaded the piece of paper in his typewriter. It was going to be a long night.

In the weeks since Brooks had paid her a visit, Frances had gone over all the things that had happened before and since Gil had died. The strain and grief which had overwhelmed her was changing into anger. The bone numbing fatigue she felt since Gil had died now became energy. She, at last, had a routine with her children, so she began to think clearer. Her father had taken Gil and Elmer's business, this was abundantly clear to her. Claude Talbot had helped to make this happen. He was no friend to her, and she knew he would side with her father without any regard to her. Her father and mother's relationship was strained, but Frances knew her mother would side with her father because this was where the money came from. Louise always had a mercenary side. As long as everything was going well, she was a supportive mother. If it appeared there was a threat to her security or income, she became a lioness.

At the centre of everything there was her father: a manipulator, a liar, and a cheat, she thought. It hurt Frances deeply to think of her father in those terms, but she could not help it. He was as strong as anyone she knew, and yet, on the other hand, he was weak.

At the church, the beautiful mixed blood girl had not recognized Jean as her father. Louise and Frances had in seconds. Frances had been so distracted and overwrought afterwards, it was not until the fire did she see Eva as her sister. She chose not to say anything at the time. There will be a time and place, she thought. Her eyes welled as she thought of Elmer's death. It had been as sudden and unexpected as Gil's. Two strong noble men, gone. Now she had to deal with lesser men. "Pine bugs," Gil had called them. She wiped her eyes and smiled, thinking of how well it described them. Gil had explained that pine bugs thrived after the calamity of forest fires because they planted their eggs in the still smouldering remnants of trees. The following year, the pine bugs are everywhere, ugly, and universally disliked by almost all the people in the North. Rejean came over and put his head on her lap. She stroked his hair and thought about how much he adored his grandfather. The future was going to be difficult, "no doubt about it," her father used to say, just to irritate her.

October was cold and wet. Every home on the reserve started using winter wood before the first snow fell. Mary, Elias, and Lucy struggled to cut wood during the days. Walter helped in the evenings and on his day off. They were barely keeping up. The band elections took place on the night of the first snowfall. Everett won the position of chief and two of his cronies won as councillors. His first motion was to have all non-status residents removed from the reserve by January 1. Some elders opposed the motion, and it was delayed until the first day of March. Eva, Luke, and Walter knew Everett would have the motion passed the next time. Mary was at a loss. Everett had not talked to her or his niece and nephew since Elmer had died. "There is so much hate in that man," Mary told Lucy.

Lucy replied, "You are in danger too, Mary."

Mary nodded her head in agreement. "I know," she said, "I know." Mary expected Everett would have been over in a minute if not for Lucy and Walter. Everett was afraid of Walter; she saw it in his eyes.

Indian Agent Price came to the reserve in early November. He did not come to Mary's house. He went to Everett's. Mary saw with satisfaction that he was limping as he got out of his vehicle. He looked nervously towards Mary and quickly went into Everett's house. Elias surprised Mary by saying, in a voice that sounded like Elmer's, "This will not be good, Mother."

Mary told Elias, "We will be alright, whatever happens." Mary was not sure she believed it herself.

An hour after Price drove away, Wilma came to her door. Mary let her in and offered her tea. Wilma looked scared and nervous. "I cannot stay; you know Everett," she said. Wilma handed Mary a letter. "I am so sorry, I don't know what is in this, but I know it is bad. That bastard Price and my husband were laughing and drinking after they read it."

To Mary, Wilma was scared and beat down. Wilma left without saying goodbye, trudging through the snow to her home.

Mary sat at the table and opened the letter. It had the official bureau letterhead. It was addressed to Everett and to her. The letter explained how Elmer had lost his status by being more than four years overseas. The letter further explained that Mary, by being married to a non-status Indian, had been stripped of her status. Furthermore, her children had lost their status as well. Mary and her children could only regain their status if she married an Indian man. It was at the discretion of the band when Mary and the children would be requested and required to move off the reserve. Pursuant to the act, it would have to be in the next 120 days. There was an address Mary could appeal to. Mary put the letter on the table. Everett will have us out before the ink dries on a letter of appeal, she thought. Lucy came in and asked what Wilma had wanted. Mary handed her the letter.

Jean had a good handle on the business now. He had men doing regular runs to empty septic tanks and outhouses. The fishing and hunting camps were lucrative for three seasons. The railway and government contracts were year-round. Residential contracts were hit and miss. Gil and Elmer had done an amazing amount of work. They had secured contracts in communities as far as a hundred miles away. The money was good, and Jean was very generous to Frances. All she has to do is be a good daughter and mind her business, he thought.

Alphonse resurfaced in mid-November. Jean did not ask a lot of questions and hired him as his foreman. Before he could start working, he sent Alphonse to Georgetown with Claude Talbot to give a statement to the police in regard to the tragic accident that killed Elmer Wabason. Claude Talbot had written the police superintendent of the region requesting a senior detective conduct the interview, citing the inexperience of Constable Brooks and the fact that a community member of Lac Ville had died in his custody. Talbot explained in the letter, "I am aware Constable Brooks was a friend of the deceased Mr. Wabason and could possibly have a perceived bias." The superintendent agreed with Talbot's assertion. The Superintendent told Sergeant McNeil that to avoid the appearance of impropriety, Constable Brooks would not be allowed in the interview. Brooks would make himself available for the detective if the detective needed him. Brooks was livid. When the detective sergeant arrived at the detachment, he told Brooks he had read McNeil's report and Brooks's follow up investigation. He did not ask Brooks any questions. It was apparent to Brooks that the detective had little time for uniformed constables and he considered the trip to Georgetown to clean up a detachment file beneath him. Brooks watched as Talbot and Alphonse walked into the detachment. Talbot was looking smug and Alphonse looking a rehearsed contrite. They removed their jackets and the detective sergeant introduced himself. Once the introductions were done, they went into the detachment interview room. Brooks could hear every word. Talbot explained he had been retained by Alphonse's employer. His client was not a sophisticated man. After the unfortunate death of Mr. Wabason, he suffered trauma akin to shell shock from the explosion and had spent the past months in isolation at a cabin north of Lac Ville. His client felt responsible for Mr. Wabason's death. The flammable material that exploded was kerosene. His client knows nothing about home brewed alcohol but has tried it on occasion. No, his client will not provide his fingerprints because in Talbot's opinion it would re-traumatize his client, who has been through enough personal turmoil as a result of this tragic accident. The detective asked a few more questions and had Alphonse sign the statement Talbot had provided. The detective thanked them for making the trip to the detachment and for clearing up any misunderstandings there might have been. As Alphonse and Talbot were leaving, Brooks made eye contact with both. Alphonse could barely conceal his grin. Talbot looked at Brooks like he was dog shit on his polished shoes. The detective went to McNeil's office. After a half an hour he came out, looked at Brooks, and said, "Best let sleeping dogs lie, Constable."

In early December, Frances and the children took the train to Winnipeg, "to do some Christmas shopping," she told her mother. Her mother had wanted to come, and Frances told her, "I would just like some time alone with the children." She had a stroller for

Francine and Rejean which, while slow, moved well enough after they arrived at Grand Station in Winnipeg. She crossed the busy street and booked a room at a hotel. Everything and everyone were within walking distance, even with the snow. Frances looked in the phone book and found a civil lawyer. The lawyer had the biggest advertisement and seemed well established. She called his office and made an appointment for the following morning. His office was only two blocks from the hotel. When Frances arrived at the office with the children, she was immediately impressed. The office was finely furnished and everything about it spoke of a successful practice. The receptionist seemed surprised a woman with small children would be seeking the services of a prominent lawyer. Frances was actually very lucky to have gotten an appointment on such short notice, the receptionist told her. The receptionist gave Frances a form to provide her personal information and when she had filled it in, took it to an office.

After ten minutes, a handsome, smartly dressed man in his early 60s came out to the lobby. He extended his hand and introduced himself. "Mrs. Bertrand, I am Kent McDonnell. How can I be of service to you?"

The children were perfectly behaved for the entire hour Frances spoke to Kent McDonnell. Speaking quickly and referring to her notes from time to time, she told him everything that had transpired since Gil had died. She wanted to know if she had any recourse legally to regain control of her late husband's business from her father. McDonnell listened and made notes. When she was finished, she felt drained. She looked expectantly at McDonnell. He put his pen down and gazed thoughtfully out his window for a moment. Without turning he said, "Mrs. Bertrand, I feel for you and all you have been through in these last months." He paused then turned back to look at her directly. "I will make some inquiries. My services are quite expensive. Will this be a problem?" he asked.

Frances shook her head; she had several thousand dollars in savings.

"If we can prove your father took advantage of you when you were vulnerable, we may have a winnable case. I will have to get permission to conduct a civil trial in Ontario because my primary practice is here," he added. "To be realistic, this will be a gamble at best. The courts do not look kindly on daughters who sue their fathers, especially if the father is providing her and his grandchildren with a steady and substantial income," he continued. "The first step is called discovery, and this will all take time. There are some more forms you will have to fill in before you leave, for billing purposes. Do you have any questions?"

"No, Mr. McDonnell, thank you for your time. I look forward to hearing from you in the future," Frances replied.

As she got up to leave, McDonnell added, "You should be very proud of your children; they are very well behaved."

Frances bowed slightly and thanked him. Frances stopped at a lunch counter on the way back to the hotel. Frances and Rejean were going to have a piece of apple pie and hot chocolate. Francine just smiled in her stroller. The fresh air agreed with her.

After Frances had left his office, McDonnell went to his rolodex. When he had gone over the form his receptionist had given him, he had seen Frances Bertrand was from Lac Ville. He wondered why she had travelled so far to seek counsel. His best friend and former lover from law school had a practice there. He found Claude Talbot's number and called him. When Claude's secretary answered the phone, she transferred the call to Claude. He picked up and heard the familiar voice of Kent McDonnell, "Claude, send your secretary for coffee, my dear old friend. I don't trust anyone in those small towns."

Claude put the phone down and told his secretary to go have coffee. She looked surprised and happily grabbed her coat and left. Claude locked the office door and returned to the phone. "Claude, I had a visit from a beautiful lady from Lac Ville this morning. Frances Bertrand. Do you know her?"

Claude answered, "Yes, of course."

Chapter 22

In the time since Wilma had brought the letter to Mary, Mary had made three trips to Georgetown. On the first trip she had visited with Constable Brooks and found the investigation into the death of Elmer was completed. Brooks had apologized and told Mary everything, including the fact Jean had hired a lawyer for Alphonse. Brooks trusted Mary with information he would have never told any other civilian. Brooks made it clear he believed Alphonse was responsible for Elmer's death. As is Everett, Mary had thought as she listened. In the end, Mary had the same feeling she had when Sergeant McNeil had assured her they were investigating. Nothing they can do will bring Elmer back. These are the ways of men, but it won't always be this way, she thought as she left the detachment.

On the same day, she made an offer on a house in Georgetown. The house was an older two story with an outhouse and a well in the back. Exactly the arrangement Gil and Elmer had been working at doing away with, Mary thought. The owner's wife had recently left him, and he was only too glad to take Mary's offer. The house was a mile from the town site and a mile and a half from the public school. It was big enough for everyone. Mary could rent rooms to Eva, Luke, Lucy, and Walter. Mary had been very frugal with the money Elmer had made. Mary shuddered to think of the scandal it would cause if people knew she had enough money to buy several houses.

On the second trip, she paid for the house and received the deed. The person in the town office looked at the seller like he was a fool. He barely spoke to Mary at all. He briskly stamped and shuffled the papers. Mary hoped this would not be the welcome she received from the rest of the townspeople. On the third trip, she brought Helen and Elias to see the house. Helen was ecstatic; she would have her own room and it had a desk. Elias was his usual quiet self. When she went to the general store in town, the owner introduced himself. He told her, "I had heard Elmer Wabason's widow was moving to town and I was anxious to meet you. If there was ever anything you need, Mary, you just ask. A man doesn't become a hero unless he has a good woman behind him. Welcome to Georgetown."

Elias did not stop smiling all the way home.

January 23, 1951, was one of the coldest days anyone could remember. It was -48 degrees without a wind. Even with the woodstove full and crackling, there was a chill in house 12. Canadians were again fighting and dying in a far-off country called Korea. The radio was on in the background, and Walter and Mary were listening to the news. Elias would laugh every time the moisture in the beams and walls froze causing them to make loud sharp cracks. Helen would shake her head. "Elias, it is not funny. This cold is cruel for the animals you know," she said.

"You are right," Elias admitted.

Mary, Lucy, and Walter were at the kitchen table drinking tea as the news cast ended. Walter had been laid off after the weather made it too cold to finish the police detachment. They did not go cutting wood that day either; that would just be asking for broken tools and vehicles in this frigid weather. "Always have a plan," Walter said to no one in particular.

Elias yelled from the bedroom, "and always take care of your kit."

Helen shushed Elias. "I do have a plan Walter," Mary said.

Mary told them she had bought a house in Georgetown. She invited them to come to live with her and the children. Walter looked at Mary smiling. "When do you want to move?" he asked.

"As soon as possible and as quietly as possible," Mary answered. "I want Everett to go through all the motions and do all the work he has to do to expel us then come to find we are already gone," she added. "It will show all those who do not already know what kind of man he is."

Lucy clapped her hands and kissed Mary's forehead. "I love it," she said.

In March, Everett and the councillors passed their motion to expel all non-status people from the reserve. He argued forcefully that as the reserve grew there would not be enough housing for the treaty members of the band. He had visited every elder, cajoling and intimidating them with threats that they would lose their houses. He broadly hinted the Indian agent would do whatever he was told by Everett. In the end, he got what he wanted. Everett and the councillors went first to Mary's Aunt Ethel. He knocked hard on the door and when Ethel answered he told her Eva would have to move off the reserve immediately. Ethel, never known for her tact, spat on Everett's boot. "Eva and Luke moved a month ago. Now I am alone. Do you want my house too?" she said and slammed the door in his face.

Everett looked at the men who were with him. They looked at the ground.

Everett would not be robbed of this triumph. He had seen smoke coming from Mary's, so she must be home. He quickly tramped through the snow followed by his men. He had not been in Elmer's house since the funeral. When they arrived, there were no curtains and the door was unlocked. He walked in and saw everything was gone. The stove was still warm. He went room to room and when he came out, he looked enraged. He brushed past the men and went to the woodshed. It was completely cleared out. Every tool, the vehicles, trailers, and every stick of wood was gone. He stopped to calm himself, then went back where the men were milling around inside the house. "Ready for new people," he said. He was not going let Mary have the upper hand in the eyes of his men.

Leaving Elmer's grave was Mary's only regret. She knew she was tough that way. Elmer's bones were just Elmer's bones. Her memories of Elmer would always be with her. Walter admired her for her way of thinking. "You would have been a good soldier," he told her.

Gabriel Cote finished articling and was now the junior partner of Claude Talbot. Claude was planning on retiring in the next few years and he would sell the firm to Gabriel if no one else offered. Gabriel loved spy novels. He read everything he could about espionage. Since the end of the war, there were many new books coming out about the exploits of agents working against the Axis. He fancied himself as an agent of sorts. He had seen many of the underhanded legal maneuvers Claude had undertaken while articling and had kept copies and records of them all. One of the most egregious things Claude had done was the way he had wrested the control of the company Gilbert Bertrand and Elmer Wabason had built from their widows for Jean. When Claude had Gabriel research the Indian Act, he became convinced that when he was on his own, his practice would help people fight its provisions. Claude representing Alphonse when he was interviewed by the police was another low. Jean, Alphonse, and Claude were laughing so hard that Jean was stamping his feet when Claude recounted the interview for him. Gabriel was in the next room, of no consequence and invisible to them, listening to every word.

After a hard, cold winter, Jean and Alphonse were ready to work the busy season. Kurt, the mechanic, was a magician when it came to the upkeep of the fleet. With Alphonse as the foreman, Jean noticed the employee turnover was higher than he remembered. If anyone quit, they did not get paid for the pay period before they quit. It was not a big deal because Alphonse always found replacement workers. Jean was concerned about the fuel costs. They had been very high over the winter, and he asked Alphonse if he had any suggestions. Alphonse laughed and answered, "I thought you would never ask." Alphonse told Jean how on every run he had been on since he started working, he would scout out dump sites. "Swamp holes, some rivers, and slow creeks were the best," he told Jean. "Swamp holes spoke for themselves. Large fast rivers would quickly wash away the sewage if there were no people around. Slow creeks would not allow the sewage to run where it could be seen and eventually would allow it to be dispersed and not a person would be the wiser." They could save thousands of dollars a year, Alphonse explained.

Jean looked at Alphonse for a moment and said, "You do it personally. Be careful, and do not get caught." Thousands, Jean thought, thousands.

McDonnell had insisted Claude Talbot send him all the contracts and paperwork Claude had completed in regard to Gil and Elmer's business. He told Claude he would review them. He would look for their strengths and weaknesses. McDonnell could then discourage Frances from pursuing her case and, at the same time, shield Talbot if she went to another law firm. It took six months before Claude sent them. The morning the papers arrived, McDonnell read them carefully. Oh, my old friend, he thought, you have been in the land of cold and blackflies too long; it would take me two days in a real court to have these nullified. It was almost twelve when he decided he was hungry. Even though he could eat in the finest restaurants in Winnipeg without reservations, he liked the all-day breakfast at the railway station. McDonnell grabbed his jacket and told his receptionist, "I will be back by twelve forty-five." The street in front of the Grand Station was one of the widest in Winnipeg. Pedestrians had to cross eight lanes to get to the front doors. McDonnell was at the sixth lane with two lanes to go until the curb when a drunk driver coming over the bridge passed a bus and ran him down. The story of his death made the local papers in Winnipeg. In Northern Ontario, it was not even news.

Frances had received only one letter from the law firm of McDonnell and Associates, indicating they had taken her as a client and had begun the process of discovery and that was a year ago. Frances had to be careful because her father had friends everywhere and they would surely inform him if she was seen receiving letters from a law office. Frances thought about what McDonnell had told her about how the process of discovery is lengthy. Frances admitted to herself that she didn't know much about the law. Still, she wondered why she had not heard anything.

The children had been keeping her busy, and admittedly she had been growing comfortable with the money her father had been giving her. Frances had secretly taken a lover to fill the void in her life. He was a quiet man who maintained the railway signals in Lac Ville. She had met him at church. He had no expectations, and he was discreet. He was what Frances needed right now.

Chapter 23

Lyle Bates, one of McDonnell's law partners, was trying to sort out McDonnell's cases. Since the funeral, the senior partner had assigned Bates to get McDonnell's case load in order. McDonnell had many clients, but his filing system was confusing and there were handwritten notes everywhere without reference case numbers. On his desk were several contracts and notes referring to a Frances Bertrand. He had boxed them up until he had written letters to McDonnell's highest paying clients first, advising he would be taking over their cases if they wished to stay with the firm.

Elmer and Everett's Aunties Ethel and Rita were sitting at the kitchen table drinking tea in house 21. Rita, looking tired and somber, asked, "Ethel, do you have someone helping you get water and wood?"

Ethel, who always looked angry to people who didn't know her, laughed and answered, "I haul my own water and Luke, or one of his guys, drops off wood when they are passing by on trucking runs. Eva arranged it."

Rita drew a breath. "What if Everett finds out?" she asked.

Ethel answered, defiantly, "He knows I told that pig, Everett, Walter sends it. Everett is still scared of Walter."

Rita smiled now as well. "I wish we all had Mary, Walter, and Lucy back."

On the reserve, the rest of the people were once again hauling water in buckets and tubs. People were burying their garbage in the woods and swamp to the west of the reserve. Shutting down the water and garbage service was Everett's way of firming his hold on the chief's position. When people complained, he blamed Mary for taking her vehicles and not telling him so he could have had replacements in place. He would restore the services just before winter with Alphonse's help, but people would pay one way or the other. He took house 12 for himself and cut down the flagpole for firewood.

With the profits from the business and money they had saved on fuel, Jean bought a share of a dealership selling new chainsaws that one man could operate. He opened a franchise in Lac Ville. Frances drove to the shop after a visit from the principal of Rejean's school. She opened the shop door and the bells hanging over the door announced her arrival. Her father was in the back with Rejean. They both came to the front, wiping grease off their hands.

Jean Armand smiled. "Well, Frances, you have finally come to see where the money is made."

Frances glared and felt guilty at the same time before replying, "No, Father, I came because my son is doing terrible in school."

Rejean stood by his grandfather and looked defiantly at Frances. "I hate school," he said. Jean smiled and said, "My grandson needs a man to show him a man's work. He loves machines and can already change spark plugs and top up oil. He can sharpen chainsaw blades. Someday all of this will be his, Frances." Frances was at a loss for a reply and Jean continued. "Those high-minded teachers at school teach him nothing he can use later."

Frances looked at Rejean, who was firmly sided with his grandfather, before saying, "He needs to learn to read and write."

Jean smirked. "He will. Just enough to make money."

The doorbells tingled and two men came in carrying chainsaws. Jean looked at them and said, "I will be just a minute."

Frances looked at her father. "Have him home for supper," she said and turned to leave.

Rejean was smirking. As the door closed, Jean Armand said in a loud voice, "Women and Indians, you got to keep them in line."

Rejean and the two men laughed.

Frances drove home frustrated and feeling helpless. Rejean did need a man in his life. It was a hard truth in this part of Northern Ontario. Frances had a gnawing feeling her father wanted Alphonse to be that man because it would suit her father's needs. She knew her father had turned more and more of the responsibilities for the sewage and septic business to Alphonse. It had always been his intention get away from the smells and grit if he was making money. Alphonse seemed to take it all in stride. "Smug bastards," Frances muttered to herself.

※

Mary, Elias, and Helen were settled into their new home. Mary got a job cleaning the school. Helen was quickly becoming her teacher's favorite student and her grades were excellent. There had been some parents who were unhappy about Indians being in their school. People were more accepting when the general store owner, Donald McCloud, explained who the family was and that they were no longer treaty Indians at a public meeting. McCloud's father and his own son were veterans. McCloud would not tolerate any discrimination to the widow and children of a veteran. Elias had a couple of fights with the local boys who were not so open-minded. At the start of every fight Elias would tell the other boys, "You may win, but you will always know afterward you had been in a fight." After a couple of the tougher boys came out of the fights with bloody noses and chipped teeth, they left Elias alone. Walter and Lucy were on Walter's trap line but came to town every second weekend. Eva made less road trips with Luke and took a job cleaning the offices of the Department of Lands and Forests.

🐜

Walter and Lucy came to the house late in October when most of the leaves had fallen and the mornings were chilly. Mary greeted them at the door. The kettle was on the stove and the tea was brewing. "Come in, I missed you two this past couple of weeks," Mary said with a smile.

Lucy hugged Mary while Walter took off his coat. Walter smiled and told Mary, "We are only going to stay the night. We want to get as many pelts as we can before freeze up."

Mary frowned. Walter added, "So we can spend more time with you this winter."

Mary smiled. "I have some news for you about your friend, Constable Brooks. He married Cathy from the tavern and after testifying at the coroner's inquest into the in-custody death of Jack Turk, he took a transfer to Sault St. Marie. He stopped in on his way out of town. He said to wish you and Lucy the best and gave me his new address."

Walter pulled his beard and said, "Good for him."

Lucy knew Walter was disappointed he did not get to say goodbye but did not say anything. "Oh yes," Mary continued. "Sergeant McNeil got his desk job in Fort William. He left a week after Brooks."

🐜

It was the third Sunday in November and it was Mary's day off. Mary saw a tall good-looking man walking in the snow up her driveway. She looked at Elmer's .303 behind the door and, reassured, opened the door before the stranger knocked. The man was surprised. He

145

was about the same age as Elmer would have been now. He had a handsome rugged face and a broad smile. "Are you Mary Wabason?" he asked. When Mary nodded to say yes, the man continued: "I am Richard Sutherland. I served with your husband and Walter Enio. I was hoping I could talk to you and Walter. Elmer saved my life many times and I need to know what happened to him so I can be at peace."

Elias, now 12 years old, almost five feet nine inches tall and solidly built, heard the talking and came to the door. He looked Sutherland up and down. Sutherland said, "No mistaking, you are Elmer's son." He stuck his hand out and Richard Sutherland shook it like Elias Wabason was a man.

Walter heard the voices and came downstairs. He broke out in a grin, "Christ almighty Richard, I never thought I would ever see you again." He grabbed Richard in a bear hug the way Gil and Elmer used to do. Mary marvelled at how the passage of time meant nothing to soldiers.

Mary invited Richard Sutherland in. He shook the snow from his boots and placed them neatly by Elias and Walter's. He hung his coat on the hanger. Elias Wabason smiled as he watched. They all went to the kitchen where the big table Elmer had built was. Everyone gathered around—Helen, Mary, Lucy, Eva, Walter, and Elias—as Richard Sutherland had them tell him what had happened since the war. It took hours, and everyone felt they had been cleansed afterwards. Richard Sutherland had the ability to draw out stories and even secrets they had all been keeping from each other. Mary finally said it was time to hear Richard Sutherland's story. Richards respectfully agreed. Richard told them, "After the war, I was a lost soul."

When he was caught in a barrage just before the war ended, every concussion from a round going off beside him took something out of him. It was like he was an empty shell. Even after the bombardment was over, the pieces of him that were jarred loose refused to come back. "I had nightmares, which caused me to stay awake for days at a time. I could not talk to anyone and avoided people. I tried to get drunk so I could sleep," he admitted. He was arrested in Red Lake for going into a bar and refusing to leave when no one would serve him. He spent 30 days in a jail in Kenora, and when he was released, he went into the bush north of Red Lake. Richard paused, remembering and reflecting before he started again, "I stayed there for a year by myself. After a year, I paddled to Moosonee and then I went south to Cochrane. I took a train to Saskatchewan and lived near Duck Lake. I took odd jobs and together with my soldier's money I always had what I needed." Richard told them his nightmares started to reside when he was caring for horses. He admired the Cree people in Saskatchewan and found some veterans he could talk to, but eventually he knew he needed to come back to Northern Ontario. He thought briefly about volunteering for Korea but decided he had been through enough.

He always regretted not saying goodbye to his brothers in arms. He started looking for Walter and Elmer in Georgetown, and after awhile had found where Mary lived. "This was how I came to be in your kitchen," he finished.

Mary smiled. "I am glad you have found us. You are welcome to stay for a while," she said.

"I think I would like that. Thank you," Richard replied.

Lucy and Helen winked at each other. Mary's cheeks were flushed, and she had brushed her hair behind her ears more times than they could count.

Chapter 24

Frances received a letter from the law of office of Kent McDonnell almost two years to the day since she had been in his office. She brought it home to the house Gil built for them before the war. After Frances had recovered enough to move back home from her parents after Gil had died, Frances decided she would never leave this house. Gil was here in every board and nail.

The letter was from a lawyer named Bates. Bates explained Kent McDonnell had been killed by a drunk driver and it was only in the past month Bates had been able to attend to her file. He apologized and offered to refund the unspent portion of her initial retainer. He went on to explain the strength of her claim against her father. Bates believed Frances had a strong and winnable case. Not only could she regain control of the company, she was also in line for substantial punitive damages, he wrote. If Frances was willing to let Bates to continue to represent her, he would not charge for the services and would instead take a portion of the settlement in line with the legal industry standards after a judgement was rendered.

Frances did not know whether to laugh, clap, or cry as she put the letter down. Things had been going well since the visit to McDonnell's office. Her relationship with her father was as cordial as it could be. The children were content, and Rejean, not so little now, loved his grandfather to the point of obsession. Though Rejean was wilful and single-minded to Frances, and it troubled her. "I am his mother I will be able to bring him around," she whispered to herself, hoping it was true. Frances decided she would wait until the New Year to answer and put the letter in her jewellery box.

Claude Talbot retired three and a half years after Elmer Wabason died. He sold the firm to Gabriel Cote for a reasonable price and a share of the firm profits for two years. He was happy to get even that. No lawyer he knew wanted to work in a backwater like Lac Ville. The train he was boarding arrived at ten p.m. The conductor escorted him to his berth as he passed sleeping passengers in the coach car. The lights of Lac Ville shone through the windows. Once he was at his berth the conductor asked for his ticket. "Destination sir?"

"Montreal," Claude replied.

The conductor punched his ticket and tore a portion off. "Dining car opens at six," the conductor said.

Claude entered his berth and pulled the window shade down as the train jolted and began to leave Lac Ville. There was no one he really wanted to wave goodbye to. As the train began to pick up speed, Claude smiled. The conductor was handsome; not very friendly though. I can finally be who I am now and live like I want to, he thought. The motion of the train put him to sleep before it reached the next village of Hillsport.

Walter and Lucy went to Lac Ville to do an estimate for a man wanting a home built. It had been four years since they had been back in the area. Lac Ville had grown in the years they were away. The police detachment was finished and occupied, and a volunteer fire hall had been built. The pulp mill had been expanded, and an entirely new neighbourhood was being built east of where Elmer had been killed. Walter framed and built houses every year after the trapping season was done. Lucy worked alongside him, which sometimes caused a stir. Wives of clients always questioned their husbands if they went to check on the work's progress too often. Lucy always had that effect on men. She could care less. She was happy and Walter was a good man. After Walter had given his quote to the man from Lac Ville, the man was only too glad to give Walter a down payment to secure his services. Walter and the man shook hands to seal the deal. Lucy told Walter, "I would love to catch some fish before we head back to Georgetown. I know a nice, secluded spot on the west side of the lake." She gave Walter a subtle wink.

They drove about a mile past the reserve before Lucy pointed out a faint road on the left. Walter pulled onto it. It was more like two-wheel ruts through the scrubby brush than a road, and Lucy laughed. "It has not changed much but looks like other people have been here this year." Lucy told Walter, "The fishing spot is a small rocky hill about a mile and half from the highway."

The bush got thicker and the hill sloped down into the lake. "The pickerel love the rock face, and we can walk on rock until we are close enough to cast," Lucy said as they bumped along the trail.

As they pulled into a small clearing, they saw some other people had been camped there recently. There was a fire pit and some garbage along the shore. Walter had been distracted thinking about the wink Lucy had given him and did not notice a one-gallon tin can among the garbage.

Everett and one of his men were checking his still on the other side of the rocky hill. They had taken Everett's boat to get there. No one would be suspicious of two men fishing, and game wardens were few and far between in this part of the country. Everett heard the truck first and he turned to his man and quietly muttered, "Who the hell is coming out here?"

The batch was almost ready, and Everett was not going to lose it to some fishermen—or worse the police. Everett grabbed his rifle and went to the crest of the hill. "I am just going to scare them whoever they are," he told the other man as he started up the hill.

Everett had gained weight over the past couple of years between his soft job as chief and the homebrew. He was short of breath after just a one-hundred-yard climb. By the time he reached the crest where he could see down into the clearing, the truck had stopped. He heard a familiar voice laughing. "Lucy," he said through gritted teeth. He saw Walter get out the driver's side and he was infuriated. He sighted his rifle on Walter. His breathing had not slowed down and he was still huffing when he pulled the trigger in rage. Walter spun and disappeared from sight. The sound of the shot was deafening as it reverberated off the rocks and hills. Everett worked the bolt to load another round. The sound still ringing in his ears. The man with Everett came running up behind him. Everett turned to look at him and Everett's head exploded in a pink mist all over the man. Everett fell at his feet. The man ran as fast as he could downhill tripping ands stumbling to the boat.

Walter was hit in the upper left arm. The bullet spun him around and he landed on the ground. The truck shielded him from a second shot. He never heard the round fired. Walter knew from the war that you would never hear the bullet that hit you. He heard the report after he was on the ground. He looked for Lucy as soon as he realized what had happened. In the seconds it took to regain his bearings, Lucy had chambered a round in his .303 and fired a round in the direction the shot had come from. He watched as she worked the bolt to chamber another round and then scanned left and right to ensure there was no more threats. Just like I taught you, he thought. He rolled over onto his buttocks and looked at his arm. It was bleeding profusely but the round only hit flesh and not bone. Lucy walked backward towards him with the rifle pointed at the crest of the hill until she heard an outboard motor start. Lucy leaned the rifle on the truck and tore the bottom of her shirt off to make a bandage.

"I think I hit whoever shot you," Lucy said, and she pulled the bandage tight. Her face grim and focused.

Walter reached and touched her face. "Show me," he said.

151

Walter stood up and took the rifle from where it was leaning on the truck.

Together they walked up in the hill as the adrenaline started to come out of them both. Lucy's shoulder hurt from the recoil and the brass plate on the butt of the stock. "I fired right in line with the birch tree," Lucy said pointing.

When they reached the spot, Lucy had pointed out they saw Everett's body. Feet pointing up towards the top of the hill and his upper body on the down slope he had bled himself dry. The round had entered the side of his head and exploded outwards. His rifle had dropped straight down into the brush. Lucy did not say anything and buried her face in Walter's chest. Walter held her for a long time before saying, "You need to go get the police."

Lucy pulled back answering, "I don't want to leave you here alone."

Walter looked Lucy in the eyes before saying, "This is no small thing for anyone to go through. I am alright until you are back."

She did not want to leave him with his wounded arm but knew he was thinking ahead like he always did. Lucy turned and went back down the hill to the truck. She drove to Lac Ville with tears flowing from her eyes. She hated Everett. The tears, she knew, were relief from the years of nightmares and degradation at Everett's hands.

The police investigation and the news of the shooting gripped the region. Even the papers in Fort William and Port Arthur covered the story. The Lakehead Tribune ran the headline: "Gun Fight West of Lac Ville, One Man Dead." Mary and the children did not attend Everett's funeral. They did go and get Wilma and her son Lawrence so they could stay in Georgetown until the police investigation was finished. Everett's oldest son, Peter, angrily refused to go Georgetown. He yelled at Wilma and Lawrence as they got into Mary's vehicle, "Go stay with friends of the people who killed my father," and slammed the door of their house so hard the window shattered.

The police found the other man who had been with Everett and he gave up the entire homebrew network on the reserve. The trail ended at Lac Ville, and no one from the town was ever charged.

Alphonse developed an ulcer during the investigation and had his bags packed for months, ready to run again if the police investigation uncovered his role. When nothing happened, Alphonse drunkenly boasted to Jean Armand, "None of the Indians would ever give me up. They know to be afraid of me. I can still do as I please." Alphonse did not mention he had not tried to resurrect his homebrew network because he was afraid to.

Finally, after the coroner's inquest, Lucy's actions were deemed justified and the matter was closed. Lucy became a reluctant hero to many women who admired her for her quick thinking and shooting skills. Those women had their own Everetts.

Richard Sutherland stayed at Mary's house for a month before he found a place of his own near town. He got hired by the fire protection branch of the Department of Lands and Forests and did work on fire towers. When he was not working, he was almost always at Mary's home. Mary's son Elias took to Sutherland immediately, and as the years passed Elias would often go to work with him when he was not in school. Richard insisted Elias finish school and encouraged him to read everything he could get his hands on. Richard told Mary one evening, "Elias is a lot like Elmer was. Maybe even better because he is a combination of the two of you. He is going to do good things in his life. Elmer would have been very proud of the man he is becoming."

Mary blushed before answering, "He has had good men in his life to learn from."

It was Richard's turn to blush.

Mary was not sure whether Richard Sutherland and her son were more like brothers or father and son. Mary was happy either way. She was not ambiguous about her feeling for Richard Sutherland. She had fallen in love with him. They had become lovers two weeks after he had come to her home. The first time they were alone, they fell into each other's arms like the act of embracing had always been meant to happen, two people meeting at just the right time in each other's lives. Helen, Eva, and Lucy encouraged the relationship though, they had no idea both Mary and Richard had already acted on their feelings. Sometimes when everyone, including Walter and Luke teased them, they would exchange knowing glances or touch feet under the table.

Mary Wabason and Richard Sutherland married in 1956. Helen graduated the same year, and with her high academic achievements she was readily accepted into a nursing college in Port Arthur. She told Mary in her soft voice, "I want to work at the Indian hospital in Fort William when I graduate to gain experience. Afterwards, I want to work at the Georgetown hospital because the city life is not for me. And I want to be where you are."

Elias Wabason was hired every summer to work on the fire crews after he turned 16 with several other young men from Georgetown. He was 6 feet tall now, and close to 180 pounds. Elias's smiles came easy, and he was even tempered. Eva told Mary, "Elias is a good-looking young man, but he doesn't even notice that girls try to get his attention."

Mary laughed, answering, "I think it is because he is shy around women, like Elmer used to be."

Elias was not shy around men. He quickly built a reputation as a hard worker and a quick study. Elias interacted regularly with the conservation officers, who everyone still called game wardens. He liked their uniforms, and their role of protecting fish and wildlife appealed to him.

It was after a small fire started by an unattended campfire in late July of 1957, when Elias was loading the tools and hoses into a ministry truck, that a conservation officer named Tom Watt said, "Young Mr. Wabason, you should think about being a conservation officer. You have the attributes. You are smart and know this land." Elias stopped what he was doing and looked at the officer for a moment. "You're not much of a talker, but I think that would change once you started doing the work," Tom said.

Elias stood thinking about what Tom had said before answering, "I had not really given it a lot of thought."

The officer countered with, "I am not sure how true that is; you watch everything and you never have to be told something twice. You work well alone." Tom paused before adding, "There are no Indian conservation officers I know of. You would be breaking a lot of ground."

Elias replied quietly, "I don't know if I am ready yet."

Tom smiled. "You're ready. Just finish school," he said.

Elias smiled and finished loading the truck, thinking to himself, I will be outdoors and I can protect the land I love. As he closed the tailgate on the truck, he looked at Tom and said, "You know what Tom, you are right. I will give it a shot as soon as I finish school."

Tom smiled back. "You're a good man. I would work with you."

After Elias graduated, he applied to the Ministry of Natural Resources for the job of conservation officer. He was deferred for eighteen months because of his age before he was hired, then trained as the first Indian conservation officer in Ontario's history.

PART 2

Prologue

The mid-spring day was warm and vibrant as Conservation Officer Elias Wabason was drinking tea from his thermos cup, sitting on the open tailgate of his ministry truck. He had just finished checking the spawning pool of a feed river to ensure no one had put fishing nets in the area and was on his way back to the office. He stopped on top of a hill, which gave him a spectacular view of the area he patrolled as he made his patrol log entries and drank his tea. The lumber company road was the only manmade scar on this area. All around him were the hills of the lower Canadian shield topped by stands of birch, jack pine, and tamarack trees. They were cut from each other by valleys with streams and rivers. From where he sat, he knew there were three small lakes and a cedar swamp all within walking distance. Elias breathed the clean air and thought, "What a gift to work in this place."

Elias finished his tea and drained the last drops onto the ground before fastening the cup to his thermos. In the distance he could hear a train on the CNR mainline. As it faded away,

Elias hesitated before getting into and starting his truck, so he could just listen to the forest. The sharp crack of a high-powered rifle startled him. He froze in place, then heard four more shots in rapid succession. As the sound reverberated off the hills and faded, Elias was sure they had been fired to the north of where he was. A rifle being fired in the north could mean a lot of things, a fisherman shooting an aggressive bear, a hunter sighting his rifle for the upcoming season (though it was still a way off), or it was poachers. Elias suspected it was poachers.

Elias knew this logging road went from the village of Chapleau and ended forty miles later at a railroad siding where the lumber company loaded the logs they cut. He was at about mile marker twenty. He had not met any trucks on his way here and there had been no other vehicles on the road at all. The company was harvesting close to the siding area. and it would be hours before the crew working there would be driving home to their camp in Chapleau.

Elias had met the foreman, Matt Willet, and most of his crew. They were a rough and ready bunch, but they were intent on making money. They were paid by the load so they would not spend any of their time poaching. The foreman told Elias, "You don't need to waste your time checking us, Chief, but feel free to drop in anytime and use our lunch shack."

Elias knew it took time to gut and dress any big game, so he had to make a decision: go in the direction he had heard the shots come from and catch whoever was at the kill site or wait here for them to drive by on their way home. If they were on the river, whoever it was would slip by him unchecked.

"March to the sound of the guns," Elias said out loud, smiling at his own quip from history. He started his truck and rolled down the hill.

Elias drove slowly, looking for the likely spots where a moose could be taken during the day. It's got to be a moose, he thought. Elias in a way hoped there was not a dead animal at the end of this inquiry, and it was just some fishermen who felt compelled to fire off a few rounds because they had not fired their rifles for a while. Some men are just like that, he thought. Elias came to a blind corner approaching a log bridge and slowed down.

James Swanson was pulling the guts and lungs from the cow moose and his buddy Milt was holding her back legs open when Milt looked up saying, "Fuck Jim, I hear a truck."

James stopped, listening for a moment. "Yep. Don't worry about it; I am a cop and we will say we hit it with the truck and had to put it out of its misery," he answered.

Elias rounded the corner and saw them. Milt let go of the legs. "What the hell, Milt?" James said, looking up.

"Game warden," Milt answered.

James stood up. "I got this," he said.

James wiped his bloody hands on his pants as Elias got out of his truck. Elias recognized James as the area sergeant for the Canadian Pacific Railroad Police. Elias had seen him a couple of times at the coffee shop in uniform, but had never spoken to him. One thing he had noticed was he never paid when he left the coffee shop. James was a big man, and he would be intimidating to anyone who did not know him. "Good morning, Chief, I am glad you showed up. You saved me a trip to your office to report this accident."

Elias, taking in the scene and knowing this was no accident, asked "Are you guys alright?"

James winked and pulled out his badge. "She came out of nowhere and I clipped her with my truck, breaking her front leg. It was awful, Chief. She would not have lasted a night."

Milt, who was now behind James feeling a little more confident, added, "She was suffering."

Elias asked, "Did she have a calf?"

Milt answered, "I didn't see one."

Elias suspected she did and it would be young and would certainly die without its mother. It was probably bedded down close. Two, maybe three of these beautiful animals will have met their fates because of these men. Elias took a step towards the moose and James put his hand up "Whoa, Chief, don't want you getting blood on your uniform, if you know what I mean. We will give you statements," he said with menace in his voice.

Elias sidestepped him. "I will get statements and I will have to seize this moose. You are not allowed to keep it," Elias said. His heart was pounding. These were the most dangerous moments in his job.

Elias had dismissed Milt as a threat. He just looked scared, and Milt knew they were in the wrong. James was 45 years old and 260 pounds. He was not about to let some novice conservation officer pinch him, a police sergeant, for an offence. Elias saw a .308 bolt action rifle leaning against a tree stump about six feet away from him and twelve feet from the moose. He turned in that direction and James said, "That's better, Chief, we don't want any misunderstandings."

Elias picked up the rifle. The safety was off. He worked the bolt and popped out the remaining round, catching it before it hit the ground. James was caught off guard. "You should ask a man before you touch his gun," he said.

"Safety was off. Can't be too careful," Elias replied as he turned towards his truck.

"What the fuck do you think you are doing?" James said loudly clenching his fists.

Elias tossed the rifle on the seat and turned towards James. "You can apply to have it back after I am done my investigation," he answered.

James's face reddened. "You little rat son of a bitch. What are you talking about investigation? We take care of each other out here. You do this and everyone will know you can't be trusted," he said.

Milt was more afraid now as the confrontation unfolded. "Let's just go, James. This guy is just a prick," he pleaded, holding James's shoulder from behind.

Elias stood his ground as Matt Willet's crew truck rounded the corner. James turned at the sound then stepped back. Matt stopped his truck. "Accident?" he asked, taking in the scene. "You okay, Chief?" he asked Elias. Elias didn't reply, keeping a wary eye on James. Matt put it together quickly. "We will give you a hand cleaning this up. Won't we boys," he said, looking at his men.

James looked at Elias and said in a low voice, "This isn't over. You better have eyes in the back of your head. Funny things happen to men who work alone in the bush." He turned, motioning to Milt to get in the truck. A moment later he peeled out, spinning his tires, and sending a shower of gravel flying.

Matt waited until the truck was out of sight before saying, "Good job, Chief. Nobody likes that guy anyway. But you will have to watch yourself now."

Elias smiled before saying, "Thanks for knocking off early. I was not sure how that was going to play out."

Chapter 25

The name "Elmer's" had been painted over on all the signs and removed from all the stationary at Gil's Septic and Sewage Service years ago. Jean Armand had increased his fleet to 12 skidders, and he had branched out to sell chainsaws, outboard motors, and boats. Jean sat in his truck at the Lac Ville Park overlooking the lake, drinking his morning coffee and listening to Johnny Preston sing "Running Bear" on his radio. He especially liked the part when the two lovers were taken by the river. Jean thought to himself, 1960 is going to very good for me.

Things were quiet in Mary's house since Helen and Elias had moved out. They came home on holidays and wrote letters keeping her informed of what they were doing. Helen's letters naturally were longer than Elias's. Mary told Richard, "I can almost hear Helen's soft voice in her words. Elias just tells a short story like he is sitting here." With Walter and Lucy working or in the bush most days, Richard and Mary spent their evenings enjoying each other's company. Mary was comfortable with the quiet and, from what Richard could tell, she did not dwell on the past.

Elias Wabason's first posting as a conservation officer had taken him south, in the Chapleau area where a huge game preserve had been created. He had his share of confrontations with people over his first four years. Elias laid a lot of charges and had been threatened with death on more than one occasion. He had developed an intense dislike of poachers and polluters. Poachers were easier to catch. Polluters, he thought, were worse than poachers because the damage they did was longer lasting and affected more people. They were often companies who had the ear of local politicians. People who depended on them for their employment were not always willing to talk. Elias had to put up with outright racism from some violators as well as his own people calling him a traitor.

Elias used skills learned from his father, Walter, and Richard to build relations with people who did not pillage the land to show them it was to their advantage to preserve and protect the resources. Elmer had told Elias more than once, "A man should listen to what is being said, and know what is not being said, and know when to talk. With some people you only talk when you need to." Walter and Richard had both told him, "Good men are comfortable in silence." Walter added, "State your honest purpose and people will fill your ears." Elias was a keen observer of people he respected when he was growing up and it was serving him well now.

The Indian game warden was a novelty to some and a wraith to others. Elias appeared where he was least expected to apprehend offenders. Elias's superintendent was a World War Two veteran and he backed Elias up whenever Elias ruffled feathers, which was often. When Elias charged a railway police sergeant for illegally shooting a moose out of season, the superintendent came to Elias's office and told him, "For your own safety, we will have to transfer you." Even the superintendent could not help him in the current situation. He gave Elias his choice of postings. Elias chose Georgetown.

Frances waited almost a year before answering Lyle Bates. It had been nearly five and a half years since Gil had been killed. She pulled the letter out of her jewellery box almost three years since her visit to McDonnell's office. She took hours to write her reply. Frances told Bates she wanted him to carry on with his work on the case. She enclosed a cheque for a thousand dollars and told Bates there was more. She was more candid than she ever thought she would be with a stranger. She wanted the ownership contested but not until she was ready. However long that took, she would retain him or his successors. She finished with the request that Mary Wabason and her children receive their fair share. The last point was non-negotiable. When Frances set her pen down, she felt a weight lifted from her chest and her mind was clearer than it had been for a long time.

Rejean quit school after Grade Eight. Nothing Frances could do could get him to go back. He was a wild impetuous young man at 18. He could fix and operate any vehicle. Rejean swore constantly and worked long days at his grandfather's sewage business. Alphonse and his grandfather encouraged everything he did. He drove too fast. He fought anyone who crossed him. He did not even bother to argue with his mother when she tried to get him to be more responsible. Rejean did what he wanted and people in Lac Ville steered clear of him if they could, except for the girls. Rejean was the spitting image of his father, Gil; to them he was a devilishly good-looking bad boy with money to burn. The corporal in charge of the Lac Ville police detachment had paid personal visits to Frances and her father with requests for them to rein the boy in before he got himself in serious trouble. Frances and his sister Francine worried constantly. Frances's father just laughed. "He is just a young man. Let him be." Frances regretted letting Rejean spend so much time with her father. Rejean never asked about his own father and ignored anyone who tried to tell him about him.

Rejean was coming back from a honey run, the term Alphonse

used for emptying a septic tank. He was speeding along the highway getting close to Lac Ville. The trailer he was hauling was empty as he had dumped the sewage in a swamp hole. He saw an elderly Indian man walking along the highway headed towards the road leading to the reserve. He drove right at the startled man honking his horn. The man had what looked like a bucket of weeds in his hands. The man jumped into the ditch. Rejean drove on, laughing so hard he had tears in his eyes. The elder got up and started gathering the medicine plants he had spilled when he jumped out of the way.

Alphonse and his grandfather were in the office when Rejean came in and hung up the keys to the truck. He told them about the old man on the road. Alphonse slapped him on the back. "You are one crazy kid," he said. Jean just smiled. Alphonse, now in his early 50s, was bald and his belly hung over his pants. He smelled like cigarette smoke, shit, and motor oil most of the time. The only time he ever cleaned himself up was when he thought Frances might be around. Alphonse had still not accepted that that ship had sailed long ago. As he said to his buddies, "You never know." Rejean and him got along very well. The kid was spirited and knew how to make money. He never acted like he was better than Alphonse, as Rejean's grandfather sometimes did. They would talk about women and who was willing to do what. Alphonse and Rejean would absolutely howl with laughter when Alphonse would talk about the mothers of the girls Rejean had been with.

Jean Armand was feeling his age, and while he thought it was funny his grandson had scared the old man on the highway, he could not help but think it could have been him diving in a ditch. That boy might be a little too wild, he thought, I taught him to be fearless and ruthless, to get what you want, and hopefully he won't want what I have before I am ready to give it to him. Jean dismissed the thought, telling himself, "I am one of the richest and smartest men in Lac Ville and the reason he will be someday as well. A proper grandfather." He had a lot of reasons to feel good about himself. He had taken control of a profitable business and had used the money to expand into other ventures. And his word counted at meetings of the local chamber of commerce.

His daughter Frances had never remarried, and rumour had it she had a stream of lovers since being widowed. She went on frequent trips and her mother Louise usually watched over his granddaughter Francine while Frances was gone. He knew if Frances was distracted and happy, she would not interfere with what he was doing. When Frances was in Lac Ville, his wife Louise took trips to Winnipeg and Fort William regularly. Jean did not currently have a mistress and admittedly he was losing interest in women. Money was his focus now. Jean almost missed Gil and Elmer because they had challenged him. The soft-shelled fools he dealt with now did not.

Gabriel Cote felt relieved after writing the final cheque to Claude Talbot to conclude their contract. Cote knew he was free to practice law the way he wanted to. He opened his office every Wednesday evening to provide legal advice and education to whoever wanted to attend. He had personally gone to all the reserves in the area surrounding Lac Ville and told the residents he would represent them if the need arose. Frances's father Jean was still his client, so he could not ethically reveal information about him to people Jean had wronged or cheated. It gnawed at him that he had to represent Jean, but Jean paid most of his bills and even if he refused to provide services to Jean, he could not represent anyone suing him because he would be in a conflict of interest. Some people in Lac Ville had expressed their displeasure when Gabriel represented Lucy after the shooting. He had been approached by Walter because, as Walter said, "I am good at many things but the law is not one of them." Gabriel refused to take any money from Lucy or Walter. Walter renovated Gabriel's house for the cost of material as a show of gratitude. Gabriel, to Jean's disgust, soon had a reputation in the area as a fair, honest, and reasonable lawyer.

Chapter 26

The year Elias Wabason was sworn in as a conservation officer was the first year Richard Sutherland could legally vote in Canada. He took everyone to the post office and made a day of it. The irony of being able to fight for a country you could not vote in was never lost on him. He was not bitter about it, though he had described the whole thing like the last campaign he fought in the war. Sometimes when they were up against stiff defences, the Canadian army would take small bits of an objective until they got where they wanted. Mary admired Richard's attitude. He firmly believed hard work and honesty would remove the inequalities his people had faced for so many years. He was promoted to the area manager for the fire protection branch and had forty men working for or reporting to him. Mary watched him as he read some reports and made notes at the kitchen table. His dark hair had slivers of white now. He talked about Helen and Elias like they were his own children. "I am honoured to be part of their lives and I am proud of them. I am proud of all of you," he told her.

Helen had worked at the Indian hospital in Fort William for four years before an opening for a nurse was announced in the Georgetown hospital. When she came for her interview, Helen told Richard Sutherland and her mother about the conditions in Fort William. It was underfunded and understaffed. Some of the doctors were dedicated and compassionate while others were only there to gain experience before moving on. Helen believed many of the people who came from northern reserves gave up and died in the hospital because it was so foreign and lonely for them. Helen broke down in tears when she described how the hospital sometimes resembled a factory. The administration had a "get them in, keep them in" approach. A high patient load was good for the bottom line when it came to funding. Helen said she did her best to make each patient feel like they were important and had been written up for spending too much time with them. She was ready to come home.

Elias Wabason had no illusions about coming home to Georgetown. He loved his job but knew he would be facing the same high workload he had in the Chapleau district. Conservation officers were overworked, underfunded, and underpaid. The Ontario government recognized the importance of protecting the natural resources in Northern Ontario. The taxpaying voters in Southern Ontario did not have the same priorities. Roads and services trumped moose and fish in their minds. Nevertheless, Elias knew his role as a protector of the land was what he was meant to do. His father loved this part of the country and was buried in it. Protecting what his father loved was Elias's way of honouring him.

When he reported to the office, he found he had inherited sixty open cases. They covered everything from a fishing camp habitually allowing overfishing by American fishermen to a report of a restaurant in Lac Ville illegally selling wild game on its menu. As he leafed through the case files to see what had or had not been done, he began to get discouraged. Some of the cases were only the original complaint with the date received written into the file. He sorted them into three piles: solvable, solvable with investigation, and for information only. Once he was done, he started reading the information files so he could conclude them or extend them. The second file was a series of complaints from the region about the illegal dumping of raw sewage in creeks, swamp holes, and some rivers. The officer he had replaced had categorized the complaints as information only and had never driven to the dump sites to document them. Elias re-classified the file and put it on the top of his solvable with investigation pile.

Elias knew from his past four years that so many investigations he was involved in were time sensitive. It only takes an experienced hunter a couple of hours to gut and load a poached animal. Nature cleaned up kill sites with great efficiency in a short period of time. A person overfishing only has to have good instincts to avoid a game warden in the bush. Elias knew he could never in his wildest dreams stop all the people violating wildlife laws. He also knew every arrest and every fine imposed multiplied ten times in the retelling. As long as people glanced over their shoulders to see if there was a game warden around, he was having an impact. Elias believed the same principle applied to corporations and small businesses. If he could charge at least two companies with pollution offences, it would be enough to deter the rest from dumping hazardous material in the bush.

Elias had never been the type of officer to ask for permission when he thought what he was doing was right. He also believed being in an office was not how things got done. He took the dumping file and drove to the farthest dump site complaint first. It was about halfway to Lac Ville on the highway. The complainant said there was a road after a rock cut by a mileage sign. The sewage had been dumped in a creek a half mile off the highway. Elias found the dump site easily enough. The stench and the clouds of flies were like a signpost. Elias got out his truck and grabbed his camera. The offender had backed a trailer in and released the contents into a small creek, which fed a river about a mile away. Both the truck and trailer had dual axles from the tire marks Elias photographed. This was probably not a local dumping his own tank, Elias noted. He searched around and found some beer bottles and garbage. They had been exposed to the elements, so they likely would not have any evidentiary value, but Elias bagged them regardless.

The sun was setting when Elias finished with the seventh site. The same tire impressions were at every site. He found more beer bottles and cigarette butts at two of the sites. The beer and cigarettes were all the same brands. He found clear footwear impressions at four sites. At two dump sites there had been two men. He got back to the office after dark. Everyone else was gone home. He threaded a paper into his typewriter, rubbed his eyes, and typed up his report.

※

Frances's mother Louise had grown increasingly short tempered and irritable over the past few years. Frances knew she was unhappy, and her arthritis impaired her mobility. She told Frances one evening, "I do not love your father anymore. You just don't know, Frances, what he is really like. And I am finished with the harsh winters in Lac Ville. I am in pain constantly from the cold. Your father doesn't care."

Frances was not surprised. As a woman, she knew from her father's treatment of her mother that their love was not sustainable. If she were Louise, she would have left twenty years ago.

What did surprise her though was how well-planned her mother's exit was. Louise told Frances she regretted leaving her grandchildren and Frances, but it was her time now. Louise had squirrelled away enough money to live comfortably wherever she chose. She had chosen Florida. She told her husband she wanted to go shopping in Sudbury, and she was taking the train. Jean half listening and not really caring, peeled seven hundred dollars out of his billfold. He gave her the money and a kiss on the cheek. Jean never saw her again. A widower from the church moved from Lac Ville around the same time. He met Louise in Toronto before they headed south. Lac Ville buzzed for weeks. Jean thought it was funny until the reality of an empty bed set in. He was getting older and took for granted Louise would always be there. He thought she was just putting on a show so he would treat her better. Jean thought the widower moving was just a coincidence until he was alone with his thoughts. The realization Louise had truly left him took him utterly by surprise.

Francine was talking to her brother Rejean in front of Frances's house. Frances had her window open and could hear Francine talking to her brother like only a sister could. "Rejean, you are becoming a pig like Alphonse. You treat Mother like she means nothing to you. Why are you being this way?" Francine asked.

Rejean answered with his own question. "Did you and Mother know Grandma was leaving before she did? If you did, I swear I will never come in this house again."

Francine answered honestly, for herself at least. "I had no idea, and what does that have to do with me and our mother? It is between our grandparents."

Rejean threw his hands up. "You women all stick together," he said.

Francine's temper rose. "That is that pig, Alphonse, and our grandfather speaking, Rejean," she snapped.

Rejean started the truck and peeled away. Francine came in the house flustered and angry. She slumped into a chair. Frances looked at her, admiring the beautiful and spirited young woman she had become. Respectful, quiet, and attentive, still not realizing what a grounding effect she had on her mother, Francine was the type of daughter any mother would want. "Francine, I have much to tell you and I think you are ready now," she said.

Chapter 27

Luke had slowed down over the years. Though he was only 49 years old, the injuries he had suffered years before when a drunk driver crashed into his truck were arthritic and he was in constant pain. His wife Eva had convinced Luke to buy two trucks and to hire drivers from Georgetown. Two trucks became four and by 1964, there were eight. Luke and Eva built a compound and a home about a mile from Mary's. Luke spent his days in the office and rarely drove anymore. Eva laughed when she told Mary he wore a tie at work. "He is so serious now," she said. They had made a good life together and Eva was as happy as Mary had ever seen her.

🪰

Lyle Bates, the lawyer who took over Kent McDonnell's files and had written to Frances over a year ago, had been practicing civil law for 35 years. He was fourth in line to being a senior lawyer at the firm. A star football player in university, he was still solidly built at 60 years of age, and unlike so many of his colleagues, he kept himself fit. His dedication to his practice and the work ethic it required took all his time and ended his marriage ten years previous. He never remarried. He used to joke with his secretary, "I tried it once and realized my true love is the practice of law."

Lyle Bates could have retired two years ago. He did not need the money. He loved the challenges of trials against worthy opponents and he did not want to give it up. Too many of his friends died within a year or two after hanging up their robes. He was sorting through his mail and he came across the letter from Frances Bertrand. He smiled as he opened it. It was more than a year since he had written her. There was another cheque in it, as well as Frances's request that Bates file a suit against her father to regain control of the company Gil and Elmer had founded. Bates was never sure why he had kept the case box in his office; perhaps he knew instinctively from the outset he could win this case. He shook his head at the fact Mrs. Bertrand still did everything through the mail. Letters were refreshingly old fashioned for an old lawyer like Bates. He opened the case box and went to work updating the work he had prepared long ago. He called his assistant and told him to make reservations at the finest hotel in Fort William. He was going to the Superior Court there to file the lawsuit personally.

Elias Wabason spent the next two weeks closing one case after another from the sixty he had inherited. He visited the fishing camp that was allowing overfishing and threatened to have their licence pulled. He added that he would post the camp's name in the post offices so camps abiding by the laws would know what their competitors were doing. He knew he could not do it, but the camp operator did not. The camp operator called him "an uppity Indian." He went to Lac Ville and posted a notice the ministry had information about wild game being sold for consumption in restaurants in the region, being careful not to name any establishments. The notice further detailed that after investigation the meat being sold was suspected of coming from disease tainted animals. The ministry cautioned people not to eat meat from unknown sources for their own safety. The notice was a total fabrication on Elias's part. It was an offence to remove Ministry notices. Elias received a call from an informant saying the sale of meat in the suspect restaurant had stopped completely because no one would order it anymore.

Elias carried his father's .303 rifle in the cab of his department truck. It was solid and reliable, and surplus ammunition was still available. It had seen his father through a war. It would see Elias through when he was working. He also carried a shotgun and a .22 rifle for putting down injured animals. He had made a rifle rack so the .303 was visible when he was in the field. He put it in a case behind the seat when he was close to the office. Conservation officers carried handcuffs but not side arms. Working alone, Elias knew he had to give the impression he was ready for anything at any time to deter the worst offenders from taking their chances with him. Elias had a knack for catching offenders while they were offending. The other officers said he had "shit luck." Elias knew his successes were from being in the field and not in the office. Good instincts helped, and luck had very little to do with Elias's apprehensions of poachers and violators. The story about him charging a police sergeant followed him to Georgetown and gave him credibility as a by-the-book game warden among law abiding citizens. There were others who were less complimentary and said, "He would charge his own mother." The talk did not bother Elias; it was part of the conscious act of making people feel he was and could be anywhere. In Elias's opinion, it helped keep people honest and protected the wildlife.

※

Frances's father, Jean, heard Elmer Wabason's son was a game warden from one of his friends who had been ticketed shooting partridge out of season. The man came into his office at the outboard motor shop with another man. He was cursing about the Indian game warden while talking. Jean came out of the office and asked what happened. The man replied, "Jesus, Jean, I was on the way home from Georgetown and I saw a bunch of birds beside the road. I thought the missus would like some for supper. I got out and shot four. Next thing I knew he was there. This Indian game warden everyone has been talking about. Waba-something. He wrote me a ticket and took my gun. He said I could apply to get it back."

Jean asked him if he had the ticket with him.

The man said it was in the truck and went out to get it. When he came back, he handed the notice of violation to Jean. Jean read it carefully and saw printed under the signature of issuer the name "CO Elias Wabason #939." Jean handed the ticket back to the man. The man asked, "Is there anything you can do? That's a lot of money."

Jean looked at the man and answered, "You can afford a hundred dollars. Pay this one. If it happens again, come and see me. Now describe this guy to me."

After his friend left, there was no doubt in Jean's mind this game warden was the son of Elmer Wabason. He had heard Wabason's widow had moved to Georgetown and he never really gave any of them a lot of thought over the years. They meant nothing to him. He had gotten their business, and they never did have the sophistication to fight him for it. Too much time had passed, and Frances had accepted her father's will. He had used the business to build others and he was a wealthy man. Why should he care if Gil's late partner's son was a low-level government employee? he asked himself. He did not hunt or fish anymore. He had nothing to fear from this name or his past, he tried convincing himself. Still, there was a feeling in the pit of his stomach he could not dismiss. The only real anxiety he felt about anything for years was when Louise left him, because he missed all the signs. He liked to be in control, and if something happened it was because he allowed it to. Louise took some of that control from him. Now he felt the same feeling of uncertainty.

The doorbells chimed as Alphonse came into the shop. "I just heard Elmer Wabason's son is a game warden and he pinched

Pierre Durant and took his gun," he said to Jean, who was standing at the counter.

Jean answered, "Old news. Pierre just left here a few minutes ago."

"Is this a thing we should be worried about?" Alphonse asked.

Jean, lying, answered, "No, just keep an eye out for him when you are working."

"Oh, I am careful, not to worry." Alphonse dismissed Elias Wabason from his mind as quickly as he had come in. If Jean said not to worry, that was good enough for him. Jean, even though he did not say it, was not so sure.

Bates carefully went over all the paperwork in the case file concerning Frances Bertrand versus her father. He read the limitations on civil action in Ontario several times. With some limited exceptions, a civil lawsuit had to be initiated within two years of the filings of the plaintiff's complaint and claim of damages. Frances had in fact retained the services of the McDonnell's law office within the two-year period stipulated by the act. McDonnell himself had requested documents from Talbot's office for the purposes of discovery and had been provided them. It was not the fault of Mrs. Bertrand that Mr. McDonnell had been killed and the claim of Mrs. Bertrand had sat unpursued for such a long period. Bates would argue before a judge of the Superior Court that Mrs. Bertrand was a lay person and could not be reasonably expected to know the nuances of the law. All further delays in proceeding were the fault of poor communications again, beyond the scope of Mrs. Bertrand's control, Bates would argue. He closed the box after taking out the statement of claim.

Bates was waiting in the ante room outside of the Judges' chambers in the Fort William courthouse. A clerk came out into the hallway and said, "Mr. Bates, the judge will see you now." Bates smiled as he stood up. The judge authorizing the lawsuit had gone to law school with him and they had remained friends for several years afterward, until their respective careers had taken them to different provinces. He would give his clerk a bonus for his impeccable research before he made the trip to Fort William.

A week later, Jean was in his office at the outboard motor and chainsaw shop when a well-dressed young man came in. The salesclerk approached him, and Jean heard him ask for the owner. Jean smiled, thinking, "rich and successful men do not deal with salesclerks." He got up and went to the counter, introducing himself while extending his hand: "I am Jean Armand, the owner of this establishment."

The man dropped a document in his hand and said, "Thank you. You have been served, Mr. Armand." He turned and walked out the door before Jean could say a word.

Jean tore the envelope open and within a moment felt as if a vice had crushed his body. He grabbed the counter and the salesclerk rushed to him. "Mr. Armand, are you alright?" he asked.

Jean, who had lost all the colour in his face, told the clerk, "Get me a glass of water."

By the time the clerk came back, Jean had regained his composure. He drank the water. He could feel every nerve in his body reacting to the fact that his own beloved daughter was suing him for everything he had built for them over the years. "In threes. Everything good and bad happens in threes; Louise, Wabason, and now this, he thought. His legs felt like lead as he walked into his office and sat down. He dialed Frances's phone, then hung up before it rang. He dialed Gabriel Cote's number and when his secretary answered, he tersely told her to have Cote contact him as soon as possible. He needed more than water now, and reached into his desk drawer for his whiskey.

Chapter 28

Helen was hired by the Georgetown hospital as a registered nurse. One doctor had opposed her being hired on the grounds she had worked in the Indian Hospital and could have been exposed to tuberculosis or other infectious diseases during her tenure there. The senior doctor asked for the opposing doctor's resignation, as he may have been exposed to TB or other infectious diseases during his time at the Georgetown hospital. The opposing doctor withdrew his opposition. Helen quickly established herself as a capable, experienced, and knowledgeable nurse. She was soon a patient favorite.

Helen was in her third year at the Georgetown hospital when six prospectors from a camp north of the highway between Lac Ville and Georgetown came in. The prospector's supervisor had brought supplies to the camp and found all of them in their tents, dehydrated, vomiting, and suffering from diarrhea. He found the crew chief lying on the core samples laid out in wooden trays. The supervisor, with great effort, loaded all six of the delirious men onto his truck and drove them as quickly as he could to the hospital in Georgetown, arriving in the early evening. Helen, being a junior nurse, was on duty by herself when they came in. She called the on-call doctor and began feeding the men fluids. Her instincts and experience told her the condition of the men was serious. She called Luke and asked him to go to her mother's and have her brother come to the hospital as soon as he could.

Helen did not want to speculate on what had caused the men to fall ill. She just wanted her brother there to help her. Elias is like our father, nothing rattles him, she thought. Elias's presence always calmed and reassured her. The doctor and Elias showed up at the same time. Elias was not in uniform, but the doctor knew who he was. "Mr. Wabason, would you be kind enough to go and get all the nurses who do not have phones from their homes and bring them to the hospital? Your sister and I will be fine until you return," he said, as he wrote down the addresses.

When Elias was done this task, he went to the home of Herbert Smits, the police sergeant. Sergeant Smits answered the door still wearing his uniform. "Hello, Mr. Wabason," Smits said, and seeing Elias looking at his uniform he added, "Small town policing, you never know when you will be called. What is going on?"

Elias told him there was an emergency at the hospital and though it was not a police matter as far as he could tell, he knew the sergeant should be on top of things. "You're a good man," Sergeant Smits said, as he put on his boots and police tunic.

The sergeant and Elias came into the hospital as the doctor came out of the examination room looking grim. He looked at the policeman and Elias with concern. "It looks like cholera. I saw many cases after the war in Europe," he said. The doctor looked older than his 65 years when he sat down. One of the nurses brought coffee for them all. The doctor looked up and said, "Thank you. That is not your job, but thank you." He looked at Elias and the policeman. In a tired voice, he said, "I do not think the oldest of these gentlemen will live through the night. I need you both to go to their campsite in the morning and see if you can seize any evidence you can find for the medical examiner. The government will want assurances this outbreak is an isolated incident."

Sergeant Smits looked at Elias and asked him if he knew where this location was.

"Only too well," Elias answered.

The policeman acknowledged him with a raised an eyebrow and made some notes.

As the doctor had feared, the oldest of the prospectors, a 58-year-old man from the Savant Lake area, died just after two a.m. The other men, younger and stronger, would likely recover.

Elias and Sergeant Smits left the hospital just after four a.m. Sergeant Smits telephoned the detachment commander of the Savant Lake area to have him send a member to notify the next of kin of the man who had died. Elias went home and grabbed his gear after putting on his uniform. He went to the police detachment and slept in a chair until first light. Sergeant Smits woke him up with a coffee as the first rays of daylight started coming in through the detachment buildings windows.

The prospector's supervisor had provided a statement to Smits at the hospital. Elias read the statement while drinking his coffee. The supervisor had selected the camp site as a base camp for the men who would be staking claims north during the fall and into winter. The camp was chosen because there was a natural divide between the area the men had dug their latrine and the creek where they would draw their water. The supervisor had years of experience in the bush. He knew how important it was to his men's health to have proper sanitation. He did not know what caused the men to become ill and he did not spend a lot of time at the camp when he realized how sick the men were. His experience told him that for an entire crew to get sick at the same time, a shared meal or contaminated water would be the cause. Smits told Elias, "The man has taken a room at the Georgetown hotel and does not want to go back to the camp until the police are done their investigation."

Elias did not share his suspicions with Sergeant Smits about illegal sewage dumping being the cause of the crew's sickness and the death of the man from Savant Lake. He wanted to be sure before he told Smits about his investigation. Elias did not yet have a full measure of Sergeant Smits. Smits seemed comfortable sharing information with him and Elias wanted to live up to the confidence Smits had shown him. Elias was certain someone from Gil's sewage and septic service in Lac Ville was responsible for this tragedy. He did not have definite proof yet. He would not say anything until he did. Smits and Elias headed out to the camp in separate vehicles with Elias leading the way as the sun rose. As Elias was driving, he could not help but think that if he made a public announcement about the illegal dumping of raw sewage in the area, he might have prevented this. He cursed himself for putting his desire to catch the offenders ahead of public safety. He vowed he would never make a mistake like this again.

When they turned off the highway and drove the two miles to the camp, the sun had completely risen. It was a warm day and there was not a cloud in the sky. They pulled into the clearing where they saw three tents stretched over wooden frames. The flaps on all of them were open. There were two camp cots in each tent. There were clouds of flies around the tents and on the areas the men had vomited or defecated before they could reach the latrines. A pair of pants stained with feces lay next to a firepit where the wearer had abandoned them. A small stand-up camp stove with an uncovered pot stood in the centre of the camp. The men had built a roof over it so they could cook in the rain. The stench caused Smits to spread Vaseline under his nose. Elias looked as he did it. Smits smiled. "Trick of the trade," he said and offered him a smear.

Elias did not really know Smits; he thought he was not like a lot of other policemen who often treated conservation officers as lesser than police officers. One arrogant young constable from Lac Ville had said, "The fish cops are here," when Elias showed up at an accident between a moose and pick-up truck. It was a cheap shot not said in jest. "Assume means making an ass out of you and me. Never assume anything," Elmer had told Elias years ago. Elias decided he liked Smits.

Smits took some pictures and made some notes as Elias looked around. Elias walked to the creek. It looked clean and was running without any apparent obstruction. He saw the trail the men used to get their water. The area had a sandy bottom and there were no weeds or rocks where they scooped from. Smits called to Elias, "Anything down there?"

Elias walked back, answering, "Nothing I can see."

Smits candidly admitted, "I am not even sure what I am looking for."

Elias knew it was time to share his suspicions. "I know what I am looking for. Follow me; your feet might get a little wet," he told Smits.

They started walking upstream following the creek. The creek was at its widest at ten feet, and for the most part never deeper than four feet. The bush was thick, and it was tough slogging. Smits tried to stay on shore but slipped off the slippery rocks twice, soaking his boots. "Son of a bitch," he swore, and took to walking in the creek.

After three quarters of a mile, Elias went up onto the bank. He wiped the Vaseline off his upper lip. "You will want to come out of there Sarge," he said to Smits. Smits knew this was Elias's territory and he was about to reveal the source of the men's illness. He smelled the waste despite the Vaseline. Elias walked higher onto the bank. When Smits caught up with him Elias pointed to a dump site of raw sewage. "It looks like three trailers full, if not more," Elias said. "You going to have to wash your pants and sterilize your boots when we get back."

Smits followed Elias until they came to a trail and vehicle tracks. Elias photographed the tracks and compared them to the sketches in his notebook. "What are you thinking, Elias?" Smits asked.

Elias explained the complaints he had inherited when he was posted to Georgetown about the illicit dumping of raw sewage. He told Smits about his investigation so far. "The dual axle truck and trailer tracks are the same as most of the other dump sites, and they have been here at least three times this month," he told Smits.

They followed the trail to the highway. The trail branched off towards the prospector's camp site about two miles from the highway. The sun had dried Smits pants and boots. "Jesus, Elias, I smell like shit now," he said. "Good work, Mr. Wabason. We will have to interview all the boys who were in the camp as soon as we get back."

"We better change first," Elias said. They both could use a bit of humour.

Gabriel Cote came into the office, and before he had even closed the door his secretary told him Jean wanted a call as soon as possible. Gabriel made a face, even though he knew it was not very professional. His secretary had little use for Jean and pretended not to notice. She liked working for Gabriel. She knew he was conflicted about representing Jean. Jean did account for a significant amount of the office's income, and she knew her job was tied with Jean's legal bills. Still, she looked forward to the day when she did not have to deal with him. Gabriel went into his office and called Jean's home. There was no answer. He called Jean's office and the salesclerk said he had left. He put the phone back in its cradle and a moment later heard the front door of the office open. A visibly upset and flustered Jean was in his office. Jean threw the statement of claim on Gabriel's desk. "Do you have anything to drink?" he asked.

"Coffee or water," Gabriel answered, as he unfolded the document Jean had thrown down. Jean grunted in disgust and pulled a flask out of his vest pocket.

Gabriel looked over the statement of claim. The first thing he saw was that his opponent was the prominent law firm of McDonnell and Associates out of Winnipeg. His heart skipped a beat. This was the same firm that had assured Claude Talbot that this lawsuit would never proceed. He was not surprised Frances Bertrand was the plaintiff. He looked over his glasses at Jean. Jean was deflated, and Gabriel knew this was when he became most dangerous. Jean caught him looking and asked, "So can we make this go away?"

Gabriel answered honestly, "Maybe, but it will take time. Have you talked to Frances about a compromise?"

Jean snorted. "I am so mad right now, Gabriel, I do not think now is the time. Besides, daughter or not she cannot have what I have built. So goddamn ungrateful it breaks my heart."

Gabriel stared for a moment, then looked at the statement of claim to avoid smiling. You, Jean, have no heart, he thought.

The next morning Gabriel called Bate's office.

Chapter 29

Sergeant Smits and Elias Wabason interviewed the men from the prospector's camp the next morning. All of them were weak and tired. They were all consistent on one fact: they drew their drinking water from the creek. It was fast, fresh, and no one saw the need to boil it before using it. There were no towns or other camps upstream of where they took the water. The fellow who had died was in poor shape from years of drinking. "He came to the camp to sober up for a couple of months," one of the men said. Only one of the men heard anything unusual. He told Smits he had been tasked to build a shelter over the outdoor stove the day before they got sick. The other men left him alone in the camp. He heard a truck on the trail coming off the highway. The truck was downshifted into a lower gear. The man checked to make sure there was coffee in the pot, fully expecting whoever was on the road to come into the clearing. The truck continued north on the trail and the man went back to work. He did not hear the truck leave the area, probably because he was sawing, he added. When they were done, they went into the doctor's lounge to take a statement from the doctor. When they entered, a man who identified himself as the District Health Officer and two other men from his office were already talking to the doctor. It was Elias and Sergeant Smits turn to be interviewed.

Elias was not comfortable with giving up details of his investigation before he had a chance to seize the evidence he needed. He listened as Sergeant Smits detailed the camp and the raw sewage found dumped into the creek to the men from Fort William. Like many bureaucrats and higher officials, they had what appeared to be an air of arrogance and smugness about them, as if the act of speaking to a mere policeman was an unfortunate and tiresome exercise. Elias and the doctor exchanged knowing glances. Talking to a small-town doctor must have been excruciating for them, Elias thought. One of the men with the health officer looked at Elias. "Do you have anything to add?" he asked.

"No sir, Sergeant Smits pretty much covered everything," he replied.

Smits winked at Elias. Smits had given nothing away about the investigation. The men from Fort William wanted this to be an isolated and unfortunate event so that they could go home and file their reports. Smits gave them what they wanted. When they left the hospital, Smits turned to Elias. "Next move is yours, Elias; this is your investigation. Just tell me what you need," he said.

Lyle Bates took Gabriel Cote's call after making him wait ten minutes. After brief introductions, they quickly got down to business. Gabriel Cote asked Bates, "Is there was a way a settlement could be worked out to the satisfaction of the plaintiff and the defendant without using the Superior Court's time?"

Bates smiled as he made a quick note. He told Cote, "Put together an offer and I will put it to Mrs. Bertrand." In his mind, Bates suspected he had already won this lawsuit. He could tell from his tone that Cote knew he was out of his league. It was a thing of beauty to Bates how when the polished and high-priced firms squared off against small town lawyers, it was like a prize professional fighter stepping into the ring with an amateur fighter. Only a miracle could change the outcome. Still, he had to entertain this young lawyer. "I hope to see your offer in a timely manner, Mr. Cote," he said before hanging up the phone.

Gabriel Cote set the phone down and leaned back in his chair. He knew he had just made a fool of himself. Gabriel struggled with the ethical dilemma of representing a man he had no use for, and the oath he had taken to practice law without prejudice. It bothered him he felt so intimidated by this law office and a lawyer he had not even met. He had not even talked to Jean about offering a settlement to Frances. He just wanted to check the waters before he did. Gabriel, being honest with himself, did not even know why he did it. Gabriel knew he was a better lawyer than this Bates fellow thought he was. The weakest part of Frances's claim was the time it took to file her lawsuit; maybe this would be what he needed to bring everyone to the table and keep this out of the courts.

Jean was sitting in the office at Gil's sewage and septic service when his grandson came in from a honey run. Rejean was shocked by his grandfather's appearance. He had not shaved, and his bloodshot eyes had bags under them. He looked puffy and hung over. "Holy shit, Grandpa. Have you been burning the midnight oil or what?" Rejean asked in a voice louder than he had intended.

Jean looked up and gestured for his grandson to sit down. "Years ago, when your father died, your mother took it hard and did not know what to do. That is when I took over," he began. "I have done well running this company. We have all done well. Your mother now wants to sue me for control of the company I have built for us," Jean continued. "May you have only sons."

Rejean was not sure what suing someone entailed. He was sure it involved the courts and lawyers. Rejean had very little use for either of them. "Have you talked to my mother?" he asked, feeling the anger flush his face.

"Not yet. First, I have to get over how angry I am and how much your mother has hurt me. Me, her own father," Jean answered.

Rejean got up and said, "I will talk to her."

Jean told him, "It is better if you do not. It is for me to do."

Rejean shook his head to disagree. "I will find out what has brought this on," he promised as he stormed out the door.

Jean let a grin creep onto his face while thinking, Frances, my girl there are many ways to fight a lawsuit and one of them is coming to your door. He turned to look out the window as a police car and a game warden's truck pulled into the compound.

"I would have stopped whoever that kid was who sped out of here if we were not on a mission," Smits told Elias Wabason as they were getting out of their vehicles.

A constable from Lac Ville who had ridden with Sergeant Smits told him, "That kid is Rejean Bertrand, a local pain in the ass from Lac Ville. Jean Armand is his grandfather."

Smits furrowed his eyebrows and gave the constable a look as if to say, "Take care of that pain, Constable."

A couple of men in the compound came out and stood by the door. A man with a German accent asked Smits, "Can we help you?"

Smits answered with a question, "Is the owner here?"

The man looked towards the office. Jean cursed as he watched Kurt the mechanic point out his office. His heart was pounding. There was no way to slip out without being noticed. Jean gasped when the game warden took off his hat. It was like seeing a ghost. The son of Elmer Wabason, he knew in an instant. As much as he said he was not worried about a low-level government employee, the truth was different now that he was looking at him. The game warden seemed very interested in the vehicles parked in the compound. He was talking to the mechanic and showing him pictures. The mechanic nodded. Jean's throat felt tight, and his palms were sweaty. The policemen and the game warden were taking their sweet time before coming into his office. Jean calmed himself as best as could. He chastised himself for being irrational. The best these government people could do was give him a fine, which he could easily pay. A fine for what he was not sure of yet, but he was pretty sure it had something to do with the thousands of dollars Alphonse and his grandson saved him in fuel costs.

✴

Frances's son burst in the door like a storm. Rejean immediately started yelling at her. "Your life is not leisurely enough mother? You need more money?" He was spraying spittle as he continued. "Why are you suing your own father? Are so unhappy and so ungrateful?"

Francine, who was in her bedroom, came out and challenged him. "What are you doing Rejean?"

"Ask your whore mother," he yelled.

Frances stayed seated at the kitchen table. She had been reviewing the copy of the statement of claim when her son had burst in. Frances held up her hand to calm both down. She raised her voice enough to show this conversation was over and said, "Rejean, you are leaving. When you are calm enough to be a man, come back and I will tell you why, and if you still think I am a whore, do not ever come back."

Rejean swallowed. His mother, who he had always taken for granted, had laid down the law. He knew he had gone too far. Still, he was not going to lose face by talking. He walked out, leaving the door swinging after a failed attempt to slam it and got in his truck. His mother did not follow him and stopped Francine before she got out the door. Shaking with adrenaline and anger, Rejean drove away. He drove to the lake before he pulled over and started to cry in frustration. He punched the dash; only his mother could ever make him do that. He was glad his grandfather and Alphonse could not see him.

✴

Alphonse looked at the creek he had just dumped five hundred gallons of sewage into. It was running slowly, and he thought, this shit is actually good for the land; a natural fertilizer. The fish will grow. He really did not care much either way. It was something he had been doing for a while and no one seemed to really care anyways. He was thinking of Frances a lot lately. Maybe he could pass everything to Rejean and start wearing a shirt and tie soon. Frances might notice him more and see what a good man he really was. A man who gets things done. Alphonse got in the truck and started it. In an hour, he would be back home. Half an hour to drive, half an hour for the paperwork, and he would be sipping a beer in the Lac Ville Tavern. Alphonse had been laying off the hard stuff because he kept getting heartburn and burped constantly. "You don't need a doctor to tell you to slow down, Alphonse," he chided himself. The flies, as always, were already swarming over his dumped load.

Chapter 30

Sergeant Smits, Conversation Officer Elias Wabason, and the constable from Lac Ville finally came to Jean's office. Jean had waited deliberately. He was not going to give them the satisfaction of coming out to the yard to see what they were there for. The first thing Elias noticed was Jean's haggard appearance. His office stunk of stale cigarettes and his desk was covered with papers, stained coffee cups, and glasses. The sunlight shining through the grimy office window only highlighted the ugliness of Jean in the place he was comfortable. This was not the same man who had come to house 12 all those years ago. Sergeant Smits handled the introductions; no hands were extended and Smits wasted no time telling Jean why they were there. When Smits told Jean that a prospector had died, Jean thought, there was a long road between speculation and proof; there were many lawyers between speculation and truth. Jean knew he had the money to put them there. Jean began to relax a little.

Jean leaned forward, staring at Elias. "And what, if anything, does this have to do with me?" he asked.

When it came to the evidence, Sergeant Smits let Elias present it. Elias took his time. He carefully recited dates and dump site locations leading up to the site where the prospector died. He glanced up at Jean every time he added a new location. Jean was now squirming in his chair. Elias's reciting of the locations was done slowly and, even with the slow delivery, he knew Jean could not form his lies fast enough if he chose to speak at all.

Jean stared at Elias as he spoke. He hated this man for being here and pointing a finger at him. He hated him for not accusing him directly of the sewage dumping that had caused a man's death. These little men are expecting me to throw myself at their mercy, he realized with some satisfaction. I will never give them this, he thought, his confidence growing. He knew now they were going too fast. They were looking for an admission of guilt or culpability. Jean was not going to give it to them. Jean held up his hand and said, "Gentlemen, I am afraid a lot of what you are saying is going over my head. If it is alright, I would like to call my lawyer Gabriel Cote in Lac Ville for some advice."

Smits and Elias did not look at each other Jean noticed. Sergeant Smits replied, "Sir, please call your counsel. In the meantime, Conservation Officer Wabason and the constable will be seizing documents. Under the powers of the Fish and Wildlife Act, they do not require a warrant, Sir. I am sure your lawyer will be familiar with the act."

Jean picked up the phone and wished Elias Wabason was as dead as his father.

When Elias left Smits and Jean in the office, he knew his suspicions were right on the money. The mechanic who introduced himself as Kurt Krieger confirmed in his heavily accented speech that there was a dual axle truck and trailer with a five-hundred-gallon tank being used for honey runs. At first, Elias found him hard to understand, and this Kurt seemed to know who he was. The mechanic did not hide his dislike of Jean and his foreman Alphonse. He told Elias, "The trailer always comes back empty. Only the foreman and Jean's grandson use it; where the contents are dumped, I have no idea." He added for emphasis, "Alphonse is a bully and a cheat and the kid, an arrogant little shit, always came back to the compound empty."

If Elias had not recorded Kurt's date of birth, he would have no idea how old he was. Kurt was about five feet-six inches tall and maybe 140 pounds. He looked like he had led a hard life. Elias speculated Kurt was one of the many former German prisoners of war who had settled in Northern Ontario. As Elias went back to the office, Kurt was smiling. Elmer Wabason's son, he thought and then muttered in German, "Die Ironie."

When Elias went to the office cabinet, he told the constable he wanted every trip sheet. He wanted to cross-reference illegal dumps to trips or honey runs. The constable knew the people of Lac Ville would do anything to know what was going on. Maybe if the constable was lucky one of the pretty single women would press him for information. Whatever happened, this was a lot better than investigating who had stolen Mrs. Woolrich's garbage can tops.

Elias located the work order for today and saw the truck had been dispatched to a location fifty miles east and Alphonse had signed it out. He looked at his watch and said to the constable, "The truck I am looking for is probably on the way back." The constable nodded in agreement.

Elias went back into the office where Sergeant Smits and Jean were sitting, waiting for Jean's lawyer to come in from town. Elias asked Smits to come out in the hallway and quietly told him, "The truck should be returning from a trip anytime."

Smits acknowledged the import of this and told Elias and the constable, "Take my police car and stop him on the highway if you can."

Elias gave him the thumbs up, and they headed out to the patrol car.

After Elias and the constable departed for the highway, Jean looked at Smits and said, "If, and I say *if*, there has been illegal dumping of waste by my company, I had no knowledge of it. Perhaps my foreman Alphonse can address the concerns of the game warden." He said the words with absolute contempt.

Smits, unfazed, replied, "I am sure your lawyer will echo your sentiments, sir."

Alphonse had to pull over on the highway. He felt a sudden and overwhelming urge to spill his bowels. He ran into the bush and sat over a log. He was sweating and short of breath when he was done. He grabbed a handful of leaves to clean himself. Alphonse felt a little lightheaded as he walked back to the truck. I must have eaten something bad or maybe the spray from the pump had gotten in my mouth, he thought. He was incredibly thirsty. All he had was some Coca-Cola in bottles. He wished for water. Alphonse had been sick before, and he had always just shaken it off. He got back in his truck and started driving. He was about five minutes from the compound when he saw a police car heading towards him. He glanced at his speed and thought nothing of it.

"That's the truck," Elias said, "let him pass." The constable looked at him. "It is better if the truck pulls into the compound yard. Then the driver and vehicle are tied directly to the business and Jean," Elias added.

The constable drove east until the truck was out of sight. He slowed down, made a U-turn, and stepped on the gas. When the police car caught up to Alphonse's truck and trailer, he was just gearing down and turning into the compound. The constable hit his lights and gave a bleep on the siren. The truck stopped in front of the garage. Alphonse recognized the constable from Lac Ville when he looked in the driver's side rear view mirror. When he looked over at the passenger side mirror, he saw Elias Wabason getting out the passenger side door. "Son of bitch," he muttered as he felt his stomach tighten and cramp again. This game warden looked identical to Elmer Wabason, the man who was killed during the fire years ago. The stories about Elmer's son being a lawman were true.

Alphonse, his mind racing, thought, I am not going to shit myself in front of these frigging people. He got out of the truck and ran towards the office. The constable, surprised, yelled for Alphonse to halt. Elias said with the hint of a grin, "Let the fat man run, he won't get over the fence," and started following Alphonse.

Alphonse ran to the toilet and flung open the door. He began to feel the same way he did the day of the fire when he passed out after the explosion. Bright white lights and a sharp pain were the last things Alphonse experienced as he fell to the floor. Smits and Jean had come out of the office because of the commotion. Soon Elias, the constable, and the men working in the compound were crowded outside the bathroom door. In his death throes, Alphonse's bowels had released. The stench was overwhelming. The constable gagged and stepped out to vomit. Elias reached down and checked for a pulse. Elias could not help noticing the three fingers of Alphonse's right hand clinched in a fist over his heart. He looked at Smits and said, "He is dead."

The young constable from Lac Ville came back in wiping his mouth with the back of his hand. "Christ, Sergeant, I don't know what happened. This guy looked like he had seen a ghost," he said.

Jean and Elias locked eyes. "Maybe he did," Elias said, quietly.

Jean went back in his office and slumped into his chair. Sergeant Smits came in and started making phone calls.

It was three in the morning before the coroner released Alphonse's body to the funeral home in Lac Ville with a tag indicating an autopsy was required and a notation: "Apparent cause of death, heart failure. Case pending." The tag was initialed by Sergeant Smits. The corporal and the constables from Lac Ville had taken statements from all the employees present and allowed them to leave earlier. Gabriel Cote had shown up and sat with Jean as Jean wrote a statement. Cote had asked to speak with his client in private afterwards. Jean growled at Cote, "Get a hold of my grandson and tell him to leave Lac Ville for a while." When the first employee released from the scene reached Lac Ville around nine p.m., he went straight to the bar. Within an hour, the news of Alphonse's death was all over town. The story grew with each telling and by midnight the story was Alphonse died when he saw the Indian game warden. Alphonse had not been afraid of the police. There must have been something else going on.

The truck and trailer had been towed to the seizure lot of the Department of Lands and Forests in Georgetown by Luke's heavy truck towing service. When Jean finally got home, he found Rejean sitting in the dark drinking his grandfather's scotch. Jean jumped when he turned on the light and saw him. "Is it true? Alphonse is dead? And you want me to leave town?" Rejean asked.

Jean poured himself a drink and sat down. "Yes, for a while until this all blows over. I will make sure the law knows you were only doing what you were told by Alphonse. Your story will be you were afraid, and I convinced you to come back and deal with everything," Jean said, thinking it had worked before. "Go to your uncle's in Fort William. Lay low. I will tell him you are coming. I will call you when it is time to come back," Jean added with mixed feelings and a sense of regret for not seeing this coming,

Rejean bristled at the thought of anyone thinking he was afraid of anything. Rejean quietly answered, "As you wish, Grandfather," and walked out the door.

Chapter 31

Elias' investigation into the illegal dumping of raw sewage took nearly three weeks to complete. Jean had stopped co-operating and all questions had to go through his lawyer Gabriel Cote. Elias issued the summons to Jean charging him with sixteen violations of the Fish and Wildlife Act. Jean took the summons at Gabriel Cote's office and never said a word to Elias when they were issued. The first appearance to answer to the charges was set a month down the road in the circuit court in Georgetown.

At the first appearance, the crown prosecutor read the indictment and the circuit judge asked Cote, "How does your client, Mr. Jean Armand, plead?"

Cote stood up, and in a clear voice replied, "Not guilty on all counts, your honour."

The judge turned to the crown prosecutor and asked him, "Are all these counts required? Could they not be combined into a single charge?"

The crown prosecutor, who also worked this circuit, replied,

"They already have been, your honour. There are 167 violations worthy of charges under this act. Conservation Officer Wabason has already pared them down and has only proceeded on the strongest and most egregious violations according to his court brief."

"I see," the judge said. "Alright, then let us proceed."

Cote filed a motion to have the truck and trailer returned. He filed a motion to have the search declared invalid. The judge in the circuit court at Georgetown was sympathetic to Jean and his lawyer, as they were small town businesspeople pitted against the Department of Lands and Forests. He split down the middle and ordered the truck and trailer returned. He upheld the search because the provisions of the Fish and Wildlife Act gave sweeping powers to conservation officers to protect the people and the environment. No trial date was set at the first appearance because Cote asked for time to present further motions. The judge adjourned the case to two weeks later to accommodate Cote and hear his motions.

Two weeks later, the next motion Cote put forward was to ask for an outright dismissal of all charges on the grounds Jean could not be held responsible for the actions of a rogue employee. The employee, Cote told the judge, had died of a heart attack. The crown said under his breath, "How convenient for your client."

What Cote could not have known when he made the motion was that the judge had received direction from the chief justice indicating there was considerable political pressure coming from the government to make an example out of the company. The local paper had written a story about how the death of the prospector was directly related to the dumping of the raw sewage. The story got picked up by the papers in Fort William and Toronto. The judge dismissed the motion saying the issue would be decided at trial.

Elias had put together a good case using the records seized at the compound to match the tire tracks of Jean's company truck to the dump sites. The biggest obstacle was the lack of witnesses. Jean had sent his grandson into hiding. Elias's superintendent and Sergeant Smits came to each hearing to support Elias. Smits, ever a realist, warned Elias that some people in the judiciary did not like the fact an Indian conservation officer had charged a prominent white businessman. He overheard the court clerks when he was in the office talking about how the case had judges talking between each other. The gist of the conversations was about how this young conservation officer was creating a lot of work for the courts and bringing charges they had never heard of or dealt with before. Now that the story was in the press there was no way to levy a small fine so everyone could move on.

After Cote became aware of the story in the papers, he went to Jean's house and told him. Jean went white as Cote told him. Without much conviction, Jean said loudly, "I don't do business with the papers. Why should they care about Lac Ville?"

For the first time in the many years he had known Jean, Cote saw he was not so certain of himself. There was no dismissive bluster about making the little government men go away. Jean solemnly asked, "What is next and what can they do?"

Cote thought, maybe this man does have some remorse and a heart, until Jean spoke. "What will people think of me? Can this prospector's family sue me?" he asked, almost whining in his self-pity.

Cote told Jean, "You need bring your grandson home." Cote would accompany him to give a statement to Conservation Officer Wabason. Then he said they should think about a guilty plea to the environmental charges before things got truly out of hand. Jean nodded in agreement. "Now, Jean, let's talk about your daughter and her claim," he finished.

Frances and Francine took a trip to Georgetown to see Mary. They had not seen each other for years. They showed up unannounced. Mary saw the car driving up her driveway and recognized Frances right away. Always on a Sunday, she thought, "something always happens on a Sunday. Mary and Richard Sutherland came out of the house to greet them. Mary could see the question in Frances's eyes when she looked at Richard. "This is my husband, Richard, and you must be Francine," Mary said.

Richard shook Frances and Francine's hands. Mary and Frances hugged each other. Mary looked at Frances, searching her face for the reason she had shown up at her home. "Come on in. It has been far too long," she said, leading them to the kitchen table.

Richard Sutherland watched as the women talked. He watched Mary's face light up and smile when Frances said something funny. He watched Frances as she spoke, her eyes sparkling and her hands gesturing. Two powerful and beautiful middle-aged women bonded by their experiences, they had a presence that filled the room. For the first hour, they talked about the children and what they were up to. Francine shifted a little awkwardly and asked if she could take a walk around the property. Richard asked the women if they wanted to be alone. Frances told him no because what she wanted to tell Mary would affect all of them at some point.

The lighthearted banter ended, and Frances told Mary why she had come to see her. "I am suing my father to regain control of Gil and Elmer's business. I believe he tricked me into signing it over to him after Gil died and Francine was born. I was very overcome, not thinking clearly and I let Elmer down. He brought money and cheques to me so I could keep the business going. I just could not," Frances started. "After the fire where Elmer was killed, the police found the car involved in Gil's death hidden in my father's old stables. My father denied knowing it was there," she finished.

Mary leaned in and Richard leaned back in his chair. Frances paused before starting again: "At Gil's funeral, I saw your friend Eva. I know she is my sister. More lies and deceit from my father. My son Rejean adores his grandfather. My father took Gil's place to create a man just like him. Hateful and angry. His grandfather has turned him against me. I just added everything together and so did my mother. My mother left a year ago."

Frances paused again to see Richard and Mary's reactions.

Richard looked at Mary. Mary half spun her teacup and said, "Go on, Frances."

Frances took a deep breath and continued. "My father has a hate for you and all your people. It made no sense, especially after I saw Eva. I think he planned to take Gil's business the moment he knew Elmer was a part of it. I have waited so long. I am sorry, Mary. None of this made sense and I did not want to see the truth. My own father," she finished, her eyes welling with tears.

Mary got up and put her arms around Frances. "What can we do to help you?" she asked.

"My lawyer says as far as anyone knows there was no written agreement between Elmer and Gil. I do not believe our men would not have written anything down. Do you know if there ever was an agreement written between them Mary?" Frances asked.

Mary shook her head and then thought of a small box where Elmer had kept all her letters to him from the war. She had packed it away knowing she could not open it without crying. "There is one place I have never looked, Frances," Mary said, almost whispering. She stood up "Did Gil keep your letters from the war?" she asked.

Frances's face lit up. "Mary, you are brilliant," Frances said, slapping her hands together.

Richard could not help smiling as he watched them. Loving Mary was the best thing that had ever happened to him. Francine came in the house and looked puzzled. "Why are you all so happy?" she asked.

Rejean Bertrand got a call from his grandfather telling him to come back to Lac Ville. Rejean was inclined to stay in Fort William. There were plenty of girls and no one ever asked for proof of his age in the local taverns. His great uncle told him to go back and sort out what had to be sorted out. Rejean reluctantly agreed. He had lost a lot of respect for his grandfather in the past two weeks. His grandfather seemed afraid of the game warden and police. His grandfather had told him for years they were nothing, men who could not make their own success, so they let others make it for them or made it on the backs of others. He would go back, but he was not about to kiss anybody's ass. Especially the cops or that Indian game warden.

Chapter 32

Gabriel Cote got another adjournment after Rejean came back to Lac Ville so the evidence he would provide could be assessed. Cote drove him to Georgetown and took him to the Department of Lands and Forests office so Elias Wabason could interview him. When they arrived, Elias greeted them and extended his hand to shake. Gabriel shook his hand, but Rejean refused. Sergeant Smits was in the office when Elias led them in. Gabriel asked why the police officer was there. Sergeant Smits replied he was there because the investigation into the death of the prospector was a joint investigation. Rejean looked at Gabriel for a moment, waiting for him to protest. When he did not, he took his seat.

Elias started by outlining the purpose of the interview to Rejean. Rejean pushed back from the desk and told Elias, "I am not stupid. I know why I am here. You want to put my grandfather in jail," he said, loudly.

Gabriel held his hand up to calm him down. Elias explained patiently and in an even voice that he was looking for the truth about the illegal dumping of raw sewage in the district. Nothing more. Elias then laid out pictures and maps of each of the 16 sites he had laid charges for. He told Rejean to read the notes attached to each if he wanted details on how the tire tracks matched up to the truck he had signed out on eight of the trips. Rejean leaned forward and looked at the papers for a while. He leaned back and said defiantly, "This doesn't mean a thing to me."

Gabriel spoke up and said, "I think what my client is saying is, is there a question related to these papers you wish to ask, officer?"

Rejean gaining confidence, leaned forward and crossed his arms over his chest. He looked Elias directly in the eye and ignored the sergeant. Elias returned his stare and asked, "Can you even read, Mr. Bertrand?

Rejean uncrossed his arms and said softly, "You son of a bitch. I can read."

Elias pushed a paper toward him and told him to read it. Rejean pushed it back. Before Gabriel could react or intervene, Elias asked Rejean what he knew about his father. Rejean shot back, "He was some big shot war hero who thought he was better than everyone else. He worked with your father instead of his own people."

Elias asked him if this was his opinion or what he had been told. Gabriel stood up and told Rejean they were leaving. Rejean sat stone still staring at Elias. His nostrils flared and fists clenched. Sergeant Smits looked at Gabriel and motioned him to sit back down.

Elias spoke first, "Your father was a war hero. He was also a man who saw men for what they were. The colour of their skin meant nothing to him if they were honourable. My father was the same. All men should be that way. Are you ready to be a man, Mr. Bertrand?"

No one said anything. Several minutes passed before Sergeant Smits spoke up. "Now gentlemen, can we get back to why we are here in the first place?"

Rejean started, "I have worked with my grandfather since I was a little boy. Alphonse was his foreman and treated me like his little brother. I was driving by the time I was ten. I was not very good at school and left in 1959 as soon as I could," he paused. "The work at the sewage and septic was dirty but the money was good. Alphonse came up with the idea to dump our loads in isolated areas to save on fuel costs. My grandfather agreed," he continued. He asked for a drink of water. Sergeant Smits poured him a glass. Rejean's hands were shaking as he took a drink. He pointed to Elias's reports and pictures. "This is not even one tenth of what we have dumped," he said.

Gabriel interrupted, "I would like a moment with my client."

It was Rejean's turn to put his hand up to Gabriel. "No, it is about time I was a man," he said looking at Elias. "Alphonse and my grandfather assured me the bush could absorb all the dumping and no one could ever be hurt by it. Alphonse told me people have been using shit to fertilize the land for years and we were helping the forests to grow. I will plead guilty to whatever charge you wish to lay, Mr. Game Warden, but I will not testify in court," he finished.

Elias put his pen down and looked at all three men before settling on Rejean. "Did you dump where the prospector died?" he asked.

Rejean answered quickly, "Yes, twice, but Alphonse dumped the last load just before the man died," he answered as he looked down at the floor. "One week apart for all three. I am very sorry," he added. He lifted his head and asked Gabriel, "Are we done? I would like to go home to Lac Ville now."

Elias nodded. "That's enough for today. Thank you for coming in," he said extending his hand again. Rejean shook it and left with Gabriel.

Smits watched them from the window as they got in their car. Without turning around, he said, "If and when you want to be a police officer, Elias, I will be the first to approve your application." He picked up his hat and added, "I better get back to the office," and left.

Mary found what she was looking for in the box of her letters to Elmer. She cried more times than she could count as she opened each folded page. Some letters she recognized and remembered.

Other letters she had forgotten what was written until she started reading them again. She found a small, yellowed paper she had never seen before. The page was lined like in a school notebook. She started reading and wondered how she could have ever doubted Elmer's and Gil's ability to have a contract. It was a simple document. Dated November 15, 1946, it read, "Gilbert Bertrand and Elmer Wabason on this date agree to start Gil's and Elmer's Septic and Sewage Company. Ownership will be fifty/fifty. All profits will be thirty-five/thirty-five with the remaining thirty to improving the business." Both men had signed it. Mary recognized Elmer's signature. She went to the store and called Frances. When Frances answered the phone, she had the same document in her hand. She read it to Mary word for word. Frances had taken her copy to the railway station where her friend worked. He said it looked like it came from an old CNR train orders book. The copy Frances had was a carbon copy, but the signatures were not. Frances told Mary the document was in the letters Frances had sent to Gilbert during the war. After Frances got off the phone with Mary, she left a message for Lyle Bates at the McDonnell law office.

When Gabriel Cote and Rejean Bertrand arrived in Lac Ville, Jean was waiting at Cote's law office. He got out of his truck and walked towards them as they were getting out of Gabriel's car. He smiled and asked, "Well, how did it go? Did you stick to what I told you?"

Looking at Rejean and Gabriel's expressions told him most of what he needed to know. Rejean walked to his truck without a word, jumped in and drove off. Gabriel unlocked his office door and Jean followed him in. Jean asked sarcastically if Gabriel had anything to drink. Gabriel surprised him by pulling a bottle of gin from his desk drawer as he sat down. Gabriel produced two tumblers and filled them to the brim. He handed one to Jean and noticed a phone message on his desk. He picked it up. After reading it, he drank half of his tumbler. Lyle Bates from the McDonnell law office wanted a phone call as soon as possible; both the office and his home number were on the message. "Christ, what now Gabriel?" Jean asked.

Gabriel finished his drink and poured another before saying, "First, let me tell you what happened today."

When Jean left Gabriel's office, he had a clear idea of what needed to be done. His grandson had let him down in the biggest way he could imagine. Rejean would never live this down with him. He had lost his grandson as surely as he had lost his daughter and wife. No matter, Jean thought, the fight ahead would make his life interesting again. He had begun to lose his fire, he realized. He was letting little people push him around. Jean did not become one of the richest men in Lac Ville by being a push over. "No, my darling Frances, I will fight you, the Indian widow, and your high-priced lawyer from Winnipeg. I will bankrupt us all before a dollar lands in your hands," he said to himself while driving home. Jean decided he would take whatever hits came with pleading guilty to the charges. He would send one of his men to explain to his clients how Alphonse and his grandson had been dumping illegally without his knowledge. He would say as a good corporate citizen he would take responsibility to preserve the good name of the company. He had long ago arranged that the services of the company had no rivals in the region. He would offer temporary discounts to ensure the clients stayed with Gil's Septic and Sewage Company. His net worth, his accountant told him, was well over a million dollars. I can ride out the storm and crush anyone in my way, he thought. He began whistling as he pulled up to his empty house.

The reporter from the Georgetown paper, Allister O'Brien, was also the owner, typesetter, printer, and delivery person. He could not let the prospector story go after his piece about the prospectors was picked up by papers throughout Ontario. He wanted to repeat his success. He received a phone call from a reporter assigned to cover the courts in Fort William. The court reporter was looking to flesh out a story. A lawsuit had been filed in the Superior Court in

Fort William regarding the ownership of Gil's Septic and Sewage Company out of Lac Ville. The reporter wanted to confirm it was the same company reported on in the Georgetown paper as being involved in allegations of illegal sewage dumping. Allister invited the reporter to Georgetown and promised a story which could help both of their careers.

Chapter 33

Gabriel Cote called Bates' home after Jean had left. Bate's tone was condescending as he told Cote about the business agreements found by Mary and Frances. "I have added Mary Wabason to the suit as a plaintiff. I am expecting an offer to settle by the end of the week, Mr. Cote. In light of this contract, I do not believe your client will have a leg to stand on," he said.

Cote felt his face flush as he answered. "On the contrary, Mr. Bates, that and everything else will be a matter for the courts. My client is refusing to even consider a settlement."

Bates replied, "Collect your fees up front, Mr. Cote, because your client will not have a pot to piss in when I am done with him," and hung up the phone.

Gabriel Cote and Jean entered the circuit court in Georgetown and changed Jean's plea to guilty to Elias Wabason's charges. A constable from the provincial police had to be called in to read the facts from Conservation Officer Wabason's court brief. Jean received a $3,200 fine and promised the judge he would carefully monitor all dumping operations in the future. Cote had moved the date of the guilty plea to a day Elias Wabason was testifying in a court in Kenora. Jean paid the fine in cash and was back in Lac Ville by lunchtime. Gabriel Cote was now free to prepare his defence for Jean in the upcoming civil trial. The reporter from the Georgetown paper got to the courthouse as Jean and Gabriel were driving away.

🐜

The discovery phase of the civil trial between Frances and Jean had started long ago when Claude Talbot sent the papers to Kent McDonnell, whether Claude had intended or not. They had sat read but never pursued until Lyle Bates took over the files after Kent's death. Immediately after receiving the revised statement of claim, Cote had submitted a statement of defence, which stopped the clock and put everything into slow motion. Gabriel Cote looked at the framed oath he took upon being accepted to the bar, which he hung proudly behind his desk. He read it every day before he sat down:

> I accept the honour and privilege, duty and responsibility of practising law as a barrister and solicitor in the Province of Ontario. I shall protect and defend the rights and interests of such persons as may employ me. I shall conduct all cases faithfully and to the best of my ability.

Jean Armand employed him and, to Cote's chagrin, employed him rather gainfully. Unless Jean Armand fired him, he would honour his oath.

Gabriel Cote's plan for Jean's defence was straight forward. He thought of it more as an exercise of re-crafting old arguments to fit new circumstances. His first area of attack was going to be on the length of time it took for the McDonnell firm to file the lawsuit. He considered Bates's argument for the reasons it took so long for the lawsuit to be filed to be self-serving to the McDonnell firm. He called Jean Armand and asked if he would come to his office. Jean told him, "I am tired Gabriel. What is you want?"

Gabriel replied, knowing Jean's need to be in control would overcome his fatigue, "I am preparing your defence. I need your input and approval."

"I will be right there," Jean replied and hung up the phone.

Five minutes later, Jean came in the door with a bottle of scotch and sat in front of Gabriel's desk. Gabriel thought Jean looked better than the last time they had talked. Jean poured each of them a drink, saying, "Claude Talbot just took my money. You are going to show me how I spend it."

Gabriel explained he would argue that while Frances may have been aggrieved many years ago, the legal time for her claim had unfortunately expired. Jean's intent in taking control of the company was not a malicious act but rather the act of a loving father. Jean nodded in agreement before saying, "How can anyone doubt that?"

Gabriel told Jean, "I believe Bates and the McDonnell law firm were close to an ethical breach for moving the suit forward at Frances's expense. I know this will outrage Bates and it could possibly throw him off his polished delivery in the opening days of the upcoming trial."

Jean replied, "I do not know this part of law. You lawyers can sort that out yourselves." Jean finished his drink and poured himself another before saying, "What next?"

Gabriel said, "My next argument will be that the recently discovered handwritten agreement or contract between Gilbert Bertrand and Elmer Wabason is invalid. Both signatories were dead. The word of the widows attesting to the genuineness of the signatures are at best prejudicial to you." Gabriel paused before saying, "Even if the signatures were accepted by the court as genuine, there was no witness to the signatures. There was no way of knowing if both parties signed the contract willingly."

Jean perked up. "Jesus, do you think Gil tricked the Indian?" he asked.

Gabriel downed his tumbler of scotch. It burned on the way down. Jean looked surprised and re-filled his glass. "Good man," he said approvingly.

Gabriel answered the last question. "That is just my point, Jean. There is no way to know. I will suspect Frances's lawyer will argue that because both parties to the contract benefited equally from the contract there would be no reason to suspect its intent was not sincere. I will counter with the argument that Gilbert Bertrand knew he could take advantage of a treaty Indian because any contracts had to be approved by the Indian agent for the area. The Indian agent, a Mr. Price, is long deceased and unable to contradict my argument."

Jean finished his drink before saying, "I have heard enough for tonight. I had my doubts about you and now I am satisfied you will earn my money."

Gabriel, surprised, replied, "There is more."

Jean said, dismissively, "You know as much about chainsaws and wood harvesting as I do about lawyer tricks. Just do right by me and my grandchildren." Jean got up, put on his coat, and left.

Gabriel sat there for a moment before drinking his re-filled tumbler, then went back to writing his notes. He wished Jean would have stayed to hear the rest of his plan for the upcoming trial. Gabriel knew he would have to attack and bring Frances's character and motives into question. He knew he would portray her as a self-centred and ungrateful daughter wanting to reap the fruits of her father's labour. The thought of doing this to a woman of such intelligence and integrity revolted him. Frances had offended enough people in Lac Ville by not being what they wanted her to be. Gabriel was able to dispose several witnesses who could testify as to her mercenary character and the weakness of her mind after Gil's death and Francine's birth. When Gabriel mentioned the witnesses to Jean, he had immediately vetoed it, saying, "I am not paying for them to have a holiday in Fort William." Mary's addition to the claim presented more of a challenge. He would have to discredit the widow of an Indian war veteran he knew very little about and by all accounts was a highly respected woman.

Gabriel would also try to limit the scope of the lawsuit. The businesses Jean had built after taking control of Gil's and Elmer's business would have been the result of Jean's business skills and had nothing to do with the success of Jean's enterprises independent of the sewage business. Therefore, they should not be considered in the proceedings. Gabriel knew Jean was an unscrupulous man, and he resented having to argue the lawsuit, but he had sworn an oath and the arrogant lawyer from Winnipeg had gotten under his skin. It was well after midnight when Gabriel turned his office light out and went home.

A couple of days later, Gabriel's secretary brought in a copy of the most recent Georgetown paper. "You might want to see this," she said as she put it on his desk. The front page was dominated by a story with the headline, "Prominent Businessman from Lac Ville Fined for Illegal Sewage Dumping." The story went on to question the appropriateness of the fine given that a man had died, and others were made sick. The reporter carefully skirted around anything which could be considered libellous when he questioned if the soon retiring judge of the circuit court was the best person to hear a case with such importance to the people in the region. The story questioned the abrupt changing of the plea in the case and why the defendant had been allowed to plead guilty almost in complete privacy. The reporter ended the story with what he thought would be a bombshell in the region. The businessman was being sued by his own daughter and the widow of a decorated Indian war veteran for control of the business that her late husband and his partner had created. Both men had died in unusual circumstances. The businessman had acquired control of the business after their deaths. Gabriel put the paper down. Clever bastard; not bad for a small-town reporter, he thought.

The story generated the effect it had intended. People in Lac Ville and Georgetown were talking about it constantly in the bars and coffee shops. In Lac Ville, both Jean and Frances had people who supported them and clearly took sides depending on who they were sympathetic to. Jean had fired his grandson and had not spoken to Frances or his granddaughter since receiving the lawsuit. When he saw them in town, he looked away or ignored them. Jean, despite the circumstances, felt invigorated and walked with a new purpose. He paid more attention to his businesses and went out of his way to be as fair as possible with his clients. He was enjoying the notoriety he felt when people whispered around him.

As winter was approaching, Allister O'Brien, the Georgetown reporter, was approached by Mary at his office. "Thank you for your work and the stories you have written about Jean Armand. My son did a lot of work on the sewage dumping case."

Allister, surprised Mary was at his office, answered "I know he did. Elias is not much of a talker though."

"I know. Once he trusts a person he opens up," Mary said. "You are a good man, Mr. O'Brien. I have one more favour to ask you."

"Anything," O'Brien answered.

Mary suggested he do a piece on her deceased husband Elmer Wabason and Gilbert Bertrand as further background to the stories he had been writing about the lawsuit and pollution in the region. Allister was only too happy to oblige. His papers circulation had doubled in the past few months. The national radio service northern broadcasting office contacted him for an interview. The reporter told Allister a human-interest story in the northern part of the province was a rare commodity and would most certainly have an audience.

Since coming back to Georgetown, Elias Wabason had been staying at the barracks at the forestry branch during the week and staying with family on the weekends. There was talk they would be shut down in the next few years as more and more of the work of the Lands and Forests Department was increasingly mechanized. Elias was a very private man and the only people he really confided in were Richard, his mother Mary, and his sister Helen—Helen especially because they were so much alike. Elias had read every story Allister had written about Jean Armand and the impending lawsuit. He knew he could not give an interview to him because the Department of Lands and Forests had someone to handle press releases in Fort William. He had been frustrated with the way the court handled his charges and was disappointed with the fines Jean had received.

Talking with Helen, he told her, "I have learned from what happened, and there will be more people like Jean as the North grows. I won't make the same mistakes again."

Helen, in her quiet voice, assured him, "You won't. Now tell me again what the police sergeant told you. You like him, Elias, I can tell."

"He is a fair and smart man, and I do like him. Besides Walter, though, I am not sure how to be friends with these men. Most of them think and see things so different from us," Elias replied. "Everything has to be a certain way instead of just what it is."

Helen smiled before saying, "Maybe we are all the same, just in a different way that we cannot see."

They sat quietly as they always did after speaking.

Elias broke the silence after a few minutes. "Sergeant Smits told me if I applied to be a police officer, he would be the first to recommend I be hired," he said.

Helen looked Elias in the eyes before saying, "I don't want you to be a policeman. You belong here. This is your home."

Elias reached over and took his sister's hand in his. "I agree. I am not going anywhere," he said.

Helen squeezed his hand, relieved. Elias was her brother, but he was also her best friend. She knew Elias felt the same about her. They did not always need to talk; it was good enough to be close. Elias said, "Spiritual insurance, blood ties, call it what you want, sister, it is the way of things."

Elias had thought long and hard about what Sergeant Smits had said to him after the interview of Rejean. He decided he was happy as a conservation officer. Elias knew there would be unique challenges and the government would never be as committed to his organization as he wished it would be. Elias loved the North, and he was in the place he needed to be to help protect it. He hoped he could stay in Georgetown to be close to Mary and Helen for at least a couple more years before getting transferred again. People in the area had come to know him as a conservation officer who was not afraid of anyone, no matter how rich or well-placed they might be.

✻

Helen fell in love with the youngest son of the owner of the general store in Georgetown. The owner who had insisted the Wabason's be treated with respect when they had first come to Georgetown had instilled the same values in his son. Scott Harris worked for the federal government. He had an office in a building attached to the town hall. His official title was Representative for the Government of Canada's Resource Development Office. He laughingly told Helen, "I am a spy making sure the mining companies did not cheat the federal government out of tax revenue." Scott quickly became a fixture at Mary's house. Richard Sutherland took an instant liking to him. Helen and Scott announced their engagement on Christmas Eve 1964. Everyone was there, even Walter and Lucy, who came in from the trap line to celebrate Christmas.

Chapter 34

Frances received a phone call from Lyle Bates in February of 1965. He told her with an excitement that only lawyers could feel, "Frances, after years of delays and legal motions, the case of Frances Marie Bertrand and Mary Wabason versus Jean Joseph Armand is set for the first sitting of the Superior Court in Fort William in March."

Francis thanked Bates and hung up the phone. She looked out her window at the snow-covered trees and the partially frozen lake. She wondered how it all had come to this. Her lawyer had discovered her father had been in financial difficulty when he had her sign the papers to turn over control of the company. "If my father had needed money, I would gladly have given him anything he had needed," she thought. The spell he had over her son was broken, but Rejean had grown accustomed to the money her father had given him. He worked at the mill now. He was unhappy and resentful over how things had unfolded. Frances knew he blamed her for some of it. Francine was quiet. She always supported her mother, to the point where she did not have her own goals or dreams. Francine had tied her happiness to her mother's. Frances hoped after the trial, Francine would find her own way.

The trial was going to be before a judge and jury. "Juries were predominately composed of men," Gabriel Cote told Jean. A 1964 decision allowing married women to be called for jury should not have too much effect on the jury selection. Most married women had better things to do than sit on a jury for weeks. The jury he believed would be less sympathetic to two women with a high-profile lawyer from a prominent firm in Winnipeg. Cote had learned Bates was not charging for his day-to-day services and was planning on taking a portion of the settlement. Cote knew this would not sit well with a jury from Northern Ontario. Jean agreed he had lived his life counting on the mindset of the men from his generation. Women, children, and Indians should know their place, he thought as he stared at the mountains of papers the preparation for the trial had created. He looked up at Gabriel. "We are keeping the pulp mills busy. Are you ready?" he asked.

Gabriel replied, "Yes, unless there is something you have not told me that the other lawyer knows and will surprise us with."

Jean pushed his thinning hair back over his balding crown. "I do not think I have missed anything," Jean answered.

Jean had doubted the fight in Gabriel for a long time. He was the only game in town for a lawyer and Claude Talbot trusted him. When Gabriel had put forward the possibility of settling out of court, Jean was going to fire him. To Gabriel's credit he never mentioned it again after Jean outright refused to even consider it.

🐝

Mary had felt restless ever since receiving the court notice. Richard Sutherland had been very supportive through everything. He knew he could not get the time off to attend the whole trial. He told Mary he would be there when he could. Richard's presence, or even his feelings, were not what was making Mary restless. She knew the trial would bring up memories and feelings which up to this point had been hers alone. Mary had done well for herself between working and buying and selling houses. She thanked God and Elmer for the bank account she had been allowed to open with Elmer's signature. Before Elmer had died, she could not legally have opened a bank account without her husband's consent and approval. Mary did not need the money if the judgement went her way. The irony of having rights after losing her treaty rights was not lost upon her. Mary did not like having whatever type of justice this civil suit would bring sitting with men she did not know. Not every white man was as open-minded as Mr. Harris the general store owner and his sons. Men like Luke and Walter were looked down upon by some men because they had taken up with half-breeds and Indians. This was the reality for all of them, Mary knew.

Mary was not one to linger over grievances. She chose to learn from them and move on. Constable Brooks and Sergeant McNeil could not bring charges for Elmer's death at the hand of Alphonse despite their best efforts and intentions. She knew she had to make a plan, and as a result, when Everett and Indian Agent Price expelled her from the reserve, she was ready and did well for her children. Mary resolved to see this through, though she could not be certain what the outcome would be. Her biggest hope was the judge and jury members would see her as a person. She knew her world was a different one from her dear friend Frances's world. Mary's mother often explained inequalities and injustices to her by saying, "It is the way of things, my daughter." For now, Mary thought, for now.

Allister O'Brien wrote a story about Gilbert Bertrand, Elmer Wabason, and Walter Enio after Mary had suggested it would provide good background to the stories he had written about the upcoming civil trial. While doing his research and interviews with surviving veterans from their regiment, he had paired with the court reporter from the Fort William paper. The reporter, Henry Ellis, was the son of a veteran and the brother of a police officer in Toronto. A picture emerged of three men who fought with determination and had been overlooked for many decorations they had deserved. Gilbert, Elmer, and Walter had on one occasion taken out the entire crews of two 88mm guns and their supporting machine guns shot by shot and man by man when their unit was pinned down. There was no officer present to attest to their action, so other than the respect of the other soldiers, none of them were officially recognised for their actions. In another action, Elmer had shot the crew commanders of a troop of Tiger tanks as they stood in their hatches one at a time from five hundred yards until all four were dead and the Tiger tanks withdrew.

Gilbert took part in the rescue of Canadian combat engineers pinned in a minefield by sniping seven German soldiers one after another until the rest retreated. Walter could be counted on to account for a German officer or signaller every day they were on the front lines. Other soldiers lost count of his contribution to the war effort. Everyone Allister and Henry interviewed independently corroborated the other accounts. Some of the officers thanked the reporters for the information. They said they had no idea why fierce resistance in those battles suddenly crumpled until Allister and Henry told them. The story was picked up nationally and re-published in the veteran's league national monthly magazine. For many people in Lac Ville and Georgetown, this was the first time they had heard the stories about the men from their towns and what they had done in the war.

Rejean Bertrand's girlfriend read the story to him when he was at her house. Rejean asked her to read it twice. His girlfriend, puzzled, asked him, "Did you not know this?"

Rejean did not answer. He got up, kissed her, and put on his coat. She watched through the window as he drove away, the headlights of his truck like halos in the cold air. Rejean stopped at his apartment and packed a bag. He had a full tank of gas. He passed his grandfather's house and the lights were out. He drove to his mother's house. He could see her and Francine through the window talking to each other. He drove away. "I will write," he said to himself. Rejean would be in Fort William first thing in the morning. He was eighteen, and he did not need anyone's permission to do what he was about to do.

Chapter 35

The day before the trial was to commence, a March storm swept through the region, dumping three feet of wet heavy snow. Frances and Francine had packed two weeks' worth of clothing and toiletries. They were going to stay at a hotel for the duration of the proceedings. The highway was down to a single lane as snow drifts accumulated in the rock cuts. Frances's friends discouraged her from going out on the highway with her daughter until things were cleared up. Frances had been told how fickle the Superior Court could be with female plaintiffs and was not going to take the chance of being the cause of a delay on the first day of a trial where a jury was in place. The weather had been mild while the snow was falling, and then the temperature dropped. Frances knew the snow was not going to melt away before she had to be in Fort William. She loaded a shovel into the backseat of her car before she and Francine set out on the highway.

Jean Armand was at the coffee shop when he saw Frances's car leaving town. His friends looked at him waiting for a comment. Everyone knew the civil trial was starting the next morning thanks to Allister and Henry's news stories. Those who were not readers could follow the trial on the radio. Jean loved the attention. He was giving these people something to talk about. He felt almost like he was the home team off to an important game. Winner take all. Jean wished the jury was from Lac Ville because he would have had this decision in the bag. Jean had worked hard bringing people onto his side. Playing the poor hardworking father so unfairly being sued struck a sympathetic chord with the middle-aged people of his church. Feeling everyone's eyes on him, Jean let them wait until Frances's car was well out of sight. He sighed and said in a low steady voice, "It is a sad day my friends, when your own daughter and an Indian woman can sue you. Learn from this, my friends, and safeguard your lives from it. Maybe the courts will bring some common sense and order back to us. I will do my best to represent us all." Jean looked at the men at his table and with smugness acknowledged how their heads nodded in agreement. He stood up, downed his coffee, and said, "I will leave around twelve, and I may come home each night. Stop by the house if the lights are on and I will let you know how it is going." He pulled on his jacket as everyone wished him good luck and safe travels.

Justice Zachary Wallace was having his coffee and looking out the window of his kitchen at the piles of snow on the street in front of his home. His wife had the radio on listening to a news story about the upcoming trial. The reporter, probably a damned communist, Wallace thought, was questioning whether women could get a fair trial in the male dominated Ontario Superior Courts. Wallace did not like how the national radio service had a habit of questioning the decisions of the government and the courts. "We are paying for them to undermine our institutions," he had told his colleagues. His wife turned and saw Wallace was listening as well. She quickly turned the radio off. "I am sorry, Zachary. I did not know you were listening. I know you do not like the news covering cases where you are presiding until they are over." she said softly.

Wallace put her hand on her shoulder and replied, "It is alright darling believe it or not this old war horse makes up his own mind after hearing the whole case."

Gabriel Cote had been in Fort William since Friday using the volumes of legal books at the library in the Superior Court. He was looking for precedents and reading case law. The lack of resources available to small town lawyers was one of the reasons lawyers from larger centres often held the advantage in civil and criminal trials. Try as he might, Gabriel could not get case law and court decisions in a timely matter in Lac Ville. His well-prepared arguments could be for nothing if a court decision made a month before in a court in another jurisdiction had ruled on the very argument he was presenting for consideration. His pride, he knew, was causing him to take this case very personally. The fake professional courtesy of Bates in the early days of the discovery process had given way to barely concealed contempt by Bates of Gabriel's legal knowledge and ability. Gabriel knew this case could very well decide if he would be contesting wills and minor disputes for the rest of his career. As much as Jean Armand was a thoroughly unscrupulous and selfish man, Gabriel still thought, he had a case worth trying.

Bates, a junior lawyer, and an assistant were staying at the same hotel as he was. Bates strutted around the lobby and lounge like he was the most distinguished guest they had ever had. Gabriel had to admit Bates cut a distinguished figure. Bates was in his mid-60s, fit and immaculately dressed even at breakfast. His voice was a deep baritone and everything he said sounded like it should be acted on immediately. In contrast, Gabriel knew he tended to speak quickly. The last suit he had bought was easily five years out of style even though it was only two years old. He knew he did not have the charm or physical presence of Bates. Not even 40 years old at five foot seven and, on a good day, 150 pounds with wild unkept hair, Gabriel knew he would not overwhelm the judge and jurors with his appearance. He needed his case to be strong.

It normally took an hour to drive from Lac Ville to Georgetown in the winter if the roads were in good shape. Frances and Francine had been crawling along for an hour and were barely twenty miles out of Lac Ville. The wind had increased, blowing the snow into a virtual white out. Whenever Frances met an eastbound vehicle, she would have to pull over as much as she could to let the vehicle pass. Everyone she met was courteous and waited until Frances was out of the snowbanks before driving on. Still, driving was arduous and Frances's shoulders were tense. The transport trucks were the worst. Sometimes they would slow to a crawl to pass, but even then Frances found herself being squeezed into the snowbanks on the passenger side of her car. On two meets, she had to rock her car to free herself from the deep accumulated snow. Even if she had wanted to, she could not turn around and go back to Lac Ville. She pressed on with Francine firmly holding the dashboard on the passenger side.

Frances had told Mary she would be in Georgetown around twelve. They were going to travel together and share a room in Fort William. Mary never liked the city. So many of the people from her reserve who had gone there had become lost and struggled afterwards, even if they came back home. Being with Frances and Francine would help her feel at least like she was not alone. She knew the storm would slow Frances down, so she was not overly concerned when Frances was late. Elias came over for coffee and to wish her luck during the upcoming trial.

"I am proud of you, mother," Elias said.

Mary blushed slightly. "This is mostly Frances's doing. I am proud of you and the man you have become, though you need a woman soon because I need a grandchild. Helen may be like I was, and I could be waiting awhile yet," she said.

It was Elias's turn to blush as he put his hands up. "I know, I know. I am just not ready yet. Maybe after this trial is over," he answered.

Mary turned solemn before saying, "I love you so very much, Elias. I know you feel you must honour your father, though you have never said it. So much has changed since he has passed. You have done more than any father could have asked. You need to live the life you choose now."

Elias sat quietly for a moment, looking at Mary. How does she see through everything so clearly all the time? he thought to himself. The love and respect he had for her was almost inexpressible. "Your right, as always. I love you very much," he replied, finally.

He finished his coffee and looked at his watch. "I have to head to the office. I have a guy coming for an interview at twelve-thirty," he said.

Mary stood and gave him a hug. Before he left, Mary asked him, "Can you come back at two to see if I am gone? I am worried about Frances and the roads. If I am not, we might have to head out on the highway to Lac Ville to check for Frances."

Elias agreed before giving her a hug and reassuring her. "Things were just slow because of the snow."

Jean threw his suitcase into the cab of his 1963 Ford one-ton truck with the dual rear tires. He was confident the snow would not give him any trouble as he headed out onto the highway. People would yield to him because of the way he drove. Jean liked to think he understood human nature. If you drove straight towards vehicles on the road they would always yield because they did not want to be involved in an accident. Most people were not fearless like he was. He was going about forty miles an hour when he passed a truck stuck in a drift. He waved and drove on. The truck driver shook his fist and carried on shovelling. The wind died down as he continued driving. The air was crisp and cold. There was some ice on the road. The chains Jean had put on his tires allowed him to keep his speed steady.

Frances was only ten miles out of Georgetown when she hit a patch of ice. Even though she was only going twenty miles an hour, she spun out. Frances took her foot off the gas and tried to correct herself. The weight of the car caused the rear end to slide into a deep drift. The vehicle buried itself almost up to the driver's side door. Frances started laughing. "It is a good thing we brought the shovel," she said. Francine looked terrified until her mother started laughing. "It will be alright we are just going to have to dig, unless some handsome men stop to help us," Frances said, winking at her daughter.

Frances pushed the driver's side door open and put on her mittens. Francine reached in the back seat and passed the shovel to her mother. "You are going to need this, mom. We should have brought two," she said.

After a half hour of shovelling, Frances was getting close to the back wheels. Francine offered to spell her out. "Take a break, mom, and let me shovel, have one those cigarettes you think no one knows about," she said.

Frances, when she put her mind to something, was not going to let anyone finish what she started. She said, "No, and I only smoke when I have a glass of wine, smart ass."

The wind picked up again and started quickly drifting snow into the area Frances had just shovelled. Francine, who was standing outside of the car watching her mother, perked up. "Mother, I hear a truck," she said smiling and pointing in the direction of Lac Ville.

Jean saw a vehicle with the rear end buried deep in a snowbank. It took Jean a minute as he geared down before he recognized it as Frances's car. He saw his granddaughter standing near the front and Frances shovelling by the back tires. Jean knew his daughter was a good northern girl and she would have everything she needed for a situation like this. At the very worst they would have to walk to Georgetown if they could not free their vehicle. Georgetown was only ten miles and there was still a good seven hours of daylight if by chance no one picked them up. Sometimes to be a good father you have to let your children learn what a trial is, Jean thought as he drove slowly by on his way to Fort William. He did not make eye contact with Francine or Frances as he shifted gears to get back up to speed.

Frances recognized her father's truck when she looked up. When it geared down, she wondered what would happen if he stopped. They had not spoken for months. Frances knew her father was vindictive and full of irrational hate but surely, he would not leave his granddaughter until he at least made sure she was alright. Francine said nothing as her grandfather drove by. Frances saw the hurt in her daughter's eyes. Frances knew they were not really in any danger but the callousness of her father to her daughter, his own granddaughter, was almost too much to bear.

※

Elias Wabason and his mother were in the ministry truck leaving Georgetown heading out onto the highway towards Lac Ville when Jean Armand drove by. Elias was going to flag the truck down to ask if there were any vehicles stuck on the highway until he realized it was Jean's truck. Mary said, "Frances must be alright. Her father would not have left her on the highway."

Elias looked at his mother before turning onto the highway and said, "We better check anyways."

Chapter 36

By Monday morning, the opening day of the trial, the snow was melting and the streets leading to the courthouse were wet and slushy. Frances, Mary, and Francine arrived with wet feet. "Not a good start, Frances," Mary said, smiling to hide how anxious she felt.

Mary had never been in a court before and she felt intimidated by the grim brick building. As they walked up the stairs to the main level, Mary saw a chalkboard with the cases being heard and what courtrooms were assigned to each case in the corridor. "Bertrand and Wabason vs. Armand—Courtroom 2—10 a.m." was neatly printed halfway down the list of cases. The hallway was full of lawyers, witnesses, detectives, and uniformed police officers. Everyone spoke in low voices. The building and formal atmosphere seemed to make them quiet and restrained. Mary began to feel more comfortable, thinking that maybe this is the place where the truth is unable to hide. If these men were this respectful of where they were, it had to be a good sign. Courtroom number two was at the end of the hall. There were two rooms on either side of a short hallway off the main corridor leading to the court. The door to the courtroom was propped open, revealing a well-lit room with dark wood on the walls. It contrasted sharply with the slate grey of the hallways leading up to it.

Lyle Bates came out of one the rooms and warmly greeted Frances and Mary. "I am glad the storm did not prevent you from travelling, ladies," he said, and led all of them into the room.

At the same time, the door to the room opposite them opened. Frances briefly saw her father as Gabriel Cote left the room. Frances noticed Bates was wearing a plain grey suit instead of the expensive suits he normally wore. He spoke quietly as he asked Mary and Frances if they were ready. Bates had gone over all of this before with them. Frances took this as another display of Bate's thoroughness. Mary and Frances both assured Bates they were ready. Mary had a feeling Bates, for all his quiet and dignified demeanour, would be the first one to raise his voice in the courtroom. "Come, let me show you the courtroom," Bates said opening the door.

Jean saw Frances as she went into the room with her lawyer. He had not heard her voice for many months and the brief glance at her pained him. Gabriel had gone to get some papers and he was alone in the room when he heard her and Mary talking as they were being led to the courtroom. Jean had worn his oldest and most worn suit to court, and he smiled thinking of how Frances would notice this the moment she saw it. Gabriel had told him he should dress normally for court. Jean thought otherwise and before he left his hotel room, he had inspected himself in the mirror. He looked like an old man in an old suit barely able to afford to come to court. It was exactly the look he had wanted. Gabriel had told him the judge would see right through his contrived appearance. The judges of the Superior Courts had seen enough ploys. "But the jurors will be the ones I need to be on my side," Jean had answered.

Gabriel shook his head and told him, "This is not the place for games, Jean." Gabriel opened the door, interrupting his thoughts. "Are you ready? It is almost time," he said.

Bates led Mary, Frances, and Francine into the court room. It was easily the biggest room any of them had ever been in, except for the church. Bates appeared comfortable and at home in court. There were two tables in front of a finely crafted wooden barrier, which was covered in boxes of papers. To the right was the raised bench where the presiding justice sat with a witness box beside it. A picture of Queen Elizabeth II draped by the flags of the country and province was behind the judge's bench. Bates told Francine she would have to sit in the gallery. There were already several people there. Most of them appeared to be reporters with notepads. Bates explained, "There are people who come to court just out of curiosity as well."

Mary saw Allister O'Brien from the Georgetown paper and nodded to him. The bailiff and the court reporter were talking to each other when Jean and Gabriel entered the courtroom and went to their table six feet from where Bates, Frances, and Mary sat. Everyone went quiet. Frances and Mary both noticed Jean's appearance. He looked shabby, old, and tired. Mary exchanged a glance with Frances and asked, "On purpose?"

Frances looked at her father again and turned back to Mary. "Of course."

At one minute before ten a.m., the court reporter went to a door at the back of the courtroom. The bailiff stood and faced the gallery. The court officer announced in a loud voice, "All rise. The Superior Court of Ontario is now open. Justice Wallace presiding."

The Justice went from the doorway directly to his seat. He sat down while scanning the courtroom. Once he was seated, the court reporter announced the audience could be seated. Justice Wallace instructed the bailiff to bring in the members of the jury. As the six members were brought in, both Cote and Bates watched them. Bates knew from previous trials that jurors are often more than slightly overwhelmed by the unfamiliar setting of a courtroom, and their first impression of opposing counsels could set the pace for the entire proceedings. Bates stood straight and made eye contact with each member of the jury as they shuffled to their seats. Cote looked back and forth between Justice Wallace and the jurors.

Bates smiled slightly. That's right, Mr. Cote, you appear uncertain and uncomfortable, he thought.

Justice Wallace surveyed his courtroom. His eyes went from the plaintiff's table to the defendants table and then to the jury. He paused for moment to view the gallery and then requested the court reporter to announce the case. The court reporter read from a paper, and when he was done, the case of Bertrand and Wabason versus Armand was underway. Justice Wallace asked both lawyers if they would introduce themselves. Bates, as the senior counsel and counsel for the plaintiff, went first and in a firm steady and confident voice introduced himself to the jury. Gabriel Cote tried to imitate the confidence and delivery of Bates. He knew he had failed the moment he was done talking. He had sounded nervous, and his voice was unsteady. Cote admonished himself afterwards and swore to just be himself for the rest of the proceedings.

Justice Wallace then asked, "Mr. Bates, are you was ready to make your opening statement?"

Bates looked towards the jury to ensure they were watching and listening to him and then at the judge. "Yes, my Lord," he answered. "My Lord and gentleman of the jury. I am here today to ask you to right an injustice done unto my clients, Frances Bertrand and Mary Wabason, both widows of decorated veterans of the Second World War, by the father of Frances Bertrand, Jean Armand. I intend to prove Jean Armand, by underhanded and illegal means, took control of a company created by the hands of the plaintiff's husbands after they died in suspicious circumstances and while his own daughter was grieving and overwhelmed by the birth of her second child." Bates paused and pointed at Jean. "Mr. Armand then used the profits from the company to build several businesses and continues to this day to profit from his subterfuge. Mr. Cote will argue Mr. Armand provided for and gave financial assistance to his daughter and his grandchildren and I will agree that, to a degree, he did. But his assistance was self-serving and only given to hide the deception he had used to take what was rightfully the property of Frances Bertrand and Mary Wabason." Bates paused again. He picked up a sheaf of papers. "I will prove there was a binding contract between Elmer Wabason and Gilbert Bertrand. This contract, discovered during the discovery process prior to the trial commencing will be pivotal to proving the company created by them was by their wills the rightful property of their widows, my clients," he said gesturing towards Frances and Mary. "Everything else you will hear in this courtroom will not change this irrefutable fact. You will hear Mr. Cote argue that the widows took too long to file this statement of claim. By the time this trial is over you will wonder why this matter, this claim, this injustice, would have ever needed to come to trial and why the defendant did not just acknowledge his duplicity and make things right with Frances Bertrand and Mary Wabason." Bates finished. He looked each juror in the eyes, starting from right to left, before turning to Justice Wallace and saying, "Thank you, my Lord," and taking his seat.

The only sound in the courtroom was pens on paper as the reporters made their notes. After a moment, Justice Wallace turned in Gabriel's direction and said, "Mr. Cote."

Gabriel stood and began, "My Lord and gentlemen of the jury. As my learned friend Mr. Bates has already said, at the end of these proceedings, you will indeed wonder why this matter has come to trial at all. My client, Mr. Armand, did take over the business of Gilbert Bertrand after his unfortunate death. He did it because his daughter was incapable of managing her own affairs. His beloved daughter was sick with grief and in the grips of what our generation refers to as the baby blues. For men not familiar with this condition, it is a state of depression which can accompany the birth of a child. In extreme cases this condition can make a mother incapable of making sound decisions and incapacitate even the strongest women. There was no way my client could know how long this state of affairs would last. Mr. Armand did what any father would have done in the circumstances. He even consulted legal counsel to be sure what he was doing was right and legal." Gabriel paused and after moment began again, "As for Mrs. Wabason, my client had no reason to believe he was obligated to her in any way for recompense. My client was suspicious of the business dealings Mr. Bertrand had with Mr. Wabason. He believed their arrangements were contrary to the provisions of the Indian Act as the law stood at the time. Mr. Armand even consulted with the Indian agent responsible for the Wabason family to ensure he was not violating the law. When my client took over the business of Mr. Bertrand for his daughter there was and still is not any legally, and I will repeat this point, legally sound document proving the plaintiff Mrs. Wabason has any claim to the damages stipulated in this claim. My sincerest wish, my Lord and members of the jury, is that at the end of these proceeding you will feel compelled to rule in favor of my client so he, as a father, can begin to mend the fences and rifts this unfounded lawsuit have created between a father and his family. Thank you, my Lord," Gabriel finished and took his seat.

Justice Wallace turned towards the jury and addressed them. "Gentlemen, I caution you that the opening statements of the plaintiffs and defendants counsel are not facts. The facts will be requiring proof. Counsel has merely outlined their respective positions." Justice Wallace paused to let his words sink in. He loved educating jurors and anyone else interested in the legal system. He never grew tired of it, no matter how many times in the past thirty years he had to do it. He turned to Bates. "You may call your first witness, Mr. Bates."

Bates stood up and looked at Mary. "I would like to call Mary Wabason to the stand, my Lord."

Chapter 37

Mary stood up. Frances smiled at her to reassure her as Bates directed her to the witness box. Mary looked at the jury members as she passed them. All the members were men. The youngest looked to be in his early thirties and the rest in their forties and fifties. None of them smiled as Mary took her seat. She turned and acknowledged the Justice with a nod. He looked to Mary like both a wise and stern man. The court clerk swore Mary in and then she turned to face Bates. "Good morning, Mrs. Wabason," Bates began.

"Good morning," Mary replied, quietly.

"Mrs. Wabason, are you the widow of Elmer Wabason formerly of the Lac Ville Indian reservation?" Bates asked.

"Yes," Mary replied. "We were married in 1929 at the community hall on the Lac Ville reservation. He was killed by an explosion while fighting the fire at Lac Ville in 1950."

Bates had to establish Mary was entitled to be a plaintiff to the jury. The court had already accepted she was, but the jury still needed to hear it. He went right to the issue at stake next. "Did your husband, Elmer Wabason, enter into a business with Gilbert Bertrand while you were married to him, Mrs. Wabason?" he asked, looking at the jury while asking the question.

Mary answered in a clear, steady voice. "Yes, they served in the same regiment together. After the war, Elmer and Gilbert started a business. They installed septic tanks, disposed of sewage, and provided firewood. They started small with a couple of trucks and a trailer. The business grew quickly. Gilbert Bertrand came to our house on the reserve quite often and they talked about the business in our kitchen many times."

Gabriel Cote stood up. "Objection, my Lord. There is no way to prove these conversations other than the testimony of Mrs. Wabason who has a vested interest in the outcome of these proceedings," he stated.

Bates quickly replied before Justice Wallace could rule on the objection. "The truthfulness of the witness is for the jury to decide on the balance of probabilities, Mr. Cote."

Justice Wallace cleared his throat and said, while looking at both Bates and Cote, "In my courtroom, I will rule on objections and I will not tolerate any deviation from this. Are we clear on this, Mr. Bates? And Mr. Cote, I will not be conducting law classes during this trial. Your objection is overruled. Mrs. Wabason, if you please, carry on with your answer."

Mary took a breath and continued. "My husband and Gilbert were like brothers. They worked long hours and I never once seaw them disagree on anything. Some people did not like an Indian man and a white man working together, so sometimes they worked separately at some locations."

Mary was looking at Jean as she said this. Jean was staring at her so intensely and with such contempt she paused so as not to break eye contact. Almost everyone in the courtroom saw the interaction. Justice Wallace's deep voice broke the spell. "Please continue, Mrs. Wabason" he said.

"Everything was going well until 1950 when Gilbert was killed by a hit and run driver. After he died, Elmer kept the business going and brought the money it made to Frances, Gilbert's widow. The vehicles and equipment for the business stayed at the business compound with exception of a truck and trailers Elmer used to supply wood and water to the reservation residents. No one gave us any information about what was going to happen after Gilbert passed, and then Jean Armand showed up at our home with a bunch of rough looking men who had axe handles and chains. They tried to take the truck and trailers, but Elmer and his friend Walter stopped them. I heard Mr. Armand yelling everything belonged to him now." Mary sat straight, bristling at the memory, then continued. "Nothing else happened until August 1950 when a forest fire was burning towards Lac Ville and Elmer and Walter went to warn the town. My husband was killed when a truck exploded. After that, I was made to leave my home on the reservation because my husband had lost his treaty rights because he was overseas for more than four years, and after he was killed the Indian agent said I had to leave because I was married to a non-status Indian. The irony is that Gilbert and Elmer were legally able to have been in business together when they started because my husband had lost his status. Which I did not know until after he was killed. Everything Gilbert and Elmer had made now belonged to Jean Armand," Mary finished.

Jean leaned back in his chair, surprised. I put much effort and money into proving that their business was illegal and it wasn't, he thought. It did not matter, though; he had still gotten what he wanted.

Lyle Bates stared at the jury for a moment and then asked Mary, "Did you know if there was an agreement in writing between your late husband and Gilbert Bertrand in regard to the ownership of the business?"

Mary answered, "I always suspected my husband would have had some agreement. I feel badly because I pushed him to make sure it was done. He always told me it was dishonourable to think they would not have done something. I just wanted to be sure for the children. He would always say a soldier's word is a soldier's word. What it was, I did not know for sure. My husband used to say a soldier's word was gold. It was not until Frances Bertrand called me and asked me to go through Elmer's papers that I found a written agreement."

Gabriel rose to his feet. "Objection, my Lord. Mrs. Wabason is referring to a document which has not been authenticated by the courts."

Justice Wallace ruled quickly. "Mrs. Wabason can refer to this document. Its authenticity will be decided over the course of the proceedings." He looked at the jury and told them, "The document Mrs. Wabason is referring to will be tested later in the trial. For now, the plaintiff's counsel is only seeking to establish a document was found which allowed Mrs. Wabason to join in this lawsuit as a plaintiff."

Jean leaned over to Gabriel when he sat down and whispered, "Let her finish. Then you can discredit her." Gabriel nodded in agreement.

Bates smiled at Mary and the jurors and asked, "Mrs. Wabason, why did you wait so many years before joining this lawsuit?"

Mary straightened her back again and looked at the jurors as she answered, "For many years after Elmer was killed, I needed to provide for our children alone. I did not know the law. Every time someone invoked or enforced a law, I lost something. I was forced to leave my home because of a law Elmer and I knew nothing about. I did not believe I had the right to try to recover part of what my husband had built until Frances Bertrand contacted me."

Bates stood as she finished and said, "Thank you Mrs. Wabason. I know this has been a long and painful journey."

Gabriel glared at Bates as he sat down. Justice Wallace asked Gabriel, "Cross examination, Mr. Cote?"

Gabriel stood up and straightened his robe. He looked down at his notes and after a pause began. "Mrs. Wabason, prior to filing a lawsuit with Mrs. Bertrand, had you ever talked to Mr. Armand to see if there was any written agreements or understandings that possibly could have benefited you or your children?"

Mary looked surprised by the question and quickly answered, "No, sir."

Bates looked at Frances wondering where Cote was going with this line of questioning. Gabriel thought he had thrown Mary off with a hint of triumph and feigned indignation. He quickly followed up with, "And why not, Mrs. Wabason? Why did you not just go to the man who had legally taken over the business you claim your late husband and Gilbert Bertrand had built and ask him if there was any of the business that you were legally entitled to? Surely such a conversation would have been a logical thing to do given your current and much belated claim?"

Gabriel looked at the jury as he waited for Mary's answer. Bates started to stand, and Frances put her hand on his forearm and whispered, "Let her answer."

Mary stared a Gabriel for a moment, thinking, I thought you were a decent man Mr. Cote, before she answered in a strong clear voice: "Mr. Armand made it clear to my husband from the moment they met that he did not like Indian people. He did not approve of Gilbert and my late husband even being friends much less being in business together."

Gabriel threw his hands in the air and looking at Justice Wallace said, "My Lord."

Justice Wallace raised his hand to cut him off and loudly said, "You asked the question Mr. Cote, and now we will all hear Mrs. Wabason's answer. Please go on, Mrs. Wabason."

Mary nodded and started again. "Both Gilbert and Elmer talked about how much Mr. Armand hated Indian people; not only Elmer, but anyone from the Lac Ville Reservation. When Mr. Armand came to the reservation after Gilbert was killed, he brought several men with him who I believe were intent on violence. After that, I knew I could never just go and talk to that man," she finished looking directly at Jean.

Jean did his best to look hurt by Mary's accusation. Gabriel looked at his notes. Jean hissed, "Enough." Cote announced he had no further questions for this witness and sat down, deflated.

Justice Wallace turned to Mary and said, "Thank you for your testimony, Mrs. Wabason, you are free to leave or you may stay in the courtroom as you please."

Mary stood, relieved, and went to the gallery.

Chapter 38

After Mary was seated, Justice Wallace looked at Bates and said, "Call your next witness, Mr. Bates."

Bates rose and announced, "I call Mrs. Frances Bertrand."

Frances stood and walked to the witness box. Frances had dressed plainly, but like Mary there was no hiding her dignity or beauty. It sometimes frustrated Frances that men could be so easily distracted. She knew in her heart, though, when it came to matters of money and the rights of men, she would still have to earn their respect. Frances was sworn in and took her seat. Bates remained standing throughout the process and when she was ready, he began with, "Good morning, Mrs. Bertrand. You are the principal plaintiff and widow of Gilbert Bertrand, are you not?"

Frances answered, "Yes, sir."

"You are also the daughter of Jean Armand, the defendant. Is that not so?"

"Yes, sir."

"Mrs. Bertrand, can you please tell the court, starting from the beginning, the sequence of events which have brought you to this courtroom today?"

Frances steeled herself and began. "My deceased husband Gilbert and I were married in 1938." A tear came to her eye and her voice wavered. "In 1941, Gilbert enlisted in the regiment from Fort William. He was overseas until September of 1945. When he came back to Canada, he was told his job as a foreman had been given to another man. He had come up with the idea to start a business just in case something like this happened. I did not know at the time, but he decided to start the business with Elmer Wabason, who he had been in the war with. They started small but the business grew quickly because they were both honest and hardworking men. Gilbert asked me to do the books, and for the first five years I kept track of everything. Gilbert and Elmer re-invested a substantial amount of the profits back into the company." Frances paused and then continued. "In 1950, I was eight months pregnant with our second child when Gilbert was killed in what I later discovered was a hit and run accident. I had a difficult birth right after the funeral, and I was not myself for a long period of time. My father volunteered to look after the business and during this period he somehow convinced me to let him take over completely. He had his lawyer complete some papers, which I signed without understanding, because I was ill at the time. There were many things I did not know at the time. Like that the vehicle involved in Gilbert's death was hidden in my father's old stables."

Gabriel shot upright. "Objection, my Lord. No criminal charges were ever laid in the death of Gilbert Bertrand and my client had no knowledge of the vehicle being in his stables. This clearly an attempt by Mrs. Bertrand to prejudice the jury against Mr. Armand."

Justice Wallace leaned back before speaking. "Mr. Cote, you will have a chance to cross examine Mrs. Bertrand. This is not a criminal proceeding, and the plaintiff is allowed to present the facts as they are perceived by them. The jury will assess the weight and truthfulness of the witness. Now, Mrs. Bertrand, please continue."

Frances continued. "My father was in financial trouble when

242

he took control of the company, and has since turned his fortunes around."

Gabriel audibly sighed. He was getting schooled by Bates. Bates did not look at Gabriel. He did not have to. I warned you, Mr. Cote, I warned you, he thought.

Frances continued. "My father rarely spoke of the business and gave me money from time to time while I was recovering. By December of 1950, I was able to piece together enough of what had gone on since Gilbert had died. I knew I needed to talk to a lawyer. Claude Talbot was the only lawyer in Lac Ville, and he was my father's lawyer. His assistant, Mr. Cote, took over Claude Talbot's practice later. I went to Winnipeg and met a Mr. McDonnell. He agreed to take my case. I did not know he had been killed in a traffic accident afterwards, and I heard nothing from his office for a long time. Several years ago, I received a letter from Mr. Bates, my current lawyer, who told me he would continue with our claim. Last year, I contacted Mary Wabason and asked her to search her deceased husband's papers to see if she could find anything in writing between our late husbands about their business together. She found an agreement in the letters she had written him during the war. Both of us had never looked at our husband's letters before, and when she told me she found an agreement, I looked at the letters I had written to Gilbert and found a copy of the agreement Mary had found."

Frances paused and Bates asked her to describe her illness after Gilbert's death and Francine's birth. Frances began slowly. "After Gilbert's funeral, I went into labour with my daughter. I do not remember very much after I learned Gilbert had been killed. I started to think clearly at the funeral. I was weak and dehydrated when I went into labour. I bled a lot and was very weak after Francine was born. I barely had energy to feed her and our son. I slept whenever they slept. Our doctor said I was overcome by grief and had what he called the baby blues, a depression arising from being overwhelmed by events. He said I needed rest and time to recover. Elmer came to give me receipts and money from the business, but I did not have the energy to process them.

When I was finally able to get out and about, I went to my house and found my papers had been gone through and all the keys to the business, which a police officer had given me from Gilbert's effects, were gone. The only person who had keys to my house was my father."

Bates looked at the jury to see if the significance of Jean's theft of the keys before any agreement was signed resonated with them. Bates would have liked things in a neat chronological order, but this was just as good. Bates would have preferred the trial be in front of a judge alone because juries acted more on emotion than law. The documents would speak for themselves, and Bates believed common sense would rule on how they were perceived. Emotions, for better or worse, would sway the jury's decision. Mary had been good. How Frances stood upon cross-examination would be very important.

Frances continued. "Once my father had the keys to the office, I lost access to everything. All the records and inventory of equipment from the period of 1946 until 1950 were removed from the site. I still do not know where they went. The building locks were changed, and the compound was secured with a new lock." Frances stopped for a moment and then said, "That, Mr. Bates, would have never happened if I was myself and healthy after Gilbert died and Francine was born."

"Thank you for your candour, Mrs. Bertrand. Once again, I know this was very difficult for you," Bates said, taking his seat.

Justice Wallace turned to Gabriel. "We will adjourn until one o'clock at which time you may began your cross-examination, Mr. Cote."

The court clerk adjourned the courtroom, and the jury was escorted out. Everyone stood as Justice Wallace left the courtroom. Bates, Frances, and Mary went back into the room they had been in earlier. Gabriel and Jean had waited until the courtroom was clear of spectators before leaving, going out the door and down the back stairs to the parking lot. Once outside, Gabriel turned to Jean and asked, "Why did you not tell me you took the keys before an agreement was signed Jean?"

Jean answered quickly. "I did not know she knew I had, and I did not think she had noticed. Either way, why is that important? I was doing it to save her business"

Gabriel countered, "It is important because it makes you look underhanded." Which you are, Gabriel thought to himself.

Chapter 39

Justice Wallace took his seat on the bench and the court clerk announced everyone could be seated. Justice Wallace was satisfied with the pace of the proceedings and as he looked over his courtroom, he saw the gallery was nearly full. This was a surprise to him, as most civil trials attracted very little interest except from the participants. "Mr. Cote, are you ready to proceed?" he asked.

Gabriel stood up and answered, "Yes, my Lord."

Frances had re-taken her seat in the witness box. She sat straight and waited for Gabriel's questions. Gabriel's opening question was, "Mrs. Bertrand what is your current source of income?"

Frances looked at Bates and then back at Gabriel before answering, "I am living off the proceeds of investments I made before and after Gilbert died."

Gabriel quickly followed with, "And if you had not launched this lawsuit would those investments sustain you in the future?"

Frances answered honestly and without hesitation. "I do not know with certainty."

Gabriel asked, "Did some of the money for those investments come from your father and his work with the company in question?"

Frances could see where Gabriel was going and answered, "Yes, a portion did."

Bates glanced at the jury. Some of the members were leaning forward and listening intently to the exchange between Gabriel and Frances. Gabriel paused and switched tack. "Mrs. Bertrand, did you allow your son to work with and for your father?"

Frances looked surprised. "Yes, my son was very wilful, and I thought his grandfather could get him focused," she answered.

Gabriel looked to the judge and with an exaggerated gesture he pointed to Jean. "Even though you had a lawsuit in progress against your father, you thought your father could help your son? I am confused, Mrs. Bertrand. How could you have trusted your father to do what was in the best interests of your son?" he finished with an air of triumph in his voice.

Frances's face was flushed, and she answered, "In spite of everything, my son Jean loved his grandfather. I could not keep him from being with him. My father did not discourage him from quitting school and involved him in a scheme which led him to be questioned by the police. I ask myself the very same question, Mr. Cote. How could I have allowed my son to be with my father?"

When she finished, she fixed her stare on her father. The courtroom was silent. After a moment, Justice Wallace asked Gabriel, "Mr. Cote, do you have more questions for this witness?"

Gabriel began again. "I do, my Lord. Am I correct, Mrs. Bertrand, in saying the success of the lawsuit filed by you and Mrs. Wabason would secure your financial future?"

Frances bristled at the insinuation, answering, "It would restore what should have always been Gilbert and Elmer's legacy to our families, Mr. Cote."

Bates smiled to himself, thinking, do not venture too far onto the ice if you do not know how thick it is. Gabriel regretted his last question and moved on to the next. "Mrs. Bertrand, is your father not part of your family? You do not have to answer that, Mrs. Bertrand. I have no further questions for this witness, my Lord," he finished.

Justice Wallace looked at Bates and asked, "Do you have any questions for the witness arising from Mr. Cote's examination?"

Bates nodded and stood up. "Mrs. Bertrand, when you and your daughter were on the way to Fort William for these proceedings did your vehicle end up in a snowbank on the highway?"

Frances answered, "Yes, we hit a patch of ice and became badly stuck."

"Did you see your father that day?"

Frances nodded and answered, "Yes, he drove by us without stopping."

Bates looked at the jury. "You and Mr. Armand's only granddaughter were stranded in a snowbank and your father drove by? How did you get out?" he asked.

Frances looked at Mary and answered, "Mary Wabason and her son came on the highway to check on Francine and me because we were late getting to Georgetown, and they pulled us out."

Bates looked at Jean and said, "I see. Thank you, Mrs. Bertrand. I am glad you and your daughter made it safely to court despite your misfortune. I have no further questions, my Lord."

Justice Wallace turned to Frances. "Thank you Mrs. Bertrand, you are free to leave or remain in the court as you please."

Justice Wallace looked at both Gabriel and Bates. "I think this is a good time to adjourn for the day. We shall see everyone tomorrow morning at 10 o'clock sharp."

The court clerk called everyone to order and they stood until Justice Wallace left for his chambers.

Bates turned and looked at Mary and Frances who were talking to reporters. He was going to intervene but instead listened as Mary told one of the reporters that she believed the courtroom setting, though it was entirely new to her, was an effective way of presenting the truth. Her humility and earnest belief came across better than any comment he could have made. Frances stood beside Mary and let Mary take the lead.

Gabriel and Jean got up. Gabriel gathered his papers and Jean muttered, "Jesus Christ, who won't these reporters talk to?"

Gabriel held his fingers to his lips and whispered, "Not here, Jean not, here."

Jean snorted and pulled on his jacket. As they left the courtroom a reporter started towards them Gabriel held up his hand and said, "My client has no comment at this time. The testimony we have heard today was as hurtful as any father can be expected to endure. I will comment on my client's behalf as the trial progresses."

The reporter stopped and wrote Gabriel's response down. By the time he looked up they had left the courthouse, Jean was angry and he was almost spitting as he asked Gabriel, "Do you think those men believed those women? Surely, they could see through their greed?"

Gabriel looked off into the distance, thinking before he replied, "I don't know. You were the one who insisted on a jury. Juries sometimes decide on emotion. We have the law on our side if we can make the jury see that."

Jean took a breath and replied, "Make sure the men see these women for what they are. Surely these men know it would set a bad example to reward women for a man's work."

"I will do my best," Gabriel answered, wishing he was back in his hotel room.

Justice Wallace removed his robe and poured himself a drink as the court clerk came into his office. His chambers were his sanctuary, the only place he let his guard down. The court clerk, Maxwell Young, had been with Wallace for years. Maxwell never initiated any conversation about the day's proceedings and Wallace respected him for that. Wallace looked at Maxwell and asked, "What did you think Max?"

Maxwell answered, "Well, sir, I believe these women have a claim, though I don't know if the jury will see it the same. I can safely say this is the first time I have ever seen an Indian in a civil trial, much less an Indian woman. I thought she was a strong witness. The daughter did well too."

"I agree. This is an unusual case. I am looking forward to the next few days. It has been moving along quite well," Wallace replied.

"Yes, sir, me as well," Maxwell answered.

※

Back at their hotel, Bates explained to Mary and Frances that the next couple of days would be about the paperwork and it would be tedious. He congratulated them on their testimony and composure. He told them he thought it was important they were in the courtroom to show their commitment to their claim. Bates left their room and went to the lounge for a scotch. His assistant and junior member of the firm was waiting. They would go over his notes before supper, even though Bates felt confident his case was going well.

※

Sam Oates stopped for a beer on his way back to his apartment. He lived within walking distance of the courthouse. The King George Hotel had a men's only barroom. The ladies' and escorts' barroom really did require him to have a lady he was escorting before he could go in. Sam ordered a beer and two pickled eggs. There were several men at a table next to his talking loudly and swilling beer. From what he could hear, they all worked in the same office and the radio had been broadcasting coverage of the trial. One of the men said he was counting on the jury to keep these women in their place, and what the hell was an Indian doing suing a legitimate businessman? Another man was more sympathetic; he supported the widows, saying the whole thing sounded like a swindle by the father. Oates sipped his beer. It was everything he could do not to join the conversation. He felt important and glad he was part of everything that was happening.

Chapter 40

As Lyle Bates had warned, the next two days were tedious, as page after page of documents were filed and disputed by Bates and Cote. Cote disputed the net worth of his client and how much Gilbert and Elmer's business was worth. Bates had done his homework and described Cote's estimates as a shell game to hide assets. Some members of the jury appeared to be nodding off at some points, especially after lunch. Bates would bait Cote into raising his voice when that happened. Justice Wallace was curious at the sequence Bates had chosen to present his clients claims. Bates was trying to prove the net worth of the defendant before he had fully established the plaintiff's right to their claim. Bates told Mary after the first day, "Prove the little lies are lies at the start and the big lies are that much easier to prove as big lies in the end."

By the end of the second day, Bates was able to prove Jean had been in trouble financially at the time he taken control of Gilbert and Elmer's business. He had substantial debts and had been on the verge of bankruptcy. When he took over the business worth

$200,000 in 1950, he turned his fortunes around and his net worth was almost two million dollars, a substantial amount, Bates pointed out to the jury, when average family annual income was $34,000. Gabriel countered with the argument a man should not be punished for being successful in his enterprises. The reporters and the jury, Bates knew from his experience, would be more sympathetic to Frances and Mary if they could prove their claim against a millionaire.

Jean marvelled at how rich he had become as the trial went on. He came to the realization he did not know how to enjoy being rich. He wanted to be wealthy for the sake of being wealthy. He could not stop accumulating money long enough to enjoy the fruits of his labour. It was good enough to make the money, and he would not hesitate to spend it all to keep it from other people, including his daughter. He did his best to look confused while the lawyers sparred. His look of surprise at his net worth when it was announced had been practiced in front of the dresser mirror in his room for two hours the night before.

On the morning of the third day, Bates introduced the agreement between Gilbert and Elmer as proof that the widows were the rightful beneficiaries by virtue of being the spouses of the principals and founders of the company. The agreement, handwritten and not witnessed by an independent third party, should have given Bates concern. Both Mary and Frances had sworn a disposition in regard to the signatures on the agreement. Gabriel Cote did not contest that the signatures were genuine. Cote instead argued the contract was not a legal document in the eyes of the court. He argued that while the sentiment may have been genuine between Elmer and Gilbert, it had no weight as a legally binding contract. This is where the irony of the law and of being a lawyer was the greatest for Bates. Bates knew most lay people did not like lawyers unless they needed them. Bates was counting on the jury member's resentment of his chosen profession. He hoped this would cause them to side with two long dead soldiers who made an agreement between men without the help of a lawyer. Bates knew the very fact most people did not trust lawyers was going to be the key to the successful acceptance of the agreement as binding. He felt vindicated when the jury members asked for copies of the agreement. That's right, put those lawyers in their place, he thought. After the jury members received the copies and started reading them, Gabriel sat down, realizing he had been out maneuvered again.

On the afternoon of the third day, Bates called a Dr. Theodore Fuller to the stand. Bates qualified his witness as a family doctor with thirty years of experience. His secondary speciality was as an obstetrician. He had delivered well over two thousand children. He had written three published papers on post-partum depression. Fuller had examined the medical records of Frances Bertrand and had interviewed her several times. Bates led him through the history of post-partum depression and how it was diagnosed over the course of Fuller's career as a doctor. Fuller patiently explained how women were regarded and misdiagnosed as mentally ill or neurotic for many years. Fuller explained that early in his career, women were committed to mental hospitals and subjected to shock treatments if they displayed symptoms like the ones Frances Bertrand had displayed after the birth of her daughter. Fuller surmised the doctor who attended to Frances was not well versed in post-partum depression and its treatment. He pointed out that in Frances's medical records, the doctor from Lac Ville had written "Baby blues" as the cause of Frances's lethargy and despondence. Fuller almost laughed at the amateur-like simplicity, then checked himself. He ventured the opinion that Frances Bertrand could have easily been taken advantage of during her bout with post-partum depression, and easily manipulated. Bates asked Fuller how many women suffered symptoms of post-partum depression. Fuller looked at the jury as he answered: as many as one in four. Most women will not seek treatment and want it kept secret because of how we have treated them over the years.

Bates waited a moment to let Fuller's last statement resonate and then stood. "Thank you, Dr. Fuller," he said and turned to Gabriel.

Justice Wallace asked Gabriel, "Do you need a few moments, Mr. Cote, or are you ready to question the witness?"

Gabriel stood up, looked at Jean then announced, "No, my Lord, I am ready." He walked towards the witness box while looking at the jury. "Dr. Fuller, are you a psychiatrist?" he asked.

Dr. Fuller answered with a hint of sarcasm. "I testified I am a doctor. I perhaps should have made it clear I am a medical doctor."

Cote quickly countered with, "Is post-partum depression a medical or psychiatric disorder?"

Dr. Fuller replied with authority, "Both actually. If after my review of the case I had been Mrs. Bertrand's doctor at the time, I would have enlisted a psychiatrist to help me help her. I would not have let her enter into any agreements or sign any papers. No ethical doctor, or in my opinion any professional person, would have allowed that."

Gabriel was visibly thrown off by the reply and stammered. "You were not there at the time and you are not a psychiatrist, that is abundantly clear. I have no further questions for this witness, my Lord."

Jean stared at Gabriel as he came back to the table. In Jean's mind, none of the men on the jury would buy the doctor's evidence. Men watched out for each other. Lawyers and doctors were among the highest paid professions, but they testified in accordance to what they were paid to in his opinion. If Jean was reading the men right, they were waiting to hear from him. They would not be disappointed, he thought. "I will tell them the truth about these people. Things will change after that. Then I will learn to enjoy the money I have made," Jean said to himself. Jean had encouraged Gabriel to bring a doctor he knew to court to counter Dr. Fuller. Gabriel had interviewed this doctor the night before. The doctor was semi-retired. In fifteen minutes, Gabriel learned the doctor thought all women were neurotic and he refused to treat Indians. Gabriel told Jean, "Your doctor friend would do more damage than good." Jean argued this was just the type of truth that needed to be heard. Gabriel finally dissuaded him just before midnight, and when Gabriel got back to his room, he had three drinks of scotch before going to sleep.

Gabriel sat down and looked at Jean. Jean had let his glasses slide down his nose, his eyebrows were raised, and he was leaned back in his chair looking at the jury members as if admonishing them. His look was like he had just heard an incredible and impossible tale. Bates looked over and then turned toward the jury to see their reaction. One of the older jurors made eye contact with Jean and he shrugged his shoulders as if to agree with Jean. Justice Wallace adjourned the trial for the day after Dr. Fuller's testimony.

On the walk back to the hotel, Bates told Frances and Mary that while things seemed to be going well, he was worried about the jury. "A couple of the members looked skeptical of Dr. Fuller's testimony," he told them. Mary asked if Jean was going to testify. Bates told her, "He pretty much has to, and from what I could see, Jean cannot wait to."

Mary looked at Bates and Frances before saying, "Then we will be alright."

Chapter 41

Bates sat in his room going over the Ontario civil court procedures until after one a.m. Gabriel Cote's client had insisted on a jury. Jean had to cover the costs, which were relatively minor—comparable to taking six friends to a hunting camp. The jury was worrisome to Bates. Simple men untrained in law and with attitudes and prejudices undiscovered would sit in judgement of his clients. Bates could make a motion to the judge requesting he strike the jury. Bates could argue the issues were too complex and beyond the comprehension of the jury members and ask the judge to dismiss them. The judge alone would rule on the claim. Bates had thought he had the jurors leaning towards finding in favour of Mary and Frances until Dr. Fuller testified. Now he was not so sure. He had not counted on the different mentality of the men in this part of Northern Ontario. Bates was used to a more cosmopolitan attitude common in bigger centres. Winnipeg, while not Montreal or Toronto, was not Fort William, and attitudes towards women were different. It was subtle, almost intangible, but Bates instincts told him he could be in trouble. The problem Bates wrestled with until his fatigue took him to sleep was whether he should make a motion to have the jury struck or gamble on Justice Wallace doing it on his own accord.

Jean was in his room reflecting on the trial when he heard a knock on his door. He got up to answer it after putting his dentures back in. He had been sipping whiskey and liked the burn of alcohol on his gums. He opened the door to Alphonse's cousin Louis. "Come on," Jean said. "Did you find it all right?"

Louis smiled and replied, "Right where you said Jean."

Jean asked, "Did anyone see you come up?"

Louis shook his head. "No, I waited until the lobby was clear and listened in the halls before I came to your door."

Jean smiled. "Very good."

Louis handed Jean a thick envelope. Jean took it and went to sit down at the desk in his room. He took out eight 50 dollar bills and handed them to Louis. "You're a good man Louis make sure no one sees you on the way out," he said.

Louis nodded and went out the door. Jean counted the remainder of the money in the envelope to be sure Louis really was a good man and smiled when he got to $14,600. If he had to, he could buy a juror or two now. He had noticed one of the older jurors was wearing a shabby old suit and had made eye contact with him more than once. Jean had seen him take the bus from the courthouse. A man his age should have a car, Jean thought. Louis will know who he is by tomorrow.

George Harrison was the oldest of the jury members. His civic address was the rooming house beside the King George Hotel. The rooming house had twelve rooms on the second floor of a laundry business. Harrison and the other tenants shared a bathroom at the end of the hall. This had been Harrison's home for the past ten years ever since his wife had died. His children had not visited him since the funeral. When he received his summons for jury duty it was the first piece of mail he had received other than his pension cheques from the railway in years. He had been inclined to throw it in the garbage because it would interfere with his time in the beer parlour. He had heard about the case on the radio and decided he would go and see what it was about. He kept a flask of whiskey in his jacket to brace him at lunch if the day went on too long. He had been mildly surprised by how interesting the trial had been so far, though he did not believe a lot of what the women and their lawyer had said. He had trouble sleeping sometimes and often sat in the men's parlour of the King George until midnight drinking cheap draft. Tonight, was no different. Harrison was just about ready to walk to his room in the boarding house when a rough-looking, middle-aged, barrel-chested man sat down at his table with a pitcher of draft beer.

Chapter 42

Day four of the trial began right on time at ten a.m. Justice Wallace was at his place on the bench and looked out over the courtroom. George Harrison and Samuel Oates were seated beside each other. Oates was no stranger to beer, but he whispered to Harrison, "Burned the midnight oil last night, eh?"

Harrison put his finger to his lips as the clerk declared the court open. Harrison felt dull and tired. He long ago had stopped getting hangovers. He reminded himself he was not a young man anymore and would take it easy tonight. The man he had met last night had bought two more pitchers of beer than Harrison was accustomed to. It was free, so Harrison was not complaining.

Bates, who looked tired to Mary, lacked his usual zeal and enthusiasm. His voice was subdued as he answered Justice Wallace's question if he was ready to proceed. Bates stood and addressed the court, "My Lord, I apologize for the lateness of this development. My associates and learned friends have been attempting to serve a subpoena on and get a disposition from Mr. Armand's former counsel, Claude Talbot. Understanding attorney client privilege, I wanted Claude Talbot to explain to the courts the authorities or statues he had based his legal documents on, because I could not find anything to explain the legality of Mr. Talbot's work based on my interpretations of the laws as they stood at the time. I received a telephone call this morning that all attempts to serve Mr. Talbot have failed and his current whereabouts are unknown. I have therefore no choice but to conclude the evidence to be presented on the plaintiff's behalf."

After he finished, he remained standing waiting for Justice Wallace's response. Justice Wallace looked surprised and Bates knew Wallace did not like surprises. "Mr. Bates, if you are suggesting there were improprieties or worse by Mr. Armand's former counsel, these matters should have been brought forward to the law society long before this claim came to court," Justice Wallace said looking directly at Bates.

Bates replied, "My Lord, what I am saying is I am not certain if there were improprieties, though my experience leads me to believe the legality of Mr. Armand's counsel in these matters was at best suspect. My firm has made the best efforts to locate Mr. Talbot and have him explain his reasoning. We waited until two months before these proceeding to attempt to locate him so he would not have time to evade or avoid service. My friend Mr. Cote was present, to my understanding, through the process but as Mr. Armand's present counsel I cannot question him on Mr. Talbot's reasoning."

Gabriel Cote and Jean exchanged glances. Gabriel had been hoping Bates would only argue the legal weight of the documents Frances had signed. Bates was implying the documents as prepared by Talbot were an illegal act. Gabriel's emotions got the better of him as he stood up red faced and said, "My Lord, if Mr. Bates is suggesting I am a party to a breach of ethics which could be perceived as an offence leading to disbarment, I want to see some damn proof."

Everyone in the courtroom was taken aback by Gabriel's outburst. Justice Wallace banged his gavel. "Order in the courtroom," he commanded. "Mr. Cote, I understand your emotion; however, I will not tolerate outbursts. Mr. Bates and Mr. Cote, as we stand at this moment, the plaintiff has no further evidence to present and the defendant's counsel I believe will need a few moments before presenting his answer to the plaintiff's claim. I think an early adjournment for lunch is in order. I will see both counsel in my chambers at one o'clock." Justice Wallace banged his gavel again, this time with a little less vigor.

The court clerk announced, "All rise," and Justice Wallace left the courtroom.

It was everything Jean could do not to smile. The $5,000 he had sent in cash had obviously made it to Claude Talbot. Jean had kept in touch with Talbot and had warned him about the trial. It made Jean physically sick to put the money in the mail and send it with a note suggesting six months in Europe would be good for him. Talbot was smart enough not to reply or leave a paper trail. The droopy eyed bastard is probably sitting on the Rivera right now, Jean thought.

Gabriel turned towards Jean still angry and quietly asked, "Your fingers are in here, somewhere, aren't they?"

Jean shrugged in the maddening manner he did when he knew he was being accused of something he would never answer to. Gabriel gathered his papers and left the courtroom without waiting for his client.

Frances and Mary watched their interaction and Frances told Mary, "I almost feel sorry for Gabriel."

Louis sat in his truck watching the courthouse, waiting for the jurors to come out. He was surprised when they came out almost an hour early. He was glad he had not waited until eleven before leaving his hotel room or he might have missed them all together. He saw Harrison walking slowly behind everyone else. He waited, not wanting to take the chance Frances would see him. He saw Frances, Mary and her lawyer come out of the court and go in the opposite direction of Harrison. Louis got out and started walking quickly to catch up with Harrison. The other jurors were well ahead of them when he caught up to him.

"Good morning, George," he said, casually.

George turned, startled. "Ron, how are you?"

Louis answered, "Good. I am just going to get a little hair of the dog. What are you doing?"

"Early lunch. The lawyers at the trial I told you about last night were arguing about something, so I have got two hours," George grunted, with a frown on his face.

"Let me buy you lunch. You're the only person I know in this city," Louis said, opening his jacket to show a flask. "Hair of the dog, George," he added.

George smiled and replied, "Lead the way." He was not that tired.

At one o'clock, Bates and Cote were outside of Justice Wallace's chambers. They did not talk to each other at all. Bates spoke to everyone else who was around in his confident and easy-going manner. Gabriel was still seething, and quite frankly he did not have a word to say to Bates. Gabriel was going over all the possible scenarios that having Jean testify could create. He knew Jean was counting on the jury to decide in his favor. Jean's belief was unshakable. Gabriel could not help but wondering if maybe Jean was right. Jean's generation was used to men winning when the law was applied to women. Jean's generation regarded Indians as an annoyance and counted on government agencies, including the courts, to side with them in disputes. The court clerk opened the office door and told them Justice Wallace would see them now. Bates went in first with Gabriel following. Justice Wallace was seated in his chair. He did not ask either of them to sit down.

"Gentlemen," Justice Wallace began. "This trial has become ugly. Mr. Bates, my examination of the documents leads me to believe Mr. Talbot did stretch the limits of the law and knowingly violated several ethics of our profession. Mr. Talbot, unfortunately, is not here to answer to these breaches. Mr. Cote, I know this puts you at a disadvantage, but that being said, I do not believe you were a willing participant or were wilfully blind to Mr. Talbot's subterfuge. Which leaves me with the quandary of how to resolve this matter. Is there any way this can be settled now that we have heard the plaintiff's claim?"

Gabriel spoke first. "My Lord, my client is adamant he wants to testify, and he will not settle. I have tried several times to persuade him to save the courts time and he has absolutely refused. As an officer of the court, I am obligated to honour my client's wishes." Gabriel did not like to admit his position in front of Bates and thought to himself, it is not because you are a better lawyer, you pompous ass.

Bates waited for a moment before replying to Justice Wallace. "My Lord, in fairness to my friend, Mr. Cote, I have to state that I believe if his client testifies, he may have a chance given the make-up of the jury. My clients have always been amicable to a settlement, and I believe if presented with one at this stage, would enter into it."

Bates did not like Cote knowing he feared the jury. Jury trials in civil cases were always fraught with peril. Wallace frowned and let out a sigh. "All right gentlemen. Court will resume at two o'clock," he said.

Gabriel left the office first with Bates following.

George Harrison was seasoned enough; the four drinks of vodka he had over lunch with his new friend Ron did not show. The cheeseburger and fries had settled his stomach down and once again, marvelling at his good luck, they were free. Oates noticed he was bit more friendly than usual and had even smiled when he came into the jury room prior to being led to court. They all rose as Justice Wallace re-entered. After they were seated, Justice Wallace began. "Gentlemen, I trust everyone had a good lunch. Mr. Cote, are you ready to proceed?"

Gabriel stood up, "Yes, my Lord. I call Mr. Jean Armand to the stand."

Jean stood up and adjusted his clothes. He shuffled to the stand and looked in every respect like a tired senior citizen wanting to be any place other than where he was.

Chapter 43

Justice Wallace watched as Jean Armand was sworn in. The awkward shuffle and exaggerated flourish when he swore solemnly to tell the truth did not hide Jean's icy resolve from Justice Wallace. He had seen the same look many times over his years on the bench from criminals and ruthless businesspeople. Jean felt the Justice's gaze and ignored it. It will not be you who will decide this, Jean thought. Jean smiled at the jury and turned to face Gabriel Cote. Justice Wallace asked Cote if he was ready to proceed. Gabriel, already standing, replied he was and then began to walk towards the witness box. He turned and looked directly at each member of the jury before asking his first question. He was not going to waste any time and went straight to the heart of the proceedings. "Mr. Armand, are you the owner and operator of Gil and Elmer's Septic and Sewage Company located in Lac Ville?"

Jean came out of his slouch and answered, "Yes sir."

Gabriel then asked, "Can you explain to the court how you came to acquire this business?"

Jean took a deep breath and began. "In 1950, my daughter's husband was killed in a tragic and unsolved accident on the highway leading to Lac Ville. My granddaughter was born after the funeral and my daughter became listless. She seemed to not care that the legacy her husband had been building was in danger of becoming insolvent. Her husband, to the best of my knowledge, was working with an Indian from the Lac Ville reserve. I am no expert, but I believed this was not legal under the Indian act, so I consulted a lawyer and the Indian agent to protect my daughter and grandchildren."

Gabriel held up his hand and Jean stopped. Gabriel then asked while looking at the jury "So Mr. Armand, you consulted a lawyer and the local Indian agent to ensure the business was legal. Why did you do this, Mr. Armand?"

Jean answered quickly, "To protect my daughter and grandchildren. Gilbert Bertrand was a strong-willed man, but he did not seem to have a mind for business. When he was killed, and I began making inquiries, he did not seem to have had a plan for the future of his family. I knew I had to act to secure their future. I asked my lawyer to make sure everything was above board and I presented the plan to my daughter which she signed." Jean paused. "After I took control, I steadily built the business and gave parts of the proceeds to my daughter. She lived comfortably, and I had no idea she was not satisfied with the arrangement until I was served this claim. It broke my heart as a father. As for the Indian woman's claim I had no idea she had any claim to Gil's business." Jean's voice rose as he looked at Mary. "No idea," he repeated.

Mary stared back at him, and Frances put her hand on Mary's forearm.

Bates saw the oldest of the jury members nodding in agreement to everything Jean said. The others he could not get a read on yet. Jean continued, "I believe I did everything I could to be a good father and a responsible man." He emphasised the word man as he finished.

Gabriel leaned towards the jury and asked, "So Mr. Armand, you had no idea there was a claim against you until you were served the notice of claim? Is that correct?"

Jean spread his hands and waited a long time before answering quietly, "Yes sir, none at all."

Gabriel had expected to ask more questions. He had gone right to the heart of the claim and realized to his own disappointment it was not as dramatic and complicated as he thought. He asked himself if he had done enough to refute Frances's and Mary's claim. As unsavoury as Jean was, he believed he had, and if Jean could handle cross examination without shooting himself in the foot this could be over soon. Gabriel looked at Justice Wallace and said, "I have no further questions, my Lord."

Justice Wallace looked at Bates and asked, "Cross examination, Mr. Bates?"

Bates rose and replied, "Yes, my Lord."

Bates was feeling the same sense of disappointment as Cote was, for as much work as he had put into preparing for this trial it was going to end with a whimper, he felt. Unless he could get Jean to make an admission his acquisition of the company was underhanded, it would be the jury who would decide if his clients were entitled to compensation. Everyone, including the judge, seemed to be done with hearing evidence and just wanted to rule on what they heard. Bates knew from experience most judges and juries made up their minds after the opening arguments, human nature being what it was. In all his years of practice, the excitement came from changing a judge or jury's mind, or keeping them on his client's side after the opening arguments. Sometimes it was just that simple. The law, with all its complicated nuances, could be reduced to a simple well-maintained argument.

Bates did not look directly at anyone when he asked his first question. He projected the question into the courtroom, so it resonated loudly and clearly. "Mr. Armand, once your daughter was herself again, after her period of grief and the birth of your granddaughter, why did you not just return her business to her?"

Jean sloped his shoulders forward and answered quietly. "I was so busy building the business, it did not occur to me my daughter could possibly want to be burdened with the day to day to operations. I thought I was doing what was right."

Bates took a step forward and said, "I see. So, when you took the keys from her home and changed the locks on the business, that was so your daughter and her late husband's partner, Elmer Wabason, would not be troubled with the day-to-day operations. Is that correct?"

Jean's nostrils flared as he answered. "I changed the locks so that Elmer Wabason could not take property that did not belong to him. He had no business being there."

Bates moved closer and, staring right at Jean, asked, "After Gilbert Bertrand died, did Elmer Wabason continue to honour contracts and obligations the company had and bring cheques and monies to your daughter?"

Jean became flustered and stammered. "I have no idea what that man did before taking control of the company to protect my daughter."

Bates looked at the jury and then moved closer to Jean. "Mr. Armand, did you ever ask your deceased son-in-law what arrangements he had with Elmer Wabason?"

Jean had his back up against the witness chair and replied loudly, "It was none of my business. Gilbert was his own man."

Bates took a step back and asked, "If it was none of your business, why did you inquire with Indian Agent Mr. Price about the legality of Gilbert's association with Elmer Wabason? That was your testimony was it not? If you did not believe there was an arrangement, why inquire if it was legal? You can't have it both ways, Mr. Armand."

Gabriel jumped up, but before he could object Justice Wallace told Bates, "One question at a time, Mr. Bates."

Bates nodded his head to acknowledge the judge. He looked directly at the jury and asked Jean, "Why did you think it necessary, Mr. Armand, to ask the Indian Agent if it was legal for Gilbert and Elmer to have a business together? It really is a simple question Mr. Armand."

Jean leaned forward and answered, "To protect my daughter."

Bates looked surprised and asked, "To protect your daughter

from what, Mr. Armand?"

Jean was focused on Bates as he answered slowly and loudly, "Gilbert was building a good business. I did not want to see it go astray because he was working with Indians if it was against the law."

Bates countered, "Did you ask your daughter or Elmer Wabason or Elmer's widow Mary Wabason what arrangements there were?"

Jean replied, "No, I did not."

"If you were so concerned about protecting your daughter, would it not make sense to ask the people most directly involved?"

Jean grew angrier and growled, "It was none of my business, Mr. Bates."

Bates turned away and stated, "None of your business, yet..." to the people in the gallery.

Jean did not hear the question or statement clearly and asked Bates to repeat what he had said. Bates turned around and repeated, "None of your business, yet you made it your business didn't you, Mr. Armand?"

Gabriel stood up and loudly objected, "Where is the question here, my Lord?"

Justice Wallace told Bates to clarify his question or move on. Bates looked around the courtroom and then asked Jean, "What did you mean when you testified a moment ago, 'I did not want to see it go astray' when referring to the business? You said 'I', did you not?"

Jean's voice went deadpan and he answered, "That's not what I meant. I wanted to protect my daughter, nothing more."

Bates looked at Gabriel and said, "You have protected her to the tune of almost two million dollars in your pocket and her having to be in this court. I have no further questions for this witness, my Lord." Bates walked to the counsel table and sat down.

Jean was excused and forgot to shuffle on his way to Gabriel's side. He stared at Bates the entire walk to his seat.

Justice Wallace asked Gabriel if he had any further witnesses. Gabriel replied that he did not. Justice Wallace adjourned court after telling both Gabriel and Bates he would rule on the original contract between Elmer and Gilbert and the length of time it took for the lawsuit to come before the courts in the morning. After his ruling, both Bates and Cote should be to be ready to present their closing arguments.

Bates thought it strange Justice Wallace would make two pivotal rulings and then expect final arguments immediately afterwards. Gabriel looked at Bates and shrugged his shoulders as well. Bates extended an olive branch and told Gabriel to have two final arguments ready depending on the rulings. It was going to be a long night for both.

Chapter 44

Richard Sutherland showed up at the hotel just as everyone was arriving from the courthouse. Frances smiled at Mary because her face lit up the moment she saw him. Mary rushed into his arms and after embracing for a moment said, "I am glad you made it. I missed you."

Richard nodded to Frances and Bates. He led Mary out the lobby door to his truck. "Let's take a ride Mary. I don't want to share you with everyone else right now," he said, opening the door for her.

They drove out of Fort William to a picnic spot on the highway. There was not another vehicle in sight when Richard parked his truck. He kissed her and got out. Mary sat watching him as Richard started a fire in the metal barbeque stand. Richard quickly had flames licking the wood and the comforting familiar smell of the fire made Mary relax for the first time in days.

Richard stood by the crackling fire until Mary got out of the truck. She walked up beside him and took his hand. Richard was staring over the flames at Lake Superior. "It is beautiful, isn't it, Mary?" he asked.

Mary looked out at the lake and replied, "It is beautiful, Richard, but it is too big. The mystery and power of it makes me nervous, and I wish I were home. It is like the city, the court, and everything that has happened in the past while. Unpredictable and beyond my control."

Richard looked at Mary and said, "I am sorry. I thought you would like the fire and the view."

Mary squeezed his hand, "I do, Richard, I do. You are a good man. You made me feel like a teenager when I saw you today. I am very happy, and the fire is perfect. I wish we were home right now. The lake reminds me of everything I have learned in the past while. Everyone has their own agenda. It is hard to predict or know who really wants what or what really lies below the surface. To me, this trial has been about righting a wrong, but what does it really mean to everyone else? Is it money, reputations, or men bouncing their chests off each other, Richard? I do not like the feeling of being used for someone else's purposes. I wish I had spoken to some elders before I came here."

Richard continued looking at the lake and answered, "Elders? I do not think the elders could have helped you, Mary. I do not remember any of our people taking part in a lawsuit. Maybe to take on the government, but not like this. This is something new, Mary, and you are at the front of it. I hope people will look at you like you see the lake. Powerful and unpredictable. A force to be reckoned with."

Richard squeezed her hand and a smile crept onto his face. Mary moved closer. It was dark by the time they got back to the hotel.

Jean had insisted on buying Gabriel's supper. As they ate, Jean was acting as if the claim was already dismissed and the costs were to be paid by Frances and Mary. Gabriel watched Jean as he talked. Jean was confident and purposeful. He used his fork to emphasize each point as he talked about how Bates had gotten nothing from him. Gabriel, already suspicious of Jean, felt uneasy, as if whatever Jean had done or was doing would drag him down as well. Jean was treating this like a hockey game. It was the most energized and animated he had seen Jean in a long time. Gabriel could not wait for this trial to be over. As soon as he could, he excused himself after thanking Jean for the meal and headed to his room to finish preparing his closing argument.

✳

Elias Wabason was having supper in the Georgetown Café when Sergeant Smits came in. Smits had taken a real liking to Elias and treated him as if the game warden was a member of his detachment. "I hear the final arguments are going to start tomorrow," he said.

Elias liked how Smits went straight to the point and did not waste time on small talk. Elias smiled and answered, "I heard that on the radio on the way over. They even pronounced our family name properly."

Smits laughed. "I know, eh? Have you heard from your mother?"

"No," Elias replied. "My mother's husband went to see her today. I don't know if they will stay in Fort William after the final arguments. I am not very familiar with jury trials and how long they take to decide."

Smits shook his head. "I have to admit, neither am I. I guess we will know soon enough though."

Elias looked at Smits for a moment before saying, "I don't know what is going to happen when this is over. If it goes against Jean, there could be trouble. He won't take it lying down. If it goes against Frances and my mother, he will be even more of an arrogant man to deal with."

Smits raised his eyebrow and said, "I was thinking the same thing myself, Elias. You sure you don't want to be a police officer?"

Elias laughed. "No, I am good, Sergeant."

✳

The night was unusually mild, and melting snow dripped down the windowpane of Frances' hotel room. Francine was reading a book while Frances was lost in her thoughts staring out the window at the city lights. Francine interrupted her thoughts by suddenly asking, "Mother, what will happen when this is over? Will you forgive grandfather, or will he forgive you? Can we still live in Lac Ville or will people hate us? And what of Rejean? What are we to do about him? I think he hates us for what we are doing?"

Frances turned to look at her daughter. Francine's eyes were brimming with tears. Frances took a deep breath; she had been thinking the same thoughts. Frances reached over and took her daughter's hand. "I will answer your last question first," she began. "Your brother Rejean will come around. Your grandfather had a lot of influence over him and it was hard for him to see what your grandfather had done. He just needs time."

Francine, with the urgency of youth, said, "We don't even know where he is right now. How can you be sure?"

Frances looked out the window again before answering. "Your brother has a lot of your father in him. He will do the right thing when he is ready. He knows how to take care of himself, so I am not too worried about him right now. As to what will happen when this is over, I cannot really say. What I can say is you, your brother, and I will be alright, whatever happens. I have already forgiven your grandfather. I just feel sorry for him now. It made me sad to know how weak he was and how cold he could be. I don't know if he really knows what love is. If things get difficult in Lac Ville we will move to Georgetown. I think we would be happier if we were closer to Mary and her family. I don't care what people think. Mary and her family have shown us more consideration and love than I imagined. I only wish I would have been closer to them sooner. Whatever happens, Francine, we will be alright, I promise you."

Frances turned to see Francine's reaction. Francine had put her book down and was smiling. "You're right, you are right," she said as she hugged her.

Louis was in the men's parlour of the King George Hotel when George Harrison came in. Louis had a pitcher of draft and two pickled eggs on his table. Louis downed a glass of beer pretending he did not notice George come in. George was not too proud to let a chance someone else was buying slip by. "Ron, how are you this evening?" he said.

Louis looked up, acted surprised, and said, "George, I am good." He gestured with his empty glass. "Sit down, my friend, and tell me about your day."

By the time the bartender called last call, Louis knew he did not need to cross the line and bribe George. George was firmly on the side of Jean. Louis knew he did not have to tell Jean this. Jean was the type of man who just expected people to do what he told them to do. Louis could just keep the thousand dollars he had in his room and no one would be the wiser. Jean had told Louis, "In the unlikely event things did not go my way, I will still have other work for you." Alphonse had been right about Jean having deep pockets, Louis thought, as he went back to his room.

Chapter 45

The anticipation for Justice Wallace's rulings was palpable in the silent courtroom after the court was declared open. Mary and Frances sat in the front row of the gallery behind Bates. Jean Armand sat beside Gabriel. Bates adjusted his tie and had two final arguments in one pile on the desk in front of him. The argument on top was the one where the rulings were in his favour. Gabriel had his two arguments in two separate piles, both facedown. Jean looked bored and had adopted his confused senior citizen look again. Gabriel warned him against it, saying his vigor on the stand the day before made the look even more spurious than before. Jean told Gabriel to lawyer and leave the rest up to him.

Justice Wallace relished these moments. He had done his research. He was confident, despite the defendant wanting an unnecessary jury, that he had found the relevant case law to support his decisions. He looked over his courtroom, took a drink of water, and started. "Good morning everyone. I would like to begin with my decision regarding the disputed agreement between Gilbert

Bertrand and Elmer Wabason. First off, I believe this was a valid agreement between two men unversed in law and contracts. The fact that Gilbert Bertrand was a white man and Elmer Wabason an Indian meant nothing to these men. I conclude that because they had served in the war together, they viewed each other as equals." Justice Wallace paused looking around the courtroom before continuing, "A lesson many of us could learn. Their agreement specified a percentage of the profits were to be re-invested in the business, hardly the wording of a contract where one partner wished to dominate the other. I believe they made this agreement in good faith, without undue influence on the part of either party and free of deceit. Therefore, I am ruling the agreement was valid at the time it was written. As for its weight in these proceeding, I find that the transfer of the company to the plaintiffs the widows Frances Bertrand and Mary Wabason would have occurred by the natural progression of our laws after their spouse's deaths. As a Justice, I know full well most people do not consider their wills if they have no reason to suspect their imminent demise. The only wills of Gilbert Bertrand and Elmer Wabason had been the wills they had completed as soldiers. I find no reason to believe these wills were not their wishes at the time of their unfortunate deaths. I rule the wills to be valid and binding."

Justice Wallace paused again looking over his glasses at Bates and Gabriel. It appeared Gabriel had the trace of a smile on his face. Justice Wallace thought that was odd given what he had just said and then continued. "As for the timing when this agreement was found, I believe the plaintiffs Frances Bertrand and Mary Wabason found their copies in exactly the manner they described. Given the circumstances of the deaths of Gilbert Bertrand and Elmer Wabason especially after surviving a war, I find it fully believable that the grief and shock of their deaths would have deterred the widows from reading letters until they were emotionally ready. It was a fortuitous coincidence the agreements were found when they were."

Bates turned to look at Frances and Mary. Both caught his eye and smiled faintly. Mary thought to herself that maybe, just maybe, this will go well. The next decision would be the one that mattered the most. Bates and Gabriel both knew it as well.

Justice Wallace paused for a drink of water and then continued. "The next and most contentious matter, especially to the defendant, Mr. Armand, and his counsel, Mr. Cote, is the length of time it took for the plaintiff to file this suit. I have with great care and diligence gone over the timeline of this action, more diligence, I may comment, then the law office of McDonnell had exercised many years ago. I do, however, find no fault on the part of the initial plaintiff, Mrs. Bertrand. Mrs. Bertrand initiated her suit in a timely manner given the circumstances. Therefore, I rule the action, while not without long and costly delays, is in fact valid and allowed to be heard and continued with until a suitable judgement is rendered."

The blood drained out of Jean Armand's face and returned with a flush of fury as he listened to Justice Wallace's decision. He looked at Gabriel and then at the jury. He saw George Harrison watching him intently as the decision was announced. Jean straightened his back and tried to look nonplussed at the ruling.

The reporters in the gallery were making notes and talking quietly. Several got up and left the courtroom. Justice Wallace cleared his throat to show his displeasure at the activity and then finished with, "My written decisions will be available to counsel as soon as I am finished. Afterwards counsel will have several hours to read them. Court will be adjourned until one p.m." Justice Wallace struck his gavel and the court clerk commanded everyone to rise as Justice Wallace left the courtroom.

Bates turned to Mary and Frances and shook their hands saying, "Those two decisions were the best we could have hoped for. Congratulations ladies. I want to read the Justice's written reasoning, so I will be tied up until one o'clock. I will meet you here then."

Gabriel and Jean leaned toward each other ignoring Bates and the women. Gabriel spoke first. "Well Jean, all we can do now is try to minimise how much damage those rulings will cause. I was not expecting this."

Jean was scowling and replied, "We have not lost yet Gabriel.

You had best get your head out of your ass and fix this." Because I already have, Jean thought, watching George Harrison leaving the courtroom.

🐜

Elias Wabason was driving out of Georgetown, heading east to check out a complaint that someone had shot a bull moose. The poacher had taken only the antlers and tongue. The rest of the carcass was just off the road about twenty miles from Georgetown. Elias was planning his investigation as he drove when the news came on the radio. "The widows prevail. Superior Court Judge Wallace makes two important rulings in favour of Frances Bertrand and Mary Wabason in the lawsuit against Jean Armand of Lac Ville," the announcer said, before going on to give the details. Elias smiled and turned the radio up.

🐜

Sam Oates and George Harrison were putting on their coats in the jury room when Sam said, "Can I buy you lunch, George? You are the only one I haven't really had a chance to talk to since this began."

George hesitated to answer for a moment and decided he did not want a drink today. "I know a good place, not too expensive, seeing how you are buying," George replied.

"Lead the way," Sam said, holding the door for him.

Louis was still in bed back at his hotel. He looked at the wad of bills he had and was wondering how he was going to spend it. He was glad he did not have to sit and drink with that cranky old man tonight. Maybe he could find a woman to spend the night with. Someone classy, like Alphonse's old flame Frances would do nicely.

Chapter 46

After reading Justice Wallace's rulings, Bates admonished himself for losing some of his confidence. He did not like that he would have to convince a jury of lay people he had already won. He knew he could do it, though. Bates would use all his considerable skills of persuasion to get the most favorable settlement he could for Mary and Frances. He had come to admire them both over the past week, especially Mary, whose quiet dignity he believed had impressed everyone.

Both Mary and Frances saw the renewed vigor and look of determination on Bates's face as he prepared his final argument. When the court was reopened, Bates stood when called on by Justice Wallace and immediately walked to the area in front of the jury. "My Lord and gentlemen of the jury. I would like to thank you for your diligence and attention over the course of these proceedings. Put yourself if you will, gentlemen, in the shoes of my clients or better yet put your spouses or sisters in their places. The young widows of two honourable veterans who started a business after serving in a terrible war together. Men who trusted each other completely and wrote an agreement without a lawyer present because of that trust. The agreement found by Justice Wallace to be legal and valid," Bates said, gesturing towards the bench. "These two men willed everything they owned to their widows while serving overseas and nothing changed their minds when they returned. Everything they owned." Bates paused and then repeated, "Everything they owned. The company they built, they owned at the time of their unfortunate deaths." Bates moved closer to the jury and continued. "So, upon their deaths the company became the property of Frances Bertrand and Mary Wabason. Mary Wabason was not aware of the agreement between her husband and Gilbert Bertrand. Frances Bertrand suspected there was an agreement and pressed Mary to search further as this date grew closer. Frances Bertrand could have proceeded without Mary, but she knew there had been an injustice. Mr. Cote will, I am sure, try to paint a picture of Frances Bertrand as a greedy woman just wanting to reap the benefits of her father's hard work."

Bates paused to let his words sink in before beginning again. "Why would Frances Bertrand do this? Why would she sue her own father and then include Mary Wabason? If she was successful without Mary, she could have potentially been a wealthy woman." Bates took a breath and looked down for a moment before making eye contact with each member of the jury. "Gentlemen, Frances Bertrand just wanted to make things right. Her father had taken the business which was rightfully the property of both women using a lawyer who is nowhere to be found and an Indian Agent who has passed away to make it legal. Mr. Armand, I am sure, never expected this day to come. He never expected his daughter to see through his duplicity and deceitful practices." Bates turned and pointed to Jean and said, "He, I am sure, never expected that one day six men such as yourselves would hear about how he operates. Six honest men with common sense would hear the facts and lift the darkness from his acquisition of a company built by honest men, and the rightful property of the plaintiffs. This man took advantage of his own daughter in her darkest hours to rebuild his personal fortunes, and he's done very well for himself, as we have heard. He totally disregarded Mary Wabason. Why? Because she was an Indian woman. No other reason."

Bates stopped and backed away from the jury before beginning again. "This lawsuit took a long time to wind its way through the system, but as Justice Wallace has ruled it is valid and that is why we are here. Gentlemen, after all we have heard, I am asking you to right this wrong. Restore the company in its entirety to its rightful, lawful owners: Frances Bertrand and Mary Wabason. The profits earned by Mr. Armand while he was in control should be split between the widows. Send a message to Mr. Armand and anyone like him. Fairness and honour will prevail. Thank you," Bates finished.

Jean stared at the jury while Bates was speaking. He began to feel anxious as he watched their heads nodding in agreement as well as looking repeatedly at him. Even the old guy who seemed to be in his corner looked uncomfortable. That Louis better not have screwed this up, he thought. Jean's thoughts were interrupted when Justice Wallace called upon Mr. Cote.

Gabriel stood up and, after adjusting his tie, began. "My client, Mr. Armand, has literally spent the last few years reeling from the accusations and claims made against him. To top it off, this case has been widely reported by the media." Gabriel gestured toward the gallery. He continued. "In good faith, and motivated by the desire to provide for his family, he built a company his son-in-law started into a viable and sustainable enterprise. He took steps which Mr. Bates has tried to paint as somehow distasteful, or worse illegal, to make sure he was doing things properly. He mentored his grandson with the full intention of turning over the company to him at some point. Does this sound like a man who is self-serving? Ask yourself gentlemen, would you have done things differently? Do you believe a man," he paused for emphasis and repeated, "do you believe a man should be punished for success? As men, we must be careful about the message we send. Should every child, no matter what their age, be able to challenge a man's success? Think about that for a moment." Gabriel stopped and waited as he looked around the courtroom. He began anew after a moment. "Mr. Armand had no idea there was a written agreement between his son-in-law and Elmer Wabason. From Mr. Armand's life experience, this was unheard of. That is not his fault, and he should not be punished for it. Think about it gentlemen: Indians were and are still in many respects the wards of the government. How was he to know any different? As the jury, you have the ability to dismiss this claim and send a message to everyone that despite the technicalities, common sense and hard honest work will be rewarded with a just verdict. Thank you." Gabriel finished and took his seat.

Jean leaned back and turning to Gabriel said, "That's it?" loudly enough that everyone heard him.

"Less is more, Jean," Gabriel whispered in response.

The jury members looked over. Justice Wallace cleared his throat, and everyone went quiet. Justice Wallace explained he was going to give his instructions to the jury. He said given the relatively straightforward issues in the suit, he would not need any time to prepare.

Justice Wallace outlined the issues quickly for the members of the jury. They did not have to be absolutely certain on the issues as this was not a criminal trial. They only had to believe on the balance of probability who was most likely telling the truth, or in other words, he explained in layman's terms, which version of the evidence they believed to be the most likely and probable. The first question they had to answer was did Jean Armand exercise due diligence, or did he take advantage of the situation when he took control of the company from his daughter Frances Bertrand? The next question was did Jean Armand knowingly ignore the possibility that Mary Wabason's husband was a legitimate partner in the original business? The third question, was Jean Armand's professed ignorance of the agreement between Gilbert Bertrand and Elmer Wabason contrived so that Jean Armand could personally benefit? Lastly, Justice Wallace pointed out that if the members of the jury believed the plaintiffs, they could rule in their favour. If the members of the jury believed Jean Armand, the suit would be dismissed. Justice Wallace asked the jury members if they understood his instructions. When the jury foreman indicated everyone did, Justice Wallace instructed the members to retire to the jury room to deliberate their verdict.

After the jury retired, Justice Wallace addressed Bates and Cote. "Gentlemen, please leave your contact information with the court clerk. Thank you for your able presentations. Court will be adjourned until the jury reaches a verdict." The court clerk called on everyone to stand and Justice Wallace left the room.

Once in his chambers, Justice Wallace removed his robe and poured a cup of coffee. His court clerk Maxwell Young came in and asked if he needed anything. Justice Wallace asked him to sit down for a moment and asked, "Maxwell, we have been together a long time. How many juries have we seen in civil proceedings over the years?"

Maxwell thought for a moment before answering. "I would say one every two years or so."

Wallace nodded his head in agreement. "Sounds about right. You know how I feel about juries in the process of civil law. This is not supposed to be about who likes who the most. It's supposed to be about the application of the law to the facts.

Maxwell replied, "I know, sir."

Justice Wallace did not say anything further, and Maxwell knew not to ask.

Chapter 47

All the jurors were at the table with their notebooks in front of them. The bailiff had filled the coffee and water urns and retired after wishing them good luck. Samuel Oates started the conversation by saying, "Gentlemen, I am of the opinion Jean Armand is a conniving thief. A wolf pretending to be a wounded sheep. He planned the takeover, and ignored anything that did not fit his plans. He executed his plan and reaped the benefits."

Another juror raised his hand. "Slow down Samuel; I think Armand just did what needed to be done. What if he had not? What would have happened to their company if he had not?"

George Harrison piped in. "The Indian was running things when the daughter was laid up. Weren't you listening?"

Samuel looked over, surprised. "George, no need for rudeness."

George looked at all the jurors and said, "This is the way I talk. Don't take offence to it. If I mean to be insulting, you will know in short order." Everyone laughed uneasily, and George continued. "I don't have a lot of use for women, or Indians, for that matter, but

I do think they were telling the truth. It had that ring to it, like when a hunter downplays a successful hunt. That Indian woman I don't think knows how to lie. Raised right, I guess. There was this nosy bastard who bought me drinks for two nights in a row just before the final arguments. He asked a lot of questions and I knew he did not just decide a cranky old man like me was his new friend just because. I think that Armand fellow sent him to snoop around." George had in a few sentences laid out his position.

The jury foreman looked at George and said, "That is jury tampering and a very serious offence. Did you tell anyone George?"

George replied quickly, "No, I did not need to. I could have caused a big fuss if I wanted to, but I am a man. I make up my own mind."

Everyone in the room went quiet realizing they had underestimated George Harrison. The jury foreman asked if anyone else had been approached. No one had, or if they had they were not saying.

When Jean Armand got back to his hotel, the clerk handed him a note. Louis wanted him to drop by his hotel room after supper. Jean read it and then shoved it in his pocket.

Samuel knew after the first hour, the judgement was going against Jean Armand. George had seen to that in the first few minutes. One of the jurors was a businessman who had a son who had been in conflict with him, and he was reluctant to set a bad precedent. The other jurors, after hearing his story, reassured him this was a totally different situation. Still, it took another hour to convince him this trial was not about him and to get back to the case before them. The last hour was spent deciding if they had a say in what the widows would be rewarded. George's final comment was, "Gentlemen, there is going to hell to pay for this. Armand and people like him will not just roll over." At just after six p.m., the foreman summoned the bailiff to tell him they had reached a verdict.

It took an hour to locate everyone and get them back to the courthouse. Jean left a half-eaten steak on his table and walked back to the courthouse with Gabriel. Frances and Mary had not eaten yet because they were nervous and wanted to wait until they were told the jury had retired for the night. Bates had taken a quick nap and felt refreshed as they all walked through the slushy streets to the courthouse. The bailiff had called the reporters at a nearby coffee shop where they were camped out to ensure they did not miss the verdict if it came early.

Justice Wallace had not left the courthouse. He had been working on a presentation he was going to make at the next annual conference of Superior Court judges where he would argue for the elimination of juries in civil trials in Ontario when his clerk knocked on his door. Justice Wallace donned his robe and waited in his chambers for Maxwell to come back to tell him everyone was in attendance.

March would have been a slow news month if not for this trial, Allister O'Brien was thinking to himself as he took his seat in the gallery. Courts and churches loved hard wooden benches for whatever reason; maybe so reporters did not overstay their welcome Allister smiled to himself to appreciate his own humour. The courtroom filled quickly. Allister saw Mary and Frances come in and gave them a nod. He watched as Jean Armand and his lawyer Gabriel Cote came in. Jean Armand forgot his old man act and walked with purpose past Bates and the women, ignoring them completely. When everyone was seated, the court clerk had everyone stand and opened the door to the chambers for Justice Wallace.

Justice Wallace wasted no time and took his seat on the bench as the court clerk announced the court was re-opened. Justice Wallace announced, "I have been informed the jury has reached a verdict. Is this correct Mr. Foreman?"

The jury foreman stood up. "Yes, my Lord," he replied.

"Very well. If you will read your verdict for the courts," Justice Wallace ordered.

The jury foreman began. "We the jury find in favor of the plaintiffs Frances Bertrand and Mary Wabason. The plaintiffs were unlawfully deprived of the business created by their late husbands by Jean Armand. The jury recommends the business and all its assets be returned in its entirety to the control of Frances Bertrand and Mary Wabason immediately. The jury further recommends fifty percent of all the profits made by Mr. Armand while he was illegally in possession of the company be forfeited to the plaintiffs under the supervision of a court ordered auditor."

Justice Wallace raised his eyebrows, thinking to himself that these men got it right, which will unfortunately weaken my argument for elimination of juries in civil cases. He then asked, "So say you all?"

The jury foreman answered firmly, "So say us all."

Jean Armand was shaking with rage as the verdict was announced. He stared at George Harrison and cursed Louis. He felt he could not count on anyone to do what they were supposed to. He turned to look at Frances and Mary with hatred and contempt in his eyes. Both women stared back, not intimidated by Jean's hostility. Gabriel whispered, "We can appeal, Jean."

Jean growled back, "Appeal? You idiot. if you could not win the first time, why would I pay you to lose a second time? I have already lost over half of everything."

Gabriel stood up and said, "My Lord, I make a motion that you strike the jury's verdict and you make a directed verdict on the grounds the jury did not understand the intricacies of the law in these proceedings."

Justice Wallace looked over his glasses and answered, "Motion denied. I believe the jury has come to a just and fair finding. You, of course, will have leave to appeal." Justice Wallace turned to the jury and said, "Thank you for your service. When the court is closed, you are free to leave." He then turned to Bates and Cote. "Gentlemen, I will meet you here Monday to work out the finer points of this settlement and appoint an adjudicator. This trial is now concluded." He looked at the court clerk who commanded everyone to stand as he left the courtroom.

The reporters noisily left the courtroom, attempting to be the first ones to announce the verdict. All of them except O'Brien, who walked over to get a comment, if he could, from either Frances or Mary. Mary looked at him for a moment and said, "Thank you for reporting this fairly."

Frances declined to say anything as she watched her father storm out of the courtroom. Bates took the opportunity to say, "Thank you, Mr. O'Brien, for your coverage of this case. I believe it has been an important case for advancing the rights of all women in this part of Ontario. It also brought important issues to attention. Post-partum depression and the way the widows of veterans were taken advantage of by unscrupulous persons including government officials was certainly highlighted. If you are interested, there will be some off the record talk at the bar in the hotel, and you are invited."

O'Brien looked surprised. "Thank you, Mr. Bates. I will see you shortly," he replied.

Jean walked quickly to the hotel, got in his truck, and drove to Louis's hotel. He stormed up the stairs and pounded on Louis's door. Louis answered with a drink in his hand. "What is wrong?" he asked when he saw how agitated Jean was.

Jean calmed down for a moment and asked, "Did you not pay the old man?"

Louis took a swig of his drink and lied, "Yes, of course."

Jean almost spit when he said, "Well, they ruled against me—including the old man. Go and get my money back." Jean felt certain Louis was as stupid as Alphonse could be sometimes and did not understand the full implications of the ruling against him. He did know Louis would do what he was told. "Get my money back," he commanded.

Louis stood still for a moment "Yes, of course. Anything else?" he asked.

Jean stared for a moment out the window. "Yes, burn the business. Gilbert and Elmer's, all of it. Make it look like an accident. Leave no evidence. Can you do that?"

Louis asked, "When?"

Jean fixed him with a cold stare. "Any time after you get my money back," he hissed, and left the room.

Chapter 48

Louis' first inclination was to drive over to where George Harrison lived and lay a beating on him. He dismissed it quickly because he had not paid him anything and there was nothing really to deny. He was just mad because he would have to return the money to Jean. He began to plan how to cause the most destructive fire he could at the business. He knew the buildings were valuable, but it was the vehicles which would be the hardest to replace. How to get them both at the same time was the quandary. He had time to think about it as he packed his things and checked out of his hotel. He would have more time to think on the drive back to Lac Ville.

Jean had gone from Louis' hotel back to the hotel he was staying in and went directly to Gabriel's room. He had calmed down enough he was sure he would not throw Gabriel out the window. When Gabriel answered the door, he looked tired and discouraged. Jean told him, "What is done is done." Jean followed up with some questions. Did he have to stay now the decision had gone against him? Could he continue to operate the business until it was transferred? Gabriel told him he did not have to stay in Fort William. He could not sell, transfer, or hide anything related to the business because the property had all been listed in the discovery phase. Jean rose, and in a rare moment of gratitude thanked Gabriel for all he had done. As Jean walked out the door, Gabriel felt relieved his time with Jean Armand would soon be done. Jean's eyes were not as good as they had been. He did not like driving at night. He made up his mind to go home first thing in the morning.

🐜

Frances and Mary were having a late supper. They could hear Bates and several men laughing in the bar next door. Neither of them had said a lot to each other since leaving the courthouse; they were tired but happy. Mary finally asked Frances, "Who do you think should run the business, Frances?"

Before Frances could answer, Francine spoke up. "The German, Kurt:, he has been there since the beginning."

Mary and Frances looked at each other and smiled, before Mary agreed. "Such a smart young lady, of course, that makes sense."

Francine added, "He is a good man. He has no love for grandfather either."

Mary laughed and said, "Elmer used to say he was glad Kurt was captured before Walter got him. Elmer said Kurt could fix anything and was never afraid of work."

Frances added, "We will ask him together when we get back. You will be there as well Francine. Since you seem to know him better than we do."

Francine said, "Grandfather used to bring me to the shop and then ignore me while he was with Rejean and Alphonse. I would sit in the mechanics bay with Kurt. He told me to be patient because someday everything would be made right. He was right."

Elias and Helen Wabason, as well as Richard Sutherland and Eva were in the kitchen at Mary's house in Georgetown when the radio broadcasted the verdict. It had only taken three hours for the jury to rule in favour of the women. Helen grabbed her brother's hand and squeezed. Richard Sutherland commented, "We will see a lot less of Mary for the next while, but it is good thing."

Within an hour, Sergeant Smits, Luke, and Helen's husband Scott had shown up to offer their congratulations. Helen, Scott, Luke, and Eva left together around 11 p.m., leaving the men alone. Sergeant Smits spoke first after the door closed. "Now what gentlemen? What do you think Armand will do now?"

Richard Sutherland replied, "He is the type of man who would salt the land rather than surrender it."

Elias Wabason agreed. "I think I will be doing some work around Lac Ville for a few days to keep an eye on things. I have two files I need to work on. How about you, Sergeant?"

Sergeant Smits winked and said, "I think a visit to the Lac Ville detachment is in order as well."

No one in Georgetown knew Wilma, Everett's widow, and Kurt had been living together. Kurt moved in with her about a year after Everett was killed. They were an odd and volatile couple. Wilma, after years of abuse at Everett's hand, was mistrustful and suspicious of Kurt even when she did not have to be. Kurt took it in stride. He was a stoic and quiet man. He loved Wilma and tolerated her children, all of whom were grown but still hanging around. Kurt was a favorite on the Lac Ville reserve because he could fix anything and was always teaching the young men. He was hard to understand sometimes because his accent remained thick. It got worse when he was excited. He would never raise a hand to Wilma or the children and the few times he was mad he would go to Gilbert and Elmer's compound to sleep. He kept an old camp cot by the oil stove. There was also stash of schnapps and coffee to keep himself warm. On the night the verdict was delivered, he had gone there about 11 p.m. and around 3:30 in the morning he heard a vehicle outside the gate.

Kurt's old bones were aching as he got up and looked out the bay door window. It was Louis, one of the guy's Jean had hired after Alphonse had died. Kurt did not like him at the best of times; now that he was disturbing his sleep, he liked him even less. The shop was dark so Louis could not see Kurt watching him. Kurt watched as Louis undid the chain on the gate and drove over to where the vehicles were parked. Louis got out and started shining a flashlight at the fueling station. He is stealing gas, Kurt thought. When Louis walked past the tanks and went back to the vehicles Kurt pulled on his boots and jacket. Louis came from the vehicles and went to the shop door, unlocking it and, using his flashlight, went to the electrical panel for the shop. Kurt picked up a wrench and crept towards the office hallway where Louis was examining the fuse box. Louis pulled out a pair of wire snips and was reaching to cut a wire when Kurt said, "What are you doing?" in a loud heavily accented voice. Louis spun around, shocked, and threw the pliers at Kurt. Kurt dodged and then saw the flash of a knife in Louis's hand. Kurt hit him in the side of the head with the wrench, knocking Louis out. Louis fell to the floor heavily and Kurt stood over him for a moment. When Kurt was satisfied he was not getting up any time soon, he went to his tool chest and grabbed some wire to tie Louis up.

After he was securely tied, Kurt sat and watched Louis, waiting for him to come to. Kurt had worked in this shop for fifteen years; he wanted some answers from Louis before he called the police. It took almost an hour before Louis opened his eyes. When he did, he immediately said, "Why did you hit me, you crazy bastard?"

Kurt looked at him for a moment, as he anticipated Louis would try to turn things around to get out of this. "What were you doing at the fuse box?" Kurt asked. He watched as Louis struggled to find an answer that would cover his tracks.

"I was not at the fuse box, old man. What are you doing here?" he sputtered.

Kurt stared for a moment before he said, "I have a good mind to put you in the cesspool and no one would ever know the difference."

Louis's eyes widened for a moment and then he regained a bit of control. "Call the police old man, we will see who will go to jail this morning," he muttered.

Kurt knew nothing about the verdict and had no idea what Louis had intended. His instincts told him he had stopped something Jean had initiated. He knew he had to call the police. Louis was a big man and strong; Kurt was not sure if he could use the phone without him getting away. He picked up the wrench and smashed it into Louis's left knee. Louis screamed in pain. Kurt looked at him and said in his deadpan tone, "Stay here. I have to make a phone call."

Sergeant Smits heard the dispatch on his police radio about a break-in in Lac Ville as he was pouring his coffee. That did not take long, he thought as he strapped on his gun belt. He called Elias Wabason to meet him at the scene. The highway was clear and dry. It would not take them long.

Chapter 49

When Elias Wabason and Sergeant Smits arrived at the compound, the corporal and constable from the Lac Ville police detachment were already there. Louis was untied and in the back of their patrol car. The constable was taking a statement from Kurt and the corporal approached Sergeant Smits, giving Elias a questioning look, as if wondering what he was doing there. The corporal was one of those policemen who considered conservation officers as less qualified than a regular police officer. The corporal knew Elias and Sergeant Smits worked closely together regardless of how he felt about it. He began by saying, "I am not quite sure what we have here, Sergeant. This fellow Kurt says Louis there came into the business about three-thirty in the morning using the keys and tried cutting the wires on the fuse box. Kurt confronted him and Louis attacked him. Kurt struck him with a wrench, knocking him out, then he tied him up and called us. What doesn't make sense is why Louis would do that. He works for Jean Armand."

Sergeant Smits looked at the corporal for a minute before

answering, "Yesterday evening, the court ruled in favor of Frances Bertrand and Mary Wabason and awarded the business to them. You did not hear the news last night?"

The corporal looked embarrassed for a moment. "I was at an accident until midnight last night on the highway. So, no I didn't," he replied.

Elias Wabason looked at Sergeant Smits and said, "Arson?"

Smits looked at the corporal and asked, "What does Louis have to say for himself?"

"He is not saying anything, except that he wants a doctor and a lawyer," the corporal replied.

Sergeant Smits told the corporal to take Louis to the detachment and detain him. "Have the doctor come to the detachment and make sure the doctor has time to tell everyone in town our business as he usually does. I want to see who shows up here and at the detachment. Your constable can stay here with Elias and I will meet you at the office in a few minutes," he directed.

When the corporal left with Louis, Sergeant Smits and Elias examined Louis's vehicle. There were rags, matches, and a gas can but they alone really did not prove anything. "Suspicious, but not proof of anything. I know and you know what was going to happen here if Kurt had not been here," Smits said.

"How do you want to handle this, Sergeant?" Elias asked.

"I am going to have a run at him at the detachment. Louis is not that smart. If Jean shows up here, tell him Louis is at the office giving everything up. Make it convincing. If he shows up at the detachment, I will radio, and you guys can clear after you collect everything," he replied.

Jean Armand had left Fort William just before the sun came up. He was almost in Lac Ville by ten o'clock. As he got close, he was hoping to see a cloud of black smoke coming from the area of the compound. He had not really given Louis a timeline but had hoped he would get to burning the business before Jean was back in Lac

Ville so he would have an alibi when the inevitable investigation took place. Either way, he thought, it will get done.

✻

The doctor was only at the detachment for about twenty minutes examining Louis. While he was there, Sergeant Smits in a stage whisper had made sure the doctor overheard his conversation with the corporal about the possibility Louis was attempting to commit an arson on Jean Armand's behalf. The doctor could not examine Louis fast enough. He recommended aspirin for the blow to the head and ice for the bruised knee. The doctor headed out of the detachment and went straight to the coffee shop. He was there when Jean walked in.

Louis sat in a chair by the corporal's, looking dejected and a bit absurd with a golf ball sized contusion on his skull. He stared at Sergeant Smits and wished he had a drink. Sergeant Smits pulled up a chair and stared back at Louis. "Rags, matches, and gas at three thirty in the morning in a business that was going to change hands from the person you worked for—that looks pretty bad," Smits said. He reached over and grabbed the criminal code, a book setting out every criminal offence in Canada and the punishments for those offences, and read the section about arson out loud. Louis avoided eye contact as Sergeant Smits read it. He flinched when Smits read the punishment section. "That's a long time to spend in jail, Louis. Especially damning is how people in this part of the country feel about fires," Smits said.

Louis straightened up. His head was throbbing. He looked at Sergeant Smits and said defiantly, "I want a lawyer."

"Yes, of course. I will get you a phone book. Gabriel Cote is the only lawyer in Lac Ville, and I believe he is in Fort William right now representing your boss, but you can try to get a hold of whoever you want," Sergeant Smits replied. He got up to get a phone book.

Jean headed from the coffee shop to the police detachment building. His heart was pounding. If Louis had talked, he would know as soon as he got in the door. He was going to use his bluster and aggressiveness to intimidate the corporal. The town cops were nothing to him. The doctor did not know Sergeant Smits and had left out the detail that he was still there. Jean thought he was dealing with the local officers. He had demeaned and undermined them in front of everyone in Lac Ville. They were wary around him, as they should be, he thought as he drove. "Still, you could never be sure what was going to happen," he chided himself. "Someone might want to be a hero."

Sergeant Smits saw Jean's truck pull up as he handed the phone book to Louis. He quickly went to the radio and called Elias Wabason. "Armand is at the detachment. Acknowledge," he transmitted.

A "10-4" came back.

Smits turned towards the door as Jean Armand stormed in. As soon as he was in the foyer, Jean loudly said, "Who has my employee, Louis. and what the hell is going on?" Jean saw the corporal and went to the counter almost shouting, "What are you doing and why?"

The corporal looked in Sergeant Smits direction and for the first time Jean realized Smits was there. Smits looked towards Louis, who was now smiling. Smits, in his police tone of voice, said, "Mr. Armand, unless you want me to throw you out the detachment door, you will lower your voice and address my officers with respect."

Jean's face revealed the contempt he had for police officers, but he lowered his voice. "There appears to have been a huge misunderstanding, Sergeant, and consequently my employee is in custody. I sent Louis to shut the power off as I had lost the business for now in a civil trial. I was not going to pay for the electricity. I cannot help if my employee is an idiot who was going to do it in the middle of the night," he said. It was a bluff; he took what the doctor had told him and hoped Louis had not talked. If he had talked to the police and confessed, then Jean knew he was likely going to be arrested as well.

It was Sergeant Smits's turn to grimace. You crafty bastard. Smits thought he would have had the time to get a confession out of Louis. He had no idea Jean had headed back to Lac Ville so soon after the verdict. Jean continued speaking. "Sergeant, I will gladly give you a statement to this effect and I am sure you will release Louis, so no unfortunate legal problems arise for the provincial police."

A threat, Smits thought. He knew with Jean's statement his already weak case against Louis was going to be dead in the water. Jean sensed his bluff had worked and he added with a hint of sarcasm and triumph, "Sergeant, given my legal troubles with the game warden recently, I had told all my employees never to talk to authorities without a lawyer present otherwise Louis would have cleared this up without my having to come to your office."

Smits knew he had lost this round. Louis was smiling and stood up. Jean looked over at him and then at the corporal before saying, "Louis looks like he has had a very rough night. I can assure you, Corporal, that being the bigger men, we will not be pursuing any charges against the man who struck Louis."

Smits told the corporal to release Louis just as Elias Wabason and the constable came in the door. Jean stared at Elias with a hatred he could barely conceal. Elias brushed past him and went over to the coatrack to hang up his tunic, making eye contact with Smits. Smits's eyes told Elias all he needed to know. Something had gone wrong, and he had to let it be for now.

Chapter 50

Jean Armand's shirt was soaked in sweat. His heart was just starting to slow down as Louis got in the truck. He looked at Louis for a moment before saying, "You really are an idiot, but I think it worked out in our favor."

Louis, looking straight out the window, replied, "If this is working out, I would hate to think what I would look like if it had not."

Jean really could care less about Louis's injuries. This big ox could still prove useful down the road, he thought as he put the truck in gear. Jean was expecting a hero's welcome, or at least everyone to admire him because he had stood up for himself. He could not wait to hear what everyone had to say about the past couple of weeks. Even though he had lost the first round in court, he stood up to the cops and put them in their place. Jean drove to the tavern. Louis did not protest even though he was tired and felt like hell. A dram of whiskey was just what he needed.

After Jean and Louis left the detachment, the Lac Ville Corporal and constable began writing their reports, because they did not really know what to say to Sergeant Smits and Elias Wabason. Smits was fine with that, and he grabbed a coffee for him and Elias. "What happened?" Elias asked.

Smits smiled his police veteran smile which said he won even if looked like he lost. It was one he saved for when his experience told him that even though things did not work out the way he had planned, there was a silver lining to what had transpired. "Elias, we have just made it impossible for Jean Armand to burn down the business, and it will gnaw at Armand until his dying days. There is no way he can destroy what your mother and Frances have won without coming under even more suspicion."

Elias looked puzzled for a moment. "We did not get to arrest them," he said.

Smits, still smiling, replied, "No we did not, but this actually works out so much better. I will explain over dinner tonight in Georgetown. Now I have a couple hours of paperwork to do."

Elias took his cue, drained his coffee, and put his tunic on.

The tavern parking lot was full when Jean and Louis arrived. A lot of men liked a beer with their lunch. The woman could have their tea in the restaurant. Jean had a grin on his face as he walked in the bar. There were about fifty men inside talking loudly, smoking, drinking or eating their sandwiches. When Louis and Jean came in, a few people looked up and then went back to their conversations. A couple of Jean's oldest friends looked away and avoided eye contact. The owner came over and asked, "The usual, fellows?" When Jean nodded yes, the owner just walked away to the kitchen.

Louis began to feel uncomfortable. He leaned over to Jean and whispered, "What's going on, Jean?"

Jean, his nostril's flaring, hissed, "They think I lost."

Louis looked at the old man and said, "You did."

Jean slammed his fist onto the table, startling everyone. "Bullshit, I lost, Louis."

Everyone went quiet and looked towards them. Jean looked around wild-eyed and shouted at the other men, "I have lost nothing. I am still rich. You are a bunch of weak women and fair-weather friends."

Men gulped their beers and got up leaving half eaten sandwiches on the tables. In five minutes, only Louis and Jean remained in the bar. The owner brought them their drinks and food. He stopped after setting them down. Looking nervously at Jean, he said "People think you made our town look bad at the trial. The people who work at your businesses are afraid for the future because of how you have been acting. The police may be afraid of you, but they are not afraid of the rest of us, and they will go out of their way to show us this. The people having been talking about this in my bar for the past few days and after what happened this morning, they are even more afraid. I am telling you this, Jean, because you have been a good friend over the years, and I think you need to know."

Jean took a swig of his beer and pushed his sandwich away. He was not hungry anymore. He looked at the tavern owner for a minute and said, "To hell with them. They will come around."

The owner cast his eyes down and asked if there was anything else Louis and Jean would like. Jean, in a lather now, snapped, "No, go wipe your counters and tables. A woman's work for a woman." Jean threw some money on the table and told Louis, "Let's go to my house. I have whiskey and the company will be better." Jean tried to conceal how weak his knees felt as he stood up. He had not anticipated this.

🐜

Bates, Mary, and Frances met for lunch the day after the verdict. Bates told the women they could head back home if they wanted. Bates or his assistant would work out the details of the transfer of the business and some of Jean Armand's assets over the coming days. It would be accountant and lawyer work so dry even he dreaded it.

Mary asked Bates if they could name a foreman for the business and begin running things. Bates replied yes, and he would ensure a bailiff would be in Lac Ville to oversee the transfer. They knew nothing of what had transpired during the early morning hours in Lac Ville. Frances said, prophetically, "My father will not take this lying down."

Bates, stirring his coffee, replied, "No, I am sure he won't, but the law is on our side."

Mary grinned at the irony of those words. It had been a long trial, not that she had ever been to one before. She longed to fall asleep in her own bed.

Lucy was fleshing two beaver pelts in her and Walter's trapping cabin. Walter was finishing skinning out two martens. The melting snow had made slogging through the bush very difficult over the last week. It would not be long until the spring break-up. Lucy did not look forward to going back to Georgetown at the end of the season. Walter would want to get back to his carpentry work. She watched him as he worked. He was a good man. Lucy felt if there was no one else in the world, she would be happy with just Walter. Walter stopped what he was doing and for a moment was dead still. Lucy looked in his eyes and saw the look that told her to not move or flinch. Walter held his fingers to his lip. He deftly moved toward the open door of the cabin and stood off to the side. He held his skinning knife low. Lucy looked over by the stove and saw Walter's .303 leaned against the wall. Walter looked over and shook his head. Lucy stood stock still.

Lucy saw a shadow in the snow coming up on the right side of the open door. A barrel of a rifle broke the plane of the door jamb. In an instant, Walter grabbed it and pulled. The intruder tumbled forward and onto the floor of the cabin. Walter was over him and had the knife to his throat in the blink of an eye. A young man, eyes as wide as saucers, looked at Walter expecting to be killed. Lucy yelled, "Walter, stop." Even though it had been years, she recognized Everett's youngest son Peter. He was smaller but his face was a spitting image of Everett's. At first Lucy was enraged and felt a fury she had not felt for a long time at the realization. Calming herself she took a breath and said, "Peter. What are you doing?"

Peter, well aware of Walter's reputation as a warrior, accepted he was had. "I came to kill you both for what you did to my father," he answered with tears in his eyes.

Lucy stood up and took Peter's gun. She removed the clip and cycled the round out of the chamber. Lucy set the gun down and looking at Walter said, "Let him up. You were very young when your father died, Peter. Let me tell you about your father so we can all finally live again."

Chapter 51

Peter, Lucy, and Walter talked until the sun went down. When Lucy got up to make tea, Peter looked at the dirt floor and avoided eye contact with Walter. Walter decided to show Peter the scars from where Everett had shot him. Peter whistled lowly, eyes wide, and said he was sorry that had happened to Walter. Walter told Peter it was water under the bridge now. Walter asked Peter if he was any good with his hands. Peter told him his mother's long-time boyfriend had taught him how to fix and build almost anything. Peter said he was hard to understand especially when he was excited. Walter looked at Lucy and then asked Peter what his mother's boyfriends name was. When Peter answered, "Kurt," Lucy and Walter started laughing. "Well, I'll be damned," Walter said slapping his knee. "I guess the war really is over for all of us." Peter did not have a clue what Walter was referring to. Walter still smiling asked Peter, "Do you want a job?"

Frances and Francine stayed at Mary's house in Georgetown for the night on the way back to Lac Ville. Frances told Mary, "I feel more at home with your family than anyone else." She dreaded going back. Frances knew there were still many people who supported her father. Not many would have the courage to say anything to her face. They would instead whisper. Small people with small minds who did not deserve a lot of consideration could still make things awkward sometimes. To hell with them, Frances thought to herself, I will do things on my own terms. She silently chided herself; she sounded like her father.

Mary was looking at Frances, trying to read what she was thinking as they sat at the kitchen table. Frances felt her gaze and smiled. "You and I are going to be busy for the next while, Mary. We can show people how a business can be run with fairness and for the good of everyone concerned," Frances said.

Mary laughed. "I am already busy, Frances what's one more thing?"

"How can we include my sister Eva?" Frances asked.

Mary almost dropped her cup of tea in surprise. Mary recovered quickly and answered, "Why don't we ask her?"

"When?"

"Right now," Mary answered, getting up to get her coat.

As they went out the door, they saw Francine talking with Elias Wabason. He was showing her the ministry truck and explaining the equipment to her. Frances looked at Mary with a smile. "In four years, she will be twenty and he could very well be a son to both of us."

Mary blushed. She knew the look on Francine's face and knew her mother's determination was part of her make-up. Mary knew her son would wait until Francine was older. He had his father's patient outlook on matters of the heart. Mary put her hand on Frances' shoulder and said, "We will see, Frances. We will see."

A few people had come over to see Jean Armand in the days after he had returned to Lac Ville. They drank his whiskey and offered their condolences. Most were just prying for information to feed into the gossip mill. Most of them did not stay long because Jean would rant and curse almost the entire time they were there. Jean felt they were all worse than useless and knew why they came over. "To gloat. To drink my booze. To see if they still had jobs," he yelled to Louis who, now unemployed, had the time to listen. "A man builds, and everyone wants what he has built," he finished.

Louis noticed that when Jean was not angry, he was getting forgetful. There were cigarette burns on the table and floor. Jean had not changed his clothes since he came back. He would stop mid-sentence and begin an entirely different one. To Louis, he had become an old man overnight. One thing Jean said was true, Louis thought; he was staying for the whiskey.

🐜

When Frances and Francine returned to Lac Ville, people were surprisingly cordial. They treated her with respect and some deference. The women in town seemed to be in awe of what Frances had accomplished. Frances was now a wealthy woman and had the ability to influence the local economy. People knew this was the new reality, whatever position they had taken prior to the trial. The irony of it for Frances was her own father had told her years before, "When people treat you as an important person, never ever correct them, my girl."

When Mary came to Lac Ville, people looked at her as an anomaly. A well-spoken successful Indian woman who would not suffer intolerance. The way she conducted herself showed humility and class. If anyone had anything negative to say, they would never say it directly to her. Mary knew in her heart there were people who would deeply resent working for women, and an Indian one was just salt in the wounds. She made it clear if anyone working at the business felt this way, they were free to leave and find other employment. Mary knew the family men would put their families first. Necessity would make the doubters give her and Frances a chance.

Kurt at first declined to accept the foreman's position. He did not really know Mary or Frances that well. Francine, while charming, was just a child. He felt a loyalty to them because of their husbands, a loyalty he thought he could return by working hard as he always did. In his mind, a promotion would take him away from the work he was doing, and no one could do it as well as he could. It took a visit from Elias Wabason to convince him to step up. Kurt had a lot of respect for Elias, and when Elias told Kurt, "As good as you are at keeping everything running Kurt, your aging knees, hands, and back are eventually going to limit your ability to do your work." The turning point came when Elias told Kurt, "I will tell my Auntie Wilma if you decline a higher paying job." By then, everyone knew they were together.

Kurt shrugged his shoulders, knowing he had no choice other than to take the foreman's job. He told Elias, "I would have to move into the shop full time if she heard that."

When Gabriel Cote got back to Lac Ville, the first thing he did was take the details of the court's instructions for the disbursement of the assets from the settlement to Jean Armand's house. He did not expect to be met with warmness or even civility. Gabriel knew he needed to get this bit of unpleasantness out of the way so he could go home and put this all behind him, for the time being at least. He would have to tell Jean after consultation with other lawyers in Fort William he knew an appeal was unlikely to be successful. As Gabriel got out of his car, a neighbour shaking his head told him that Jean has not been out of his house since he had returned from Fort William. Gabriel thanked the man and knocked on the door. Louis answered. The stale air from the interior hit Gabriel flush in the face. Cigarette smoke and sweat hung in the air. Gabriel walked in and saw dozens of empty beer and liquor bottles in the living room and on the kitchen table. Jean was in a lounge chair looking out a window facing the lake. "Who is here, Louis?" he asked without turning around.

"Your lawyer," Louis replied.

Jean stood up. He looked at Louis and told him to clean up the house. Gabriel was shocked at Jean's appearance. He had the same clothes on as he had when he left Fort William. He was unshaven and looked like hell. Jean said, "Have a drink. I just have to clean up." He turned and went into the bathroom.

A half-hour passed before Jean came out of the bathroom. He had showered, shaved, changed his clothes, and brushed his teeth. Louis saw the old fire in Jean's eyes. "Are you going to bill me for the half an hour I made you wait, Gabriel?" he asked.

Gabriel shook his head. Louis had cleaned the table off and they all sat down as Gabriel opened his briefcase.

It was almost dark by the time Gabriel was finished. Jean signed documents and had listened carefully to everything Gabriel had told him. They had drunk almost three-quarters of a bottle of scotch while going over everything. Gabriel's cheeks were flushed. Jean looked like he had been drinking water. Jean asked several times how the handover could be done without further complicating matters. He compromised on several issues and suggested ways to make the process as painless as possible. Gabriel could not believe he was talking to Jean Armand. Jean pulled his chair closer to the table and asked, "So that's it then, Gabriel?"

Gabriel answered, "Yes, I think we covered everything."

The old Jean came back in a flash. "Good. Send me your bill and then I don't want to ever see you again. You can leave my home now," he said, menacingly.

Louis stood up, happy to see his old boss again and ready to do violence onto Gabriel if ordered to. Gabriel loaded the papers in his briefcase and left the house without turning around. Once outside, he looked skywards and said, "Thank you." He had been fired.

Chapter 52

The coming of spring revitalized everyone. Jean Armand acted as if nothing had changed. He ran the businesses he still owned with renewed energy. People in Lac Ville noticed he went out of his way to be fair in his dealings with everyone. His constant scowl was replaced with an expression that, if nothing else, was neutral. He was hard to read now. Frances and Jean still had not spoken to each other. In a small town like Lac Ville, the animosity between them was well known. No one ever asked either Jean or Frances about the other. The priest came to both of their homes offering to act as an intermediary. Jean showed him the door. Frances politely declined the offer.

Frances, Mary, and Eva had gotten a crash course on Gil and Elmer's Septic Service from Kurt and the other workers. All but three stayed on with the company. Mary hired three young men from the Lac Ville reserve to replace them, including Wilma's son Peter on Walter's recommendation. Mary suggested they buy uniforms for the men suitable for the work they did, so the men did not ruin their own clothing. Frances agreed, adding it also made them look more professional. Frances and Mary co-signed a cheque for baseball equipment and sponsorship of the baseball teams from Georgetown, Lac Ville, and the Lac Ville reserve.

The women used their influence and money to create several services in their communities, much to the disgust of Jean. He confided to Louis, "They are very free with my money. They will not last long."

The most popular innovation was the free shuttle service the women created to take people to medical appointments. It went as far as Fort William. Eva co-ordinated the trips. Sometimes the shuttle caused people who had never been together before, like the residents from the Lac Ville reserve and the town of Lac Ville, to spend time together.

Mary was troubled by the fact Frances never mentioned her son, Rejean Bertrand, who had left Lac Ville before the trial and had not been heard from since. As a mother, she knew this would be breaking Frances's heart. Mary was at Frances's house going over their plans for a community day in June when Francine burst into the house with a smile. Francine had gone to the post office to check the mail. She had several letters in her hand. She put them on the table and handed one to her mother. "It's from our Rejean," she said, excitedly.

Frances took it and saw the return address was Cornwallis, Nova Scotia, and the post mark was from an army post office. She knew the emblem from Gilbert's letters all those years ago. Mary sat quiet as Frances opened the envelope. Frances's hands were trembling. Frances took the letter and unfolded it. Francine impatiently asked, "What does it say?"

Frances read the two enclosed pages in silence. After a long pause, she said, "Like his father, not much of a writer." They all started laughing. Frances put the papers down. "Rejean has joined the army. He is in basic training right now. He says he was accepted into the Royal Mechanics and Engineers because he was good with machines. He hopes to come home after basic training before he starts his trades training. He misses and loves us all," Frances said.

Mary and Francine hugged Frances. Frances was smiling and crying at the same time.

Eva was in the post office posting the shuttle schedule when the door opened behind her. She turned out of instinct and found herself face to face with Jean Armand. They both froze in place as they made eye contact. Eva took a breath and was going to turn away when Jean spoke, "Eva, you have certainly grown into a beautiful woman. Like your mother was." Eva felt a surge of emotion and pain wash over her. Every sense was on high alert as she stared back at Jean Armand. He seemed stuck for words for a moment. He glanced around to be sure no one else could hear him. "Eva, I am your father," he said.

Eva's eyes flashed in anger as she answered, "You are nothing to me. My mother loved you." She brushed by Jean and went out the door.

Jean turned and watched as she got in her truck and drove away. The postmaster, unseen behind a shelf, let out his breath quietly in disbelief at what had just happened. He could not wait to tell his wife.

Within a week, everyone in town knew Frances and Eva were sisters. Frances told her daughter before someone in town did. Francine was ecstatic. She always thought Eva looked like her mother with darker skin. She always felt comfortable and relaxed around her. Frances explained to her daughter, "I long suspected my father was Eva's father, but I waited until he confirmed it before I said anything to anyone. It feels good now the truth is out. I wonder what people would talk about in this town if they did not have our families." Frances laughed as she gave Francine a hug.

Since the death of Everett, the reserve outside of Lac Ville had shrunken to a population of just under 300. Some of the young people left to look for work and many of Everett's cohorts moved to reserves where there was still cheap alcohol to be had. The remaining people had transformed the reserve into a quiet well-run community. The chief was a young man named Roger Ferris. Ferris had spent ten years working for the City of Fort William. He had started off in sanitation and ended in the parks department. He took what he had seen and experienced back home. His first moves where to re-establish the water distribution and garbage collection. He organized the younger people to remove derelict cars and any last remnants of the time Everett was in charge. He had heard many stories about Elmer and Mary. What they had done and what had been done to them. Ferris had written Veterans Affairs to have a soldier's headstone put on Elmer's grave. The wooden cross marking where Elmer laid was worn and faded. It sat forlorn and unvisited for many years, except by Roger who trimmed the grass around it in the summer. Even though Georgetown was only a short drive away and Mary was frequently in Lac Ville, Roger never approached her. He was not sure why exactly. He believed it was out of respect. She was a strong woman. Roger believed they would meet when they were supposed to.

Being Elmer Wabason's widow, Veterans Affairs contacted her when the request for a soldier's headstone was received. Mary was surprised anyone would have taken the trouble to apply for it. Mary missed and loved Elmer, but she had never thought there might be people other than her family that would want to commemorate and remember him. Her grief and remembrance were very personal matters to her. Mary felt she would have done a strong man like Elmer a disservice to share the pain of his passing with everyone else. Elmer used to say to Elias when he was a boy, "When someone passes on, salute, mean it, and move on." She was deeply moved by the gesture, and more so when the caller told her it was the chief of the Lac Ville reserve who requested it. She called Elias, Helen and Eva and told them they were going back to the Lac Ville reserve in the morning to meet the chief.

Jean quietly sold his skidder and pulp equipment business to a rival company from a town east of Lac Ville in June. In July, he sold his chainsaw and outboard motor franchise to a young man from his church. The condition of the sale was the businesses had to keep the name Armand's for a year. The rumour around Lac Ville was both buyers got a bargain because Jean was losing his facilities. A woman from the church told Frances, "Your father is getting forgetful and walks with a shuffle now." Frances had seen him out and about town. She had noted he was slower and stooped over as well. He still refused to acknowledge her and acted as if he did not even see her. Her father was an unbelievably stubborn and vindictive man who would rather lose his mind alone than admit he was wrong. Frances wondered if she should make the effort for herself and her children. Her priest encouraged her to do it. Frances, busy with the company and her philanthropy, kept putting it off.

In September, Jean put his truck in reverse instead of a forward gear and crashed in the front of his own home causing a great deal of damage. He left the truck running and went into his house. The neighbour called the police and Frances because they thought he was drunk and possibly injured. Frances arrived first and found her father in the kitchen. He stared at her blankly when she came in. Frances felt tears well up as she asked him, "Father, are you alright?"

Jean snapped, "Of course I am alright."

Frances knew she had waited too long. Jean did not know who she was. A constable from the Lac Ville detachment came in the door. The constable had been in Lac Ville for about a year and knew most of the story of Jean and his daughter. He looked at Frances for a cue. Frances looked at him and asked if he had shut Jean's truck off. He nodded he had. Frances said, "I think my father needs to go to the hospital."

The constable quietly said, "I think it is for the best."

A month later, Frances walked through the door of Gabriel Cote's law office. Gabriel was shocked. They had not seen each other since the trial. Gabriel took a breath and said, "How can I help you, Mrs. Bertrand?"

Frances sat down and replied, "I need to have power of attorney over my father so I can manage his estate while he is in the care home."

Gabriel took out a pad of legal paper and answered "I see. Well, let's get started then." Frances looked straight ahead as she started talking.

Acknowledgements

I would like to acknowledge Heather Campbell and Mitchell Gauvin and all of the staff at Latitude 46 working so hard to bring books to life in Northern Ontario and beyond. Your work has allowed me to bring a story to life which I hope honours the many strong characters, many of them World War Two veterans and their wives, I met growing up in Oba and all-over Northern Ontario.

A special thank you to my wife Christine and to all of my family. Thank you for your patience and support.

Miigwetch//Thank you